"We'll never know if you don't try, will we?"

"I'll tell you what," he said. "I'll make a deal with you."

"What kind of a deal?" Miriam's expression was cautious.

"I promise to do everything you say…to try my hardest…for a month. If I'm not much better by then, you agree to quit."

Miriam stood very still, considering before she spoke. "I can't speak for Tim. Just for myself."

"*Yah.* Just for yourself."

"Who's going to decide whether or not you're much better?" she said. "You?"

His jaw hardened. She wasn't going to make this easy.

"No," he said abruptly. "How about…Betsy?"

Her lips twitched. "Don't you think Betsy has her own reasons for wanting to be rid of me?"

He raised one eyebrow, a gesture that used to work with the girls. "If you're really making progress, you'll have won her over by then. What's wrong? Don't you have any confidence in your work?"

She seemed to wince at that. After a long moment, she nodded. "All right. It's a deal."

A lifetime spent in rural Pennsylvania and her Pennsylvania Dutch heritage led **Marta Perry** to write about the Plain People who add so much richness to her home state. Marta has seen over seventy of her books published, with over seven million books in print. She and her husband live in a beautiful central Pennsylvania valley noted for its farms and orchards. When she's not writing, she's reading, traveling, baking or enjoying her six beautiful grandchildren.

Carrie Lighte lives in Massachusetts next door to a Mennonite farming family, and she frequently spots deer, foxes, fisher cats, coyotes and turkeys in her backyard. Having enjoyed traveling to several Amish communities in the eastern United States, she looks forward to visiting settlements in the western states and in Canada. When she's not reading, writing or researching, Carrie likes to hike, kayak, bake and play word games.

MARTA PERRY

CARRIE LIGHTE

A Promise to Heal

2 Uplifting Stories

Nursing Her Amish Neighbor and
Caring for Her Amish Family

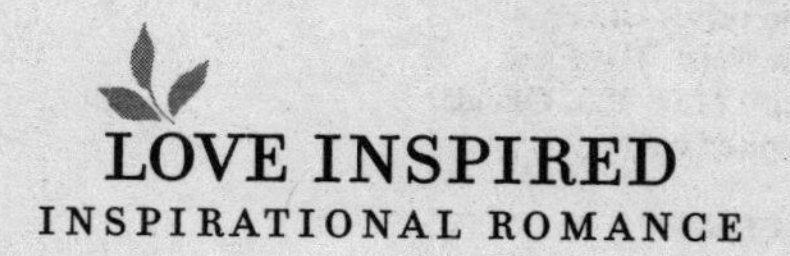

LOVE INSPIRED®
INSPIRATIONAL ROMANCE

ISBN-13: 978-1-335-50830-0

A Promise to Heal

Nursing Her Amish Neighbor
First published in 2021. This edition published in 2023.

Caring for Her Amish Family
First published in 2022. This edition published in 2023.

For questions and comments about the quality of this book, please contact us at CustomerService@Harlequin.com.

Harlequin Enterprises ULC
22 Adelaide St. West, 41st Floor
Toronto, Ontario M5H 4E3, Canada
www.LoveInspired.com

Printed in U.S.A.

CONTENTS

NURSING HER AMISH NEIGHBOR

Marta Perry

This story is dedicated to all those who work toward healing in the world. And, as always, to my husband.

For if ye forgive men their trespasses,
your heavenly Father will also forgive you.

—*Matthew* 6:14

Chapter One

Matthew King heard the footsteps on the back porch and knew his father had finally come home. He'd been over at the Stoltzfus place next door long enough…talking about Matt, he felt sure. It was dark already, although the daylight lingered long on these August evenings.

Daad would come into the old farmhouse quietly, not wanting to wake the household, and especially Matt, sleeping on the first floor since the accident.

But Matt wasn't asleep. He didn't sleep much anymore, not unless he took those little white pills that the doctor had prescribed. And he didn't even have them at hand. Daad had insisted they be kept in one of the kitchen cabinets, maybe afraid of what Matt might do if they were too easily accessible.

However appealing oblivion might be, even on the worst days, he'd never take that way out. It would be too hard on his parents, as well as being a violation of their faith. He wasn't sure he even cared about that any longer, but they did.

Matt shoved the pillow up behind him, his gaze wandering around the room. They'd put him in the sewing room, so he could be on the ground floor. The quilting frame was still propped against the wall, and the sewing machine, covered with a sheet, sat in the corner. Inconveniencing everyone, that was what he was doing. Better if he had died in the accident, like David.

The familiar pain and grief swamped him, only to be chased away by rage. Better if he had died *instead* of David, that was what he thought. And certain sure better if that reckless drunken teenager had killed himself instead of David. But no, he'd walked away with hardly a scratch, while Matt's family's lives were changed forever.

Forgive, said the church. But this wasn't something he could forgive. The bishop came to see him, praying for him, sitting endlessly beside the bed. *Time*, he'd said. *Give it time. God's purposes will become clear. Our job is just to obey.*

But all the time in the world wouldn't make this any better. David was gone.

The back door closed softly, and he heard Daad's quiet footsteps cross the wide boards of the kitchen floor and stop. He must have walked to the hall and waited, looking and listening. He'd see that the light was still lit in Matt's room. He'd come in.

Sure enough, the footsteps approached. A slight

tap on the door was followed by the door opening, and Daad stepped inside.

"Everyone else asleep?" he asked.

Matt shrugged. "They went up a half hour ago. Whether they're sleeping, I couldn't say. Well, did you convince Miriam to take on the hopeless case?"

He could hear the bitterness in his voice. He wanted to take it away, but he couldn't.

Daad's weathered face tightened. "It is not hopeless. Nothing in God's creation is hopeless unless people make it so. And yah, Miriam has agreed to come and help us."

"Maybe she can help Mamm. She can't help me." His jaw set. "And she won't be around very long."

He'd make sure of that.

Daad's lips quirked in what might have been a smile. "Wait and see. You may be surprised."

Matt shook this off impatiently. "That little thing? Shy and serious and afraid of her own shadow? She's not going to make any difference to me."

He was being unfair to Miriam, he knew. And Daad knew it, too. That's why he was frowning, but he didn't say anything more about Miriam. Instead he glanced around the room.

"Do you need anything before I go up?"

Just a new pair of legs, he thought, the bitterness engulfing him. But he wouldn't say it. Daad had enough to bear without him pitying himself.

He shook his head. "Good night, Daad."

"Good night, son." His father went out quickly,

probably glad to leave the sound and smell of the sickroom behind.

Matt shoved at the pillow again. Daad might be confident about Miriam, but he figured he knew her better after growing up next door. She was a sweet kid, but there was no way she'd get him to do anything he didn't want to do. And he didn't want to waste his time on exercises that wouldn't make him the man he'd been before.

No, Miriam could try her best. But he was a hopeless case, and the sooner she accepted that, the better it would be for both of them.

Miriam Stoltzfus walked along the edge of the pasture that stretched between her parents' farm and that of the King family, trying not to think about what she'd gotten herself into. The August sun beat down, hot already though it wasn't noon yet, increasing her discomfort.

Most of that discomfort came not from the temperature, but from her own feelings about accepting this new challenge. After all, she'd just returned from a lengthy stay with relatives out in Ohio, helping with a new baby, then with her aunt's recovery from surgery, and then…

She'd as soon forget what had happened next.

In recent years, word had gotten around in the close-knit Amish communities that Miriam Stoltzfus, still unmarried at twenty-six, had a gift for helping out when folks were sick or injured, and the requests had been thick and fast in the past year. She'd come home hoping for a rest, only to be confronted by Abel King, who was distraught over the loss of one son and desperately worried about the recovery of the other.

The two families had been neighbors for generations. It wasn't possible to turn down a request like that. So here she was, approaching the King farmhouse, more than apprehensive about what she was going to find. Her own confidence was at an all-time low, and Matthew King had certain sure never lacked for that quality. If he didn't want her here—

With a silent prayer for help, she paused at the screen door.

She hadn't timed that very well, since their family was obviously getting lunch on the table. But Abel spotted her and waved her in.

"Wilkom, Miriam. Will you join us for a bite?"

Elizabeth glanced up from the stove at the sound of her husband's voice. She didn't speak, but Miriam was shocked at the sight of her. Elizabeth's worn, pale face seemed to have been wiped free of all emotion. She moved mechanically, ladling chicken potpie into a bowl for serving. It was if she'd turned her inner self off, leaving only the outer shell.

Miriam collected herself with an effort. "No, denke." She tried to smile at Abel, tried to sound normal. "I ate before I left home. Don't let me interrupt you. Can I help?"

She glanced around the kitchen, in some ways a

replica of theirs next door, with its wooden cabinets and long oak table, except that this table was oval instead of rectangular. And smaller. The King family had been much smaller than theirs, with Matt, David and Betsy the only children. Betsy stood at the counter near the stove, putting dishes on a tray—for Matt, obviously.

As if feeling her gaze, fourteen-year-old Betsy looked up and murmured a welcome, but the wariness in her blue eyes seemed to deny the words.

Curious at her reaction, Miriam crossed the kitchen to her. Betsy had buttered two slices of bread and cut them into small pieces, and now she was cutting up the morsels of noodles and chicken in the potpie.

Odd. From what she'd been told, she'd thought Matt's injuries were mostly to his legs.

Trying to be helpful, she reached for the tray. "Why don't you go ahead and eat, Betsy? I'll take this—"

"No!" Betsy grabbed the tray and jerked it away from her. "I'll take Matt's meal. I always do." The accompanying glare suggested Miriam had better back off.

"If you want," she said, keeping her voice mild, but she didn't back away. She wasn't going to be intimidated by a teenager. "But I did come to help with Matt, after all."

Betsy's eyes widened. She spun, zeroing in on her father with a look of outrage. "You didn't say anything to me about this." Her voice rose. "I can take care of Matt perfectly well. I don't need anybody's help."

So Abel hadn't told anyone about his plans—or at least, not Betsy.

A glance at Elizabeth didn't make things any clearer. Either she hadn't known, or if he'd spoken, the words hadn't registered with her, caught as she was in her frozen state.

But Betsy was the immediate problem, not her mother.

"That's enough, Betsy." Abel sounded weary. "We need more help. You shouldn't spend all your time with Matthew. Your mother needs your help with the house and garden."

"Matt's recovery is more important!" she flared.

"Yah, it is." His voice had hardened. "Miriam has had experience in taking care of injured people, and she knows how to work with the therapist."

"Matt doesn't want—"

"Enough," he repeated. He didn't raise his voice, but there was no doubt that he'd meant it. After a moment's hesitation, Betsy turned away, silenced.

Abel's reaction might not have helped Miriam in Betsy's eyes, but maybe nothing would have. Betsy clearly considered Matt's well-being her responsibility.

As for Elizabeth, she didn't even seem to have noticed that anything had happened. She just moved from the stove to the table like some sort of machine, and Miriam watched her with shocked pity.

She'd told herself that her only job here was to help Matt, but it seemed clear now that she wouldn't be able to do that without becoming involved with the rest of the family. Her heart sank at the enormity of the task.

Betsy, seeming to sense victory about lunch, at least, picked up the tray defiantly and started down the hall. Miriam moved just as quickly, right behind her. When the girl turned to glare, she just smiled.

"I'll hold the door for you." Before Betsy could react, she moved past the pantry and opened the door leading to what had been Elizabeth's quilting room. It was the only space downstairs that could have been turned into a room for Matthew.

Betsy gritted her teeth, but she gave a short nod and passed into the room. She reached for the door, obviously intending to shut Miriam out, but Miriam slipped inside and closed the door, never letting go of her smile.

Matthew sat on the bed, propped against pillows. He'd clearly been expecting only his sister, because after one shocked look at Miriam, he turned his head away quickly.

Not quite fast enough, though. The right side of his face, with his even features, strong jaw and well-shaped mouth, looked much as usual, except for the pallor and strain that was evident. But the left side—

Her breath caught. A jagged scar ran down his

face from the outer corner of his eye to his mouth, twisting it out of resemblance to the right. Her heart winced at the pain he'd been through.

Betsy hesitated a moment, as if waiting for an outburst, and then scurried over to him, setting the tray on a bedside table. "Your favorite thing today—chicken potpie. I've cut it up to make it easier for you to eat."

He grunted, and she seemed to take that for agreement. Betsy began spreading a napkin over his chest, as if he were a messy toddler.

Not wanting to precipitate another outburst from Betsy, Miriam looked around the room while observing them in brief glances. Matt was ignoring her, although he certainly knew why she was here.

That was all right. She intended to watch this time, see what the situation was, and talk to the therapist. That would give Miriam enough to think about for her first visit.

When the room had been Elizabeth's quilting room, it was constantly in use. Elizabeth's beautifully designed, colorful quilts had been very popular at craft fairs and auctions, and her family had beamed with pride when one fetched the highest price at last year's spring auction.

But now the quilting frame was shoved against the wall, actually gathering dust, something that was ordinarily unheard-of in Elizabeth's spotless house. A basket and several blankets were piled atop the treadle sewing machine in the corner, making it clear that it was unused, as well.

It wasn't a bad room for someone recovering—bigger than most bedrooms, with two windows on the side and one looking out the back, so that Matt would have views both of the meadow between their two farms and the normally busy farmyard and barn behind the house.

He didn't act as if he enjoyed the views, though. He stared at the walls even while his sister fussed over him, holding the bowl at what seemed to Miriam an awkward height.

Did Matt really need someone to help him eat? He didn't seem to, but he submitted tamely to Betsy's fussing, darting a glance toward Miriam once or twice, as if to be sure she saw that he didn't need her help.

Finally he pushed Betsy's hands away with an annoyed movement. "That's enough," he muttered.

"Come on," she coaxed. "Just a few more bites, please? You can do it." She spoke as if he were a two-year-old.

Had he been putting up with that? He must have been, she supposed. But something, maybe Miriam's presence, made him object today.

"I said it was enough. Take it away and stop fussing."

Looking hurt, Betsy collected the tray. Once again, Miriam held the door. Then she closed it behind Betsy and turned to him, steeling herself for trouble.

"Well? Tell me you're not shocked at the change in me." His tone was edged, taunting her to say no.

"Just a bit," she said mildly. "I guess you have changed. You didn't used to expect people to wait on you."

It took him a couple of seconds to get what she was saying, and then his face darkened with anger.

But before he could speak, the door opened again, revealing Abel, gesturing to her. The argument Matt clearly wanted to have would have to wait. Well, thinking out what he wanted to say would at least keep him from staring at the walls.

She couldn't count on help from Matt's mother or sister, it seemed, but she wouldn't give up. Matt had her to deal with now, and she'd push him for his own good. She stepped into the hall. An Englischer stood waiting behind Abel, watching her with a twinkle in his brown eyes—undoubtedly the physical therapist.

Matt glared at the door, feeling as if his thoughts ought to burn right through it. Nothing happened to the door, and he resisted the impulse to throw something at it, just to make clear how he felt.

When his ire lessened enough so that he could concentrate on something else, he realized he could hear the murmur of voices from the hallway. Miriam's was one, that was certain sure, and after a moment, he recognized the other as that of Tim, the therapist.

He gritted his teeth. He should have known Miriam would be expecting to talk to the therapist. Probably Daad had set it up that way. He hated the idea of anyone discussing him, especially those two.

And he also didn't like what Miriam had implied with her smart comment. Apparently she wasn't as quiet and shy as he'd always thought, to talk back to him that way.

What had she meant, anyway? Did she think he was making too much of his physical problems? Or that he was pitying himself?

No, he didn't need Betsy's fussing over him, but it wasn't Miriam's business. Besides, it seemed to make Betsy happy to do something for him.

He'd gotten that far in his figuring when someone tapped on the door and opened it.

"Hey, Matt, are you ready for me?" Tim Considine didn't wait for an answer, just came in with his usual good cheer.

"Ready as I'll be..." Matt stopped, frowning, as Miriam slipped in behind him. "What's Miriam doing here? I don't need an audience when you're working on my legs."

Tim quirked an eyebrow as he shook his head. "Come on, now. Miriam has signed on to help with your daily workout. She has to see how I want it done." Tim grinned. "No need to worry about her. She's done this before, right, Miriam?"

"That's right." Miriam's pleasant face might have shown a little wariness now. Maybe she knew he had an outburst waiting for when they were alone. And maybe that wariness meant a little pushing would convince her this wasn't going to work.

"I'm not worried. And I don't need anyone to help me."

"Can't fool me." Tim shoved back the sheet, his hands moving deftly along Matt's legs. "You haven't done a single exercise since last week, have you?"

Matt set his jaw. Just about anything he said would be a lie. He had endured the exercises Tim pushed him through, but he certain sure wasn't willing to do any extra ones.

"Right." Tim read the answer in his face. "This time you'll have someone to help you through them."

An objection came to his lips, but Tim shook his head. "Your father says you agreed to this. Isn't that right?"

He didn't have an answer to this one, either. Maybe he'd have to put up with Miriam for a few days. But with a little effort, he ought to be able to make the experience unpleasant enough that she'd quit herself.

Contenting himself with that, Matt nodded.

"Okay, let's get busy." Tim rubbed his hands together. "Come over here where you can see what's going on, Miriam."

As she moved closer, Tim started in on his routine. This time he explained what was happening while he went, showing Miriam exactly what was wrong and how to work the muscles. Matt discovered he was listening just as Miriam was, understanding a little better what was happening with his useless legs.

"You want to push to the point of resistance, ease up and then repeat. Let's try four or five repetitions of each exercise this week." His easy grin came again as Miriam scribbled notes on a pad. "Not so little that he doesn't have to work, but not so much that he tries to throw something at you."

Miriam's answering smile suggested that she knew Matt wanted to do just that. "I'll duck if I have to."

"Right. Now just put your hands where I had mine, and you can try it."

Before Matt could protest, Miriam's hands had replaced Tim's, grasping his leg firmly but gently. Hers were smaller than Tim's, but he was more aware of them. He could feel their warmth through the loose pants he wore.

He had to admit she seemed capable enough, and she moved his leg exactly as Tim had done.

"How's that? A little farther?" She studied his face as if she'd read the answer there.

Gritting his teeth, he nodded. His muscles screamed in protest, but he sure wasn't going to let Miriam know it.

Tim moved on through the exercises, showing, teaching and then watching as Miriam did the same. Only once or twice did he have to stop her and correct something. Matt found himself annoyed by Miriam's ability. He didn't want her working on him.

He didn't want anybody doing it. Why couldn't they just leave him alone? He was useless no matter what they did.

As for Miriam…well, he suspected she had to know when she pushed his leg to the point of pain, but she wouldn't let it show in her face, any more than he would. They had that in common, at least.

"You can feel how strong his leg muscles are, even now," Tim was telling her. "But it's important that we work on the arm strength, as well. We don't want him to lose muscle mass because of lack of use."

Miriam nodded. "It's encouraging that he's so strong to begin with, ain't so?" She didn't glance at him, but Matt thought a faint flush of color moved through her cheeks.

"Yes," Tim said. He patted Matt's arm in a friendly way. "Gives you a much better chance of getting off this bed and busy again."

A spark of anger flickered in Matt. "Will it get me back in the fields again, where I need to be? Because if not, it doesn't matter to me."

Tim drew back, startled by the bitterness in his voice, and Matt regretted losing control. It wasn't Tim's fault, but…

"It matters to other folk." Miriam's voice didn't lose its gentleness, but there was a thread of disapproval he could certain sure hear. "Like your parents, and your sister, and a bunch of other people who care about you."

"All right," he growled, knowing the rebuke was

justified, but he was annoyed all the same. “Are you about finished?”

“Just the massage left.” Tim glanced at Matt’s legs and hesitated.

Matt figured he knew what was in his mind. Last week Tim had helped him remove the pants for the massage. Well, he certain sure wasn’t going to have Miriam doing that. And it looked as if Tim had figured that out for himself.

“Maybe your father could help with this,” Tim began, sounding doubtful. He must know how busy Daad was with no one to help him on the farm.

“That won’t work.” He’d sooner do without the massage than add something else to Daad’s workload.

“Suppose we spread the sheet over his legs and do it that way,” Miriam suggested. “It will work better than nothing.”

“Not a bad idea. Let’s give it a try.” Between them, they spread out the sheet. “You’ve done massage this way before?”

“Yah. The last…” Her voice faded, and she took a breath. “The last young man I helped had badly swollen, painful joints, and the massage eased his pain.”

Tim nodded, and they went off onto a technical discussion of what had been wrong with that person, probably someone she’d helped while she was out in Ohio. Matt didn’t bother listening, because he was too busy wondering what had caused that sad expression on Miriam’s face.

Who was he? And why did the mention of him bring that mingling of pain and embarrassment to Miriam's face? If he wanted a way to get rid of her, it might be worthwhile for him to find out.

Chapter Two

Miriam had avoided the angry encounter Matthew had undoubtedly looked forward to by the simple method of walking out with the therapist. After consulting with him and assuring Abel that she'd be back in midmorning to do the first of two workouts each day that Tim recommended, she'd headed for home. She'd been shaken enough by seeing what had become of the Matthew she'd known. She hadn't needed to stick around and be a target for his obvious displeasure.

The lively conversation around the supper table kept her thoughts occupied—with her six younger brothers, there was never any lack of chatter, even though Aaron was married now and had his own small house on the property. That still left five others ranging from eight to twenty to keep up the noise level.

No, she certain sure wouldn't talk about Matthew

over supper. She'd wait until she could be alone with Mammi.

Eventually the kitchen cleared out, since there were evening chores to be done. Miriam and Mammi automatically began to tackle the dishes. After the final banging of the back door, her mother gave her a questioning look.

"Are you going over to see Matthew tomorrow?" A slight shadow of doubt crossed her face as she said the words.

"Not until midmorning." She raised her voice above the rush of hot water into the sink. "Tim, the physical therapist, wants me to do two workouts a day—one in midmorning, one in midafternoon. I'll try to do whatever I can to help with him in between."

"I hope..." Mammi paused, and Miriam saw the doubt in her eyes. "I hope it works out."

"What is it, Mammi?" She reached over to clasp her mother's hand with her soapy one. "You're worried about this, ain't so?"

Mammi squeezed her hand. "Ach, I'm being foolish. But after the bad time you had, I was looking forward to having my daughter here so I could just baby you. You need a rest from taking care of people. I thought we could pick out material for a new dress, and can corn relish, and..."

Miriam didn't know whether to laugh or cry. Her mother had been thinking the same way she had... that those sweet, ordinary things of life would feel wonderful good after the trials she'd experienced lately.

"We will, Mammi. I promise you. Whether I end up being able to help Matthew or not, we'll make time for us to do things together."

"Good." Mammi wiped away a tear. "I can't very well take any of your bruders shopping with me, ain't so?"

The thought made Miriam chuckle, but that fact was a bit sorrowful, too. Mammi had really wanted another girl or two, Miriam knew, but she'd ended up with six boys. Boys, she always claimed, weren't quite as satisfactory in producing grandbabies for her. Not that Miriam had many hopes of doing that either at this point. Still, Aaron's wife, Anna Grace, had a good chance at it.

"Mammi, I know you've been over at the King place often enough to get an idea of how things are going. Do you think I'll be able to do anything with Matthew?"

Mammi wiped a bowl slowly, her face thoughtful.

"I'm not sure what's happening with Matthew since the accident, and I don't know that anyone else does. I guess it's natural that someone who's always taken his strength and good health for granted would be shaken by losing it all at once, but he's not even trying. He ought to see what it's doing to his father, it seems to me."

Even that mild a criticism was rare from Mammi,

who always saw the best in everyone. It sounded as if Matt's whole personality had changed.

Well, she'd seen that for herself. "Maybe he needs a little more time," she suggested. "He's grieving for his brother, too. Maybe even feels responsible since he was driving, though how he could have avoided that drunk driver, I don't know. Still, I have the physical therapist on my side, at least. We'll gang up on him if we have to," she added lightly.

Her mother managed a smile, but Miriam could see that she was still worried.

"I just don't want you to be hurt. If you don't get anywhere with Matthew, it won't be your fault, any more than what happened with your aunt's neighbor was."

Miriam winced at the reference to her painful experience in Ohio. Poor Wayne. She couldn't help but wonder how he was faring, despite being told in no uncertain terms to stay away from him.

"I can't do more than try," she said, wishing she could chase away her mother's worry, to say nothing of her own. "You know what Daad always taught us kids. That if we failed at something, we just had to try again."

"Some things it's better not to try again. Like the time Sammy climbed up to the barn roof," Mamm said. "Your daad certain sure didn't want him to try that again. Some things are best not repeated."

"I remember, only too well. I'm the one who had to go up and talk him down." She grinned, remembering the expression red-haired Sammy wore when she'd finally eased him back down to the ground. He'd been proud as could be, right up to the moment when Daad had taken the switch to him for being so foolish.

"Sammy hasn't changed, for all that he's ten now," Mamm said, trying to suppress a smile. "Your daad caught him trying to ride that old mule the other day."

"What happened?" She remembered the mule—the worst-tempered creature that God had ever created, Daad always said.

"It ran him right into the barn wall and then kicked him for good measure. Your daad thinks that might teach him a lesson, but I don't believe anything ever will." Mamm looked exasperated.

"He's still trying to find something his big brothers haven't done, I guess. That's what it is to have older siblings."

That made her think of Betsy, the baby of the King family. Surely it would be possible to get Betsy to see that babying Matthew wasn't helping him.

But her job would be Matthew, not Betsy. Nor their mother, who was so lost in her grief.

"About Elizabeth..." she began tentatively.

Mammi shook her head. "I've tried to get her to talk about it, but she just can't. You know how she always doted on David. You'd think it would have been Betsy, the youngest, who was the one she'd spoiled, but it was always David."

Miriam remembered. "I don't believe it was possible for anyone to spoil David. He had such a sweet nature."

"No, it didn't spoil David," Mammi agreed. She frowned, as if groping for an answer to a riddle. "But I was thinking more about Betsy. This has been hard on her. She's the only one of the kinder who was untouched by the accident."

Miriam found herself shaking her head. No, surely Betsy hadn't been untouched by the accident. It had turned her whole family upside down and would have affected her in ways she might not even recognize. Maybe…

She reminded herself again that Betsy wasn't her job. But she had a feeling that between them, both of the remaining King siblings were going to try her fragile confidence to the breaking point.

Miriam hurried along the edge of the pasture toward the King place the next morning. She'd have to pick up her pace to be on time, but she'd valued an early morning conversation with her mother too much to rush it. Mammi understood people, and she'd known Elizabeth and Abel all her married life. Maybe, with both of them thinking about it, they'd see some way to help them. As for Matthew, it seemed he was going to be her responsibility.

With her forehead furrowed in thoughts of Matt, her brother Joshua, coming toward her, had almost reached her before she realized he was there.

"Finished helping Abel already?" She knew he'd headed out before dawn to help Matt's father get crates of vegetables hauled to the co-op for the produce auction.

Joshua stopped, smiling down at her—he'd been enjoying looking down at his big sister ever since he'd passed her in height. At seventeen, he probably wasn't finished growing yet, either. And she still had to go through it with Sammy and the twins.

"Yah, we're done for now. I said I'd come back later to help Abel with the fencing."

"Maybe I'll see you there later, yah?" As she took a step, Joshua put out a hand to stop her.

"Can you wait a minute? I want to ask you something."

As far as she could tell, Matt wouldn't care if she ever got there, so she decided to stop worrying about it. "For sure. What is it?"

She studied Josh's face, noticing the maturity that had become more evident in the months she'd been away. As the middle of seven children, he'd always been quieter than easygoing, popular Daniel, three years older, and Sammy, almost seven years younger, the energetic schnickelfritz who was always into everything. He wasn't one to whip out an answer. If you wanted to know what was on Josh's mind, you had to wait patiently.

"It's Abel," he said finally. "He wants me to come work for him—like a regular job, I mean, not just helping out."

He stopped there. It seemed something about the offer bothered him, but she wasn't sure what.

"If you don't like that sort of work..." she began, but he shook his head vigorously.

"It's not that. I like it. Even better than dairying." He darted an apprehensive look around, as if afraid Daad would hear him. Their branch of the Stoltzfus family had been dairy farmers for three generations.

She waited. There was more, or else Joshua wouldn't wear that line between his brows.

"Abel wants to pay me," he said, all in one breath. "I don't know...well, we're neighbors. I'd help him anyway. It feels funny him wanting to pay me for it."

Probably only Joshua, with his sensitive conscience, would worry about such a thing. She squeezed his hand. "I think it's all right. Naturally he'd pay anyone else he hired. If you want to do it, it seems like a gut job for you."

When he looked unconvinced, she added, "Talk to Daad about it. He'll know the right thing to do, ain't so?"

"Yah, that's true." A smile wiped away the line. "Denke, Miriam." He squeezed her hand in return, his blue eyes cleared of worry, and then trotted off toward home, his burden lifted.

It was a small thing, she knew, but Miriam felt satisfied in a way she hadn't in quite a while. She shouldn't have stayed away so long, letting her little brothers grow up without her. They counted on her.

This was where she belonged…in this valley, with the people who knew her and cared for her.

Reminding herself that she had someone to help today, she hurried on across the field.

Miriam's muscles tightened as she thought ahead to what awaited her. Matthew had been annoyed with her the day before, and he hadn't had an opportunity to vent that annoyance. The Matt she'd known and grown up with had never held on to a grudge overnight, but Matt as he was since the accident…well, she couldn't be sure of his reaction. And if there was one thing she disliked, it was confronting someone.

To her surprise, Elizabeth was out in the garden, and even more surprising, Betsy was with her. Apparently Abel's words had borne some fruit. If Betsy could get her mother to take an interest in things, that would help both of them.

Waving to them, she hurried inside, reaching the door to Matt's room slightly out of breath. She paused for a moment, collecting herself, tapped lightly, and opened the door.

"You're late." Matt shoved himself up onto his elbows to level the words at her, and Miriam had to smile. If annoyance with her produced that much energy, maybe she should annoy him every day.

"Yah, I am, a little. Sorry. I met Joshua coming over."

That distracted him, as she'd hoped, giving her a moment to assess his condition today. He seemed to have a bit more color and life in his face, maybe the effect of having something to complain about.

"Joshua told you about Daad's offer, ain't so?" He sank back on his pillow.

"Do you mind?" She moved a little closer. She'd learned to read feelings on people's faces since she'd been home nursing, but Matt managed to evade her with his closed expression.

His hands clenched into fists. "If I weren't stuck in this bed, Daad wouldn't have to be hiring anyone to help him."

There was the crux of the matter, and Miriam knew she'd have to meet it head-on if she were to help him.

"No, I guess not. If the accident hadn't happened, a lot of things would be different." She grasped his right leg, wondering how much he'd cooperate without Tim standing beside her.

He jumped in response, but then he seemed to force himself not to react. His eyes narrowed.

"Aren't you going to accuse me of self-pity? Or... what was it you said yesterday? Of wanting people to fuss over me?"

Miriam forced herself to adopt the calm mannerism that she used with complaining patients. "I suspected you wanted to yell at me over that. Go ahead, if you want."

That seemed to disarm him, and he gave her a reluctant smile. It changed quickly to a wince as she lifted his leg.

Noting it, she regretted she hadn't warned him before the movement. "Let's start with some leg stretches, yah?"

"Seems like you already started." He was gritting his teeth. "I was going to say it's no fun yelling at someone when they've given you permission."

Miriam was cheered by the trace of humor in his voice. That was more like the Matt she remembered. "That's why I did it," she said lightly. "You know, you can tell me to ease off whenever you think I'm going too far," she reminded him.

"Would you listen?" he retorted. "Never mind, don't answer that."

"We do want to increase the angle of lift before Tim comes back, ain't so?" She eased the right leg down and moved around to the left. She'd come back to it for more exercise once he was warmed up.

He didn't answer, and she gave him a questioning look. He was eyeing her. "You'd like to please Tim, yah? He's a good-looking guy."

What was on his mind now? Did he intend to tease her about the physical therapist? If so, he was really on the wrong track.

"You're the one who's supposed to please him." His earlier comment about his father having to pay someone to help out came back to her. That might be a way to get him motivated. "You don't want your daad to have to pay for extra therapy sessions, do you?"

"I don't want him paying for any," he snapped, his fragmentary good humor gone. "You don't need to remind me of what I'm costing my family. But if I can't be the way I was, what use is it?"

Well, she'd wanted him to be motivated, but that was the wrong reaction. "If you can't do what you did, you might find you can be useful in another way," she said. She watched his face to see how he took that idea, but once again, he'd frozen her out.

Well, she'd come back to it. "Let's push you up on the pillow a bit before we do the bent leg stretches. Okay?"

Taking his silence for assent she bent to help lift him at the same moment he reared up on his elbows. Their foreheads cracked together, and she closed her eyes. When she opened them, his face was inches away…close enough to see every tiny line, to feel his every breath.

Her own breath caught in her throat, and she forced herself to push away from him. "Sorry." She managed a shaky smile. "I didn't mean to knock you out."

Matt didn't speak, and his face was unreadable. But if he really thought she was attracted to Tim, he was on the wrong track.

Wait a minute, she warned herself. She wasn't attracted to anyone. It was completely unsuitable to feel anything for either of them.

Matt rubbed his forehead, trying to get his mind straight. He hadn't expected that…well, that closeness with Miriam, even if it was accidental. She was looking at him, a bit anxious, and he had to say something.

"Tim never cracked his head on mine," he muttered.

"Well, you probably never interfered with his moving you."

That was completely different, as far as he was concerned. Tim was a professional, and a man, and there wasn't any shame about letting him help.

"Just tell me what you want me to do, and I'll do it myself. It'll probably be safer."

Miriam's lips twitched. "Learning how to move patients is part of being able to help them. You don't need to be afraid I'll drop you. Or that I'll hurt myself."

Her talent for figuring him out was mistaken this time. Fear wasn't what bothered him. The truth was, he didn't want Miriam helping him move because that made him too aware of his own weakness. He didn't think he'd say that to her, though.

"I'd have said you were too shy to do any such thing. What happened to the quiet, soft-spoken Miriam I used to know?"

She had taken hold of his leg again, this time moving his bent knee toward his chest. Once that had been taken for granted. Now it hurt so much he clenched his teeth.

"Easy," she said, bringing his leg back a few inches. "You're trying too hard to do it yourself. Let me move your leg for you. We're just working on flexibility." She pressed it again, very gently. "As far as shyness is concerned…well, I figured out that if I was going to help people, I sometimes had to be firm, even if I didn't feel it."

He breathed a sigh of relief as she eased his leg down and then started on the other one. "So that's just a mask you wear, yah?"

Miriam smiled. "You sound pleased. Do you think that will make it easier for you to push me out?"

She understood too much, he decided.

"I wouldn't do that," he said, and then wondered if that sounded as phony to her as it did to him. "I agreed to let you work with me, didn't I?"

"Yah, you did."

It seemed to him that she didn't sound convinced. It was almost as if she knew perfectly well what he had planned. He didn't like it.

Before he could figure out whether or not to deny it, the door opened, and Betsy burst in. "What are you doing?" She glared at Miriam as if suspicious of her actions, making him remember Miriam's comment about him enjoying Betsy fussing over him.

"Exercising," he said shortly. "Maybe you should go help Mammi." Not that he thought Miriam was right, but still…

"I already did. And anyway, if I watch, I can help if Miriam can't be here sometime." The smile she gave Miriam didn't convince him, although it might have convinced someone else. Betsy was up to something. Or maybe she just didn't want anyone else taking over what she considered her job.

"That's a gut idea," Miriam chipped in unexpectedly. "We're just going to start on some exercises for arm strength. Did you notice the attachments Tim rigged up overhead?"

Betsy nodded, moving a bit closer, while Miriam groped over her head, standing on tiptoe to point out the handholds of a couple of sets of cords.

"Tim said he wants you to start working with these this week. Eventually you can use them to help you sit up and to get in and out of bed."

He wanted to say that he didn't consider that much of a prize for hard work, but decided it wasn't worth it, especially with Betsy standing right there.

Was that why Miriam had been so interested in involving Betsy in what she was doing? Did she think his little sister's presence would make him try harder?

Actually, he'd begun to count on Betsy's willingness to do whatever he wanted. He wanted her on his side, not Miriam's, even if she thought what Miriam was doing was for his own good.

"For now, let's just do a few strength exercises." Miriam put a handgrip in each of his hands. "Try pulling yourself forward and up, as if you're going to sit up in bed."

He nodded, his muscles tightening as he pulled. And pulled. "Wouldn't have thought it would be so hard," he gasped. What had happened to him while those doctors were operating on him and keeping him under all that medication?

"It takes time to come back from lying in bed," Miriam said, as if she knew his thoughts. "I've heard a therapist say a week of exercise for every day in bed." She'd moved closer, and as he tried again, she put her hand on the middle of his back, pressing.

He could feel how much easier that made it to pull up. And he could also feel the shape of her palm and the warmth of her skin through the thin cotton of his nightshirt. He looked at her, feeling that awareness move between them.

"Here, let me help." Betsy charged in, inserting herself between him and Miriam.

Jealous? He couldn't be sure.

"That's right." Miriam, unruffled, moved Betsy's hand slightly. "Good. Now don't push. Just use your hand for a little extra support. We want his muscles to work but not strain."

"Yah, I see. I can feel it." Betsy sounded pleased, her antagonism slipping away.

With the two of them behind him, he couldn't see either of their faces. But he didn't like the idea of them ganging up on him.

"Betsy, do we have any lemonade?"

"I don't think so. Do you want some? I can make it." All her eagerness to please him rushed back.

"We could all use some after we finish here, ain't so? Why don't you make a pitcher?"

"Right away." She hurried off.

"Don't worry about it." Miriam seemed amused. "She's still your willing servant."

"That wasn't the idea," he said stiffly, his temper flaring that she could read him so easily. "In case you haven't noticed, it makes her happy to do things for me."

"I noticed." She looped the handles back up over the bar and pulled down a pair of stretchy bands. "As long as she's helping you to get stronger, I don't object."

"Stronger." He almost spat out the word. "Stronger for what? None of this is going to do any good. It's useless. I can't be the person I was."

She seemed unaffected by his anger. "We'll never know that if you don't try, will we?"

He glared at her for a long moment as a thought formed in his mind. He turned it over, looking at it from all angles. Would it work?

"I'll tell you what," he said. "I'll make a deal with you."

"What kind of a deal?" Miriam's expression was cautious.

"I promise to do everything you say…to try my hardest…for a month. If I'm not much better by then, you agree to quit."

Miriam stood very still, considering before she spoke. "I can't speak for Tim. Just for myself."

"Yah. Just for yourself."

"Who's going to decide whether or not you're much better?" she said. "You?"

His jaw hardened. She wasn't going to make this easy.

"No," he said abruptly. "How about… Betsy?"

Her lips twitched. “Don’t you think Betsy has her own reasons for wanting to be rid of me?”

He raised one eyebrow, a gesture that used to attract the girls. “If you’re really making progress, you’ll have won her over by then. What’s wrong? Don’t you have any confidence in your work?”

She seemed to wince at that. After a long moment, she nodded. “All right. It’s a deal.”

Chapter Three

Over the next couple of days, second thoughts came back to haunt Miriam. Had she backed herself into a corner by coming to that agreement with Matt? Still, what else could she have done when he challenged her?

The truth was, if her work didn't have any good results in a month's time, there was no sense in Abel continuing to pay her for coming.

The fact that Abel was paying did give her pause. In a sense, she worked for him, not Matt. Should she tell him what she'd done in agreeing to Matt's demand?

Neither she nor Matt had said they would keep the deal to themselves, but she couldn't help feeling that it had been a private agreement between two childhood friends. If it worked as she hoped, it would be well worth it. Abel would be too pleased to care how it had come about.

So far Matt had been fulfilling his promise, although it was early days yet. She couldn't complain that he wasn't trying. In fact, when she saw how hard he pushed, she wanted to tell him to ease off.

Today's morning session was going well, with Matt using the stretchy bands to build muscle strength back in both his arms and legs. He actually seemed interested in using the bands, maybe because it pitted him against himself. She'd always thought him competitive.

"Good work," she said, rolling them back when he'd finished. "If you keep that up, you might be able to move to the next tighter bands by Monday."

He shrugged, leaning back against the raised slant of the hospital bed. "Such excitement. Will they be a different color?"

"As a matter of fact, they will."

His question had been sarcastic, she supposed, but it made her think of something that might be more exciting. She glanced around the room, with its sewing and quilting equipment shoved back against the walls and covered with sheets, like so many mounds of snow.

This room didn't have much to express the personality of the person living in it. Or to make it more cheerful and welcoming. Why hadn't she seen that before?

The door opened, admitting Betsy with a tray. "Lunch is ready, Miriam. Mammi says to come."

Leaving Betsy to cope with getting Matt to eat as

best she could, Miriam walked into the kitchen and took her place at the table.

Once the silent prayer before the meal had finished, Miriam continued to sit quietly, mentally rearranging furniture, until Abel put down his fork and looked at her.

"Was ist letz? Is something wrong, Miriam? You are not usually so quiet. And you're not eating."

She'd been making a special effort to encourage Elizabeth to talk since she'd been coming, and Abel must have noticed. She hurriedly picked up her fork.

"I was just thinking that maybe we could do something to make Matt's room more cheerful since he spends so much time there. Is there anything in his bedroom that maybe could be moved down?"

Abel looked blank, as most Amish men would when confronted with the idea of decorating. "I don't think..."

"His bookcase." The words, coming from Elizabeth, were so surprising that Miriam had to look again to be sure it was she who had spoken. Normally she didn't say anything unless prompted.

"That's a gut idea," Miriam said quickly, willing to encourage Elizabeth no matter what she suggested. "Maybe he'd like to read in his spare time." *Instead of staring at the ceiling*, she added to herself.

Betsy, who'd come back to join them once Matt was finished, seemed torn between discouraging the idea because it was Miriam's and trying to cheer her mammi.

Before she could decide, Miriam plunged into involving her. “What do you think, Betsy? Would we be able to bring the bookcase down between the two of us?”

“Yah, for sure.”

She’d apparently decided to be encouraging. She wouldn’t want to suggest there was anything she couldn’t handle.

“Actually,” she continued, “I could bring it myself if I took the books out first. You don’t need to help me.”

Miriam just smiled. “I’d like to help. We’ll have to decide where to put it. Any ideas?”

“What if we moved the sewing machine?” Once appealed to, Betsy seemed to be all in with the idea. “We could put it in the dining room. We don’t use the dining room unless a lot of people are here, I mean, like…”

Like the day of David’s funeral, Miriam finished for her. That would have been the last time there were many people in this house.

Elizabeth didn’t move, but she seemed to retreat into herself, and Betsy looked stricken and guilty. Miriam reached out under the table to pat the girl’s hand in sympathy. She hadn’t meant any harm.

“Yah, a gut idea,” Abel said firmly. “You girls can do that after you eat. I must hurry. Joshua is coming to help me finish the fencing.”

Joshua, after consulting with Daad, had agreed to start working daily, but on the days of the early trip to the co-op, he usually went home for a few hours afterward. To sleep, Miriam thought. Like most boys his age, he always seemed to need sleep.

Elizabeth had slipped away from the table after eating hardly enough to keep a bird alive. Miriam looked after her, concerned. She'd make herself sick if she kept that up.

Miriam joined Betsy in clearing away after lunch. "Shall we go ahead and wash the dishes?" She'd always found washing dishes together conducive to sharing. Anything that made Betsy cooperative was certain sure worth doing. She didn't want to be struggling against Betsy, as well as Matthew.

"Let's do the bookcase first," Betsy said, looking eager. "I want to see his face when we take it in."

"Okay. I'll follow you." She'd been upstairs in the King house, but not for years. Had Matt been sharing a room with David? She didn't know.

But when Betsy led the way in, it seemed clear that this was Matt's alone. Like most Amish bedrooms, the room contained only necessary items. Matt's clothes hung on pegs on the wall, along with his winter felt hat and several pairs of suspenders. The shoes he didn't have a reason to wear now were lined up beneath the clothes, and Miriam's throat tightened at the sight.

Otherwise, a chest of drawers that would hold everything else he needed stood against the wall opposite the twin bed that was topped by one of Elizabeth's creations—a beautiful sunshine-and-shadows quilt in shades ranging from pale yellow to orange and rust and brown. It was like looking at the hillside in autumn.

Betsy was already kneeling in front of a two-shelf bookcase that stood beneath the window. Miriam hurried to join her. She pulled out an armload of books.

"It's the *Little House* books." Betsy sounded intrigued, as if she'd like to dip into them again herself. "Mammi read those to us when we were small."

"You liked the one about the Big Woods best."

Betsy jumped in reaction at finding her mother standing behind them. "And David..." Elizabeth stopped, struggling for a moment. "David liked..." Again she stopped.

Betsy brushed away a tear almost angrily. "He liked the prairie one. He wanted to hear it over and over."

Elizabeth's tears were flowing now, and to Miriam's surprise, she didn't freeze into herself again. Surely it was better for her to express her emotion rather than pretend it wasn't there.

"Yah," Elizabeth whispered. "He loved it." She moved blindly over to the chest, her back to them.

Betsy was busy stacking books to clear the bookcase, so Miriam picked up the first of several carved wooden animals arranged on top. "Should we take these downstairs, too?" She held up a very life-like bear.

Betsy looked up. "Yah, I guess. He made that one last winter."

"Matt did?" She hadn't thought Matt had an interest in anything that required sitting still.

Betsy nodded, standing up. "Okay, it's empty. Let's take it down. I'll go backwards."

She suspected that Betsy meant that she didn't trust Miriam to take the more difficult part of the job, but she ignored the jab, if that's what it was. Her mind revolved around this new facet of Matt's personality. Maybe it was one that would help his healing, if only she could approach it in the right way. She had to consider that and maybe even talk to Tim about it.

Matt stretched tired muscles and relaxed back against the pillow behind him. He hadn't realized how much it was going to take to live up to his promise about exercising. But he'd do it, if only to prove that he was right. He could pull on those stretchy bands all Miriam wanted, but at the end of the month, he'd still be unable to do any of the things he used to. Then Miriam would give up and go home.

For just a second, his conviction wavered. Having Miriam pop in and out to pester him did make the days go a little faster. Still, it didn't change things. He was useless. He'd been able to do the work of two men without tiring, and now he tired out pulling a couple of elastic bands.

He gritted his teeth. If he could take David's place in the accident right now, he'd do it in an instant.

Realizing he'd tensed his muscles again, Matt

forced himself to relax. He couldn't rest all keyed up. If he could stop his thoughts from going round and round, maybe he'd even be able to take a nap.

He used to think naps were for babies. Now they were a prize to get him through the days.

Something thudded out in the hallway, followed by a spate of giggles, no doubt from Betsy. She used to giggle all the time, but he hadn't heard the sound since the accident. Now there was a scrape of wood against wood.

"Ouch, not so fast." Laughter threaded Miriam's voice, too, and someone bumped against the wall.

"What are you doing out there?" He shoved himself up against the pillow, thoughts of his nap evaporating. "Sounds like the house is coming down."

The door popped open, and his sister backed in. She turned a laughing face toward him and knocked whatever she was carrying against the door.

"Wait and see," she said. "If Miriam quits steering me the wrong way."

"You're the one who's steering," Miriam retorted, pushing the door back with her elbow.

It was the bookcase from his bedroom that they were manhandling between them. "What are you doing with that? It belongs in my bedroom."

"We thought it might be more useful down here for now." Miriam swung her end of the bookcase around, and they settled it against the wall close to the bed. "This way you can have your books handy to read. In between exercising, of course."

Miriam's cheeks were flushed with the effort, and her blue eyes sparkled. Betsy had lost her sulky look, and she wiped her forehead with one hand still grinning.

"Whew. It's hot for furniture moving, yah? I'll get the first load of books before I melt."

"I don't want..." he began, but Betsy was already gone.

Miriam lifted her eyebrows in a question. "You don't want what?"

"I don't want my furniture moved around. You can just take that right back where it belongs."

Miriam plopped down on the chair Mammi used at the sewing machine. "I don't think I can. Not until I rest a little. What's wrong with having it down here?"

Nothing, except that it was your idea, he thought. "I don't want anything changed."

He probably sounded as stubborn as a child, but it was true. There was no sense in changing things around, making even more trouble for the family because of him. He'd caused enough problems.

Miriam met his gaze with a firmness that seemed new to the girl he remembered. She must have learned that during her home nursing. He didn't like it.

"If you're right, you won't need a bedroom upstairs, ain't so? Your mamm can use it for something else. Maybe for her quilting, ain't so? But if I'm right...well, Betsy and I will be wonderful happy to take everything back upstairs for you."

Betsy came in, laboring under an armload of books. She plopped it down next to the bookcase, and she and Miriam both dived in, starting to put books on the shelves.

"Do you want the books arranged by author?" Miriam, engrossed in what she was doing, barely glanced his way.

"I want..." he began, and realized there was no use in telling them again that he didn't want anything changed. Once Betsy had the bit between her teeth, she wouldn't quit. But he knew well enough who'd inspired this business. He glared at Miriam. "Yah, I guess if you're so set on doing it."

He was tempted to say he wouldn't be reading them anyway, but he wasn't so sure that was true, now that he thought about it. Reading might pass the time better than staring at the ceiling.

The two girls chattered away about books for a few minutes, and then Betsy went off to get another load. He glanced at Miriam again and realized she was putting his carved animals on top of the bookcase.

"Don't bother with those. They're not good enough for anybody to see."

"Too late. I've already seen them." She held up the bear that he'd made last winter during the long evenings. "I love this one. You really made him look menacing."

"Would have been great if that was what I'd intended."

He hadn't meant it to be funny, but when he saw the laughter in her eyes, he couldn't help smiling , too.

"Let's say the bear wanted to be that way," she said, getting up. "Right?" She turned her head at voices from the kitchen. "Sounds like someone has come to visit. Shall I see who it is?"

But he'd already recognized one of the voices. "I don't want to see them." He must have sounded as panicked as he felt, because Miriam's eyes widened. "Hurry and stop them."

"But if it's someone who wants to see you—"

"No!" He all but shouted it. "For once will you do what I tell you?"

Her face paled at the anger he couldn't control. "Yah, for sure. Don't worry."

Miriam scurried out, probably glad to get away from him, and closed the door behind her. He grasped the edge of the hospital bed so hard the metal felt hot under his hands. Would she stop them?

The murmur of voices got louder for a moment, and his jaw clenched. If he could just lock the door, he'd be safe, but he couldn't get to it. He was helpless…helpless to avoid all the people he didn't want to see, and more importantly, that he didn't want to see him.

Miriam stood for a moment with her hands behind her on the door to Matt's room. Whoever was in the kitchen, Matt definitely didn't want them to visit him. Was he like that with everyone? Or was this someone special? She didn't think she'd ever seen him quite so desperate, and his feelings had touched her without words.

No matter who had come, it was up to her to turn the visitors away, she supposed. She doubted that Elizabeth could muster enough firmness. She headed for the kitchen, trying to remind herself that she was the one in charge of the sickroom now.

The two women who'd come in seemed to fill up the kitchen with their movement and chatter. Miriam hadn't pinpointed the voices, but she knew the women now that she saw them, just as she knew every person in the church district. Liva Ann Miller and her mother, Dora. No wonder it seemed so noisy in here—they were two of the most talkative women she'd ever met.

"Ach, here's Miriam, back from Ohio after such a long time!" Dora swept over to her for a quick embrace, her cheek not quite touching Miriam's. "Look, Liva Ann, it's Miriam. You're helping out, ain't so, Miriam?"

Miriam took breath to answer, but Dora surged on. "We heard you were back, and I said to Liva Ann, depend on it, Liva Ann, Miriam Stoltzfus will be helping out with Matthew, and sure enough, here you are."

"Yah, it's nice to see you, Miriam." But Liva Ann was looking right past her toward the door to Matt's room. "Such a gut thing you're here. I know you're a big help to dear Elizabeth. We brought a pineapple upside down cake. That's Matt's favorite, and I made it just for him. I'll go in—"

She took a step toward the hall, but Miriam moved to block her way. "I'm afraid that's impossible just now." She tried to emulate the tones of the visiting nurse she'd met out in Ohio—calm, pleasant, but admitting no argument.

"Oh, but Matt will want to see me. And the cake." Liva Ann held it up as if it were a pass to get into the room.

Miriam shook her head, smiling. She darted a glance at Elizabeth, but she looked helpless. And Betsy, who could probably stand up to anyone, had chosen this moment to disappear.

"I'm sure he'll love it, and his mamm will make sure he has some for dessert tonight. Right now he's resting. He's on a strict schedule, you know, for meals and therapy and rest."

"Ach, he can't be sleeping, not with the noise we're making." Dora laughed heartily. "My gross-mammi always did say, 'Dora, your laugh is loud enough to call the cows home from pasture,' and she certain sure was nice. Just give Liva Ann a peep in the door. A look at her pretty face is sure to cheer him up—"

"Not now." Miriam was shaking inside, but she stood firm. "We'll tell him all about your visit." She tried to vie with Dora's endless line of chatter. "It was sehr gut of you to come."

Seizing the cake and putting it on the table, she shepherded them toward the door, making sure Liva Ann didn't dart around her. "His therapy session is scheduled in half an hour, and we must get ready. So nice to see you both."

"But—" Dora began, but Elizabeth, apparently stirred into life by the prospect of getting rid of them, had opened the door. Miriam, arms spread wide to corral them, ushered them out.

"Goodbye. Greet your family for me." She closed the door and held on to the latch for a moment, half-afraid they would attempt another entry.

But Liva Ann was tugging at her mother. "Come on. I told you he didn't want to see me. You never listen to me. Let's go home."

Miriam stood at the screen door, watching the buggy carrying Liva Ann Miller and her mother turn onto the main road and disappear. Liva Ann's words to her mother had been odd. If she hadn't seen Matt, how did she know he didn't want to see her?

With a sigh of relief that they were gone, she glanced at Elizabeth, who sank down onto a seat at the table. Betsy, who'd appeared with another arm-load of books too late to help, patted her mother's shoulder.

"What was all this?" Miriam asked. "Why was Matt so…so frantic about not seeing them?"

It was Betsy who answered her. "Didn't you know about Liva Ann? Matt was courting her before the accident."

Miriam shook her head, a little surprised at that pairing. "I was in Ohio at my aunt's for most of the last year, remember? I'm pretty sure nobody mentioned it in the letters I got."

She considered Matt's visitors. Easy enough to see what attracted him to Liva Ann, with her huge brown eyes fringed by long lashes and her pink cheeks. With the purple dress she wore, her coloring made her look like a pansy.

Matt had recognized Liva Ann's voice, all right. And he hadn't wanted to see her.

"But if they were courting..." She pushed away the reflection that Liva Ann was awfully young for him. "Hasn't he seen her at all since the accident?" She asked the question of Betsy, but surprisingly it was Elizabeth who answered.

"No, not once. She came to the hospital, but he wouldn't see her. We thought maybe when he was at home, he'd change his mind." Her voice shook a little on the words. "If only he'd see her..."

"He won't." Betsy sounded scornful. "Why would he? All Liva Ann ever thinks about is how pretty she is."

"Betsy, that's not kind." Elizabeth roused herself to scold. "She's just..." She couldn't seem to find the word, so Miriam filled in for her.

"Immature?" She actually thought Betsy had described Liva Ann very well, but she ought not say so.

"I suppose." Elizabeth frowned down at her hands, pressed on the tabletop. "She's not what I would have chosen for him," she burst out as if relieved to say the words. "But I'd be glad for anyone who would help him."

Miriam didn't say anything. At least today's events seemed to be bringing Elizabeth out of the cold shell she'd been inhabiting.

As for Liva Ann, it seemed doubtful that someone as young and frivolous as she was would be of much help in this situation, but maybe she was wrong. Besides, maybe what Matt needed was someone pretty and flirtatious who'd distract him from his troubles. If he refused to see her, well, he had his reasons.

Elizabeth looked at her almost pleadingly. "Don't you think it would be good for him to see her? Maybe, if you talked to him..."

"I don't think he'd listen to me," she said hurriedly. But then, because Elizabeth was looking at her so pleadingly, she added, "If...if I see a way to do it, I'll encourage him. All right?"

Elizabeth actually came close to a smile at that. "Denke," she whispered.

It was a good thing she couldn't see the reluctance Miriam felt to do any such thing. As for Miriam... well, she really didn't want to look too closely into her reasons for not encouraging their romance.

Chapter Four

On Sunday morning, Miriam was up before dawn, along with the rest of the family. Everyone had to move even earlier on worship Sundays, since the cows had to be taken care of, breakfast cooked and eaten, everyone cleaned up and ready to leave for the drive to the farm where worship was being held.

The older boys had matured enough over the past year that no one had to help them…except for trying to get Joshua away from the mirror. As for the three youngest ones, they dallied around, finding every excuse to be late, until Mamm raised her voice. Then they were suddenly ready and waiting.

Mammi exchanged exasperated looks with Miriam as she shepherded her brood out to the buggy. “If they could do it after I shouted, why couldn’t they do it before?”

“Is it any comfort to know that they will eventually grow up?” Miriam reached out to disentangle the twins, who were trying to climb into the buggy at the same time.

"I'll be too old to care by then," Mammi muttered, and then broke into smile. "Just you wait and see."

Shaking her head, Miriam climbed in after her. Once again, very carefully, Mammi was hinting about the grandchildren she'd like to have. It seemed more and more unlikely to Miriam that she'd be able to provide any of them.

The buggy reached the end of the lane, and Daad stopped to let Abel King's buggy go past, carrying only him and Betsy. Mammi shook her head as they pulled in behind.

"Poor Elizabeth. I'd be wonderful glad to stay with Matthew so she could go to worship, but she keeps saying no."

Miriam patted her mother's hand. "I know. I would, too, but I'm afraid she's not ready to go anywhere. It's a challenge even to get her out in the garden."

Mammi shook her head. "All we can do now is pray for them and wait."

That was probably so, although Miriam knew Mammi would rather do something more active to solve the problem. She understood… It was how she felt, too.

By the time they had gone two miles, they'd caught up with a long line of Amish buggies moving in the same direction. Miriam found something almost prayerful in that steady progress of the community toward worship, and she knew the others did, as well. Even the twins stopped squabbling in the back seat.

Worship was at the home of her cousin Lyddy's family today, so she would have a chance to spend time with Grossmammi, who lived with them. She hadn't seen enough of her since she'd returned. Or of her female cousins, Lyddy and Beth.

Miriam felt a burst of excitement at the thought of her cousins. They wouldn't have much chance to talk until after worship, but surely at some point today they'd be able to catch up. She might not have sisters, but her two cousins were just as close. They'd known each other since they were babies, often in the same playpen, and the round-robin letters they'd exchanged while she was away didn't make up for talking in person.

When they reached the farm, Sammy hopped down to join the other boys who were serving as hostlers today, taking care of the horses and buggies. John Thomas, the bolder of the eight-year-old twins, tugged at Mammi's sleeve.

"Can we sit with the other boys today, Mammi? Please?" He asked the question every worship Sunday, but Mamm and Daad hadn't shown signs of weakening yet.

Her mother touched his cheek. "Not today. Soon Daadi and I will have a talk about it."

John Thomas opened his mouth to argue, but Miriam caught his eye and shook her head at him. Would

John Thomas ever learn that it wasn't a good idea to argue back? Probably not. Miriam gave him a consoling pat as she stepped down.

"Soon," she said. "It will take longer if you argue."

He didn't look entirely convinced, and his lower lip protruded, but then a smile warmed his blue eyes, and he tugged at his twin's hand. "Come on, James. Don't be so slow."

Miriam glanced toward the barn, where folks were already lining up for worship, women on one side, men on the other. There was a low murmur of voices from the men, but on the women's side, the murmur rose to a buzz. Miriam caught several people looking at her, and her stomach seemed to turn over.

They couldn't have heard anything about what happened in Ohio, could they? Surely not. Her relatives wouldn't talk about it.

Her mother nudged her forward. "We'd best get lined up."

Miriam froze for a moment and then moved automatically. "Mammi, people are staring at me." She kept her voice to a whisper but still looked around to be sure no one heard.

Her mother's calm glance seemed to take in all her thoughts and fears. "They're just happy to see you home again, ain't so? Komm."

Telling herself she was too sensitive and Mammi was right, Miriam moved on toward the place where younger women stood in the line. But if she was convinced, why were her fingers clenched so that her nails dented her palm?

Her cousin Lyddy, standing with the oldest of the unmarried women, wiggled her fingers at Miriam. Lyddy would be moving up to the married women soon, since she'd be marrying Simon Fisher sometime this fall. It hadn't been announced yet, but anyone who saw them looking at each other across the width of the barn would know it.

Lyddy clasped her hand when she slipped into place next to her. Her cousin Beth, a couple of places away from them with the married women, reached back to touch her hand, smiling.

A year older than Miriam, Beth had been married and widowed before she was twenty, but now she wore a contented glow of happiness after her remarriage. Miriam was the only one left who hadn't found somebody to love.

She chased the thought away. She had a full life without marriage, didn't she?

Her thoughts flickered back to the memories of what had happened out west, and her muscles seemed to tighten in response. She'd filled her life with service to others, especially those who were recovering from illness or injury. She couldn't let one failure ruin everything.

A hush fell over those waiting as the lines began to move. The barn where she had played so often as a child would have been cleaned and cleaned again in preparation for worship. This couldn't totally eliminate the scent of a barn, but somehow that seemed right, too. They worshiped in the spaces where they lived and worked, because worship was part of daily life.

Once they were inside, and she was seated next to Lyddy, Miriam's sense of being watched seemed to vanish. Grossmammi, seated two rows behind her with Mammi, sent one of her sweet smiles toward her, and farther down the row, Anna Schmidt, who'd been their teacher in school ages ago, smiled and waved.

As the vorsinger sang the first notes of the familiar first hymn, Miriam relaxed and lifted her voice. She was home, where she was loved and cherished. No one would think badly of her here, would they?

It wasn't until she was alone with Lyddy and Beth in the farmhouse kitchen after lunch that the subject of her visit to Ohio came up.

"So, how is Aunt Etta?" Lyddy asked, plunging a platter into the hot water in the sink. "I guess recovering from a hip operation is no fun."

"No, it's not, but you know how Aunt Etta is...always laughing and joking no matter what happens."

Aunt Etta was not actually their aunt—really a second or third cousin, she supposed—but in the wide-ranging genealogy of the Amish, she was family. She belonged to their parents' generation, so it seemed natural to refer to her that way.

Miriam smiled at the memory of her patient. "As

soon as the physical therapist started her on exercises, there was no holding her. My job ended up being to keep her from doing too much."

"A bit different from working with Matthew King, I guess." Beth seized the platter to dry before Miriam could reach it. "I've heard he's being…well, difficult. I'm not criticizing," she added quickly, and no one looking at her sweet face could think it. "It must be terrible, losing his brother that way."

Miriam nodded. She always tried not to talk about the people she thought of as her patients, but it was natural for folks who knew the family to be concerned.

"Yah, it's hard for him to focus on his own healing when he's grieving David." She thought briefly of her bargain with Matthew, wondering again if she'd done the right thing. "But he has been working with the physical therapist well enough."

"And not so much with you?" Lyddy said, her eyes twinkling.

"Well…he's not as wholehearted about it as I'd like." She was silent for a moment, overwhelmed by her need to help Matthew for his own sake, but also for hers. If she failed him the way she'd failed young Wayne…

She tried to force the thought away, but her eyes filled with tears. The dish Lyddy was washing clattered in the sink, and in an instant both of them had their arms around Miriam.

"What is it, Miriam? I knew something was wrong

when you came back all of a sudden like that." Beth dried her tears gently with the corner of a tea towel.

"You can tell us." Lyddy patted her shoulder. "You know that."

Yes, Miriam knew it, and she realized she'd had this at the back of her mind all morning. She never had been able to keep anything from her cousins, and they'd never failed her.

She sniffed and wiped her eyes with her fingers. "I was going to come back as soon as Aunt Etta was better, but you know how it is…they kept wanting me to stay. I'd finally made arrangements to leave, but then another family in the church district asked if I could help them for a time. They have a boy, only fifteen, Wayne."

She seemed to see the pale, thin boy, his joints so painful he could hardly move, his face drooping with sorrow. "He has what they call an autoimmune disease. Sometimes he'd be fine, but then he'd go downhill again, and he was having a bad spell right then. They needed someone who could take over for the mother for a few weeks, stay with him, help him with his exercises and treatments."

"So you said yes." Beth said the obvious thing.

Miriam nodded, her throat tightening. "Poor boy, not able to do what every other teenager took for granted. I was glad to help."

Lyddy patted her shoulder. "Something went wrong, yah?"

"Yah." She hesitated, but she needed to say it. "I

didn't realize he…he was getting attached to me." She swallowed with difficulty. "Too attached. He thought he was in love, thought…well, all kinds of things that weren't real. And it all exploded when I finally realized and tried to talk to him about it."

Beth put her arm around Miriam's waist. "It wasn't your fault," she said firmly, and Lyddy nodded.

"It *was* my fault," she said, angry at herself. "I should have seen. If only I had realized sooner…but I didn't, and there was a scene. His mother said terrible things about me. Wayne was so upset. If I could have talked to him, maybe I could have helped. But his parents wouldn't listen. They were sure it was all my fault. They said I'd made him even worse."

Her voice choked with tears. She couldn't say anything else, but she didn't need to. They hugged her and wiped away her tears, and Beth said loving things while Lyddy said silly things just to make her laugh instead of cry, like always.

Finally Miriam mopped her face again. "Ach, it was silly for me to fall apart like that." She gave them a thankful look. "But I'm glad I did. I wrote to Mamm and Daad about it, but that's different from actually saying it out loud."

How strange that was, but it was true. Just saying the words aloud was sort of like removing a painful thorn—it hurt, but at least maybe then it could heal.

Beth hugged her again. "You have to put it behind you. You couldn't have known what would happen. What does your mother say?"

"She thinks I should just talk about it openly to people. After all, folks here are bound to learn about it through relatives out there. She says it would be easier."

"Well, then, that's what you should do." Lyddy's way was to charge at any problem. Miriam had known that would be her advice.

"I know, I know. You're right, and Mammi's right, but I just can't do it. Well, look at me—I'm falling apart just telling you."

"Don't you think it will be easier once people know?" Beth asked gently.

"I guess."

"After all, you said this was the first time you'd really talked about it." Beth was quietly persuasive, as always.

Miriam nodded, but as relieved as she felt, she didn't really agree. She should have known, shouldn't have been so confident she could help. And she just couldn't go around talking to people about it.

Well, there was no danger of her being overconfident now. She didn't have any confidence left.

The sound of a footstep on the back porch shocked her into awareness of her state. Someone was coming, and here she was with her eyes probably swollen and her face tearstained.

"I can't let anyone see me like this," she gasped.

Lyddy was already pulling her toward the hall. "In the pantry, quick, and shut the door. We'll get rid of whoever it is."

"It's all right," Beth whispered. "Go."

Miriam hurried around the corner and into the pantry. She got the door closed just in time, but she could still hear the voices in the kitchen. Hear and recognize. It was Hilda Berger, and Hilda was well known across the county for the way everything she thought came out of her mouth. Without a pause to consider, some said.

Miriam hugged herself and prayed Hilda wasn't looking for something in the pantry.

"But I made sure Miriam would be in here with the two of you," Hilda exclaimed. "I haven't had a chance to talk with her since she came home from Ohio. I have some kinfolk out there, you know. Maybe she even met them while she was there."

Miriam closed her eyes and hoped for the best. The shelf full of canned applesauce pressed against her back.

"She was here earlier," Beth said vaguely.

"You'll catch up with her, I'm sure." Lyddy, a little bolder, spoke out. "Maybe you can find her with her family."

"Yah, I guess you're right." She must have moved toward the door, because the sound faded a little. "Ach, I'm forgetting why I came. I'm supposed to take out another quart of applesauce from the pantry." Her voice had become louder, and Miriam slid behind the door, patting her face in the hope it would chase away the traces of tears.

There were rapid footsteps, and a hand brushed

the door. "I'll get it for you, Hilda." Lyddy must be right outside.

In another instant, the knob turned. Miriam grabbed a quart of the applesauce, and when Lyddy moved, Miriam thrust it into her hand. Lyddy grabbed it, still talking, and seemed to steer Hilda away.

Miriam closed the door silently and leaned on it, eyes closed. She knew who Hilda's relatives were—her Aunt Etta had introduced them. Even if Hilda could be avoided, it wouldn't help. Hilda's cousin was even more of a chatterer than Hilda was. There was no chance at all that she wouldn't tell Hilda all about it. And what Hilda knew, everyone would know.

By the time of Miriam's late arrival on Monday morning, Matt had worked himself into a bad mood. It wasn't that he wanted her here or looked forward to her company. He'd be just as happy to see her quit. But if she took on a job, she ought to be on time.

He'd been awake since five. He'd heard Miriam's brother and Daad talking outside as they loaded the wagon to take vegetables to the co-op. August was the busiest month on the farm—sweet corn, tomatoes, peppers—they were all at their peak now. And he couldn't help. He had to lie here and listen to someone else doing his work.

When Miriam tapped, his answering shout no doubt told her that he was irritated. She came in, closely followed by Betsy, who seemed to think she had to keep an eye on him, as if he were a toddler.

"You're late."

Miriam looked at him, and her expression startled him. It was almost as if her thoughts were so far away that she didn't even register his sharp comment. Then she blinked, and her clear blue eyes focused on him.

"I'm sorry. I've no good reason, except that I ran into Joshua outside." A smile touched her lips and was reflected in her eyes. "He had to tell me all about how many dozens of ears of sweet corn they took to market this morning. According to him, people were lined up waiting to get at it when they'd barely finished unloading."

Her voice seemed to fade as she reached the end of what she was saying, as if she sensed his mood. But she couldn't know she'd touched a sore spot.

"Josh likes his job, does he?" He made an effort to put some enthusiasm into his voice.

Seeming reassured, she nodded. "He says he feels like an outsider in the family, thinking more of crops than of cows. But I know Daad's okay with it."

He couldn't help smiling at that thought. Still, Miriam's daad had other sons ready and eager to run the dairy business, unlike his own.

Miriam reached up to pull down the cables he was supposed to use to sit up and eventually, so Tim said, allow him to get into a wheelchair on his own. Matt gritted his teeth. "You're not going to start with that, are you?"

She looked surprised. "Why not?" She glanced up again. "Although if I can't reach them, they're not going to do much good. How did they get up so high?"

"I didn't like them dangling over me. I told Betsy to get them out of the way."

"Maybe Betsy can get..."

Before she could finish the thought, Betsy turned away. "I think Mammi's calling me." In another moment she was gone.

Miriam looked after her, shrugged and picked up the stool that stood against the wall. "What does Betsy have against being helpful?"

"Nothing," he said quickly, trying not to feel embarrassed. "I guess she knows I don't like that exercise much."

"All the more reason to get it over with first," she said, putting the stool next to the bed and stepping up. "Ain't so? My grossmammi always says to do the hardest thing first and the rest of the day will be good."

"Your grandmother never had to waste time on something that..." His complaint withered and died when he looked up at Miriam.

She was leaning against the bed for balance as she reached above her head for the handles. She'd been close to him before—she could hardly help it when she worked with him. But he'd never had this kind of a look at her before. Sunlight streaming in the east window brought out golden highlights in the hair he'd always thought mousy. Her position, arms raised, outlined her slender figure, and her cheeks were flushed with the effort, making him think of ripe peaches.

"I guess we could shorten the exercises this morning," she said as she climbed down, pulling the handles to their full length. "After all, Tim will give you a hefty workout this afternoon." She looked at him again. "Matt?"

Brought back to the moment, he shook his head, trying to banish her image from his mind. "Nope. I can't have you saying I'm not living up to my part of the bargain. Do your worst."

That surprised her into a smile that lightened her expression. "I'll do my best," she corrected him. "And so will you." She put the handles in his hands, her touch sure and firm. "Let's do a few partial sit-ups."

As he rose up, pulling against the handles, she moved closer to put her palm on his back, helping him. He had control of himself now. He wasn't going to lose track of what he was doing because of Miriam.

But he found himself studying the curves of her face, only six inches or so from his. Was it his imagination that once again she didn't look quite as calm and peaceful as usual? He couldn't be sure.

"Something wrong at home?" he asked abruptly.

She blinked. "No, nothing. Not unless you count Sammy finding new ways to risk life and limb and trying to get the twins to follow him in mischief."

"Sammy's what? Ten, now? He'll probably grow out of it."

"If he lives long enough," she said. "Between climbing to the barn roof and fighting with the goat, he has Mammi at her wits' end, she says."

He had to smile. It seemed, whatever the problem was, it wasn't at home. With his red hair and constant grin, Sammy had always looked…not for trouble, he guessed, but for things that seemed to lead him into it. Anyway, why should he care what had put that worried look in her eyes?

They moved on through another set of exercises, and he couldn't rid himself of the thought. What was distracting her? It shouldn't bother him, but it did.

"How was worship yesterday?" The question popped out without his thinking about it, but in an instant he saw that it was the right one. Her hand tightened on his arm, seeming to communicate without words.

In another moment, her face smoothed out. "Fine. It was gut to see the familiar faces again. I missed all of you while I was away."

The words were the right ones, but the feeling beneath them wasn't, he felt sure. He studied her face, searching for answers.

Miriam seemed to feel his scrutiny, and she shrugged as if to shake it off.

"That wasn't very convincing," he said. "You want to try a different response?" She could tell him to mind his own business, but he didn't think she would.

Looking down, she stared at the soft exercise ball she was squashing between her fingers. Finally she shook her head. "I was glad to see everyone, but by the time I'd answered the same questions about my time in Ohio twenty or so times, I guess I was a little tired of it."

"They're just trying to catch up, ain't so? You didn't get up to anything out there you have to hide, did you?"

He expected her to either deny it or turn it off with a joke. Instead, she went completely still, her eyes dark with pain. In another moment, she was shaking her head and smiling.

"Not a bit of it," she said, her voice light.

But it was too late. He knew what he'd seen. Pain.

Chapter Five

Miriam arrived at the King place Tuesday morning to find Abel waiting on the back porch steps. He stood up as she approached, nodding in his grave way. Was he waiting for her to hear her report from the therapist's visit the previous day? Anyone could see at a glance how heavy a burden Abel carried, but he had hope, even so.

"I'd be glad to talk with you a moment, Miriam." He hesitated. "It's about Joshua."

Miriam rearranged her thoughts as quickly as possible. She hadn't expected that, and a flash of concern went through her. Was he going to say that Josh wasn't living up to expectations?

"Yah, of course." She tried to hide her concern with a smile. "I hope he's doing all right."

"Ach, yah, more than all right." For an instant the lines in Abel's face seemed to relax. "I was wondering… I would speak to your daad first, but I thought you might know. If he has plans for Joshua, I wouldn't say anything, that's for sure."

The more Abel said, the more confused she felt. "Plans? Do you mean for today?"

He actually laughed a little at that, shaking his head. "I'm that ferhoodled, I'm saying it backwards. Josh has been a wonderful gut help to me. I wondered if he would want to make his job more permanent. But if your daad has something else in mind for him…"

There was a tentative note in his words that she began to understand. What would the future of the farm be without Matthew and David? She hesitated, not wanting to speak for anyone else, although she did know that Josh was happy with his work.

"I haven't heard Daad say anything about it. I expect he knows Josh's heart isn't in the dairy business, though. He knows most things."

Abel nodded. "You know how I'm fixed without David and not knowing how much Matthew will come back." His voice choked on the words, and he looked as if he regretted starting this talk.

"Yah, I know. I'm sorry," she said hastily. "It's hard to make any plans, not knowing. But you can be sure Josh is happy here, and if you want to talk to him about…well, anything, I feel sure Daad wouldn't mind."

Her heart hurt for Abel, and for an instant she had an unreasonable anger with the boy who'd been so reckless. If he had known how many lives his foolishness was going to affect, would he have believed it?

"Gut, gut." Abel seemed satisfied with what was really only half an answer to his question. "I was sorry to miss Tim when he was here yesterday. Has he said anything about Matt's progress?"

He looked so in need of hope that Miriam would have done anything to reassure him. "It's early days yet, you know. The damage to Matthew's legs…well, the doctor would talk to you about it, I'm sure. Tim talks in terms of what we should do this week, or maybe next week."

She was running out of optimistic things to say, and it was almost a relief when the screen door slammed open. Betsy stood there, scowling at her.

"Matt wants to know why you're not in there working."

"Betsy." Abel didn't raise his voice, but it was stern enough to send Betsy back a step. "You will not speak that way to Miriam or anyone else."

Betsy's expression became mulish. "Matt said—"

"You heard me."

Miriam wondered for a moment if he'd scold his older son. Probably not, even though the words were probably his.

"I'll come now," she said cheerfully. "Unless you wanted to say anything more?"

"No. Denke, Miriam. That was helpful." Abel turned away, his thoughts obviously running ahead to the work to be done. She didn't suppose it was really very helpful, but what could she say? What could anyone say about how much Matt would recover?

Betsy managed to slam the screen door again when she went inside, and Miriam opened it gingerly, hoping the hinges would hold up. Reminding herself that Betsy was dealing with a lot of changes in her young life, she resolved to be pleasant. Or at least, patient with her.

"What were you and Daad talking about outside?" Matt demanded the moment she went into his room.

She should have been prepared so she wouldn't be standing there like the dressmaker's dummy Mammi fitted dresses on. She didn't want to be the one to say his daad was thinking of bringing Joshua in permanently. It would be like telling him he was never going to recover.

In the end she replied with part of the truth. "He was sorry to have missed Tim yesterday and wanted to know what he said."

"Well, what did he say? You and Tim were a long time in the kitchen yesterday. Or was that a social visit?"

Matt seemed to be in as bad a mood as Betsy. Still, he had a bit more of an excuse for it. Ignoring his implication about her and Tim was the only way to handle it.

"Just the usual discussion of plans for the week." She released the brake of the wheelchair and rolled it closer, then picked up the stool and carried it over to the side of the bed.

"And what are those plans?" Matt eyed her preparations warily.

Maybe it would have been better for Tim to have discussed it with Matt. Miriam put some enthusiasm into her voice. "Tim thinks we should work on your ability to get into the wheelchair on your own." At the rejection on his lips, she held up her hand. "Not right away. I just brought the wheelchair over to give you an idea of how it's done."

"I'm not trying to get into that thing with just you to help me. We'd both end up on the floor."

Relieved at the trace of humor in his voice, she smiled. "It's the goal. We're just taking steps toward it." She got up on the stool, leaning against the edge of the bed. "And Tim says you should start going out to the kitchen to join the family for meals."

His reply was quick and sharp. "No." He glared at her. "You think I want to take away everyone's appetite?"

Miriam looked down on him from her perch, honestly baffled for a moment. And then she realized he was talking about his scarred face—the scarring she didn't even see any longer. Maybe it was time to see what scolding would do.

"Don't be ferhoodled," she snapped. "Nobody minds that. And for some reason I don't understand at the moment, they really want to enjoy your company while they eat. Must have something to do with loving you, I suppose."

She stretched up, reaching for the handles that

seemed to be completely entangled. A quick glance back at him showed him looking equal parts surprised and embarrassed at her words. Well, that was good. He ought to be embarrassed.

Her groping fingers touched the handles, and she stretched further to take a grip with both hands and pull. They didn't come. Exasperated, she looked up, giving them a good tug.

For an instant she thought she'd brought the whole ceiling down. The handles struck her face as she teetered off balance and then fell heavily, half on the bed, and her head struck the footboard.

"Look out!" Matt lunged forward as Miriam fell, but his muscles betrayed him. His hand fell short, and the sound of her head striking the footboard echoed in his head.

"Mamm! Daad!"

But already he heard footsteps pounding in the hall. The door flew open. Mammi and Daad rushed through, followed by Joshua and then Betsy.

Miriam moved, hand against her head, and he managed to grasp her sleeve. "Don't move. Not until my mother takes a look at you."

Mammi hurried to Miriam, putting one arm around her and tilting her head back gently. The lump on her forehead was growing larger and redder while he looked at it.

His mother clucked and stroked her forehead. "Hush, now, Miriam. It will be all right." She looked up and raised her voice. “Don’t just stand there. Betsy, go and wet a dishtowel with cold water. Wring it out thoroughly and bring it. Someone move the rocking chair over here next to Miriam.”

“I… I’m all right,” Miriam murmured. “You don’t need…”

“Just let me take care of you. Rest, now.”

Daad carried the rocking chair, and Joshua rushed to help him, his face white. As they set it in place, Matthew caught his father’s eye and knew they were thinking the same thing. The woman snapping out orders was Mammi the way she used to be, before tragedy struck. It was wonderful good to hear her taking control again, even at the cost of a lump on Miriam’s head.

“Denke, Elizabeth.” Miriam’s voice was weak, and she allowed her brother to lift her from her awkward position. He settled her gently in the rocking chair.

She patted his cheek. “I’m all right. Don’t be upset.”

“Who, me?” He managed a light tone, but it trembled a little. “I know how tough you are.”

Her smile flickered. “What happened?” She was looking at Matt now for answers. “It felt like the ceiling fell on me.”

“Not quite. The hook holding the cords pulled loose from the ceiling.” Matt glanced toward the floor. “Where did it go?”

Daad picked up the cords and handles from the

bed, making sure the hook wasn't there. Meanwhile Josh scrambled on the floor in search of the hook, crawling under the bed.

"Here it is." He crawled backward from under the bed, holding it up. "Funny it came out like that."

"Yah." Daad took it in a work-hardened hand, brushing off the bits of plaster that stuck to it. "I put it in myself. It should have been able to hold Matt, let alone a little thing like you, Miriam." He frowned, looking from the hook to the hole in the ceiling. "I'm wonderful sorry, Miriam. That's certain sure. It's my fault."

Betsy had returned with the wet cloth and an extra towel, and Mammi pressed it gently against Miriam's forehead. "Denke, Betsy." Mamm was so focused on what she was doing that she didn't look up at Betsy.

But Matt did. He saw an expression on his sister's face that startled him. She wore a small, sly grin.

It disappeared when she spoke. "I guess you won't have to do those exercises today."

For a moment he didn't understand, and then he saw it. Betsy knew he always complained about those particular exercises. Maybe she'd decided on a way to keep him from having to do them.

No, that couldn't be true. She surely wouldn't have set out to hurt Miriam, would she?

He was frowning at his little sister, trying to figure it out, when she seemed to feel his eyes on her. The color came up in her face. She turned away quickly and had gotten a couple of steps toward the door when he spoke.

"Hold on, Betsy. What do you mean by that?"

She turned around slowly, and suddenly everyone was looking at her. He could see the moment at which she decided to bluff.

"What? I didn't mean anything." She must have seen the doubt in his gaze. "Really. I just thought you'd be glad…"

"Glad to have Miriam get hurt when she's trying to help me?" He had to muffle himself not to shout. "What was in your mind to do such a thing?"

"Betsy, is this true?" Daad looked as if someone had hit him, and Miriam was close enough to Matt that he could hear her sharp intake of breath.

For an instant longer Betsy held out. Then her expression seemed to crumble away. "I didn't," she protested. "I mean… I mean… I just untwisted the hook a little bit. I didn't mean for anyone to get hurt. Not Miriam, not anyone. I didn't think she would. I just… I just wanted to help Matt."

"*Help* me?" he repeated.

He felt the urge to shout again, but something stronger prevented him. Why was he blaming Betsy? What she said was true enough. He'd talked carelessly about hating those exercises and wishing he didn't have to do them. He looked aghast at the result of his stupidity. He should have known better.

Daad looked solemnly at Matt for a moment—

long enough for Matt to hear the things he didn't say. Then he turned to Betsy.

"Miriam *was* hurt," Daad said soberly. "And you are responsible. I would never think a child of mine would do such a thing."

"But I didn't mean it. And anyway, Matt shouldn't have to do anything he doesn't want to." It was a feeble attempt at defiance, and she looked ready to cry.

Daad went on as if she hadn't spoken. "Go to your room, and don't come out until I say to. And while you're there, think about how you'll feel if you must go before the church and confess that you have injured a sister."

Betsy's face went white, and Miriam murmured an instinctive protest. But Daad's face said no argument would sway him. Betsy spun and fled. They heard her footsteps pounding up the stairs.

Miriam pushed herself up to standing…a little wobbly, but standing. Her face was very pale, and the red mark stood out like a light. She looked as if she wanted to say something about it to Daad, but Matt shook his head, and she subsided.

It would do no good now. Later, when Daad had cooled down, he'd speak to him.

Miriam seemed to understand his unspoken message. She moved closer to the bed. "We must get busy. There's no reason not to do the rest of the exercises now."

"Not until you've had a sit-down and a nice cup

of tea." Mammi gathered herself together and took Miriam's arm. "Come along now."

Before Miriam could move, Matt closed his hand around her wrist. She looked at him, eyes wide and startled, and he could feel the pulse stuttering under her skin.

"I'm sorry," he said softly. "I should have known better than to complain in front of Betsy."

Miriam shook her head slightly and then stopped, touching her forehead as if it had been a bad idea. "It's all right." She let Mammi lead her away.

But it wasn't all right, and he knew it. He'd caused her injury as sure as if he'd done it himself. And what was just as bad, she'd fallen within inches of him and he couldn't help her. He was useless, totally useless.

Miriam sank into a kitchen chair, relieved to sit and be quiet for a moment. Elizabeth didn't speak as she hustled about the kitchen heating the kettle and getting out tea. Finally she set a brimming mug in front of Miriam and sank onto the chair at the end of the table.

"What else can I get for you? Some toast or a piece of shoofly pie?" She watched Miriam anxiously.

Miriam managed to give her a reassuring smile. "Nothing else, denke. I'm all right, really."

"I can't tell you how sorry I am for what Betsy did. I should have known, should have realized…" Her words broke on a sob.

"Ach, don't." Miriam clasped her hand, patting

it. "I understand." At least, she thought she did. Betsy was trying desperately to claim her remaining brother, afraid of losing him the way she lost David.

Elizabeth sniffed and dabbed at her nose with a tissue. "If you understand, it's more than I do. That child..."

"Betsy's grieving," she said firmly, knowing that, at least, was true. "I'm sure she didn't mean to hurt me. She was just trying to help her brother." She hesitated, not wanting to open any sore places in poor Elizabeth's heart. "She is missing what her family used to be, ain't so?"

Looking at her, Elizabeth's attention seemed to be caught. "You think so? But what she did—"

She nodded, patting the older woman's hand again. "I've already forgiven her. I just wish I could do something more to help."

Elizabeth blinked away tears. "Denke, Miriam. I'm the one who must help her. I see it now."

Did she? Miriam sincerely hoped so. This whole family needed help, but it was more than she knew how to do. One good thing had come out of this morning's mishap, anyway. Elizabeth had awakened from her self-imposed isolation. If only this awareness would last... She murmured a silent prayer that it would be so.

She gulped down the rest of her tea, hearing a few thuds accompanied by the rumble of men's voices from Matt's room. "I must go. Matt should have at least a short exercise period this morning."

When she walked back into Matt's room, it was to find Matt sitting up on the bed, apparently supervising while his father and Josh finished installing the apparatus again.

"There," Josh said, attaching the end hooks that Abel handed to him. "All done."

He stepped down and grinned at Miriam. "I guarantee it won't come down again."

"And she'll know who to blame if it does," Matt said with a wink at him.

"Yah, just me." He pushed the stool back in place while Abel took the toolbox, and he looked over at Miriam. "We looped the cords over this hook above the bed, so you don't have to go climbing on anything. Give it a try."

Smiling at her little brother's obvious pleasure in his work, Miriam went over to the bed, finding that she could easily reach the handles and lift them off.

"Terrific. Denke."

Abel started for the door and then paused, looking at her. "Are you sure you wouldn't like to go home and rest? We can get along without you for the remainder of the day, if need be."

"Not at all. I'm ready to work, and so is Matthew."

Matt's lips quirked at her comment, but he didn't speak.

Joshua started to follow his boss, and then he detoured to give Miriam a quick hug before leaving. "Take care."

She stood looking as the door closed behind them,

and then she turned to Matt, shaking her head. "I wouldn't have believed how much my little brother has changed in just the months I've been away."

"He's not so little anymore," Matt commented.

"Yah, but it's not just that. It's a change in himself. He was always so quiet and reserved that it was rare to know what he was thinking. Now…now he's talking to me about himself and not embarrassed at all."

"You're better friends now that he's growing up." His eyes were shadowed for a moment, and she guessed he was thinking about his brother.

"I'm sorry I missed some of the growing up." She considered those months when she was away. "I guess any change in the family affects all of them."

Matt studied her face, maybe trying to read what was behind her words. "That might be aimed at me, ain't so?"

She felt her cheeks grow warm. "I wasn't really thinking of that. Should I apologize?"

"Not necessary. It's right about us, too, and our change is a lot harder to deal with. Betsy…well, she shouldn't have done it, but I guess I can understand, a little."

Miriam nodded, relieved that, like his mother, he was seeing a bit more clearly. "She really wants to hold on to you now."

"Maybe so." He didn't seem convinced. "Well, I've learned my lesson about complaining, anyway. I guess I'll have to save it for when we're alone."

"You could give it up altogether," she suggested with a twinkle in her eye.

"Yah… I don't think I can manage that. But Betsy needs to understand that the exercises are the right thing for me, even if I complain." He smiled a little. "So we've learned something about my sister, and all it cost was a black eye for you."

Startled, Miriam's hand flew to her eye. "What do you mean? I don't have a black eye. It's just a lump on my forehead."

"Today it's a lump on your forehead. By tomorrow it will be swollen around your eye and turning a lovely purple color."

She stared at him, seeing his smile. "You're joking. You can't be serious."

"I might be teasing you, but I'm not fibbing. That big lump on your forehead is going to go down to a black eye and most likely a bruise on your cheek, too. Trust me. It's happened to me more than once."

Miriam put her hand over her eye again, trying to imagine what it was going to look like. It was easier to imagine how her brothers were going to tease her.

"You don't have to sound so happy about it," she informed him. "It could have been you, you know. If those handles had hit you in the eye…"

"But my therapist's helper protected me, isn't that right?" He was smiling, and his eyes twinkled for a moment.

Then, slowly, his expression grew more serious.

His hand closed on hers. “I’m sorry you got hurt. Sorry I wasn’t the one who protected you.”

Their gazes locked onto each other, and it seemed to Miriam that the world around them pulled away, leaving only the two of them in a private circle of their own. She could hear his breath moving in and out, feel the warmth of his hand, and her own breath caught.

She couldn’t be the only one feeling this. She couldn’t. How could it only be on her side?

Chapter Six

By Thursday morning, Miriam was dumbfounded at the results of her black eye, which had appeared on schedule just when Matt had predicted. Everyone she encountered seemed compelled to comment on it, either teasing or openly curious, so she was grateful to stay at home when she wasn't at the King house.

Not that staying home let her avoid comments. The older boys found it a subject for teasing and jokes, with Daniel, in particular, coming up with a new joke about every hour. Josh, having been there for her accident, was more protective, while Sammy was speechless for once. The twins were the most surprising—they took one look at her and burst into tears.

Even now, and she started off to work, she found two pairs of small arms twining around her waist. Exchanging amused glances with Mammi, she bent and kissed one blond head and then the other one.

"I'm off to work, but I promise to be careful today. No more accidents, right?"

"Right," John Thomas and James answered in chorus.

"All right now, you two. Get off to your chores and let Miriam go. She'll be home to supper, and you'll see her then."

Mammi waved them off with her dish towel, and then came to give Miriam a hug of her own. "I wish..." She stopped and started over. "Are you sure this is the right job for you? Maybe Abel could find someone else."

"Are you trying to lose me my job?" she said lightly, aiming to chase away the concern on her mother's face. "I'm fine."

"This time," Mammi said, touching her cheek.

"Honestly, Mammi, after the way Abel scolded her, I'm quite sure Betsy isn't going to attempt anything else so foolish. I just wish I could find a way to help her." The children didn't know about Betsy's role in her accident, but she'd had to tell Mammi and Daad.

"Your tender heart will lead you into trouble one of these days," Mammi chided. "You have so much sympathy for everyone else, but you don't spare any for yourself."

Miriam blinked. "I don't need sympathy, Mammi. I'm doing what I was meant to do." She gave her mother a quick hug. "Now I'm off before it gets any hotter." She scurried out the back.

As she took off on the path along the pasture, the August day settled on her like a heavy blanket. It was going to be even hotter by the afternoon, but clouds were massing on the western horizon, promising storms before the day was over.

She touched the bruise on her face. It wasn't throbbing the way it had yesterday, at least, but she couldn't see that it looked any better. Maybe it was worth it, considering the way Matt had been pushing on his exercises since Tuesday. She'd thought he was cooperating earlier, but now he seemed determined to show her and Tim what he could do. Yesterday he'd gotten into the wheelchair with minimal help, though getting back into bed was more of a challenge.

She was happy with his progress, and Tim would be, as well. She just wished she knew how Matt himself felt about it.

Betsy wasn't around when Miriam got to the house, but Elizabeth greeted her with what was almost a smile. "Your face is looking better today, ain't so? I hope it doesn't hurt too much."

"I'm fine." She resisted the urge to put a shielding hand over her eye. It struck her suddenly that she ought to understand better Matt's reaction to his damaged face. It wasn't vanity, she thought. The idea that people were staring at you was enough to make her stomach twist anyway.

Elizabeth nodded, but she looked doubtful. "Is there anything you want help with today?"

Miriam hesitated. "Not really, but I would like to get Matthew out here to the table for lunch. What do you think?"

Elizabeth's faded hazel eyes filled with tears. "Ach, Miriam, that would be wonderful gut. Do you think we can?"

"We'll give it a strong try." She smiled, relieved at Elizabeth's reaction. Elizabeth had said *we.* She had come a long way since the first day Miriam was here, and that was fine to see.

When she went into Matt's room, he took one look at her black eye and winced, turning his face away.

"No need for you to be embarrassed," she said lightly. "I'm the one who has to answer all the questions and deal with the smart remarks. I've decided that a black eye brings out the joker in people."

He seemed to force himself to look at her. "Sorry. I wish I'd been wrong about it. What kind of jokes?"

She shrugged as she prepared the exercise apparatus for use. "Did I have a fight with the broom when I was sweeping? Did I walk into the barn door? Nothing really very clever, but everybody has to make a comment."

"Maybe that's because they know it's not permanent. Not like this." He gestured toward the scarred side of his face.

Miriam paused before handing him the weights he was working with today. "You probably won't believe it, but I really don't see it any longer. I don't think your family does, either."

"You're right. I don't believe it." He grabbed the weights from her and began to lift them, frowning.

"That's too bad." She corrected his arm position. "That you don't believe it, I mean. But there's one thing this has taught me—that I'm just as self-conscious about my looks as the next person. I keep wanting to hide it."

"You're not going to fight with me today, are you?" His lips twitched in a smile. "Why are you being so understanding?"

"I'm not." She smiled in return, relieved that at least he could talk about his scarring. "I'm saving arguing for something bigger. Let's try the side lifts now."

He didn't pursue the topic, and she was glad. She had a feeling he was going to battle the idea of going out to the kitchen for lunch. What would be the best approach? Reminding him that Tim had instructed him to? Pointing out that his family wanted it? Or as a last result, suggesting it was selfish of him to insist on having lunch brought to him?

She still hadn't decided by the time they had finished the exercises. Well, maybe she should…

Matt caught her hand as he gave her the exercise bands he'd been using. "Okay, you may as well tell me. Do you think I don't know when you're plotting something? What is it this time? Some new way of making me miserable?"

"Are you talking about your body or your disposition?" She kept her voice light, reminding herself that part of her job involved touching him. It was no different just because he'd been the one to initiate that handclasp.

"Both," he said shortly. "They go together, ain't so?"

Matt had a way of going right to the heart of the matter, and it felt as if he was always a step ahead of her. Maybe it was just impossible to surprise someone who'd known you since childhood.

She moved the wheelchair into position next to the bed, and he glared at it. "Not this again."

"Yah, this. You're doing it really well now. Don't you like doing something you've mastered?"

"You make me sound like a trained animal," he muttered, but he maneuvered into position, swinging his legs off the bed. "Do I get a treat when I do it?"

"Of course." She couldn't keep from smiling at that. He might not consider it a treat, but he should.

Without asking anything more, he moved into the process, going through each step Tim had impressed upon them. When she reached to help him, he shook his head. "I'll do it myself."

For an instant she felt panic. Was she pushing him too far, too fast? Before she came up with an answer, he'd done it, and he wheeled himself a few feet from the bed. He was trying to show nothing, but she could read the satisfaction in his eyes.

"Wonderful gut!" She felt like clapping, but he probably wouldn't appreciate that.

He grimaced, yet she knew better. "So, what is my treat?"

"You get to go out to the kitchen and have lunch with the family."

She grasped the handles of the wheelchair and held her breath for the argument.

He waited a moment too long before he answered. "What if I don't want to go?"

She started pushing. "You do want lunch, don't you?"

Grabbing the wheels, he stopped the chair abruptly, twisting his head to look at her. She smiled at him, but she knew she must look both scared and hopeful.

She watched the stubbornness drain out of him, and finally he nodded. "Okay. Let's try it."

With a singing heart, Miriam pushed the chair toward the kitchen.

Matt discovered he was holding his breath as he was propelled into the kitchen. Why was he so ferhoodled about something so ordinary? Foolish—that's what it was. Just because he hadn't been out here for a meal since he came home from the hospital…

The rest of the family was already seated at the table. Daad, beaming, jumped up to pull a chair away to make room for the wheelchair, and Mammi smiled with tears in her eyes. Betsy managed to look both sulky and glad at the same time, which was quite a trick. Miriam could be right about her.

Miriam's brother Joshua, grinning, helped her move the wheelchair into position. Matt caught him giving his sister a wink. Looked like he considered this an accomplishment. Did everyone in the community have an opinion about what he should or shouldn't be doing?

"Have some potpie." Miriam passed him the yellow earthenware bowl Mammi always used for chicken potpie, and other bowls began circulating around the table.

They must have had silent prayer before he got out here, he realized. Had his mother been praying for this moment? Maybe so, because right now she looked as if someone had given her a present. The least he could do was try to behave normally and act as if he were glad.

That meant joining in the conversation. Josh was asking Daad about the tomato baskets for market. For just an instant, Matt imagined it was David asking the question. David, who wasn't ever going to be here again. Angry at himself, he forced himself to focus.

"Good crop of tomatoes this year, Daad?"

His father looked enormously pleased at his asking the simple question. "Yah, yah, some nice big slicing ones, as you can see." He nodded toward the plate filled with rich red slices of beefsteak tomatoes.

"The sauce tomatoes are gut, too," Josh volunteered. "My mamm's been making quarts and quarts of sauce this week. Ask Miriam." He grinned. "She goes home from here and jumps right into hauling canning jars around. The kitchen is like a hot bath."

"We haven't even started." Mammi looked stricken, as if she'd been failing in her duties.

"I'm sure you have plenty left from last year," Miriam intervened. "Didn't I see them on the shelves when I went down in the basement?"

The upset look faded from his mother's face at the reminder. "Ach, yah, that's true. Still..." She seemed to be mentally counting out quarts of tomato sauce and juice.

"We don't need any more," Betsy said quickly, clutching at Miriam's comment, probably because she saw herself dragged into the canning operation Mamm usually had going this time of year.

Matt decided it was time to switch off the subject. "What did you end up putting in the north field, Daad?"

"Just letting it lie fallow this year. I'm thinking it might be good for cabbages. You ought to take a look at it. Maybe..." He let that trail off, maybe not sure what Matt's reaction should be.

As for him, all he could do was cringe inside at the thought of venturing even that far. Why did folks keep pushing him? He couldn't be any use to Daad even if he did go look at the field. Just because he let Miriam bulldoze him into coming out for lunch didn't mean he wanted to go anywhere else.

Before he could find a nice way of saying he didn't want to, Josh had already jumped on the idea. "We could easily put a ramp up to the porch. Remember, Miriam, when we built the ramp for Grossdaadi? It worked fine to get a wheelchair outside."

"That's an idea," Daad said, and Matt could see his enthusiasm building.

"I don't think I need it," he said firmly. "Besides, you've got plenty to do without building ramps."

Josh didn't seem to catch the message of his frown. "No problem," he said lightly. "I can get Daniel and Sammy to come over one evening and do it."

"It's none of your business." Betsy butted in with a glare at Miriam, as if this conversation was her fault. "It'd be too much for Matt."

"Betsy." Daad didn't have to say more than her name to shut her up. She was already in trouble over Miriam's injury.

Matt would have to do something about Betsy. Somehow he'd have to convince her that...well, he didn't know. Maybe Miriam would have some idea how he could get her to let go of her determination to protect him.

"Anyway, it would be too hard for anyone to push me that far over rough ground." He hoped he said it with enough finality that they'd get the message.

"Miriam, what about that battery-powered scooter you were telling us about in one of your letters?" Josh asked. "You said that guy you worked with could get all over the place using it."

"I... I didn't realize I'd mentioned it."

There it was again, Matt realized: That sense of

something uncomfortable, even painful, about Miriam's time in Ohio. What had happened to her out there?

"It would have to run off the electric, wouldn't it?" His father was frowning at the idea.

"That would be out of the question for us," Matt added quickly.

"The scooter is battery-powered."

Miriam wasn't looking at him when she spoke. Maybe she hadn't intended to bring this subject up at all until Joshua forced it. Why?

Daad looked interested. "But you must have to charge the batteries, ain't so?"

"Yah, but the…the family I worked with had figured out a way to charge the battery using the milk cooler. In fact, the family bought two batteries for the scooter so one could be charging while the other was in use."

"Do you know where they got it, or what kind it was?" Daad had taken a piece of paper and a pencil from a kitchen drawer and was jotting down notes.

"I'm afraid I don't, but I expect Tim would know all about it, if you wanted to talk to him. Or I could call to find out."

Matt realized he had to stop all this before Daad spent a lot of money he couldn't afford on something that wasn't going to give him his legs back.

"I don't want a power scooter." He was trying to say it firmly, but it came out sounding loud and more angry than he'd intended.

Nobody said anything for a few moments, and he felt, without anyone saying anything, that they were disappointed in him. The weight of that disappointment was heavy on him.

"Sorry." Joshua's face grew red. "I just thought you might be interested."

Now he'd succeeded in embarrassing Joshua, who was only doing his best to help out. Daad's disappointment was obvious, and as for Miriam…

He couldn't mistake the look on Miriam's face. She was angry. In fact, she looked ready to tell him exactly what she thought of him for picking on her little brother. Her expression reminded him irresistibly of a moment on the schoolyard when she'd flown out after one of the older boys for hassling a smaller child. She'd been angry then, too.

When it came to defending someone who was smaller and weaker, quiet, gentle Miriam had had no fear. He'd try not to forget that again.

A rap on the screen door announced the arrival of Tim, breaking an uncomfortable silence. Miriam got up quickly, relieved to have an excuse to move, but Abel had already gone to the door and was greeting him.

"Komm, sit. You'll have a cup of coffee, yah?" Abel pulled up a chair.

"Well, since my client is still having lunch, I guess I will." Tim smiled impartially around the table.

"Matt, I'm glad to see you out here for your lunch. That's a good sign."

Matt looked about to say something negative, but Elizabeth set coffee and a slice of apple pie in front of Tim. "Yah, very gut," she said, smiling at Matt with a look of pride. Whatever Matt had on the tip of his tongue, Miriam thought he swallowed it.

Tim murmured his thanks for the pie and coffee, taking a big bite of pie before he said anything, and then it was to praise the apple pie.

"My mammi makes wonderful gut pie," Betsy said, darting a look at her father as if to be sure he noticed her being polite.

But Abel had his mind on something else. "You would say that Matt is making gut progress, ain't so?"

Tim nodded, and Miriam had a feeling he was trying to decide how much to say. He wouldn't want to make any predictions about recovery. She was certain of that. "Progress is always good." Tim hesitated. "Injuries like Matt's can take a long time to heal."

"Very long," Matt added. "Months."

"Sure, but now the bones have come together well enough that we can really work on rehabilitation. You should start to see faster progress, even if it seems like a long time to you." Tim spoke with the air of one who had heard all the complaints his clients could come up with. "Trust me."

He looked at Matt as if expecting some response,

but Matt just set his jaw stubbornly. Miriam didn't have any trouble interpreting that look. If they couldn't make him the way he was before, he wasn't interested. If only she had something encouraging to say…

But Tim took a last taste of pie, said thanks again, and stood up. "Miriam and I need to talk about the upcoming exercises, so we may as well do it first, while Matt finishes lunch." He nodded to the door. "Let's take a little walk to help me digest that wonderful pie."

Miriam followed him outside, feeling Matt's eyes on her as she went. Sooner or later, he'd be wanting to know what they'd talked about.

Tim took a deep breath as they headed toward the barn. "I've been stuck inside all day, and I'm glad to smell some fresh air for a change. And get away from town for a bit." He glanced sideways at her. "Good work on getting Matthew out of that room to eat lunch with his family. I want to hear about it. But first, tell me how you got that black eye."

She'd known that would be coming. "It was nothing. I yanked on the overhead cords, and they came down suddenly and hit my forehead. That's all."

He gave her a skeptical look. "You're sure that's all you want to say about it?"

"I'm sure," she said firmly.

Tim's concern wasn't allayed. "If it was Matt…"

"Oh, no. He had nothing to do with it. Really."

He nodded, accepting it but not fully convinced, she thought.

"Okay, if you say so. Anyway, getting him out with other people is great. Did he give you a fight about it?"

"Not as much as I expected. But then over lunch, someone mentioned taking him outside, and he had all sorts of objections to that." She sighed. "I know I shouldn't push too hard, but if I don't, he wouldn't move at all."

"Not unusual," Tim said. "The longer a patient has been down, the harder it seems to get him to tackle anything different. Their room becomes a refuge, and they're leery of what will happen if they go out. Of course, all that time in a hospital bed would discourage anyone."

"Especially someone who's so used to being active and working outside." She gave a fleeting thought to Matt the way he used to be. "I know his mood isn't really your job..."

"But it is." Tim stopped, turning to face her and looking steadily into her eyes as if to impress his words upon her. "A lot of recovery is mental and emotional. If that holds the patient back, then it's our business."

"Ours?" She wasn't sure she liked the sound of that.

He grinned. "You'd better face it, Miriam. He's not going to talk to me about what's causing his attitude. But you've known him all your life, so I hear. If anyone can get him talking, it's you."

She shook her head, doubting it. "Maybe his parents would be better."

"Sometimes that works, but not in this case. Their feelings must be awfully close to the surface after losing their younger boy. It might cause more harm than good." He gave her a sympathetic look. "I know you don't want to, but unless you know someone else he's close to, it comes down to you."

A sense of helplessness swept over her. "I wouldn't know where to start."

Tim shrugged and started walking again. "His attitude could be due to any number of things. Maybe more than one. In this case…well, I read up on the accident. Terrible thing."

"Yah, it was." She'd grieved for David's lost life even though he wasn't part of her family. "David was such a fine, loving boy." She was afraid her emotions were near the surface, too.

"Any negative feeling can hamper recovery. Fear, loneliness, loss of confidence, grief, even guilt." He stopped again, studying her face. "All I know is, if you can get him to realize what it is and accept it, he'll be able to move forward."

And if not? She followed Tim, heading back, and she noticed something at one of the windows. The curtain fluttered as if it had just been moved. As if someone had been looking out, watching them.

Chapter Seven

Miriam was up and moving early, but she hadn't gained any wisdom during the night. She still had no idea how to get Matt talking about his feelings. What's more, she had to admit that she was almost afraid to try.

Thankful that she didn't have to help with the milking as she had when the boys were too young, Miriam hurried to the kitchen. Mamm was already cooking hot cereal and had eggs ready to go as soon as the milkers came in.

"Miriam, I just remembered… I saw Beth when I went to town yesterday. She says what about having a cousins' picnic on Saturday at her place? I told her I'd have you call her." She shook her head. "I don't know how I could have forgotten last night."

Miriam gave her mother a hug and took over the cereal. "Maybe it's because there are so many of us that we talk you silly."

"Ach, you know I love it. But it does get a bit noisy around the table, yah?"

"It does. Especially since Josh is talking so much. He's really become more outgoing, ain't so?"

Mammi nodded, getting a pitcher of milk from the gas refrigerator. "He's growing up. Feeling more sure of himself, too." She paused, turning to Miriam. "You should be free to go Saturday afternoon. You can't be working all the time."

"I'd love to go. I guess I have been concentrating pretty hard on Matt and his family."

"You need a break," Mamm said firmly, giving her a searching glance. "Is something worrying you about Matt? Or the others? If there's anything I can do, I will."

"I know, Mamm." After all, she'd learned how to care for her neighbors from her mother. "Not really worried so much as wondering how to do something the therapist wants."

"Didn't he show you how?"

She shook her head, smiling a little. "If he could, that would be easy."

Was it right to talk it over with Mamm? Surely it was, especially if her mother could help her see what to do.

"Tim says that Matt's attitude is holding him back from healing. He thinks it would help if I could get Matt to talk about it. But I don't know if I can. If I ask him directly, I know he'd just be angry."

"Yah, that's certain sure." Mammi's forehead

wrinkled. "The only way I can see is to listen when he does want to talk." She hesitated, seeming troubled. "Are you sure..."

"What?" She lifted the pot from the burner, hearing voices coming across from the milking shed.

Her mother reached out to touch her cheek lightly. "I wouldn't want you to be hurt." The look she gave Miriam squeezed her heart.

"If it helps Matt...well, I guess I have to do it anyway. You always say that the job God puts in front of us is the one we must do. No matter what."

"I guess I do think that," Mammi said, her expression rueful. "But it's different when it's my child who might be hurt."

She had only time to exchange an understanding look with Mammi before the boys came in clamoring for breakfast, and the moment was over. But still, she felt comforted.

Since every option she could think of to get Matt talking was a dead end, Miriam decided the sensible thing was to focus elsewhere. She walked along the field, feeling the warmth of the morning sun already hinting at the heat coming later. That room of Matt's would be stifling by afternoon. Maybe she could persuade him to go out on the porch if there was a breeze.

She considered the likelihood of his agreeing. Just because she no longer saw the scarring on his face, that didn't mean he wasn't sensitive about it. If she promised to take him inside immediately should anyone come, maybe he'd go along with it. All she could do was try.

And keep on trying, she reminded herself. Working with Matt was certain sure not as easy as working with her aunt had been. And the answer to that was surely that God hadn't promised it would be easy…just that He would be with His servants.

To her pleasure, when she arrived, she found Matt in his wheelchair at the kitchen table, a mug of coffee in front of him.

"This is nice to see…" she began.

Betsy jumped in before she could finish. "I helped Matt come out." Her tone implied the words she didn't say… *We don't need you.*

Miriam just smiled at her. "That's great, Betsy. I'm so glad."

Betsy didn't look as if she believed that. Too bad, because it happened to be true. If everyone in contact with Matt started pulling in the same direction, they could surely do great things.

"Seems to me I deserve some credit. After all, coming out for meals was my idea." Matt smiled up at his mother as she refilled his coffee mug.

His idea? Miriam seemed to remember it differently, but she was too pleased and amused to say so.

"You'll have some coffee before you start working, ain't so?" Elizabeth was already pouring it, not waiting for an answer.

"Denke. Better to have the hot coffee now than

later. It feels as if it's going to be a scorching day," she commented.

"That probably means that Mammi is going to bake bread, just to heat the kitchen up even more." Matt's teasing tone brought a smile to his mother's face.

"I don't see you rejecting the bread, ain't so?" She patted his shoulder, and Miriam realized that for a few minutes she looked like her old self again.

Good job, she thought, watching Matt's face. It was the first time she'd heard him make any of the easy, laughing comments that usually flew around the kitchen whenever a family was gathered. Just that simple thing had lightened the atmosphere of the kitchen so that it seemed the heat didn't matter at all.

Elizabeth moved off, following Betsy toward the hall to tell her something, and Miriam took advantage of the moment.

"That was gut, teasing your mamm that way. You made her happy."

She thought at first that he was going to snap back at her, but he didn't. He frowned down at his hands on the table.

"David used to tease her a lot. He always knew how to make people smile."

She nodded, brushing away a tear even as she smiled. David had had a gift that way.

Matt set his mug down and turned the wheelchair away from the table. "If I can make her smile..."

he paused, his voice husky "...well, it's the least I can do."

With a push of his hands, he set the chair rolling toward the hall. She got up quickly, her mind spinning even as the wheels turned.

What did Matt mean by that? Yah, it would help his mother if he did so, but why did he say it was the least he could do? She found herself questioning Matt's every comment, looking for what it meant. And not understanding it.

By the time they were finishing lunch, Matt felt as if he were melting in the wheelchair. And that was nothing compared to the way Daad and Josh looked, although Daad's weathered face didn't show much reaction. Joshua was redder than any apple, but he still managed to smile as Daad got up from the table.

Knowing it would do no good, Matt still had to try. "Daad, how about knocking off early today? This heat's bad for anyone to be working in." He wanted to add, *especially someone your age*, but Daad would explode at the suggestion that he couldn't keep up with what he used to do.

"Ach, we're used to it, ain't so, Josh?"

Poor Josh couldn't do anything but nod.

"You'll take the jug of water with you," Mamm said firmly. "Sit down in the shade every so often. We can't—" She stopped short, but Matt knew just what she would have said. *We can't lose you, too.*

Silence spread around the table, and he noticed

Miriam take a quick look at him. She wouldn't see what he felt, because he'd learned how to keep his emotions hidden.

Miriam seemed to know him better than he'd ever have thought, but she couldn't know this. No one would know that he was eaten up with guilt inside for all that this family had lost. If he'd pulled over farther, if he'd seen the car earlier, if he'd been a bit smarter, a bit faster…

After a few more minutes at the table, Daad and Josh were gone. Mamm and Betsy were clattering dishes in the sink, while Miriam came to grasp the handles of the wheelchair.

"What about going out on the porch? It's shady now, and there's a breeze. It will be much cooler than inside."

He grasped the wheel before she could move him. "If anyone comes, you get me inside at once." His words were sharper than he'd intended, but maybe it was just as well. Miriam had to understand there were things he wouldn't do.

"If that's what you want." She pulled the wheelchair away from the table and moved him toward the screen door. In response to a gesture from Mammi, Betsy hurried to hold it open.

"Denke, Betsy." Miriam's voice was as soft and peaceable as usual, but Betsy only glared.

Daad had insisted that Betsy apologize to Miriam, but maybe he should have left it alone. Saying the words hadn't changed what was in Betsy's heart, it seemed. And Matt guessed Miriam was willing to forget it.

Miriam settled his chair in a shaded spot where a breeze from the west provided intermittent cooling, and then she drew another chair over to sit next to him.

"You can digest your meal where it's slightly cooler before we start on your afternoon exercises." Miriam raised her face as the breeze came again, letting it lift strands of silky hair.

"Too bad we couldn't convince Daad to do the same." He watched Daad and Joshua walk across the field, Josh carrying a coil of wire and a handful of tools. "Mending fence is hot work."

He brooded, looking after them, then darted a glance at Miriam. "Aren't you going to try convincing me that I'm still of some use to the family?" Bitterness was acrid in his mouth.

She shook her head. "Maybe you're not, the way you mean. Not right now. But there's more to being part of a family than the labor you provide."

"Or don't provide," he said flatly. "Daad needs help to keep the farm going, and there's not a single thing I can do." He discovered he actually wanted her to argue with him, just for the doubtful pleasure of proving her wrong.

"Maybe not now, but nobody expects you to until you're healed."

"I expect it," he snapped. "Now is when Daad needs me. And don't bother talking to me about your brother. Josh is a gut boy, but Daad needs his own son. David is gone, and I'm useless."

He looked at her to find her studying his face as if trying to read his thoughts. That steady gaze made him feel uneasy. Was she thinking he sounded like a spoiled child? He did, of course, but the guilt that gnawed at him had that effect.

When she didn't speak, his discomfort grew. "Well? Aren't you going to convince me that one day I'll be back the way I was before?"

"I can't, because I don't know it. Nobody does." Her expression was serious, as if everything he said deserved attention. "I just know that if you do your therapy, you'll be better than you are now. If you don't, you won't."

"So you and Tim and the doctors say, but it doesn't help." He nursed his bitterness, letting it grow. "If someone had taken the keys away before that kid got into the car, I wouldn't be here. If I'd swerved sooner, or pulled off the road so he could pass..."

"You can't prevent an accident with wishful thinking." Miriam seemed to be holding on to her quiet tone with an effort. "It was an accident. No one intended it to happen."

"Is that supposed to make me feel better?" he snapped.

Miriam stood up, startling him.

"Leaving me?" He couldn't blame her if she did, and it would be a relief not to have to live up to her expectations. He was beginning to wish he'd never made that promise.

"I'll go and get the equipment ready for your exercises. Maybe that will put you in a better mood."

He looked up, ready to argue, but she'd already gone into the house before he could find a word. He heard her say something to Betsy, heard a snarled response from his sister.

"I thought you might like to work through the exercise routine with your brother," Miriam said patiently. "Then you could help him with it when I'm not here."

"Why? He doesn't want to waste time on those stupid exercises. He told me so. Why can't you leave him alone?"

"Because I want him to get better, and that's the only way to do it." Miriam's voice rang out clearly as he turned toward the screen door.

"That's what you say."

If Daad could hear Betsy, she'd be in for another punishment. And if he sat here and did nothing, he'd be helping her get into trouble.

With a wave of shame, he realized that Betsy wasn't nearly as rude to Miriam as he had been. He grabbed the wheels and shoved himself toward the door, reaching it in time to see the two of them staring at each other.

"That's enough, Betsy. Do what Miriam says."

She spun toward him, startled. "But I thought you

didn't want to do those stupid exercises. That's what you said."

He had to force the words out, and they almost choked him. "Yah, I said it. But I was wrong."

Well, he had been. Not because he had much hope for the exercises, but because he'd agreed to them. Still, he hated to admit his fault with Miriam standing there staring at him.

By Saturday afternoon, showers had chased some of the oppressive heat away. As Miriam walked along the path into the woods with her cousins, laden down with picnic baskets and a jug of lemonade, she felt her spirits lift.

"I feel as if I'm about eight years old again," Miriam said. She smiled as Beth, ahead of her, glanced back over her shoulder.

"You don't look much older," Beth said.

"Wait a minute." Lyddy poked Miriam from behind. "I'm younger than Miriam by three whole months, ain't so?"

"Maybe she thinks your approaching marriage makes you look older," Miriam teased.

"Well, I feel eight, too. And the raspberry bramble that just caught my apron is probably the same one that did back then."

"More probably its great-great-granddaughter." Miriam felt like skipping along the path downhill to the stream, but most likely she'd end up flat on her face if she did. There seemed to be a lot more tree roots snaking across the path than there used to be when they were children.

Still, it felt safe and familiar, walking down to the creek in the heat of an August day, eager to plunge her feet into the cool water. And there it was, rippling over the rocks that it had smoothed and flattened over years and years, since long before any of them were born.

"Here we are," Beth said as she stepped onto the oblong flat rock that jutted into the creek, causing the water to swirl around it. This had always been their picnic spot…the place where they'd sit and eat jelly sandwiches and whoopie pies, then take their shoes off and dangle their feet in the water.

Miriam paused to set the jug of lemonade she carried in the small pool created by the rock, wiggling the jug to be sure it wouldn't tip over. As soon as she drew her hand away, a flurry of minnows swam around it as if thinking it a strange newcomer to their watery home.

When she rose, Lyddy was already spreading a blanket for them to sit on while Beth started to unpack the picnic basket. Tradition said they'd eat first, talking about what everyone had been doing and then wade in the creek, catching minnows and the occasional crayfish.

"What do you think, Miriam?" Beth held up a packet of sandwiches. "Ham salad or pickle and egg?"

"If there's no peanut butter and marshmallow

crème," she said, mentioning a favorite gooey treat from childhood, "I'll have half of each."

Laughing a little, Beth doled out the sandwiches, and talk began to ripple back and forth, just like the water chuckling past. They knew each other so well, and yet they never ran out of things to talk about. Anyone would think they'd already said everything there was to say, but anyone would be wrong.

Eventually, after tales from Beth about the silly things that happened in the store she ran with her husband, and the latest funny thing her son had said, Lyddy turned to Miriam.

"Your turn," she said. "We really want to know how Matthew King is doing. Are you ready to throw up your hands yet? Or has he tried to kick you out?"

Miriam smiled, relaxing back on her elbows, her legs stretched out on the cool rock. "You ought to know I've never been one to give up," she said. "Although Matt does try my patience from time to time."

"From what I remember about Matt, it would be more than just trying," Lyddy said, wrapping her arms around her knees. "He's one who always got his own way, or he'd know the reason why."

"Well, he usually thought he was right about whatever it was, and as often as not, he was right," Beth pointed out.

"He'd do even better if he set all that determination toward getting well, but he is doing better. This week we got him to join the family for meals, and yesterday he actually sat out on the porch for a gut long time. He was cross, but he did it."

"That's wonderful gut," Lyddy exclaimed. "From what I'd heard, I thought he'd never be out of the bed again."

But Beth was studying Miriam's expression. "What's wrong? That should make you happy, ain't so?"

"It does," she protested. "Well, mostly."

"Then what?" Lyddy turned from watching the minnows flitting around in circles.

"Healing is more than just physical." Miriam struggled for the words to explain the thing she knew but had trouble rationalizing. "It's…being well inside yourself. Not arguing with God about it, but accepting and moving on."

"It's a lot to accept," Beth said softly. "David… well, everyone loved David. And Matt was driving."

Miriam nodded, a lump forming in her throat. "Grief is natural, but I think Matt actually blames himself for the accident. He won't listen to anyone telling him otherwise."

"Like you?" Lyddy clasped her hand for a moment.

"Maybe I shouldn't have pushed, but it just seemed so wrong to me." She wasn't sure whether she was trying to justify it to them or to herself. "An accident is an accident. It's something nobody can predict is going to happen. If you could, you'd prevent it. Nothing he could have done would have made any difference. I'm sure of that."

She could hear the passion in her voice and knew she was giving away her feelings with every word. It couldn't be helped, and at least she was saying it to Beth and Lyddy, knowing they would understand and not tell anyone.

Lyddy straightened, shoving her feet out in front of her as if she intended to jump up and do something about it. "But that's ferhoodled. The police blamed it entirely on the driver. That boy had been drinking, and he was driving too fast. My daad heard one of the policemen say that if it hadn't happened there, it would have been somewhere else."

"It's no good telling Matthew that. He persists in thinking he could have prevented it. It's tormenting him, and I really believe it's keeping him from getting well."

"Yah." Beth's voice was soft. "It's sort of like you, blaming yourself for what happened with that boy you took care of."

Miriam could only stare at her in disbelief. Beth—gentle, understanding Beth—couldn't be saying such a thing. "I'm… I'm not. And anyway, it's not the same thing at all."

"Isn't it?" Beth exchanged glances with Lyddy, and she realized they'd talked about it privately since the last time she saw them. "You had no idea what was happening with that boy, so how could you have prevented it?"

"It was my job to understand," she said stubbornly. "You can't compare the two things."

"Matt probably feels it was his job to keep David safe, but he couldn't," Beth said.

Lyddy clasped her right hand again, and Beth took her left. They sat there, linked, not speaking. Not doing anything but letting the words sink in.

Beth was mistaken, she told herself firmly. She might have wonderful insight into other people, but this time she was wrong.

A small voice spoke in the back of her mind. *What if she isn't wrong? What if you're caught up in futilely replaying the past, just like Matt is?*

She wanted to believe Beth was mistaken, but the more she thought of it, the more it wondered her. If what Beth said was true, what could she do about it?

If she couldn't heal herself, how could she hope to heal anyone else?

Chapter Eight

By Monday, Miriam was eager to dismiss all her questions and get back to work. Whatever her own problems, they couldn't keep her from doing her best for Matt.

Sunday had been off-Sunday, when worship wasn't held in their church district. Families either got together to enjoy one another's company or went to another district to worship. In their case, they'd entertained her mother's side of the family. Much as she loved them, it had been stressful.

Mammi was the youngest by far of her family, and with five older sisters to host, she had spent the afternoon mediating the inevitable spats they had whenever they were all together. Miriam had never been able to understand why they couldn't just enjoy being together, but when she'd said that to Mammi once, her mother had laughed and said the sisters *were* enjoying themselves. Squabbling was their means of conversation.

Maybe so, but it wasn't so pleasant for the onlooker. And it wasn't much better when they united, only to wonder audibly why Miriam wasn't married yet.

After all that, Miriam gave her mother an extra-warm hug when she left for the King place on Monday morning. She probably needed it.

Miriam arrived to find that Elizabeth had put Matt and Betsy to work snapping beans at the kitchen table. Before she could comment, he'd pushed the wheelchair back from the table.

"Sorry, Betsy. You'll have to finish. Miriam's ready to put me to work."

"No fair," Betsy said, grinning. "You always have an excuse not to do kitchen work."

It was good to see Betsy smile after the way she'd been for the past few days. "I wouldn't let him get away with it if I were you," Miriam said, joining in the teasing. "Besides, he's exercising his fingers, ain't so?"

"Yah, for sure." Betsy put a strainer full of beans in his lap before he could protest.

Elizabeth handed Miriam a mug of tea fixed just the way she liked it. "You must have had a nice time with so many visitors yesterday," she said. "I noticed all the buggies pulled up by the barn."

She sounded a bit wistful, as if longing for the days when she had done so, and Miriam noticed that

Matt's face tightened. He'd be blaming himself, she guessed, for his mother's lonely day.

"*Nice* wasn't the right word," she replied quickly. "It was my mother's family. My aunts argued all afternoon."

Elizabeth actually chuckled at that. "They always did, especially Evelyn and Lizzie. What was it this time?"

"Aunt Evelyn's granddaughter had a new dress, and Aunt Lizzie thought the color made her look like an eggshell. Or maybe it was the other way around."

"It wouldn't matter to them, as long as they had something to fuss over," Elizabeth said.

"I'd rather have a quiet Sunday afternoon," Matt said abruptly. He pushed the strainer over to Betsy. "Anyway, Grossmammi was here, so we had company. Now isn't it time we were getting to work?"

"Yah, for sure." Miriam took another swallow of her tea and set the cup down. "Let's go."

No sooner had the door closed behind them than Matt turned on her. "I guess you think I should encourage my mother to invite every relation we have to come here and stare at me."

If he was looking for a fight, she wasn't going to indulge him. Besides, they both knew he'd only said it because he felt guilty. She'd begun to think that he took out his unhappiness on her because he certain sure didn't want to hurt his family.

"Your mother was glad just to have your grandmother here."

He shrugged, looking embarrassed. "Yah, she was." He seemed to struggle for a moment. "Sorry I snapped."

With no reply but a smile, she got out the weights Matt had begun working with. "Let's try the three-pound ones today." She handed them to him.

He grabbed them with more energy than he usually showed and started on the round of arm exercises. Maybe he'd work off the rest of his ill feelings that way.

Actually, she could understand how he felt about seeing people. After all, she'd experienced it herself with all the comments about her fading black eye the previous day. Every relative had wanted to hear the whole story until she was tired of telling it.

Still, Matt would have to get over that particular feeling if his family was ever to have a normal life again.

Trying to change the mood, she waved toward the wood carvings. "What would you think about setting up your wood-carving tools? You might like that better than snapping beans."

"Neither of them is much help to anyone." He met her eyes and shrugged. "I'll think about it."

The door opened just then to admit Betsy. "The beans are done. Did Matt tell you how I made him work out on Saturday?"

Miriam smiled at the enthusiasm in her voice. "No, he didn't. How about it, Matt? Did she push you?"

Matt surrendered the weights. "She did. I think she's been taking lessons from you and Tim."

Miriam liked seeing how Betsy blossomed at the compliment from her brother. "We were just talking about getting out his wood-carving equipment. What do you think?"

"Great. Remember, you promised to carve a cat for me when you had time. I know right where the tools are."

"I said I'd think about it," Matt protested, but more as a matter of form than anything serious.

"Don't bother thinking about it. Just do it," Betsy prompted. "That's what Grossmammi always says. Let's finish the exercises, and then Miriam can help me carry the table and equipment down from the attic."

"Sounds good to me." Miriam waited for another protest from Matt, but it didn't come. He actually looked enthused about it. For the first time, she felt optimistic about his recovery.

So it turned out that fifteen minutes later, having finished the first round of exercises, she and Betsy were toting a heavy table awkwardly down the attic steps.

"I know this is the right thing to do," Betsy said. "Once the wood-carving stuff is set up, he won't be able to resist. He..." She stopped while they made the turn at the bottom.

As they moved into the upstairs hallway, the sound of voices below came floating up. "Sounds like someone is here." Setting the table down, Miriam took a step toward the stairs, trying to determine who it was.

The voices became louder, and she and Betsy exchanged looks, recognizing the voices. Miriam felt her heart sink. "Liva Ann," she murmured.

"And her mother," Betsy added. "We'd better go down and help Mammi."

For once they were on the same side. They scrambled toward the steps, but even as they did, Miriam feared they were too late. That loud, cheerful voice sounded as if Liva Ann's mother was barreling right through Elizabeth.

"He'll love to see Liva Ann," she announced. "We'll go right in. Come on, Liva."

"Hurry," Betsy said. They scrambled down the stairs, but before they could reach the bottom they heard a shriek, a slamming door and then a crash.

Matt stared at the door, his hands clenched into fists, his stomach churning. She'd taken one look at him, and that had been enough to make her shriek. He heard Liva Ann muttering while her mother scolded, her voice fading as they apparently left the house.

He let out the breath he'd been holding. They were gone. How had they gotten in here?

The doorknob turned. He reached out and grabbed the nearest hard object...the flashlight that lay on the bedside stand. The door opened a crack and Miriam's voice floated through.

"I'm coming in. Don't throw anything."

The door swung open. Miriam came inside, her feet crunching on broken glass. She looked down and stepped clear of the remains of the canning jar he'd thrown. The daisies it had contained were scattered across the broken glass.

If Miriam said one word—

She turned back toward the hall. "Betsy, hand me the broom and dustpan, please."

Betsy apparently did, because a moment later Miriam was back, closing the door and beginning to sweep up the glass without comment.

For some reason, even her silence infuriated him. "If you were part of that, you'd better have a bigger dustpan."

She paused, looking at him. "Don't be foolish. You know I wasn't. Betsy and I were carrying a table down from the attic. And don't blame your mother, either. Dora Miller simply charged past her as if she weren't even there."

"Sorry," he muttered.

"Those were the daisies Betsy picked for you." She was still scolding. "You'd best tell her you're sorry."

His annoyance flared like a fire with dry kindling. "If someone screamed at the sight of you, you might throw something, too. At least I waited until she shut the door."

"Liva Ann? Yah, we could hear the screech from upstairs."

"I didn't have time to turn away." He glared at her, but Miriam seemed unaffected. "Liva Ann got the full effect of this." He smacked his palm against his scarred cheek.

Miriam kept on sweeping. "She doesn't seem to have much self-control, does she? But she's pretty young. She'll probably be better when she's older. Look at her mother."

"I don't want to look at her mother," he said, exasperated. "What does she have to do with it?"

"I'm just saying that she wouldn't scream. When Liva Ann is a little more mature…"

"I don't intend to wait until Liva Ann is more mature. Why are we talking about it?"

Miriam shrugged. "I was just pointing out that she'll probably have her mother's nerve when she's older. If you're going to marry her…"

"I'm not. I'll be happy not to see either of them ever again. If they come back, I'll throw something heavier than a canning jar full of daisies."

She stared at him for a moment, and a smile tugged at her lips. "I take it you're not heartbroken. You're just mad."

"Wouldn't you be?"

Miriam bent to sweep the glass into the dustpan. "If I loved somebody, it would be painful."

"You're trying to make me admit that I didn't

love her." He rolled the wheelchair closer and took the dustpan while she stood up.

"Well, you didn't, did you?" Her smile was more definite now.

He tried to hang on to his annoyance. He couldn't. To his astonishment, he discovered he wanted to laugh.

"I guess not." He chuckled. "But that was a spectacular way of finding out. That screech she let out..."

He wrapped his fingers around her wrist, feeling her pulse thud against his skin. He couldn't seem to find anything more to say, but he didn't want to let go.

Someone opened the door cautiously, and he pushed the chair back to empty the dustpan. Betsy looked around the edge of the door, and his mother appeared beyond her, both of them looking apprehensive.

"Everything all right?" Betsy's eyes were wide.

"Yah, it's over," he admitted. "Just watch for any glass."

"I think I got it all," Miriam said, not looking at him. She turned to Betsy. "Maybe we should get that table we left on the stairs."

In a moment she was gone, and he was left wondering what she was really thinking.

Mammi patted his hand. "Ach, I'm sorry. That woman—" She fought to control herself. "She just pushed right past me like I wasn't there. I'm sorry. I should have stopped her."

"Don't be sorry." He clasped her hand. "Maybe it was for the best. At least they won't come around anymore."

"But you…she hurt you."

He shook his head slowly. "Actually, it didn't hurt. It just made me mad. Miriam said that meant I never loved her at all."

Mamm actually smiled. "I never did think Liva Ann was the right girl for you. Maybe it's for the best."

"She can go back to her rumspringa parties and flirt with the boys," he said, realizing that prospect didn't bother him in the least.

"Who's going to rumspringa parties?" Betsy came in, walking backward and carrying one end of the chair.

"Liva, I hope," he said. "She should find some nice boy to court her."

"As long as it's not you," Betsy declared. "She's too silly for you."

Miriam had appeared with the other end of the table, and they set it against the side wall next to the bookcase.

He looked from one face to another. "It sounds as if all of you have the same idea. You must be right." He rolled his chair toward the table. "This will be perfect. Did you find the boxes with the tools?"

"I'll get them," Miriam said, moving quickly.

He was about to say that Betsy could do it, but

Miriam was already gone. Was it his imagination, or was she trying to stay away from him?

Maybe she hadn't liked it when he'd grasped her wrist. He hadn't meant to offend her. It was just a friendly touch. He hadn't meant anything by it. Had he?

Miriam could only be thankful that Tim would be coming in the afternoon. That way, she didn't have to be alone with Matt, something too dangerous for her self-control. Dealing with this morning's events had been enough for one day.

Conversation bounced around the table during lunch as everyone seemed to react cheerfully to the fact that Liva Ann was out of their lives. And mostly, it seemed, that Matt didn't care a bit about losing her.

The lively chatter proved to be a useful distraction for Miriam from those moments when Matt's hand had encircled her wrist. His touch had gone right to her heart. Her breath had caught in her throat. Everything she thought she knew about herself turned upside down, and it still hadn't righted itself. All she could do was hope that he hadn't realized what was happening to her.

Miriam heard her name and surfaced, hoping no one realized she hadn't been listening. Josh was speaking, and it seemed he'd asked her a question. She hadn't the faintest idea what that question had been.

"There comes Tim," he said, glancing toward the

window that overlooked the lane. "I'll ask him. He'll know exactly how the ramp should be built."

"You don't need to." Matt sounded as if he was trying to stop a flood with his bare hands. "I don't want..."

He stopped, because no one was paying attention to him. Josh was getting up from the table and carrying his dishes to the sink. In a moment, Abel had followed him.

"I can stop by the lumberyard and get the planks you need," Abel said. "It's wonderful kind of you and your brothers."

"There's nothing the boys enjoy more than making a big mess building something," Josh said.

Miriam had caught up with the conversation by now. Josh was determined to build a ramp off the porch for Matt, and his enthusiasm had pulled his brothers along on the project.

Josh grinned, turning from the sink. "Daad said he was sure he had enough planks for it. I'll check with him and bring them over next time."

Matt might as well save his breath, because it wouldn't change Josh's enthusiasm. Besides, she could see that Abel was just as eager. There'd be a ramp off the back porch before many days had passed.

Good. Matt would soon have no excuse not to join the world again.

Tim's van had pulled up by the porch, and he was calling for someone to give him a hand. Josh hurried out, followed by Abel. In another moment, Betsy had scurried after them.

Clattering and banging came floating in from outside. Miriam decided that whatever they were doing, they had enough help, so she finished clearing the table. With an expression that said he was giving in to curiosity, Matt wheeled himself to the door where he could see.

"What is that thing? Miriam?"

She came to look over his shoulders at the unloading that was in progress, but she'd already figured it out. "Parallel bars. So you can get upright again."

Miriam had turned to look at him when she spoke, and she couldn't miss the expression on his face.

"I don't want to use them," he muttered, and she didn't know if his words were born of fear of trying it or just plain stubbornness.

Deciding there was no comment she could make that would help, she ignored him, clattering the dishes to sound as if she were busy.

Something thudded onto the back porch, and then Betsy opened the door and held it wide. "Okay?" she called, probably to Tim.

"Right." Tim sounded cheerful. "Easy does it. We'll have to decide on the best place to put it."

Tim and Josh appeared, handling the set of bars between them. Miriam heard a sharp intake of breath beside her.

He was afraid, Miriam realized. Afraid of trying something new. Afraid of failing.

"You don't have to try it until you're ready," she said quickly. "I don't think Tim will push you on it."

"Good." Matt sounded as stubborn as ever. "Because I'm not ready." He folded his arms across his chest in a sign of conviction, but Miriam noticed how tightly clenched his fists were.

Meantime they had wrangled the apparatus into the kitchen and set it down for a consultation about where it might go. Aside from not being in the kitchen, Elizabeth didn't seem to mind where it was, and they eventually decided it could go next to the wall in Matt's room.

At that point, Miriam joined them, and when Abel and Josh hurried off to get some tools, taking Betsy with them, Miriam had a chance to tell Tim what was troubling her.

"Don't you think this is pushing him too fast?" She gestured toward the bars. "He doesn't feel he's ready."

"I know." Tim lowered his voice, stepping closer to her. "We'll move slowly, of course. Remember when we talked about the things that hold him back? I realized that maybe holding out a goal in front of him might have the opposite effect. Don't you think?"

Miriam hesitated for a moment, and then she realized what was happening to her. She had become too involved with Matt, and she cared too much. Her own emotions were getting in the way of what was best for him.

Forcing a smile, she nodded. "I'm sure you're right."

Tim studied her face carefully, probably knowing something was wrong. She waited for him to tax her with being too involved, but he didn't.

"Don't worry. We'll coax him into it, one baby step at a time. Remember, we can't guarantee anything, but we'll do everything possible to get the best result for our patient."

It was a reminder that she needed, she knew. Matt was a patient, and she had to see him that way. She couldn't let anything interfere.

For the rest of Tim's visit, she watched, along with Betsy, as he worked with Matt, demonstrating each new exercise slowly and carefully, showing Matt the brace that he hoped would stabilize his more seriously injured leg enough to allow Matt to stand.

They were getting into new territory this week, and she realized that Betsy was watching and listening to the description of each exercise just as carefully as she was. She felt a wave of gratitude for the girl. She'd come so far from her initial antagonism that she'd turned into a great help.

Miriam caught Betsy's eye as they each had a try with putting the brace on themselves to see how it felt. Betsy cared about her brother. That caring had been behind her attitude all along. It had just been misdirected at first. Now that she understood what was best for him, she'd be invaluable.

"Okay," Tim said at last. "Good work, Matt. Just

your massage left to finish off the day, and none too soon, I'm sure you're thinking."

Matt gave a rueful smile. "You discovered a few muscles that I'd forgotten about, I'll say that for you."

Tim laughed, taking a mock punch at Matt's shoulder. "That's the way to look at it. Try some heat on it after your massage. You'll be ready to work on it again tomorrow."

Miriam walked out with Tim to hear his final instructions for the next few days. When he went off to give Josh a few tips about the ramp, she went back inside slowly. Her thoughts had been spinning so much that she felt as if she should curl up in a ball until they stopped, but there was no time for that. Her patient was waiting for his massage. Somehow she had to isolate her feelings and do it.

But when she walked back into Matt's room, she found that Betsy was already doing it. Startled, she paused. Before she could say anything, Matt spoke.

"Betsy can take care of this today. You're already late getting finished with all that's been going on. She'll even take care of the heat packs."

"I'm doing it right, ain't so?" Betsy said anxiously.

"Exactly right," Miriam said. Now her thoughts stopped spinning and landed with a thud. She had betrayed herself. Matt had recognized her rush of feelings when he'd touched her. He'd probably been embarrassed, unsure how to handle it. How to let her know that she was wrong.

So he was trying to let her down easy, holding

her at arm's length. Telling her without a word that there could be nothing between them.

She couldn't control her blush, so she turned quickly away, trying to hide the color in her face as he had tried to hide his scar.

"I'll be glad to get off home." She walked steadily to the door. "I'll see you tomorrow."

Tomorrow, when she'd have figured out a way of controlling her feelings. Tomorrow, when she'd become adjusted to the fact that she was in love with Matthew, and he felt nothing in return. How was she going to deal with it?

Her future was just what it had always been, she assured herself as she walked quickly toward home. She would help other people heal. It was what she'd always wanted, and she would keep on doing it.

But now she knew that she could never heal herself.

Chapter Nine

Miriam and Betsy stood on either side of Matt, ready to help him stand. But Matt wasn't cooperating.

"We can wait until Tim arrives to do this one." Sitting in the wheelchair, which they'd pushed up to the bars, Matt planted his hands on the arms of his chair, as if he planned to stay there no matter what.

"You heard the message. Tim said to start without him, and he'd get here as soon as he could. That's right, isn't it, Betsy?"

Betsy nodded. She'd gone to the phone shanty when Tim didn't arrive at his usual Thursday time and found his message. "He said he was delayed at the appointment before ours. He didn't sound very happy about it."

"So, he's obviously late. We don't need to start with this exercise."

Miriam was more than a little disappointed. After

what had been a shaky start to the week on Monday, she'd thought they were back to their friendly, patient-and-helper relationship again. Now why was he balking?

"You know why Tim wants you to do this after your warm-up stretches." Miriam said it as patiently as she could, but her exasperation probably seeped through. "Always do the hardest thing first." She found herself smiling as the memory popped up in her thoughts again. "According to my grossmammi, that's the rule for everything, not just exercises."

Betsy giggled. "Grandmothers have good advice for every subject, ain't so? Our grossmammi certain sure does." She nudged her brother. "You know she'd say the same thing."

"Maybe she would, but..."

"What's wrong? Can't you think of another excuse?" Betsy had gotten rather bossy with her big brother now that she thought it was her job to cheer him on.

Miriam decided she'd best intervene before it turned into a brother-sister battle.

"You may as well tell us what's really wrong. We're not giving up unless you give us a genuine reason." She grasped his arm firmly to help him up, and he jerked away.

Her face must have reflected the dismay she felt. She really had ruined things with her reaction to his unexpected touch on Monday. If Matt wouldn't let her touch him, she couldn't do her work. She'd have to quit.

"All right, I'll tell you." His lips quirked. "You'll drop me."

His sister swatted him. "Listen, the two of us are a match for you any day. Ain't so, Miriam?"

Her tension drained away, leaving a smile. It wasn't a good reason, but it was better than thinking what she had been.

"That's certain sure. Besides, we put the mats down. Even in the unlikely event that we let go of you, you'll have a soft landing."

"Judging by my sister's expression, it's not that unlikely." He extended his arm to Miriam. "Okay, I'll risk it if you'll keep an eye on Betsy."

"Nobody needs to keep an eye on me." Betsy grabbed his other arm. "Now quit stalling and get going."

Betsy might think she didn't need supervision, but Miriam watched to be sure her grip was correct. "You can use the bars to help as much as you want. You know you can count on your upper body strength."

"That's from all the hay bales he's tossed around," Betsy put in, bracing herself. "Ready?"

Miriam nodded. She had to hold his arm so closely that it pressed against her rib cage. Trying to block out every sensation, she counted down. "Three, two, one, lift."

In another moment he was standing, each hand

clasping a bar. Cautiously, he straightened, putting more weight on his hands.

She watched his face, looking for any sign that he should be lowered back to the wheelchair. But he looked triumphant. Surprised at himself, but triumphant.

"Let go for a minute," he demanded.

Miriam exchanged looks with Betsy. He seemed to be standing easily, and his grasp on the bars was firm. With a silent prayer, she nodded. Gradually she and Betsy loosened their grip, but Miriam kept her hands in position to grab him.

"I'm doing it." There was no mistaking the surprise and pride in his voice, and her heart sang.

"You definitely are. And that's about enough for the first time." She took his arm, just as the door opened.

"Wow." Tim grinned at the sight that met his eyes. "So this is what happens when I'm late. If I'm not careful, you won't need me at all."

"I'm not that far along." Matt eased himself back and let them help him sit down. "But it surely feels wonderful good to stand by myself."

Tim looked as happy as if it had been him. "Maybe I'll have to be late more often." His expression changed. "Scratch that. I shouldn't even joke about it. If it happens again with the same job, I'll… well, I don't know what I'll do."

"Problems?" Miriam asked, and Matt turned his chair slightly so he could see Tim's expression.

She could see the struggle on Tim's face. He was so frustrated that he looked ready to burst if he couldn't vent to someone.

"Okay, here it is without names. My last patient was a woman just home from the hospital after hip surgery. She and her husband had been instructed that she could not be left on her own yet." He grimaced. "When I got there, the husband was already in his car and ready to pull out of the driveway. I wanted to give him some instructions, but he sped away before I could. I guess he figured if I was there, he didn't need to be."

"The poor woman." Miriam's heart ached for her. "Is he the only person she can rely on?"

"Apparently, but you haven't heard half of it. The appointment was for one hour. I like to allow plenty of time to talk to the patient, especially the first visit. So the hour passed, and the husband wasn't back. I waited—I couldn't possibly leave her by herself."

"She must have felt terrible," Betsy said. She was obviously trying to imagine any of her family doing that, and failing.

"She kept urging me to leave, saying she'd be okay. But no way was I doing that. Anything could have happened to her. Forty-five minutes later, he showed up."

"I take it you gave him a lecture." Matt moved his chair back a little, facing Tim more completely.

"More than that. I told him his insurance wouldn't pay for the time he'd wasted, and he would be charged personally for it." He grinned. "That got him serious in a hurry. I won't have any more trouble with him, though his wife might." Looking better for having told the story, he patted Matt's shoulder. "You're one of the fortunate ones. You have people who love you to help."

Miriam froze for an instant. Tim didn't mean that the way it sounded, of course. But at that moment, she felt she'd like to hide.

A wave of energy powered Matt through the rest of his therapy session, so much so that Tim firmly removed the weights from his hands. "I can do more…" he began, but Tim shook his head.

"Enough. Just because you got on your own two feet doesn't mean you can tackle a mountain." He handed the weights to Miriam, and she stowed them on the bookshelf.

"It's nice to see though, yah?" Her warm smile seemed to congratulate Matt.

It also reminded him of the agreement they'd made about his therapy. He just might have to admit that Miriam had been right. After a session like this, he wasn't going to give up now.

"Come on, Tim. Admit it. I'm doing better than you thought I could." He swung the wheelchair around to follow Tim to the kitchen.

"I think you're looking for a compliment." Tim's usual smile widened. "You deserve one. You're doing great. So is your support team."

Matt glanced from Betsy to Miriam as he propelled himself into the kitchen. "That's certain sure. I couldn't do without them."

Betsy dashed away a tear and gave him a throttling hug. "You'd better not try."

Hugging her back, he looked at Miriam to find she'd turned away, but he couldn't miss the fact that she wiped her eyes, too. When she turned around, she had banished any sign of tears.

"Just don't get overconfident," she cautioned. "We don't want any accidents." For an instant her voice seemed to tremble on the words.

Or had he imagined it? No, there was something—some emotion that she was hiding behind her gentle smile. He opened his mouth to ask when he was interrupted by a crash out on the back porch, followed by male laughter.

"What's going on out there?" He set the wheelchair in motion and got to the door first. Then reality set in, tempering his euphoria, when he had to wait for help to manage getting out the door.

Miriam pushed him outside. "This was going to be a surprise, but my brothers can't do anything quietly, ain't so?"

"We could have," Josh protested, "if we hadn't brought Sammy with us."

Ten-year-old Sammy turned to Matt with a grin, mischief lighting his freckled face. "It wasn't my fault. It was Daniel's. He was being so bossy that I told him to do it himself."

Daniel took a mock swipe at him, and he ducked away, laughing and still talking. “We’re building you a ramp, Matt. Then you’ll be able to get back to work.”

Matt sensed Miriam freeze, as if she held her breath, waiting for an explosion from him.

But Sammy was just a kid. He joked with Matt the way he would with his older brothers, and it was impossible to be upset at anything he said. He reached out to tap Sammy’s straw hat, tipping it over his eyes.

“Big talk,” he said. “Let’s see you do some work. I can probably still work harder than you, even in this chair.”

Sammy just grinned with his usual good humor. He reminded Matt so much of his own younger brother than his heart seemed to stop for a moment.

Someday would he be able to remember David without the flood of guilt and grief? He didn’t think so. He guessed he would have to learn to live with it.

“Much as I’d like to join the work party, I’ve got another visit yet this afternoon.” Tim rested his hand on Matt’s shoulder. “Don’t quit working. But don’t try doing things on your own—that usually backfires.”

Matt jerked his chin toward Miriam and his sister. “My guard dogs won’t let me. You can count on that, ain’t so?”

“Just try it,” Betsy said, overhearing. “I’ll land on you like a wagonload of hay bales.”

“Good for you.” Tim lifted his hand in goodbye as

he strode off to his van, and Matt could almost see his mind shifting again to his next patient.

Miriam moved toward the door. "If you're going to stay here and supervise, I'll finish putting the exercise equipment away."

Matt nodded. "Don't let it worry you. Betsy will keep an eye on me."

"I'm sure of it." Laughing a little, she swung the screen door open.

Moving the chair to a better angle, Matthew could see the whole process. Obviously, the Stoltzfus boys had planned this carefully. They'd brought the parts of the ramp already assembled in the wagon that was pulled up on the grass, and with many hands available, they were putting it together. If it had been a barn raising, it couldn't have been better planned.

The ramp would go out from the porch at a gentle slope, then turn toward the lane and end just where buggies usually pulled up. He'd thought to stay for a few minutes, just to show he appreciated it, and found he couldn't pull himself away. Instead he watched it take shape and longed to have a hammer in his own hand.

"So, who was the designer?" he called. "Someone knew just how to go about this."

Daniel gave Josh a shove. "This guy. He talked to Amos Gaus about the one he made for his grandfather, and together they figured it out."

"Yah, but you did most of the carpentry, with Sammy's help."

Sammy blushed bright red, and the others laughed.

"If you can call it help to nearly nail his shoe to the plank…" Daniel teased.

Watching them work, Matt let his mind stray back to the day when he'd rejected the whole idea of a ramp. It struck him how selfish that had been. They were smiling, their voices light and joking. They were enjoying the job, not just because it was a change in the routine but because they were doing something good for someone else. He'd have let his own stubborn pride rob them of that pleasure and satisfaction.

It was as if he looked in a mirror, saw himself, and didn't like what he saw. He'd not just been selfish, he'd been self-pitying…hiding in his room when he should have been sharing his family's grief and helping them.

No more of that. Maybe it had been the elation of finding he could stand alone, but his plans had changed. No more reluctance. He'd do everything he could to keep improving, even if it didn't get him where he'd like to be.

He owed it to all the people who cared about him. And he owed it to Miriam to tell her that their stupid agreement was over. When they'd made it, he'd been using it as a wedge to get Miriam out of his life. But Miriam was the one who'd helped him get this far. She deserved an apology.

Spinning the chair around, he headed for the door, and Betsy scurried after him. "What are you doing?"

"I need to talk to Miriam for a bit. Give me a hand with the door."

"I can get her—"

He shook his head. "I'd rather go in. I won't be long."

Obediently, Betsy pulled the door open and gave him a push over the slightly raised doorstep. "Just shout when you want to come back out."

He nodded, engrossed in what he was going to say.

Miriam was sliding the bars back against the wall. She obviously didn't hear him, and when she turned, she nearly tripped on the chair.

"Easy," he said, catching her arm. "You were making too much noise to hear me."

An outburst of hammering came from the porch, and she shook her head, smiling. "I couldn't compete with that. Do you need me?"

"Just to tell you something. About that agreement we made—remember that?"

For just an instant he thought she'd completely forgotten it. Then the puzzlement in her face faded. "I don't think our month is up yet, is it?"

"I don't need a month. You win."

"Are you sure you want to admit it?" she asked lightly, but pleasure brightened her eyes.

"Certain sure." He frowned a little. "Look, I know what Tim was thinking—that I'll never be back the way I was. But if I can't be that, at least I can be useful. I want you to stay. Unless you're tired of my complaining."

"Never that. As long as you need help, I'll stay." Something serious darkened her clear eyes for a moment. "Maybe it'll make up for things."

Her expression troubled him. "What do you need to make up for? You've done nothing but help people."

Miriam shook her head a little. "Nobody's that good. Nobody gets through without some scars, even if you can't see them, even if their intentions are good."

He studied her face, wishing he could see beyond the calm facade. He realized he still held her arm, and he let his hand slide gently down to her wrist, reluctant to let go. "I'm not convinced."

"It doesn't matter." She tried to shake it off. "I've had a failure or two. But if I can really help you, well, maybe it will make up for the ones I couldn't help."

He still wasn't satisfied, but he knew her well enough to understand she didn't want any more questions. So he nodded and squeezed her hand, then thought he probably shouldn't have.

"I'll do my part," he promised. He wanted to know who it was Miriam thought she had failed, but unless she decided to confide in him, he'd never know.

Miriam moved away, a fixed smile on her face. This was too difficult—being with Matt every day, being close and hiding her feelings for him. It was easier when he snarled at her. She could take that. But when he smiled, when he expressed interest and concern, it was just too difficult.

But difficult or not, she had to manage. She was committed to help him for as long as he needed her.

A burst of laughter and cheering from outside was a welcome distraction. She hurried toward the door. They were calling for Matt.

"You're wanted out here. I'm afraid they're going to make you try it."

Matt wheeled himself across the kitchen. His movements were more sure every day, she realized. He'd probably be able to go in and out without help soon. She held the door and then followed him.

Her mamm and daad had shown up while they were inside, Mamm with a basket that probably contained food. She would think that any celebration ought to include food, and certain sure the boys were celebrating.

Matt must have seen her mother about when she did, and in what was probably a reflex, he turned his face away. So, he didn't mind her little brothers seeing him, but apparently a woman was different.

He surely couldn't think Mammi would shriek like Liva Ann. Miriam learned over the wheelchair and spoke in a low voice.

"Don't turn away from Mammi. If she can stay calm when the boys have been intent on mangling themselves, she's not going to be upset by a nice clean scar."

He glared at her for an instant. Then he nodded, and a smile tugged at his lips. "Guess you're right at that," he said, but it still seemed to take an effort for him to turn to face Mammi and speak to her.

A familiar pain cramped her heart. How could he think that a scar made him any less of a person? She longed to reach out and touch it soothingly, and the impulse was so strong that her palm actually tingled.

She pressed her hand firmly against her skirt, trying to chase away the feeling.

"It's finished," Sammy announced, standing at the entrance to the ramp. "Look!" He stepped aside, gesturing with a flourish, and making her wonder where he came upon that idea.

"You don't need to take the credit," Betsy teased, and in a moment they were shoving one another like the childhood playmates they'd always been.

"Behave yourselves," Mammi said impartially to both of them. She handed the basket to Elizabeth. "Just a little snack for everyone," she said.

"Ach, whoopie pies," Elizabeth exclaimed. "That's Abel's favorite. I'd best make sure some are put back for him before the young ones eat them all."

"He's coming now," Miriam said. "Don't let Matt start until his daad is here. I'll run and tell him."

She hurried out the lane, not so much because she thought they'd start without him, but because she could see his expression. He must have been out to the mailbox, judging by the envelopes in his hand.

He stared at a paper open in front of him, and his face was so grim it startled her.

He didn't look up until she had almost reached him, and then had to blink before he seemed to register that she was there.

"Ach, I'm sorry, Miriam. I didn't notice…" He ran out of words, and the paper trembled in his hand.

Alarmed, she grasped his arm. "Are you all right? Was ist letz?"

He finally seemed to see everyone gathered around the ramp.

"The ramp is finished," she explained quickly. "They want you to come to see Matt try it. If you're all right…"

"Fine, I'm fine." He stuffed the paper into an envelope and put it underneath the copy of the Amish weekly paper. "It's about the trial. The boy who hit Matt and David." His voice shook as his hand had, and he took a breath. "It maybe will start as soon as next week."

Her thoughts made a leap to all that might mean to Abel and Elizabeth, indeed to all of them. But especially Matt.

"I must think about how to tell them." He clamped his lips on the words.

"Do you want me to…to make some excuse?" She gestured toward the house.

"No, no, I must go." He forced a smile and took a few steps forward before glancing at her. "Don't say anything to Matt."

"No, for sure I won't."

"Gut." He gave a short nod and then headed for the porch.

Miriam hurried along behind him, trying to wrap her thoughts around what this might mean. At the very least it would upset everyone. And Matt…

Matt hadn't come to terms with what happened. Maybe he never would. What was this going to do to his progress, which had seemed so bright just a moment ago?

Chapter Ten

By Friday morning, Miriam realized she had to talk to someone about the trial or burst. She'd spent a wakeful night, worrying, praying, and worrying and praying over and over.

Daad and the boys didn't seem to notice anything. They were still talking about how much fun it had been to build the ramp and watch Matthew use it.

"He can go anywhere now, can't he, Miriam?" John Thomas, the bolder of the twins, appealed to her.

James leaned over to whisper in his ear, and a silent conversation seemed to pass between them.

"John Thomas says not everywhere. But can't he?" Two pairs of round blue eyes fastened on her, looking for the final word.

"He can go several places he couldn't without the ramp. But some things will still be hard, like going over rough ground, or getting into a buggy, or going up into the hay loft."

"So we must pray for him and help him any way we can," Mammi added, always ready to teach her young ones what it meant to be a neighbor.

The twins nodded solemnly, and Miriam and her mother exchanged glances, sharing a little amusement mixed with a great deal of love.

As her mother's gaze lingered on Miriam's face, Miriam realized she hadn't hidden her worries entirely. No one else might have noticed, but Mammi always did.

"If I had a pulley and a rope, I could figure out a way to get Matt up to the loft." A spark of excitement lit Sammy's eyes, as if he pictured trying it out himself.

"No." Daad's voice was firm.

"But, Daadi..."

"No, Sammy. And don't go trying it on yourself, you hear?"

Sammy nodded, convinced and disappointed.

Miriam had to hide a smile. Mammi always said that Sammy had more dangerous ideas in one day than the rest of the kinder did in a year.

Eventually Daad and the boys scattered to their morning chores, and Miriam stacked dishes quickly. "I'll help with these. I have time before I leave."

A few minutes later, her hands plunged into the hot soapy water, the words spilled out.

"You know something's wrong, yah? Did you hear about the trial?"

Mammi rinsed a plate and started to dry it. "So that's it. I thought it might be. I heard something when I was in the grocery store yesterday. How is Matthew taking it?"

"He doesn't know yet." She scrubbed the oatmeal kettle so hard that soapsuds splattered her face, and she had to rub them away with her wrist. "At least, he didn't when I left. Abel had gotten a letter about it, and he dreaded telling him."

"He's worried about it, and no wonder." Mammi's forehead wrinkled. "Those poor things. To have to go through hearing all about it again just when they were starting to heal…it seems unfair."

"Yah, it does. It will hurt all of them, Matthew worst of all, maybe. I think he imagines sometimes that he could have avoided the accident. That's foolish, but no amount of telling can change his feelings. Physically he's been doing so well, but…"

Mammi patted her shoulder. "Ach, I know. You've worked hard to help him. You're afraid it will set him back, ain't so?"

"For sure." Her heart seemed to twist. "Yesterday he was so encouraged after he managed to stand on his own. He told me he'd do everything he could to get as well as possible. He just wants to be useful."

Mammi nodded, understanding. "It will be gut for him to feel he's able to help, even if he can't run the farm by himself. It would be for anyone. When we can help, we feel valuable."

Miriam reflected that her mother's understanding of people had shaped how she raised her children. Somehow she'd never seen that in her before, and she'd certain sure never appreciated it. Mammi had taught all of them that being useful was what God wanted of us, even if no one else ever appreciated it.

Miriam rinsed a dish and put it in the rack. "You didn't tell me what people were saying at the market."

"No." Mammi hesitated for a moment. "Most folks I talked to were feeling bad for the King family. But I heard someone had written to the newspaper saying that the Amish buggies were a danger on the road."

Temper flaring, Miriam slapped a bowl into the drainer so hard she feared she'd broken it. "I don't know why people think they have to say such things. If Matt heard that, he'd feel even more responsible, and it's not fair. After all, that boy had been drinking."

He'd been just sixteen, almost the same age as David. Boys balancing on the edge of being men, swaying first one way and then the other and sometimes falling. Like Wayne, the boy she'd worked with in Ohio. Her heart ached for all of them, including the young driver.

Mammi seemed to be reading her thoughts. "Drinking or not, I don't suppose he meant to do wrong. He was young and reckless, and his parents must have been worrying and praying about him, just as we do about your bruders."

"I know." Miriam wiped her eyes with the corner of a dishcloth. "I guess there's not so much difference between parents, whether they're Amish or Englisch. Now all of it will be in the newspapers, and everyone will talk about it."

Wiping the last plate, Mammi set it down carefully. "Has Matthew been able to forgive him?"

No need to ask who she meant. "I don't think so," she said unhappily. "I know the bishop has been coming to counsel him, but Matt…well, he's holding on to the pain, I'd say. When Tim asked me to try to find out what's holding him back, I didn't have much trouble seeing that his lack of forgiveness was part of it."

"Part?"

"Yah." Miriam dried her hands slowly, her thoughts busy. "He feels guilty, I know that. Guilty and useless."

"That's a hurtful combination. Hurtful to him, I mean."

"Yah." She held back for a moment, and then the words burst out. "What can I do? It's like…like watching an accident happening and not being able to stop it. The trial will come, the King family will go through their pain and grief all over again, and I'm afraid Matt will go backwards instead of forwards. Back to staring at the ceiling in bitterness."

Mammi turned to her, dropping the dish towel.

"My sweet girl, you can't stop what's going to happen. All you can do is help them through it. Matthew depends on you—I could see that yesterday. Even if you're just there to stand beside him, it will help."

Would it? Miriam was frozen with doubt. Was she wise enough, strong enough, to make a difference?

Then her mother's arms went around her, hugging her tightly, and she knew she had to try.

The new day was cooler, making everyone more energetic, and Matt still hung on to the hopefulness he'd found the previous day. He didn't have any illusions about becoming the man he'd been before the accident, but if he could improve enough to be of some use around the farm, he'd try to be satisfied with that.

He wheeled himself out of his room, maneuvering the chair easily. He'd go out on the porch and try out the ramp again. Maybe surprise Miriam by being outside when she got there.

The house was so still that he thought no one was in the kitchen. Then he heard Mamm's and Daad's low voices. He was about to speak when he heard what Daad was saying.

"He has to be told, Elizabeth. Better he hears it from us rather than anyone else."

"No one would tell—" Mammi began.

"Would tell me what?" Matt propelled himself into the room with one powerful push of the wheels. "What has happened?"

Mammi looked at him, pressed her lips together, and turned away. Tears had welled in her eyes, alarming him.

"Daad?" He shoved his chair closer. "Was ist letz?"

"We've heard something about the accident. The driver is going on trial—you know that, yah?"

"I know. The police said they'd pass on what I told them about what happened."

He gritted his teeth together. He'd still been in the hospital then, hardly over the shock of the accident. Just beginning to understand how badly he was hurt.

"They say it may start as early as next week or the following one." Daad frowned at the paper he held in his hand and then thrust it toward Matt. "You'd best see what it says for yourself."

Matt stared at the letter, forcing his mind to absorb it all before he reacted. But he couldn't, because after the news about when and where it might happen, he saw something more.

"This says they want to talk to me. The district attorney's office will send someone to ask me some questions." He fluttered the paper. "Why? What do they think I can tell them that I didn't say before?"

Daad shook his head. "Maybe something wasn't clear. I thought… I hoped, anyway, that the driver would admit his guilt. That it would all be settled quickly instead of—"

He seemed to choke on the words, and Matt finished for him. "Instead of dragging it all out again.

Making us relive it. Putting it in the newspaper so everyone is talking."

The emotions that spurted up seemed strong enough to power him out of the chair, even out of the room. Why? Why did they have to go through it?

"That is justice," Daad said heavily, answering the question Matt hadn't asked out loud. "Our faith tells us to cooperate with the law unless it runs against God's law."

He knew that just as well as his father did, but rebellion still roiled in him. He turned away, not wanting Daad to see the feelings in his face, and his eyes caught a bit of movement through the screen door. Miriam stood there, her hand raised to the handle, her eyes wide.

"You might as well come in. I suppose you've heard about this already."

Miriam stepped inside, her gaze going from Daad's solemn face to Mamm's tearful one and then to his, no doubt showing anger.

"I'm sorry. I've come at a bad time. Do you want me…" She gestured toward the door, a question in her voice.

"Stay, please." His father had contrived to sound calm. "Matthew shouldn't miss his therapy because of this." He held out his hand to take the letter, but Matt shook his head.

"This says I'm supposed to tell them when someone can come and talk to me about the accident."

His mother made a soft, pained sound and reached

out as if groping for support. Before he or Daad could do anything, Miriam had gone to her, clasping her hand.

"It's all right, Elizabeth. You won't have to talk to them."

He wanted to flare up. To ask her what she knew about it. But whatever she knew or didn't know about the legal system, she'd known what to do about his mother.

"Yah, that's right, Mammi. Why don't you sit down? Is there any coffee left from breakfast?"

"I'll get it." Miriam helped her mother sit at the table, and in another moment had brought the coffee, pouring for Mamm and Daad. She held the pot out to him questioningly.

He shook his head, and she set it down.

"I'll get the equipment ready while you talk," she murmured.

"No, stay." He wasn't sure why he wanted her presence. Maybe because she could probably stop him before he upset Mamm any further. Or maybe for him, because she would understand.

"You'll have to talk to this person," Daad said. "It wouldn't be right to refuse."

Matt had to push down a tangle of emotions so he could speak calmly. "I can't tell them any more than I said before," he repeated. "I wish they'd leave us alone." He slapped his hand down on the table.

Daad shook his head. "We must do what's required." He passed his hand across his eyes as if to shut out the pictures the letter must have brought to mind.

Matt had a few of his own, pounding to get in. Seeing the buggy smashed on top of him. Hearing the horse whinny in pain. Trying to turn his head, to see David. And—

His hands clenched into fists. "I can't forgive, but I don't want revenge. I just want to be left alone."

Daad shook his head again. He was right, of course, but the rightness of it didn't change Matt's feelings.

"If you talk to this person, you might be able to find out what's going to happen," Miriam said.

He shot an angry look at her. She winced, but she went on.

"It would help all of you to be prepared for it, ain't so?" Miriam said softly, probably expecting a harsh reply.

Matt glared at her. He didn't want to be prepared. He wanted to shout the words at her.

But he had just enough control to think that maybe she had a point. If they understood what was coming, it might help Mamm, if not him. Maybe they could even get her to go to her sister's place until all this was over. If she and Betsy could be kept away from the whole thing, it would be easier to stand.

Was that what Miriam had meant? She looked so calm that he felt an instinct to rattle her. He wanted to throw something across the room and smash it. Smash it the way his fragile hope had been smashed.

He remembered her reaction to the jar of flowers. It would take more than that to rattle Miriam. That gentle, peaceful exterior of hers hid a core of iron.

By the time they were nearing the end of Matt's afternoon exercises, it seemed to Miriam that the King family had begun to adjust to the trial looming ahead of them. She could hear voices and the clink of jars from the kitchen where Elizabeth and Betsy were making corn relish. Abel and Joshua had vanished toward the upper field after the noon meal, talking easily about the work to be done.

As for Matt, he was concentrating fiercely on his attempts to take a step or two holding on to the bars. Beyond that concentration, she had the sense that his emotions were bubbling up, still ready to explode.

"Let go," he demanded, his arms rigid, muscles straining. "I can take a step without you holding on to me like I'm a baby trying to walk."

"And if you fall and crack your head against the bar? It'll be my fault. I don't want everybody mad at me." She understood his frustration, but his mind wasn't in the right place just now to take chances.

"Tell them I insisted. Tell them I knocked your arm away. Tell them anything, but let me try at least one step."

Maybe she'd best let him try. If she didn't, he'd probably be doing it the instant her back was turned, and nobody would be there to break his fall.

"If I do, I'll stay close enough to—"

He was already shaking his head. "Stand back. I'll take my chances."

"I won't," she said flatly. "Either I'm in a position to grab you, or else I'll take the bars away entirely."

Matt glared at her, and she glared back. After a moment, his expression began to falter. His lips twitched. "Never met such a stubborn woman," he muttered. "All right. If you get hurt, don't blame me."

"I'm supposed to say that." She moved closer, her hand pressing on the long, flat muscles of his back. She took a shaky breath and braced herself. "Say when you're ready, and I'll let go."

His chest moved as he inhaled a deep breath. She focused on his arms. As long as they didn't fail him, he'd manage. Even if he faltered, he should be able to catch himself.

"Now," he said, waiting until he felt her hands move away. He looked down at his weakest leg, frowning in grim concentration. Muscles tightening, he forced his foot forward. Straining, he brought the other up to meet it.

Delighted, she grasped him again. None too soon, as his left arm began to buckle.

"There, now. Enough." She pulled the wheelchair up behind him, using her foot. "That's great."

He let her lower him back to the chair. "I did it." He said the words evenly, with no hint of yesterday's triumph and exhilaration. She felt a different determination in him now, and his face settled into fierce lines.

Miriam pulled the chair away from the bars. "Now relax. Do you want some juice?" She nodded toward the bottle on the bedside table.

"Yah, guess I could use some." He leaned back, and when she put the glass into his hand, his fingers trembled a little. Small wonder. It was all she could do to keep hers steady.

He drank deeply, and then looked at her, his eyes studying her face. "You're worried. Why?"

She could only be honest with him. He'd recognize any attempt to steer him away.

"I'm afraid this hassle about the trial will hold back your progress. It's a pretty big distraction, ain't so?"

His face clouded. "Makes all of us remember too much. No, that's not it. I certain sure haven't forgotten anything that happened that day, but it was like a…like a mist, I guess, shielding it. Now—"

Matt fell silent, his lips clamping on the word.

His pain seemed to ricochet through her, clamping around her heart. "I know," she said softly. "Even when the memories are good ones, it makes your throat get tight and your eyes sting."

"And these are all bad. No, no that's not right. Even that day, even minutes before the car hit, we were laughing." His voice roughened, but he went on. "David was teasing me about not getting married yet. Saying he'd better hurry up and start courting someone so Mammi wouldn't worry about not having grandchildren."

"I can almost hear him. He always had laughter lurking in his eyes, ain't so? That's why everyone loved him."

Now her voice was choking up. Matt reached out, clutching her hand so tightly it hurt.

"He was so young. He had everything to look forward to. It's not fair."

"I know, I know," she murmured. Her thoughts raced to other young boys who stood balanced between childhood and manhood. "Boys that age are on the edge of turning into men, and sometimes they're so daring or so careless you wonder how they'll make it."

"David wasn't daring," he said quickly.

"No, but the driver was. He wasn't much older than David."

She winced as his grasp became even tighter.

"Are you saying I should forgive him?" Anger broke into his voice.

"Ach, Matt, that is between you and God. But I can't help thinking that he was just a boy, too. And now his life is wrecked, and his parents are grieving." She shook her head, trying to hold back tears. "It seems too big for anyone to heal it but God."

Matt seemed to mull over her words. Then he shook his head. His grip loosened, and he looked down at her hand with a muffled exclamation. "I'm sorry." He smoothed gentle fingers over the angry red marks.

"It's all right." She tried to draw her hand away,

but stopped when she saw that now he seemed to draw some comfort from her touch.

Matt let out a long breath. “Daad says we must forgive.” His eyes darkened, not in anger but in pain. “I can try to understand what they’re feeling, but I don’t know that I can ever forgive.”

Chapter Eleven

Matt had been up early on Saturday morning, watching from the window as Daad and Joshua left for the co-op. Sales would be brisk today, and they didn't want to miss the buyers. Restaurant owners wanted the freshest of the produce for their weekend customers, and they'd be there in force.

The house seemed unusually quiet after the breakfast dishes were done, and he found he was waiting for the sounds of Miriam's arrival. Funny, to be so eager for something to happen. For a long time after the accident, he hadn't noticed or cared. Now he was restless, eager to be doing, if only he could find something useful.

He was about to head out to the porch when he heard a sound from the living room. For a moment his brain couldn't identify it, but even as he turned, he knew. Someone was crying. The sound was muffled, but unmistakable.

His heart lurched. If it was his mother, he was helpless. Comforting Mammi would be such a reversal of their roles that he couldn't imagine coping with it. Still, he had to do something. Steeling himself, he pushed the chair toward the room.

The wheelchair made little sound as it rolled forward. The person who sat on the floor in front of the cupboard clearly didn't hear him. It was Betsy, bending forward over clasped hands, her bowed back shaking with the force of her sobs.

Matt moved closer, wheels bumping against the boxes of games and puzzles she'd obviously pulled out of the cabinet. He reached out to clasp her shoulder.

"Was ist letz? Are you hurt, Betsy?" What could there be about puzzles and games to make her weep?

She jumped in reaction and shook her head, not looking at him.

"Something is making you cry. Komm, tell me about it. Troubles are easier to bear when they're shared, ain't so?" His own words startled him. They sounded like something Miriam would say. Or Mammi, before the world had shattered.

A stubborn shake of the head was Betsy's only answer. She mopped at her face with the backs of her hands, and then seemed to realize that she had to say something.

"It's nothing. I'm okay."

She obviously wasn't, and he'd run out of things to say. He longed for someone else to walk in and handle this…someone like Miriam or Mammi. He even looked toward the door. Nothing.

"Where's Mammi?" She'd know what to do.

"She…she went across the road to take some tomatoes to Great-Aunt Alice. And some shoofly pie."

That explained her absence. Mammi's aunt and uncle occupied a small house back a long lane across the road, and normally she made regular treks to check on them, usually carrying food. It was encouraging that she'd begun to do it again, but he could wish she'd waited a day or two.

Betsy stacked several games. "I'm supposed to clean up the cabinet while she's gone. I'd best get it done." She grabbed the stack and turned to shove them back on the shelf. As she did, something fell from her lap and landed in front of him.

His stomach lurched. Not just something. It was a carved wooden fish—the brook trout he'd carved for David's birthday last year. He remembered the feel of it in his hands even without touching it…the way he'd used the smallest of his chisels to add the tiny ridges that were the scales. He bent to pick it up.

A year ago David had still been with them. He'd loved to fish…loved walking up the creek in the early morning to the pool where he always found some "brookies."

His fingers moved on the curve of the fish's back, remembering David's expression when he'd unwrapped it. "Where…" He cleared his throat. "Where did you find this?"

"It was behind the boxes. I don't know how it got there." Tears threatened to fall again. She screwed up her face in an attempt to hold them back. "Remember? You said you were going to make your gifts from now on, and David said he'd have to remind you."

"Yah." His voice was husky. Betsy remembered even better than he did. He held the fish a moment longer, and then he leaned forward and dropped it in her lap.

"You should keep it. He'd want you to have it. Komm, let's get this stuff put away before Mammi gets back." He handed her a game at random, trying not to look at the fish. He'd longed to keep it himself, but he thought maybe his little sister needed it more.

A glimpse of movement through the front window alerted him. "Here comes Mammi. I'll finish these. You run upstairs and put some cold water on your eyes. No sense worrying Mammi."

Betsy scrambled to her feet, holding the fish against her. Impulsively she leaned forward to press her cheek against his, and then she was gone, running up the stairs.

It was simple enough to shove the remaining games in and shut the door on them. He was back in the kitchen by the time Mammi came in.

"Your aunt and onkel send their love," she said, putting her basket down. "Do you want anything before Miriam comes to start your exercises?"

He shook his head. "I think I'll wait for her out on the porch."

But when he reached the porch, he headed straight for the ramp and started down. Miriam would be here soon, but there was something he wanted to do first. He reached the bottom of the ramp safely and headed toward the shed next to the lower level of the barn.

The lane wasn't so bad—there was enough gravel on it to give some stability to the chair. Lots more arm muscle required to move, but doable.

Then he turned to the grassy slope that led to the shed, got about three feet and stuck. Muttering to himself, he bent to check the wheels, only to find the right front one had hit a soft patch and sunk in. Just a little, but enough to stop him.

He leaned the other way, pushing the wheels, feeling the strain on his arm muscles. The chair tilted… he thought for an instant he was going over. Then someone grabbed it, pulling it as he leaned back.

The chair settled, and Miriam let out a long whoosh of air. "What are you doing?"

In an instant, Miriam regretted the sharpness of her tone. She leaned against the chair, trying to calm the shakiness that set in once she knew Matt was all right.

"Just give me a hand." He pointed. "There. The shed. Get me over there." He slapped the side of the chair in frustration.

Miriam pressed her lips together. "Wheelchairs

aren't great on rough ground. Whatever you want, can't I get it for you?"

He didn't answer—just planted his hands on the wheels, gripping them so hard she could see the cords of muscle on his forearms. "Are you going to help me or not?"

Maybe counting to ten would help. Or maybe not. "Okay. We'll both have to push."

It actually wasn't as bad as she'd feared. Apparently the wet spot he'd hit was the only one, and the wheels bounced over the clumps of grass to the shed.

"There." She started to reach for the door latch, but he was ahead of her. He leaned out of the chair to yank it open.

The only light in the interior was what came from the door and slipped through the cracks between the boards. As Miriam's eyes grew accustomed to the dim light, she realized it was a wood storage, stacked along the back wall with split firewood.

"I hope we're not going to build a fire," she said. "I think it'll be hot enough without it."

Matt's concentration finally wavered, and he looked at her as if he saw her now. "Yah, I don't think we'll need one." His expression eased, but he still seemed intent on something. "Look over on the left wall. See that old fruit box?"

"You want something from it?" she asked as she stepped inside, holding her skirt away from the cobweb that draped the opening.

"Just pull the whole thing over here so I can see

it. Or do you need some help?" His tone was teasing, as if with his target in sight, he didn't need to snap out orders.

She'd grasped the end of the box by then, and she looked back at him. "I don't think I'm that weak."

She gave it a yank and dragged the box out into the light. This time she'd managed to hit the spider web, and she had to brush it from her skirt and then wipe the remnants from her hand onto the grass.

The box was half-full of what seemed a miscellaneous collection of wood…most of the pieces fairly small, some of them twisted roots, some knotty bits of misshapen limbs. She stood and looked at it as Matt bent to scrabble through them.

He looked up at her and lifted his eyebrows. "You don't understand yet? But you were the one who mentioned wood-carving, ain't so?"

The light dawned. "Yah, for sure. But are these the pieces you picked out to carve?"

Matt chuckled at the doubt in her voice. "You don't just start with a block of wood. At least, I don't." He picked up one piece, turning it over in his hands and running his fingers along its curves. "My grossdaadi taught me. He always said that the figure was already there in the wood. You just had to see it. Then you take away all the parts that don't belong."

She loved the way his face warmed when he talked about his grandfather. They must have been close in the way that sometimes happened between generations. Her own grandmother was close to her that way.

He picked up another piece and put it in her hands. "Go on, take a good look at it. Turn it around and see what you can feel with your fingertips."

Miriam tried, but it might have been easier if his hand weren't guiding hers, warm against her skin.

"Feel that bump there, and the other one on this side." He guided her fingers. "Think about what might have that shape in it. Or this part that sticks out, and then curves under."

It seemed to take shape in her mind as he talked. The rounded part, almost like a jaw. "I see. It's like a head, or maybe a face."

"Gut. What kind of head? What could the bumps be?"

"Horns? Ears?" She laughed. "I don't think I'm very good at this."

"You're doing fine." He squeezed her hand and released it, taking the wood piece. "This might be a deer's head, or even a rabbit with the ears standing up. Once you decide, then it's not hard."

"It would be for me, I'm afraid. What made you decide to start on this?"

His face sobered, the laughter fading from it. "Betsy." He hesitated a moment. "She found a fish that I had carved for David's last birthday. It brought up a lot of memories."

"For both of you, I guess." She studied his face, wondering how much she should question.

"Yah. Funny," he said, but his expression said it wasn't humorous. "I was thinking that I'd like to keep it, and then I saw her face. She needed it more than I did."

"That was thoughtful." She couldn't keep herself from resting her hand on his arm. "She's struggling, I think."

"Yah. Anyway, I remembered I'd intended to make something for her next birthday, but by then..."

She understood. By then they were all grieving, groping their way through pain.

"Betsy would love to have it anytime. It doesn't have to be a birthday gift. What will you make?"

Matt fingered the piece of wood that he'd picked out. "You know what I see in here? Not a deer or a rabbit, but an owl." He turned it the other way, so that he could trace a flat round area with a few smooth, smaller rounds inside it. "There's the face, and here are the eyes. Don't you see?"

To her surprise, she did see the face of an owl emerging from the wood. She glanced at his intent face.

"It means something special?" she ventured. "The owl?"

He leaned back in the chair, seeming to look back in time. "Betsy might not remember. But I think she will. David and I took her walking up in the woods when she was maybe five or six. We came upon a barn owl sitting on a limb just over our heads." He smiled, picturing it. "She was so excited because it was just like an owl in a story Mammi had been reading to her, with its white face like a heart."

She nodded, understanding. The same book was probably on her family's shelves, too.

"Usually they fly away at the sight or sound of people, but this one just sat there for another minute while she talked about it. Then it swooped away." He shook his head, smiling. "She must have talked about it for a week, and Mammi had to read the book to her over and over."

"You remember. I'd say she'd remember, too."

He released the brake on the chair. "Just shove that box back inside the door and let's go in. I want to start on it."

She did as he asked, then flipped the latch on the door.

"We'll go inside, but carving will have to wait until after your exercises."

"Carving first," he said, his eyes laughing at her.

"Exercises first," she said firmly, giving the chair a push.

"Bossy," he muttered, but he was smiling.

His smile was infectious, but Miriam had even more making her happy. Despite the looming pressure of the trial, Matt had seen someone else's pain. More than that, he'd done something about it.

She murmured a soundless prayer that this might be a good step towards healing, both for him and for his little sister.

* * *

Matt couldn't figure out why he was in such a good mood right now, not when the trial was hanging over them. A month ago he'd have said he couldn't feel that way unless he was back to normal, and now he was celebrating the smallest step forward.

He studied Miriam's face as she got everything ready for his workout. He couldn't deny that Miriam had something to do with the change in him. Her faith in his progress must have been contagious, that's all. He certain sure couldn't have drummed it up by himself.

The question of the lawyer, the looming shadow of the trial…well, they were still there. But for the moment, he could shove them into the back of his mind and concentrate on what was in front of him.

The worries of the day are enough for the day. That was what his grandfather used to say. He'd been right.

"Ready?" Miriam indicated the rack of hand weights. "Let's get started."

As they worked their way through the exercises, Matt considered how much his opinion of Miriam had changed over what was really a short time, compared with the fact that he'd known her all their lives.

"I always thought you were so quiet. What changed?"

Laughter lit her eyes. "Maybe you just weren't noticing before. Or my brothers were making too much noise. Sometimes it wonders me how Mammi can know each of us so well when there are so many of us, but she does."

He considered that. "I'd have said the same about Mammi, but..." He struggled with what he wanted to convey. "It seemed like she got lost when David died."

Miriam paused, putting down the exercise band she was holding. "I guess that's right. She was confronted with something so bad that she didn't know where she was for a while."

"I didn't make it any easier. I must be about the worst person you've ever worked with, yah?"

Smiling, she shook her head. "Not even close. You never met the boy I worked with out in Ohio." She sobered, her clear eyes shadowed suddenly. "He shook my confidence more than anything else." She shrugged. "But there's no use dwelling on spilled milk."

Matt grasped her hand before she could turn away. "Something happened...something that upsets you when you think about it. If you want to talk..."

She looked down at his hand, but she didn't pull away. "I don't think it's a good idea."

"Why not? I've unloaded on you plenty."

"That's different," she said quickly. "You're the patient, and anything that troubles you can affect your progress."

"And you're my friend, since we were about three or four. Isn't that just as important as being a patient?"

Her face lightened as she seemed to hear the affection that was behind the words. "Yah, well, I guess. Maybe I'd just gotten too confident. The boy was hard to work with at first. He was only fifteen, and he was cut off from everything his friends were doing. He had an illness that affected his joints and muscles. Sometimes he'd be better, his mother told me, but then he'd get worse again. But I felt like I was making good progress with him."

"Something happened?" he asked gently, knowing by her expression she was getting onto shaky territory.

"I guess I'd been thinking about him like he was one of my little brothers. Then I found out that he… well, he had a crush on me. And he thought I felt the same about him."

"Poor kid." He spoke automatically, and then realized the meaning of what he'd said. To be thinking that Miriam—sweet, strong Miriam—loved you and then learning you were wrong would be devastating.

He wanted to say something of that to her, but he couldn't. He couldn't because he was beginning to see something he hadn't even guessed at, and he had to know for sure before he spoke.

While he sat there, silent, she must have decided that he wasn't interested, because she shrugged, and her voice changed. "Well, it's not such a big thing, I guess, but it certain sure damaged my confidence. I thought I'd found my gift, you see, and I'd stumbled badly. His parents were so angry—"

"But even if you made a mistake, well, that doesn't mean it isn't your talent. You're still learning, ain't so?"

"I hope." Her fingers tightened on his hand for a moment. "I want to do the thing God put me here for."

"Yah." It struck him that she was saying what he'd been feeling. "But what happens if you really can't do that thing any longer?" The bitterness sprang out of hiding and nipped at him. That was where he was.

"I don't know, Matthew." She didn't pretend not to understand him. "Maybe you have to find a different way of using your gift. Or maybe you have another gift that's equally important."

"Maybe." But he doubted it.

As if she thought it was time to distract him, she put away the equipment they'd been using. "Why don't we take a break and get your carving set up?"

Without waiting for an answer, she pulled out the table they'd pushed against the wall, and set out the wooden piece they'd brought in and the roll of tools. "What else do you need?"

He didn't intend to be switched away from the conversation, but in spite of himself, the sight of his materials stirred a need he hadn't even recognized he was feeling.

"This is enough to start with," he muttered, unwrapping his tools and smoothing them with the soft fabric of the case. He drew out his favorite knife, and it felt comfortable and familiar in his hand.

He glanced up at Miriam and smiled, liking the way her face lit in response.

"Good?" she asked.

"Yah. This one's what I use most often."

She leaned closer and reached out to touch the blade.

"Careful, it's sharp."

She drew her finger away after touching it gingerly. "I'll say. I hope you're careful with it."

"You get used to working with it." He smiled. "The first time Grossdaadi let me use it, I cut myself in the first five minutes. Mammi was mad, but Grossdaadi just said, 'This time he'll be more careful,' and I was. You can't work with it if it's not sharp. See?" He made the first slice, and a sliver of wood curled away. "Like butter."

Once started, it came back to him. His hands remembered the use of the tools, and a satisfaction he hadn't felt in months seeped through him.

Miriam moved, murmuring something about helping his mother, but he shook his head and pointed with the knife. "Sit and relax. You don't have to be always working."

She subsided onto the chair, seeming perfectly content to sit still and watch. In fact, there was a quality of stillness about it that was soothing.

They sat without talking as he worked and she watched. The figure had just begun to emerge from the wood. And then the door burst open and Betsy propelled herself into the room, her face excited.

"You won't believe it, Matt. There was a message on the machine from the courthouse. It was some lawyer, and he said he'd be here to talk to you on Monday morning." She sounded impressed. "What do you think of that?"

He didn't speak for a moment. Nothing he said could match Betsy's excitement. He found he was looking automatically at Miriam for her reaction.

She looked the way he felt—as if something that had been looming over them was here.

Chapter Twelve

Miriam sat on the backless bench in the Gauses' barn on Sunday, trying to concentrate on the voice of the bishop. Unfortunately she wasn't having much success. The heat of the late August day didn't trouble her, despite the red faces of those around her. At least a slight breeze came through the double doors that had been slid open. No, it was her restless heart that caused the problem.

Next to her, cousin Lyddy fidgeted a bit, controlled herself and then looked across to the opposite side of the barn where Simon Fisher sat with his little daughter. Miriam understood. Lyddy was longing to be with Simon and his daughter, soon to be hers, too.

Happy as she was for Lyddy, that didn't keep her mind away from Matt. They had been having such a blessed, peaceful time together the previous day, with Matthew carving while she sat and watched the deft, sure movements of his hands.

But then news of the lawyer's visit had exploded all their peace. Not that Matt had reacted openly, but she could sense his feelings without the need for words. Matt was torn between a resurgence of his anger, the pain of his grief and probably the endless struggle to forgive.

She heard again his voice saying he didn't think he could forgive. But if that was true, how could he move on with his life? And how much would that inward struggle affect his physical recovery?

She could no longer tell herself she was interested only as his aide, because she knew it wasn't true. She loved him—loved him in a way she'd never imagined it would be possible to love someone. Every day it continued to grow.

Maybe nothing would ever come of that love. She'd had no indication that he felt anything but friendship for her. But if she could help him become whole again, that was enough reward for her.

She slid to her knees for the final prayer and blessing. Then, as people began to move, Lyddy smiled and spoke. "I'm wilted, I think. But look at Grossmammi. She's as fresh as a daisy. How does she do it?"

Miriam glanced behind her and saw what Lyddy meant. Grossmammi was already talking with her cronies, while around them the men began carrying tables and benches out under the trees. Not a strand of her snowy-white hair was out of place, and her skin glowed with the joy she felt at being here.

"Maybe that's the fruit of a good life," Miriam suggested, and Lyddy laughed.

"Then we might be in trouble. Seriously, how is Matt doing? I see Abel and Elizabeth are both here this morning."

"He's improving," she said, with a silent prayer that it might continue. "Yah, they left Betsy in charge this morning."

"Was that a gut idea? She can be so flighty at times."

Not any longer, Miriam thought. The accident had pushed her to grow up in a hurry. Maybe too much so.

"I'm sure she's glad to be relied upon," Miriam said. "She really loves helping Matt. I just hope Elizabeth isn't fretting to be home."

"It's gut for her to be out after all this time," Lyddy said, and they both watched as friends surrounded Elizabeth, all eager to greet her.

"Time to get busy," Lyddy said as they stepped out into the open. "I said I'd help carry things to the table."

"I'll come, too," Miriam said, pausing a moment to enjoy the fresh breeze that cooled her face. It rustled the corn stalks in the nearest field so that it sounded as if they talked to each other. She amused herself for a moment, thinking what they might say, and then headed for the farmhouse in Lyddy's wake.

She had almost caught up when Nola Frey hurried to her. Miriam stiffened, ready for anything. Nola, like Hilda Berger and one or two others here, had relatives in the community Miriam had visited. She'd probably have heard any rumors that were going around by now.

But Nola was smiling, at least. "Ach, it's gut to see you this morning, Miriam. My cousin wanted me to say she was sorry not to have a chance to visit you again before you left. She said you went all of a sudden."

There was a questioning note in the comment that Miriam didn't miss. She planted a smile on her face. "I'd actually planned to leave weeks earlier, but I stayed on because another family needed some help. But I was wonderful eager to get home by then. It felt like years."

"I see." Her eyes were still curious. "But surely..."

"Goodness, I promised to help bring the food out. I must get busy. My best to your family." She hurried off before she could be stopped.

As she scurried away, she let out a long breath. Nola had been fishing, no doubt about it, but at least Miriam hadn't lost her poise. Maybe Nola would have forgotten about it by the next time Miriam talked to her, or some new exciting story would replace it.

She crossed paths with Lyddy, who carried large baskets filled with sandwiches. "Better hurry, or everything will be done," she teased.

"Right, I will." Even as she neared the door, she passed several younger girls carrying more sandwich fillings and two more with large dishes of gelatin salads. Lifting a hand in greeting, she slipped up the steps to the porch and reached for the screen door. And then she froze at the sound of her name from within.

"...says that Miriam is devoted to helping Matthew get well. She said you wouldn't believe how much help she is with him."

"The end of it will be that he'll marry her," another voice declared.

Someone else exclaimed at that. "Surely not. I thought it was Liva Ann..."

"That's all over, I hear. She couldn't stand marrying someone all scarred up like that, with her being so pretty and all. But Miriam wouldn't mind. After all, she doesn't have so many choices, not at her age. If she's ever going to get married, this is her chance, and she won't hesitate to grab it. You'll see..."

Miriam couldn't listen anymore. Shaking, she moved silently the porch and stopped at the nearest table, hanging on to it for a moment to steady her ragged breathing.

So that was what people were saying. That Matthew was her last chance, and she'd be foolish not to grab him.

She drew in a steadying breath. If that were so, she wouldn't marry at all. Better to live alone the rest of her life than to be married only for her nursing ability to a man she loved with all her heart.

The tension in the air Monday while they waited for the attorney to show up, Matt decided, was like waiting to be released from the hospital. The whole family sat around the table, seeming unable to start anything else until this was over. Even Daad had allowed Josh to begin the day's work without him and sat drinking a third or fourth cup of coffee.

At a step on the porch, Daad's hand jerked, and the coffee sloshed over.

"It's Miriam," Matt said quickly, recognizing her step. He'd known she'd get here before the attorney would.

She came in, hesitating as the door closed and she realized everyone was looking at her. "Is something wrong?"

He shook his head. "No, but you can help me settle something. I don't think the rest of the family should be in on my discussion with the attorney, especially Mammi and Betsy."

"We are your family and David's," Mammi said quickly. "I, at least, should hear what he says. Betsy is too young—"

"No, I'm not!" Betsy was offended, that was certain sure.

Miriam seemed to understand instantly what he wanted. She moved quietly to his mother and touched her shoulder, smiling at Betsy to include her.

"It will be difficult for Matthew to talk about the accident to the man, ain't so? And even more painful if he knows you are hearing it, too. He will have trouble talking in front of you. You understand, ain't so?"

Miriam had said exactly the right thing, as he'd known she would. Mammi hesitated, looking from Miriam to him, and then at Daad.

"Miriam is right," Daadi said. "We don't want to make it harder on Matthew than it must be."

Mammi hesitated, undecided, and then the sound of a car pulling up grabbed everyone's attention. They listened, hardly breathing, Matt thought, as he approached.

In another few moments, the man from the district attorney's office was at the door, opening it in response to Daad's invitation to enter.

His youth was the first thing that struck Matt. For sure too young to be a qualified attorney and working on something like this.

As if in response to Matt's thought, the young man stammered, trying to introduce himself. "I... I'm Robert Forman, from the district attorney's office. I'm here to see Matthew King."

He was slight and fair, looking as if he hadn't grown into his fine suit yet, and he had the sort of fair skin that blushed easily, making it a fiery red as he realized he was the target of so many eyes.

"I'm Matthew King." he said. It was up to him to deal with this, he knew. "These are my parents, Abel and Elizabeth King." A pause ensued while young

Forman shook hands with Daad and nodded with the effect of a bow to Mamm.

"And here is my sister, Betsy, and Miriam Stoltzfus, who is..." He paused, unsure how to refer to her. Helper, friend, something more? "...my aide," he finished.

"I won't keep you any longer than I have to," Forman hurried on with what sounded like a prepared opening. "I appreciate your letting me come and see you." His gaze lingered on the wheelchair.

Matt shifted his weight, uncomfortable with his stare.

Maybe aware of his reaction, Forman flushed again. "If we can go over the facts of the accident and the statement you made, that will help us with our case. Is there somewhere...?" He looked around, clearly searching for privacy.

Daad rose. "We all have things to do, so we will leave you here." He nodded to Mammi and Betsy, and after a moment's hesitation, they got up.

Miriam stirred, started to rise, and Matt stopped her with a hand on her arm. "I prefer that my aide stays with me."

"Um, yes, fine. I'm sure it's good if your aide is here, in case you need her." Forman flushed again and then sat in the chair Daad pulled out for him, setting his briefcase on the table and opening it.

The outside door closed behind the rest of the family, and they could hear the murmur of voices as they walked away.

Forman seemed to pull himself together, and Matt wondered how many times he'd done this sort of thing.

"Now, if you would just tell me about the accident the way you remember it, I'll follow along in the statement you signed when you were in the hospital. That way if you've remembered anything additional, I can make those changes."

Matt nodded to show he understood, but his nerves tightened. This wouldn't be easy, going through it all again. At least it would help that he'd talked through some of it with Miriam.

It struck him that he hadn't asked Miriam if she was willing to be here. He looked at her. "If you don't want…" he began.

She shook her head. "It's fine. I'd rather be here." Her eyes were apprehensive, but she patted his arm reassuringly. Maybe he was being selfish, but he accepted her help. He'd known he could count on her.

Forman spread his papers out on the table and clicked his pen. "Now, if you'll just tell me about what you remember in your own words, that will be fine."

He cleared his throat and plunged in, like jumping into an icy pond.

"I was driving the buggy, and my brother, David, was sitting next to me. The road is hilly and curvy, but we were going slow, you understand?"

Forman nodded. "I took a ride over there to see the site."

"Good. We were talking, and I heard a car coming up behind me. It sounded as if it were coming pretty fast. So I steered the horse closer to the edge of the road..."

That much was easy. But as he talked his way through what had happened, the events became more and more vivid in his mind. Forman didn't speak, sometimes making a mark on the typescript in front of him.

Matt kept his voice was steady while he talked about the car striking the buggy, even of finding himself tangled in the wreckage, but he gripped Miriam's hand as if his life depended on holding on.

When he reached the moment that he'd glimpsed David's twisted body, though, his voice finally broke. He stopped, struggling for control.

After a moment, he glanced at the attorney and was surprised to see an expression of satisfaction on his face. What was there in this terrible telling to make anyone satisfied? He was suddenly repelled.

Miriam spoke, maybe to give him time. "You can see that this is difficult, Mr. Forman. Since you have his statement already, is it really necessary?"

"Knowing the injured person makes a much stronger case against the defendant, don't you see?" he said eagerly. "If the jury hears the story from someone who suffered, they'll feel his pain."

Matt's revulsion deepened. "I don't want to make anyone else feel this way."

"Well, of course not," Forman said quickly, as if

sensing he'd made a wrong step. "But you see, hearing directly from you makes it more likely that the defendant will get a harsher sentence. You'd be surprised at how lax juries can be."

"No doubt." He'd mastered his voice again, but not his feelings. They tumbled around in him confusingly, but one thing was suddenly very clear. "But they will not hear it from me. You have my statement of what happened. I don't want to testify."

That seemed to catch the attorney off guard. For an instant, Forman gaped, speechless. "But…but we thought for sure you'd want to speak. I know that sometimes Amish won't do it, but with the loss of your brother and your suffering—surely you want to see the defendant get a good stiff jail sentence for what he did."

"No." He knew his answer was final.

Matt found he was thinking about something Miriam said. Something about boys that age, boys like David, like the driver, even like her brothers, balancing on the line between being carefree, careless boys and being men.

He was vaguely aware of Forman talking, trying to convince him, but it didn't matter. An accident could have been caused by any boy that age doing something stupid…any of them. His brother, hers… He couldn't do anything to help take the rest of that boy's life away from him.

The attorney ran out of arguments. "You're sure of that?" he asked.

"I'm sure. The law has my statement and will have to do with that. The driver will be held accountable according to the law, and we'll all get on with our lives."

Forman nodded, accepting his decision. "I understand, I guess." He sounded like a real person now, instead of one reciting a familiar speech.

"You do, don't you?" Miriam's voice startled him, she'd been so quiet. "If Matthew had to testify, if his family had to listen to it…well, that would be punishing them all over again."

Forman was intent upon her words. "When you put it like that, how could I help but understand?" His face relaxed, making him look no more than sixteen or seventeen himself.

"Good." Miriam smiled gently at him, as if he were a child who'd gotten something right.

He cleared his throat. "Well, I'd better tell you what might happen next. Since we won't have your testimony, the district attorney will probably agree on a plea bargain with the boy's lawyer. That means he'll admit he was at fault, and there will be a judge to decide the appropriate penalty." He looked a little anxious. "Do you understand?"

"I understand." Matt exchanged glances with Miriam. She looked relieved, and he realized that was what he felt, too. The heavy cloud that had loomed over them was gone.

"You shouldn't be troubled anymore, then. Although you might be asked if you want to make any statement to the judge."

He nodded, ready for the man to be gone.

In another moment, he had his wish. Miriam showed Forman to the door, standing there until the car turned and moved off down the driveway. Then she came back to him, smiling.

"You made up your mind, ain't so?"

"Yah." He struggled for a moment, knowing there was more he wanted to say, but not sure what or how. "I guess it is possible to forgive."

Chapter Thirteen

Miriam could only be thankful that this, at least, was over. Matt had not only stood up to the ordeal, but he had reached a decision, and with it, she hoped, the beginning of some peace.

She turned back to him from the screen door. "He's gone, and I see your mamm and daad coming." Another look told her that Matt was exhausted, and no wonder. She felt as if she'd been pressed through the wringer, and she didn't have Matt's painful memories.

Hurrying over, she put one hand on the table as she bent over him. "You…you must be tired out. Some coffee?"

He leaned back then, seeming to force his eyes to stay open. "Don't bother. I'm all right." He caught her hand as if to stop her, and she couldn't help but wince.

Startled, Matt moved it gently in his as he saw the red marks of his fingers. "I did that? I didn't know…"

"It's all right," she said quickly. "The marks will be gone by tomorrow." She tried to draw it away, but he held it in his, his finger tracing the marks with a featherlight touch.

"Matt..." she began, but couldn't find anything to say. Her throat was so tight she wouldn't have gotten words out anyway.

Matt's face twisted suddenly, as if he were hurt. Then he lifted her hand to his lips and kissed it, so quickly that it was over before she could react.

Footsteps sounded on the porch, and then his parents came in, looking at him with anxious eyes. Miriam drew her hand away and hid it in the folds of his skirt. No one else must see or exclaim.

Matt turned to his parents, somehow managing to smile. "It's all right. It's over. Where is Betsy?"

"Sulking," Abel said briefly. "She's hurt because you didn't let her stay with you, but it was no place for her."

It didn't take much for Miriam to fill in the rest of what had happened with Betsy. She'd been angry not only because she was excluded but also because Miriam had been allowed to stay. Maybe she would be blaming Miriam for it. Well, that was probably better than blaming her parents.

Abel moved to put his hand on his son's shoulder. "Are you all right?"

"Yah." Matt seemed to steel himself for what he had to say. "The man wanted me to go over what I'd said before. And then he wanted me to testify at the trial." His lips twisted. "He said that would make the jury punish the driver more. I told him I wouldn't. That's all."

"But..." Abel must have wanted more details, but he seemed to recognize that now wasn't the time. "That's gut. You have done what the law required. But it is not for us to judge others."

Elizabeth wiped tears from her face and nodded. "The Lord says we must forgive, as He has forgiven us." Her expression quivered, and she turned away. "I must find Betsy." She went out, moving quickly.

Abel looked from his wife to his son, as if not knowing who to go to.

Matt made the decision for him. "Komm, Miriam. Let's get on with the exercises."

Relieved, Miriam hurried to open the door for him. Maybe she was being a coward, but Matt was the one she'd been hired to help. He had to come first.

When she began to organize the equipment, she actually had to stop and think about what to do first. It was as if her thoughts had been whipped up with a giant eggbeater.

Matt seemed equally distracted. He looked at her, then away. "Don't...don't do anything that will make you hand hurt. I can pick up the weights myself."

What was he thinking about? Was he remembering the moment when he'd pressed his lips to her palm? Was he regretting that he'd done it?

Maybe she ought to say something light about it,

but how could she? So she contented herself with beginning the familiar routine.

Matt seemed to move through the exercises automatically, his mind elsewhere. At last they'd reached the bars. He was holding on to them, trying to force his leg to move forward, when suddenly he stopped. She grabbed hold of him, bracing herself to bear his weight. If he fell—

He shook his head. "I have it. Bring the chair."

Pausing only to be sure he could support himself, Miriam pushed the wheelchair into place behind him. He sank into it, gripping the arms.

Possible explanations flew into her mind. "What is it? Do you feel dizzy? Sick?"

"I remembered."

She blinked, not following him. "Remembered what?"

He shoved the wheelchair around and gestured to the straight chair against the wall. "Sit down. I need to talk."

Matt was so intent that she didn't hesitate to do what he said. When she brought the chair, he moved so that they sat facing each other, knee to knee. His expression alarmed her, and she leaned toward him.

"You're sure you—"

Cutting her off with an impatient gesture, he began to speak. "Listen. When I was going over it all with the lawyer… I kept feeling like there was something more I should say. Something I should remember."

"Are you sure you don't want your daad to hear this?" She put her hand on his arm, and felt it as rigid as a steel bar.

He ignored the question except for a quick shake of the head. "There…when I stood up…it slid into my mind. The rest of the memory…what happened after I saw that I was trapped."

He didn't even seem aware of her now, but she didn't dare move. "I heard it," he said. "I heard someone crying."

Her voice was stuck in her throat. "David?" she whispered.

"No, not David. It was him…the driver."

"But he wasn't hurt…"

"He was crying and crawling into the wreckage." He went on as if she hadn't spoken. "He saw me. He struggled toward me. The tears were on his face, and he kept saying, 'I'm sorry, I'm sorry,' over and over again. 'I didn't mean it. I'm sorry.' He said it the whole time. He kept pulling things off me so he could drag me out. He kept saying it. 'I'm sorry.'"

She didn't know what to say. Was it better or worse for Matt that he remembered more? She didn't know, but she knew that Matt himself was on the verge of tears.

"It's all right." She murmured the words as gently as if she were comforting a child. "It's all right."

He met her gaze then, and his eyes were clouded with tears. "He was just a boy. He looked like a little kid who'd hurt himself. He looked like David."

His face crumbled then, and he reached for her almost blindly. Her arms went around him, and she cradled him close, feeling his labored breathing and the salt tears on his face. Her cheek was against his wounded one, and she stroked his hair and kissed him gently, longing to make everything better, and knowing she couldn't.

He turned his head, just a little, and then his lips touched hers. His arms tightened around her. He kissed her with a kind of desperate longing that made her gasp, and then grasped her heart and wouldn't let go.

This is where I belong. The thought shocked Matt into awareness. He threw himself back in the chair and stared at Miriam in consternation. What had he done? Had he lost his head entirely?

"S-sorry," he stammered. He knew his face must be barn-red. "I didn't mean… I mean…"

He'd better shut up, because he wasn't making any sense. And Miriam was staring at him with her eyes so wide and dazed it was as if she didn't know where she was.

He released the brake and shoved the wheelchair back away from her. He cleared his throat. And his mind still couldn't fathom what had just happened.

He'd kissed her, and somehow he had to make that right. Miriam was a friend, a neighbor, someone who'd helped him immensely and done her best for him. He might have wrecked all that with one careless action.

No, not careless. There'd been nothing careless about it. He'd needed someone. Miriam had been there, helping, as she always was. If she…if they…if there could be anything more between them…

Miriam rose, turning away from him as if she couldn't look at him. Pain shot through him at the hurt he must have caused her. What was she thinking?

Marriage? They weren't teenagers. He couldn't kiss her casually. Not that it had been casual.

No, she wouldn't think he meant marriage. She was more sensible than that. He couldn't marry. He had nothing to offer anyone now, and Miriam knew it.

He had to say something. "Miriam, I… I didn't mean that to happen. You've been so good to me…to the whole family. I don't want to mess this up."

There. That at least sounded as if he had a brain in his head.

With her back still to him, Miriam straightened. She turned toward him slowly, and her face was composed now. "It's all right." Her voice trembled, and then steadied. "I know you didn't mean anything. Forget it, and I will, too."

Despite her words and her expression, Matt knew that things were not all right. Her hands clasped each other so tightly that her knuckles were strained and white. But what else could he say?

"Denke," he murmured.

She walked a few steps away from him, fiddling with the exercise bands as if she needed something to occupy her hands. She shook her head, and then she spoke.

"Do you think you'll need to do something about what you remembered?"

If her voice quivered a little, he guessed it was only natural under the circumstances. The line of thoughts opened up by her question had him feeling shaky, as well.

"I hadn't thought of it that way." He tried to find his way through the confusion in his mind. "Do you mean tell that lawyer?"

"Yah. Maybe...maybe it would make a difference in the trial. I mean, if they knew that the driver tried to help you."

"Yah, yah, you're right. And the others..." He gestured toward the rest of the house. Then he shook his head. "I don't think I can go through it again right now."

"I understand." Miriam's voice was gentle.

His gaze was drawn to her face. "Could you... could you find Daad and tell him the gist of it? So maybe he can help me figure out how to handle it? I know it's not fair to ask you..."

She broke in before he finished. "For sure. I'll go and find him now."

Judging by the speed at which she hurried to the door, he guessed that she was eager to get away from him, at least for the moment. He couldn't blame her, because he felt that way himself. He had to think… about her, about what was going to happen, about what she meant to him.

By the time Miriam reached home that afternoon, she felt as if she'd run miles and climbed several mountains. Had she done the best she could to help Matt's family deal with the upcoming trial? And, just as important to her, what was she going to do about Matt? About the fact that Matt kissed her, combined with her love for him and his…what? Friendship? Reliance? What was it he felt for her, or did he even know?

Mammi was in the kitchen, as usual. She took one look at Miriam and reached for the refrigerator door.

"You look as if you're about to drop from the heat. Sit down. I've got some iced tea all ready for you. And there's a fresh batch of oatmeal cookies on the cooling rack."

Miriam veered toward the counter to grab a couple of cookies and then sank down on her chair. Mammi set a tall glass in front of her, then fetched one for herself and returned to the table.

"There, is that better?" she asked after Miriam had taken a long drink. "You look like you needed it."

"I did." She held the cold glass against her forehead. "Today that lawyer came to talk to Matt. It was upsetting to everyone."

"Including you." Mammi patted her hand. "I can see that, too."

She nodded. "The lawyer insisted that Matt go over everything he remembered from the accident. It was clearly hard on Matt to relive it. I wanted so much to make the man stop."

"I suppose I haven't thought about that part of it." Mammi frowned, considering. "We say justice should roll down, but what if the justice causes more harm to someone who's been hurt already?"

"That's just what I felt. And then he assumed Matt would go into court and tell it all again. He acted like it was all routine." She caught back several angry things she'd like to say.

"He was very young, and I guess he was just doing his job. Matt said no. He'd done what he should, but he wouldn't go and testify against the driver." Tears stung her eyes at the thought. "He forgave him. He thought he never could, but he did."

"Ach, I'm wonderful glad." Mamm's fingers tightened on her arm. "If he can forgive, then he's on the way to getting over it."

"It's not easy," she murmured, seeing the pain in Matt's face again. "But it's best for him. For all of them."

She almost went on and told Mammi about the decision Matt and his parents had made, that they would tell the district attorney about how the driver had tried to help. She caught herself just in time. That news wasn't hers to share until they'd done it.

Before Mammi could ask the question that lingered in her eyes, feet thudded on the porch, and the three youngest boys barreled in. They were wet and muddy—they'd obviously been cooling off in the creek.

"Ach, what have I told you!" Mammi jumped up, scolding. "Go back out right now and wash off before you come tracking mud into my kitchen. Go on." She made a shooing motion, but then she grabbed Sammy before he could leave and turned him around to face her.

"What is this?" She touched his face, where a red bump was swelling as they watched. "Another person with a black eye in this house? How did you get this?"

Sammy wiggled, trying to get away from her hand. "Just a bump. It's nothing."

The twins exchanged glances and began backing out the screen door. Without seeming to look at them, Mammi responded.

"You two stay right here."

"But Mammi, our dirty feet—" John Thomas had a righteous tone that didn't fool anyone.

"What do you know about this?" She fixed them with a maternal frown.

"Nothing," John Thomas said glibly.

James wasn't so accomplished. He blushed, stubbed his toe into the floor, and murmured, "It wasn't our fault."

"All right, I'll tell it," Sammy said. "You two

would mess it up." He turned to Mammi, with a side look at Miriam that seemed full of a warning she didn't understand.

"Some of the guys came over to get in the creek with us. And one…"

"Out with it. Who, and what did he do? Have you been fighting?"

"Not exactly fighting." He grinned. "I just ducked him to make him take back what he said. And he hit my eye with his elbow by accident."

"Who?" she repeated, implacable.

"Jimmy Frey," he said reluctantly.

Miriam blinked, suddenly right in the middle of it. Jimmy was Nola Frey's boy.

"What did he say?" Mammi was firm about knowing it all.

"It was something about me, wasn't it?" In that moment, Miriam realized how foolish her worries about what had happened in Ohio were compared to real problems. "It's okay. Tell us."

"It was dumb. He said he heard that Miriam got into trouble because of some guy while she was out in Ohio. And I said she did not. And he said it again, so I ducked him in the creek. And I'm not sorry," he added defiantly.

Miriam had never realized how hard it must be to convince a boy of the value of nonviolence. She wanted to laugh, but Mammi wouldn't appreciate it.

"Listen, it's okay." She went to put her hands on Sammy's shoulders, realizing how tall he'd gotten in recent months. "He's just got it all mixed up. There was a boy I was helping when he was sick, and he just acted silly. He got a crush on me. That's all it was." She hesitated. That was all a ten-year-old needed to know, anyway. "You understand what a crush is?"

Sammy considered. "You mean like when I took all those flowers to Teacher Gloria when she took over our classes that time?"

Mammi gave an odd sound that might have been a cough or a laugh.

"Yah, just like that. So you don't need to duck Jimmy in the creek anymore. But you can tell him the truth…that the boy had a crush on me, but I didn't do anything wrong."

"I knew you didn't do anything wrong," he told her loudly. "And if he says that again—"

"Well, he won't say that again, will he, once he knows the truth?"

"I guess not. But I would, if he did."

Miriam decided not to take that on. "Go on out and get washed, the lot of you."

Mammi nodded. "Go."

The door slammed behind them, and Miriam was unable to restrain the laughter. "Poor Jimmy. And it's all so foolish. You and Daad were right all along. I didn't do anything wrong, and I shouldn't have tried to hide it."

Mammi put her arm around Miriam in a tight hug. "Yah. But it's not nice to have people gossiping like that, and I'll be setting Nola Frey right just as soon as I can."

"You don't need to."

"I do." She seemed to look forward to it. "Was it just Sammy that made you see?"

"Not just that." She shook her head. "I was self-centered, thinking so much about the fact that I had been humiliated. It was foolish in comparison to what other people have to fret about. I'm ashamed of myself."

She wouldn't be thinking about it any longer, she knew. That was one thing learned from this time with the King family. And if she had to leave her job only half-done because of what she felt for Matt, well, she'd do it. She could have a satisfying life without marriage, even if she didn't see how right now.

Chapter Fourteen

Matt had plenty of things to fill his mind, but he'd tossed and turned through the night, thinking about Miriam. And he still hadn't come to any conclusions.

Was it even possible to make things right with Miriam? She'd said she'd forget about that kiss, but he suspected she couldn't. If they'd both been teenagers, a casual kiss wouldn't be out of line. But at their age, it meant something far more serious.

He'd punched his pillow a few times during the night each time he came to that conclusion. The pillow had survived it, but he hadn't found any answers.

Fortunately the family had been occupied during breakfast by the revelation of what had happened between him and the driver of the car. Mammi was obviously relieved. She hated to think ill of anyone, no matter what they'd done, and his revelation of the boy's attitude and his efforts to help had dissolved whatever barrier was left in her to forgiveness.

It wouldn't be right to say she was happy. She was still grieving for David and probably always would be. But there was a peace about her that he almost envied.

He was far from being at peace, at least with himself. He glanced at the clock as Mammi and Betsy finished the breakfast dishes. Miriam would be here soon, if she were coming. But would she?

"I believe I'll go out on the porch to wait for Miriam." He pushed his chair to the door, and Betsy came hurrying to help him.

"You'll like it," she told him. "The air is nice and clear today."

"Like fall?" He rolled onto the porch.

She shrugged. "Maybe. The kids will be going back to school soon." For an instant Betsy looked as if she wasn't sure what that meant for her. She'd finished her schooling in the spring, and he realized he'd no idea what she wanted to do next.

"What about you?"

She shrugged. "I was thinking about asking to be a helper at school, but maybe…well, maybe I'm needed here more."

"Because of me." He didn't really have to ask why. Her life had been changed, too, he reminded himself. But maybe that plan, at least, could be saved.

He caught her hand and squeezed it. "I think you ought to go ahead and try for a job at school. Look at me—I'm doing better every day. And you'd be a good teacher's aide."

"Do you think so?" Her face brightened in an instant.

"Yah, I think so." He patted her hand. "Go after what you want, okay?"

She hesitated and then nodded. "I guess maybe I will." She skipped back inside, all smiles.

You're spreading cheer all over the place, he told himself wryly. Now what about trying to make things better with Miriam?

He turned the chair, looking toward the path by which Miriam came. Maybe he should make sure she understood he couldn't marry anybody. That might ease things between them if she had any feelings for him. Or would she find it insulting? He suspected he didn't know as much about women as he'd thought he did.

He'd probably been foolish enough to think he did because of his popularity with girls like Liva Ann. But Miriam was a completely different person from Liva Ann—a grown-up, with a mind and a determination and a full heart to share.

Matt was still trying to figure out what to do when he caught sight of Miriam's slender figure moving toward him along the path that bordered the field. He watched, aware of a funny disturbance in his heart, almost as if it tried to tell him something.

Shoving the thought away, he wheeled himself down the ramp so he could meet her at the driveway. The trouble was that the closer she came, the stronger the feeling grew, and the less able he was to deal with it.

He was almost relieved when she was close enough to talk to so that he was forced to make a decision. Pretend that nothing had happened and carry on as usual?

He knew suddenly that he couldn't. It wasn't fair to Miriam to pretend he hadn't kissed her. It wasn't fair to himself, either. If he had feelings for her, the best thing was to confront them.

Miriam came up to him, her smile strained. "Are we going somewhere before we start on your exercises?"

"Not exactly. I think maybe we should talk a bit first."

"If this is about what happened yesterday, I'd rather not," she said quickly, actually taking a step back.

That decided him. They couldn't go on like this, no matter what.

"We have to. Please, Miriam." He gestured toward the seat under the apple tree. "Let's go over to the bench and talk. No one will bother us."

She stiffened, as if she would refuse to move, but then she nodded. Seizing the back of the chair, she helped him maneuver it across the lawn to the bench in the shade.

At his gesture, she sat down and looked at him, her eyes wary.

He drew the chair over so that he faced her—knee

to knee, the way they'd been during those moments when he'd lost control of himself.

After taking a deep breath, he plunged in. "I know you said we'd just forget about what happened between us, but we can't. Or anyway, I can't. I didn't plan it, but it happened."

"I know that," she said in a rush. "Please, Matt, can't we just get back to work on your exercises? I don't want to ruin that by mixing up personal feelings in it. You're doing so well."

He shook his head, feeling the need to explain… to apologize… He wasn't sure what, but he knew he couldn't pretend it never happened.

"Look, I… I can't deny that I have feelings for you. You've…well, you've brought me back to living again. But I can't offer you anything."

He was doing this badly, saying all the wrong things. He should have stuck a bandage over his mouth. But at least her expression had softened a little.

She leaned forward, touching his hand gently. "I'm not asking you for anything, Matt. I want to help you. Any other feelings I have…" she stumbled over the words "…well, that doesn't affect my work. I won't let it."

Other feelings. He repeated the words silently.

"I just want to be sure you understand." He drew in a breath and fought for the words. "Whatever I feel, I know that marriage isn't for me. I can't support a wife, I don't have anything to offer, and I won't take pity."

* * *

Miriam sat rigid for a long moment, staring at Matt. His words had been bombarding her heart, with every word seeming to add another blow.

But this…this was the last straw. The only thing she could do was either break into a storm of weeping or explode in a display of temper. And she wasn't going to cry in front of him.

She shot to her feet. "What do you mean? I haven't asked you to marry me. And you certain sure haven't asked me."

"Look, I…"

"And if I did want to marry you, it would be because I love you." She swept on, carried by a wave of feeling too strong to be denied. "That's the only reason I'd marry anybody. As far as I'm concerned, loving doesn't have anything to do with what somebody has to offer or whether that person has a beautiful face or two good legs. It has to do with loving the whole person, the way they are inside. That's what I—"

She stopped, knowing she was on the verge of telling him she loved him. Still, if he didn't realize it by now, he wasn't paying attention. She'd left him speechless, and she couldn't go on much longer. Soon they'd just sit and stare, like two statues.

"I'm going home," she announced. "I'm taking the day off. If you want me to come back to work tomorrow…well, just let me know."

No more…she couldn't handle any more. Miriam

wanted to run, but she wouldn't let herself. Walking away, she was shaking inside, but her legs kept on moving. She could only hope that she could get to the haven of her room before her family asked her questions.

Matt figured he couldn't have made any more of a mess of that conversation if he'd intended to. Somehow he'd said all the wrong things. He'd just wanted to give both of them room to pull back, but he'd managed to hurt Miriam and chase her away.

After struggling to turn the chair in the grass, Matt finally got it done and moving, which was an accomplishment if he'd felt like celebrating. He tried to spot Miriam, but she'd already vanished around the curve in the path.

By the time he was nearing the ramp, Betsy had spotted him, and she came running to help. With her assistance, he reached the porch, where he stopped.

"Is Mammi here?"

"No. Don't you remember? She was going to help at the cleanup day at the schoolhouse. Do you need her?"

He shook his head. What he wanted was to avoid any questions, so it was just as well she'd gone out. But there was still Betsy to deal with, and he felt sure she'd have something to say.

"Where's Miriam? Why did she leave you out here by yourself?" She studied his face. "You hurt her feelings, didn't you?"

Annoyed, he frowned at her. "You're getting awful sassy, you know that?"

"I'm growing up, you mean. Well, what did you do?" She put her hand on the arm of the chair as if to keep him from getting away before he'd answered.

"Nothing." Neither of them believed that. "I didn't mean to do anything. I was just explaining why I figured I wouldn't get married. I mean, that's out of the question."

"Why?" Betsy didn't let go. "I mean, why couldn't you get married? You were going to marry Liva Ann, weren't you?"

He shuddered at the thought of how unhappy they'd have made each other. "No," he said firmly. "Anyway, that doesn't matter. Just let me get to my room."

Betsy stepped back and then went and opened the door for him. "I still say you hurt her feelings. After all, she loves you."

"She… What makes you think that?" He turned his face away, not wanting her to read his expression. "Did she say so?"

"She didn't need to say so," Betsy said scornfully. "Me and Mammi both saw it over a week ago. And we thought it would be a good thing."

How much else, he wondered, had he missed about what went on behind his back?

"Listen, Betsy, be serious."

"I *am* serious," she protested. "Ask Mammi if you don't believe me. Miriam loves you, and you ought to ask her to marry you. There's room for both of you here, right?"

"I can't," he said automatically.

"Well, why not? Miriam doesn't care about that scar, ain't so? She's not like Liva Ann. And you love her, don't you?"

The question hit him like something exploding over his head. Was that what was the matter with him? Did he love her?

The answer filled his heart. He loved her. It had been her all along, and he hadn't seen it.

Panic swamped him. If he'd lost her—

He grabbed Betsy's arm. "Where's Daad and Josh?"

"They went to the lumberyard, and then they're going to stop at the school. Why? What do you need? I can do it."

"Looks like you'll have to." He thought quickly. Sending a message wouldn't help. He had to get over there and find Miriam before it was too late.

The buggy? No, he wouldn't be able to get up into it without Daad to help. But the pony cart...

"Can you get the pony cart out and harness Dolly? Quickly?"

"Yah, sure I can. Why? Where am I going?"

"Not you. Or at least not alone. Me. I have to get over to see Miriam right now."

Betsy looked at him, understanding growing on her face. Breaking into a huge grin, she whirled and sped toward the barn, moving so fast it was as if she hardly touched the ground.

He took the wheelchair back down to the road. He'd have gone to get the pony himself, but if the wheelchair scared Dolly, they'd be that much longer getting there.

So he waited with what patience he could muster, hands clenched. He should have been thinking about how he would get into the pony cart, but his thoughts were completely revolving around Miriam.

There was no real need to rush, he told himself, but he didn't believe it. He had to get to her, to tell her. This time get it right. This time tell her that he loved her.

It seemed forever before Betsy came back driving the pony cart, but it couldn't have been more than a few minutes. She set the brake, climbed out, and ran around the cart to help him.

"What's the best way to do this?" She grabbed his arm as if planning to pull him into the cart by sheer force.

"Slowly." He mentally measured the distance up to the cart seat. He could do it. He had to. "It's a good thing I put the brace on my leg this morning," he said. "Just get me as close as possible to the seat, but facing forward."

She wiggled the chair into position and stopped when he told her. "What are you going to do now?"

"Help me stand, first. Then, when I'm in position, I want you to go round and get in the other side. You put your arms around my chest and pull me toward the seat while I push myself up."

Betsy hesitated. "You sure you're not going to get hurt? Daadi would kill me if I let you get hurt."

"He wouldn't. Just remember that if you don't help, I'll do it myself."

That convinced her. Using the side of the cart with one hand and the arm of the wheelchair with the other, he managed to get to his feet with her help.

"Now hold on tight while I get on the other side." Betsy patted his arm and scurried around the cart.

He was concentrating too hard to speak. He'd stay upright. He had to. He was backed against the cart, feeling the seat with one hand, when Betsy clambered in. In a moment, her strong young arms circled his chest.

"Okay," she said, once satisfied with her position. "Are you ready?"

"Ready." Hands braced, he used his better leg to push against the cart wheel, levering himself up and over while pulling with his hands. Betsy, breathing hard, pulled him too, bumping his back against the side bar.

He seemed to be balanced in midair for a moment, pushing and straining, the sweat pouring off him. Then Betsy gave a huge pull, he shoved as hard as possible, and he dragged himself onto the seat, sprawling across it.

"Good girl, Dolly," he breathed. "She didn't move an inch. And good for you." He clasped Betsy in a one-armed hug, busy holding on with the other. "Just pull my legs in or they'll be dragging on the ground."

By the time she'd done that, he was sitting up. The pony cart, with its memories of dozens, maybe hundreds of trips, seemed to welcome him. He reached for the reins, but Betsy beat him to it.

"No way. You've done enough for one day. What Miriam is going to say, I can't even guess." She slapped the lines, and Dolly moved off. The pony cart bounced over every little bump in the drive on the way to the road and Miriam.

Matt held on tight. He didn't have to guess about what he wanted Miriam to say. He wanted her to say yes.

Chapter Fifteen

By the time she'd reached the privacy of her room, Miriam discovered that the urge to cry had left her. Something about walking all the way home had drained it away, leaving her…empty. That was the only word she could think of that fit.

She wanted to be angry with Matt, because that would be easier. She knew exactly what he was thinking. He didn't want people to see him this way. He'd pushed away all the progress he made, convincing himself that he wasn't whole enough to gain a woman's love.

He already had it. Didn't he realize that? They could build a life together—a good life that included his family and her family and the farm…

But not if he didn't love her. Not if he didn't believe she could love him.

Trying to distract herself, she walked to the bed and slumped down on it. She should find something to do with herself. Mammi had gone to the workday at the school, of course, and Daad and the boys were out about the farm. They probably didn't even realize she'd come back. But they would, and she'd have to explain herself.

Miriam pressed her fingers to her temples, feeling the pounding of an oncoming headache, no doubt from suppressing her tears.

She stared at the hooked rug Grossmammi had made for her bedroom, all deep rose and soft green. It had been an act of love, and just pressing her feet against it brought her grandmother's love flowing around her like a hug.

How long she sat there, she didn't know, but eventually she heard a sound out in the driveway—voices. Before she could go and look, feet came pounding up the steps. Was someone hurt?

She hurried to the door in time to catch the twins. "What are you doing? Is something wrong?"

John Thomas grabbed one hand, and James the other, and they tugged.

"You have to come. Right now!" John Thomas was so excited he was nearly jumping. "Hurry!"

"Yah, hurry," James added. "Matt is here. He wants to see you."

"Matt? He can't be. How would he get here? If this is a joke—"

"No joke. He's here, and he wants you." Her brothers dragged her forward, with John Thomas being the spokesman, as usual. "Now, now, now!"

Her heart thudding with a mixture of fear and excitement, she rushed down the steps, the boys getting in her way and nearly sending her headlong. They raced ahead of her across the kitchen and out, slamming the screen door, but she wasn't far behind them.

She shot outside and then stopped, unable to believe what she was seeing. The pony cart stood in the driveway, with Dolly cropping peacefully at the grass along the edge. Impossibly, Matthew sat in the cart, his gaze fixed on her.

"Aren't you going to say anything?" he asked, his voice gentle. There was something in his eyes that she hadn't seen before…something that set her heart pounding so loudly, she could hear it.

"I… I don't know what to say." She moved to the pony cart, brushing Betsy and the twins out of her way. "How? What?" She gestured helplessly.

It was Matt, the old Matt—sure of himself, cheerful—who smiled at her. "Come up here and I'll tell you all about it." He held out his hand to her. "Because if I get down, I'll never get back up again."

Could he actually be laughing at himself, the way he used to? She reached for his hand and felt him pull her into the cart.

Matt looked at her, started to speak, and then stopped. "Betsy," he said loudly, "there's too many people around here."

Betsy giggled, then grabbed a twin by each hand. "Come on, guys. Show me the chickens, okay?" She led them away despite John Thomas's loud objections.

Then they were alone, sitting close together, and she couldn't think of a single thing to say. She stared down at her hands, clasping themselves in her lap as if independent of her.

"Wouldn't you look at me, Miriam?" His voice was low, just for her. "I can't tell you I love you unless you do."

Her gaze leaped to his before she could think about it. "You… What did you say?"

"You heard. It's what I should have said before. I love you." He put his hands over hers, and his touch immediately stopped their straining. "I didn't even realize it, and it was there all along." He touched her cheek, running his finger lightly along the curve to her lips.

Her breath stopped, and all she could do was look at him with her heart showing plainly in her face. "Are you sure?" she murmured.

"Very sure."

His head bent, and his lips closed on hers, warm and confident and loving. The world seemed to spin around them and then draw slowly away, leaving them locked in each other's arms as if they were the only people in the universe.

Miriam could hear his heart beating, sure and steady. She sensed the feelings flowing back and forth between them…love, passion, longing, friendship, caring. She had known she loved him, but she'd never imagined it would be like this.

Slowly he pulled back far enough to look at her.

"Now that we have that settled, will you marry me? I don't know what we'll live on or how well I can hope to be, but I know I want the future, whatever it is, to be with you."

She caressed his scarred cheek. "Yah, I'll marry you. In fact, if you hadn't asked me, I might have had to ask you."

He chuckled, his voice low and his arms tightening. "I'd like to hear that."

"And I know just how we'll live, no matter how well you become. We'll live on the farm, and we'll share our families. With Josh's help, one day you'll be running the farm yourself."

"You're sure of that?"

"I'm sure." She traced the line of his smile. Smiles had been scarce for a time, but now it was her job to be sure he smiled often. "One day we'll have sons to help you work the farm…maybe one of them named David, if you want."

He nodded, his eyes shining. "Mammi and Daad would like that. But how about a girl?"

"Yah, there has to be a girl," she said lightly, loving the way he sounded when he laughed at her, and the way his voice rumbled in his chest so she could feel it. "My mother and your mother will demand it, don't you think?"

"They will." He caught her hand and brought it to his lips for a kiss. "Ach, Miriam, life doesn't always turn out the way you expect it to. Are you sure you're willing to take a chance on me?"

"I'm sure," she said, feeling it with every heartbeat, every breath. "Whatever comes, we'll deal with it together, with God's help."

His smile was very sweet.. "Yah. We will." It sounded like a promise.

She glanced over his shoulder. "Here come the twins, and your sister, and my daad, and my other brothers. I think you'll have to be ready to take them all on as part of your family."

"That sounds like a great idea." He followed the direction of her gaze, smiling.

She watched as they reached the pony cart. Daad didn't seem to need any explanations. One look at their flushed faces must have been enough. He reached out and grasped Matt's hand, smiling, while the boys climbed in the back of the pony cart, eager to be part of whatever happened.

Two families would become one—one noisy, funny, sad, troublesome, loving family, with God in control. She couldn't think of anything better.

* * * * *

CARING FOR HER AMISH FAMILY

Carrie Lighte

For my dad, who keeps his word

Be ye therefore merciful, as your Father also is merciful. Judge not, and ye shall not be judged: condemn not, and ye shall not be condemned.

—*Luke* 6:36–37

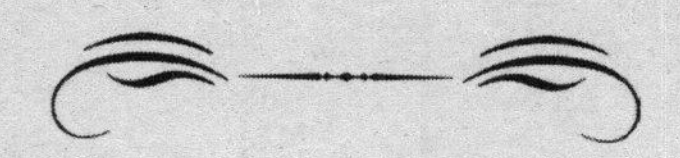

Chapter One

At twenty-seven, Anke Bachman was a year older than her sister-in-law, yet Velda was lecturing her in the same tone she used to admonish her four little children.

"You know what the Bible says, Anke. Whoever is a friend of the world is the enemy of *Gott*." She furiously scraped the remnants of mashed potatoes from the inside of a large pot with a spatula.

"*Jah*, that's true," Anke replied. "Yet it also says that people who don't provide for their own *familye* have denied their faith."

"But your *schweschder* left our *familye*!" Velda emphatically waved the spatula in the air, splattering little blobs of potatoes on the floor. Her husband, Ernest—who was Anke's brother—was as calm as Velda was excitable. Seated at the table, he was quietly sipping tea and eating a second slice of sour-milk cake. The little ones had been so tired they'd gone to bed immediately after supper, but Anke feared her sister-in-law's voice would wake them again as she exclaimed, "And Clara didn't just leave our *familye*, she left our faith!"

Anke didn't need a reminder: she'd been lamenting her youngest sister's rebellious lifestyle ever since Clara ran away during her *rumspringa* a little over five years ago. In all that time, there wasn't a day that went by when Anke didn't pray that Clara would repent and return to her family's home in New Hope, Maine. Or at the very least that she'd call or write to let them know she was okay.

Her prayers were finally answered last week when her sister sent a letter requesting Anke meet her on Saturday in a little diner on the edge of town. "Please come alone," she'd written. "I have something very important to discuss with you."

For days after receiving the note, Anke was filled with hope that Clara wanted to discuss coming back to her Amish community. The possibility made her so ecstatic that her feet barely touched the ground.

But that was before Anke had seen her.

And it was before she'd heard Clara's story.

When they'd met, Anke almost hadn't recognized her sister. Clara's flaxen hair was cut shorter than a boy's and streaked purple. Her ears were pierced six or seven times, she had a tiny gold hoop in one nostril and she was wearing ripped jeans and a hooded black sweatshirt. But even more alarming than her accessories or clothes was how old and hardened her face had appeared. Her eyelids were so puffy that her baby-blue eyes looked half the size they used to be. Or maybe that was because she was scowling.

She'd allowed Anke to hug her for a long time, but Clara hadn't returned her embrace. When Anke had finally let go, her eyes brimming with tears, Clara had swiftly stepped to the other side of the table. Gesturing to the middle-aged dark-haired *Englisch* woman seated at the booth, she'd announced, "This is Yolanda, my sponsor."

"Sponsor?" Anke had repeated numbly, trying to understand why Clara had invited a third person to meet with them when she'd specifically requested that Anke come there alone.

Clara quickly delved into an account of what she'd been doing since she'd left home, admitting she'd originally run away because she'd become pregnant during her *rumspringa*. Four months later, she gave birth to a baby boy she named Will. She and her *Englisch* boyfriend were together until about a year ago, when he'd broken up with her and moved to California, claiming he was too young to be a dad and he didn't want anything to do with her or their child.

After he left, Clara had been so sad and lonely that she'd turned to alcohol for comfort. It didn't take long before she was addicted. Her drinking had led to such irresponsible behavior that a judge had told her if she didn't participate in a residential recovery program, she'd have to put Will in foster care.

Although Clara had recited the details of her life

as unfeelingly as if she'd been reading items off a grocery list, they were so painful and shocking for Anke to hear that she'd struggled not to wince.

Dear Gott, *you've brought my* schweschder *and me together again for a reason*, she'd silently prayed as Clara was speaking. *Please help me respond to her in accordance with Your will, no matter how disappointed I am in her behavior.*

After hearing Clara's story, Anke assumed the reason she'd wanted to meet with her was because she needed money. Anke didn't know how much a residential recovery program cost—she wasn't even sure what it was. But she did understand what it felt like to be separated from one's child. Granted, Clara wasn't actually Anke's daughter, but she had raised the girl after their parents died when a car rear-ended their buggy nine years ago. Even though Anke's and Clara's circumstances were completely different, Anke didn't want her sister to have to endure the kind of heartache Anke had suffered when Clara had run away.

"I've been making aprons and putting them on consignment at Millers' Restaurant, so I've built up a savings account. It's not a lot, but you can have it all," she'd offered. "If you agree to let me tell our *bruder* about your predicament—he might be willing to help, too."

"I don't need your money. I'm not a *beggar*," Clara had snapped. She'd sat back against the booth seat and crossed her arms over her chest, clearly offended.

"Maybe not, Clara, but you *are* in need," Yolanda had interjected pointedly. Anke hadn't understood what she'd meant, but her remark seemed to have an effect on Clara's attitude.

For the first time since she'd arrived in the diner, Anke had caught a glimpse of how vulnerable her little sister really was. Her voice quavering, she'd said, "I'm sorry. I appreciate the offer, but the costs are covered by the state. What I really need is for you to watch Will while I'm in the program. It's only for six weeks. Please, Anke? I'm desperate. I don't want him to wind up with strangers. What if I never get him back?"

That's exactly how I've *felt all these years* you've *been away*, Anke thought. She'd told Clara she'd have to pray about it. She'd also have to discuss it with Ernest and Velda since they all lived in the same house.

The dwelling was technically Anke's; as the eldest sibling, she'd inherited it the year her parents died. But Ernest and Velda had been living in it with her ever since they got married, and Anke considered it as much theirs as hers. She couldn't have possibly made a major decision that would affect their entire household without consulting them first.

She'd anticipated that Velda would have reservations, but she hadn't expected her to get worked up into such a tizzy. Trying to show her sister-in-law she understood her concerns, Anke started to say,

"Clara was on *rumspringa* when she left, so she's not under the *bann*, but—"

Hands on her hips, Velda interrupted, "That doesn't mean we should *wilkom* her with open arms! Especially since she hasn't indicated any interest in repenting and putting her *Englisch* lifestyle behind her."

"Please allow me to finish expressing my thought," Anke replied softly. "What I was going to say was that even though Clara was on *rumspringa* and she isn't under the *bann*, I don't approve of the way she's been living any more than you do. And *neh*, she hasn't indicated an intention to leave the *Englisch*."

Anke paused, thinking, *She hasn't even really admitted remorse—I get the sense she's only going into the recovery program because she has to.* But her prayer was that the Lord would change Clara's heart, as well as her actions. She continued, "However, I'm not asking you and Ernest to *wilkom* her back into our home. I'm asking you to help me watch her *suh* here for six weeks. What his *mamm* has done isn't *his* fault. And there's nothing in our *Ordnung* which would prohibit us from providing a temporary home for him, considering his age and circumstances."

Velda spluttered. "The only reason there's nothing in our *Ordnung* prohibiting it is because the situation has never *kumme* up before! And that's because everyone knows better than to invite *Englischers* to live in one's home."

"The Nisley *familye* rents out their *daadi haus* to

Englischers for three months during fishing season," Anke reminded her.

"*Jah,* but that's not the same as breaking bread with them day after day," Velda countered. "I don't want an *Englisch bu* introducing our impressionable *kinner* to the temptations of the *Englisch* world."

"I understand your concern, Velda," Anke responded sincerely. "But Will is five years old, so he's impressionable, too. It's possible that your *kinner* might demonstrate the virtues of *our* faith to him. And perhaps by caring for Clara's *suh*, we'll win her back to our *familye*."

Having finished his cake, Ernest put down his fork, wiped his mouth with a napkin and finally spoke. "I want Clara to return, too, Anke. But I'm also very concerned about the influence Will might have on our household. Just because it's permissible for him to stay with us doesn't mean it's advisable. I believe we ought to do what we *know* is best for our household, instead of what we *hope* might turn out best for our *schweschder* and her *suh*."

Although her brother's reasoning made sense, Anke wasn't ready to give up. She didn't want to push Ernest and Velda to violate their consciences, but neither could she ignore her strong belief that caring for Will was the Godly thing to do. *If we lived in separate* heiser, *this wouldn't be an issue*, she thought.

Suddenly, she was struck with a solution that seemed so obvious she didn't know why it hadn't occurred to her sooner. "I could stay in the *daadi haus* with Will!"

"That place isn't fit for you and a *kind*," Ernest objected. "Even *I* wouldn't want to sleep in there, especially not in February."

Situated on the northern corner of the property, the little structure had been home to Anke and Ernest's grandparents before they died some fifteen years ago. On occasion since then, the Bachmans had used the small dwelling for visiting relatives they didn't have room to accommodate in the main house, such as when Ernest and Velda got married. However, two years after the wedding, a tree limb fell on the roof and the damage had been patched over, but not thoroughly repaired. The inside of the house needed restoration, too.

But Anke had already come up with the perfect plan. "I'll have a frolic on *Samschdaag*. The *menner* can repair the roof and the *weibsleit* can help me clean it inside. It'll be nice and cozy when Will arrives next *Muundaag*."

"All the available *menner* are helping Omer Wilford build his workshop this *Samschdaag*, remember?"

"Oh, that's right. The *weibsleit* are having a quilting bee at Lena's, so they won't be available to help me, either." Anke tentatively proposed, "Would you be comfortable allowing Will to stay in this *haus* with us until the following *Samschdaag*?"

"Neh," Velda objected vehemently. "I wouldn't be comfortable with that at all."

Ernest agreed with his wife's sentiment. "It's okay if our *kinner* play with Will on occasion, but staying at our *haus* for five nights? That doesn't seem prudent. What if he grows too accustomed to us and then doesn't want to leave to go live in the *daadi haus*? It will be upsetting for him as well as for our *kinner*."

Anke bit her lip, refusing to be defeated. It dawned on her that she could withdraw the money from her savings account and pay someone to work on fixing the place up during the week. Surely there was someone in the New Hope community who needed an income as much as she needed his carpentry services. "All right, I'll find someone who's willing and able to make repairs to the roof before Will arrives."

"Like who? Your suitor Keith Harnish?" Velda boldly inquired, even though most of the Amish in New Hope generally didn't discuss who they were dating, not even with their family members.

"Keith is *not* my suitor," Anke insisted. Although it was true that she had agreed to walk out with him about a month ago, she'd quickly decided it had been a mistake to say yes to his persistent requests to court. Like the other two men who'd courted her in her lifetime, he just didn't seem to understand that caring for her family took priority over going bowling on Saturday night or for a buggy ride on Sunday afternoon. She'd felt that way when she was raising Clara, and she felt that way about helping

Ernest and Velda care for her nieces and nephews, too. Anke didn't blame any of her suitors for feeling frustrated with her; they wanted to get married and have their own families, not play second fiddle to hers. She'd come to realize it wasn't fair to a man for her to accept an offer of courtship, knowing she had little time or inclination to develop a relationship with him.

That was especially true now, because until Clara completed her recovery program, Anke's primary focus was going to be giving Will a healthy, happy, loving Amish home. In fact, in this instance she believed her singleness was a gift from the Lord. *If I had* kinner *of my own, I might be as protective of them as Ernest and Velda are of their brood*, she thought. *And then who would care for little Will?*

"Don't look so embarrassed," Velda teased, clearly in a better mood now that she could rest assured her *Englisch* nephew wouldn't be living in the same house as her children. "Every *weibsmensch* needs a little romance in her life."

Not me, Anke thought. *All I need is a* gut *carpenter—and preferably one who can start working on the* daadi haus *right away.*

"We're sure having one fierce cold snap," Josiah Mast's brother Victor remarked on Tuesday afternoon as his horse pulled the buggy onto the main road leading toward the New Hope bus station. It was the same station Victor had picked Josiah up at when he'd arrived yesterday; now they were headed back there so Victor could catch a bus to Upstate New York. "At this rate, the ground won't thaw until July. I'm *hallich* you're here, but for your sake, you probably should have waited until April to *kumme*."

Josiah had moved from a small 'istrict near Arthur, Illinois, to New Hope to work for his brother, who owned a fence-installation business. He was aware that Victor wouldn't have any customer orders to fill until the weather warmed, but Josiah was eager to relocate to Maine. "I actually think this timing works out well for all of us. I'll be here to care for your livestock while you and Laura are away. And I can lay your new floor in the kitchen without worrying I'm getting underfoot."

Last week, Laura, Victor's wife, had rushed to Upstate New York after her father suffered a stroke. Now that it was clear she'd need to extend her stay to help during his recovery period, Victor was going to join her. So Josiah would be staying alone in their house in New Hope.

"It's *wunderbaar* that you'll be working on the floor while we're gone, but won't you feel lonely here on your own?"

"*Neh*, I'll be fine." Actually Josiah was looking forward to some solitude, especially after feeling as if he'd spent the past year under scrutiny from both the *Englischers* and the Amish in his community.

It all began last winter on a day a lot like this one, when he was traveling past a golf course and he spied his girlfriend Jana's sixteen-year-old brother, Stanley. The teenager and a couple of his *Englisch* pals were standing around a bonfire, watching their friends take turns racing snowmobiles nearby. Aware they were trespassing and they might get into trouble with the police, Josiah had pulled over to offer Stanley a ride home.

To his consternation, when he got out of the buggy, Josiah noticed the teenager had alcohol on his breath. Stanley was on his *rumspringa* so the church might not have held him accountable for this transgression. However, his father, Emery, was a deacon and he didn't tolerate alcohol consumption by anyone under any circumstances. Understandably, Stanley seemed chagrined to have been caught drinking and he refused to go home.

Josiah was just about to get back into his buggy when he heard a loud shout: one of the passengers had fallen off the snowmobile. The driver just pumped his fist in the air and sped off, causing the *Englischers* standing near the bonfire to laugh, without any apparent concern for the passenger's well-being. So Josiah ran down the hill to see if the youth was okay. He was, but he'd twisted his ankle and Josiah had to assist him back to the bonfire.

Meanwhile, someone must have notified the golf club manager that there were trespassers on the property, because he'd arrived in his car. By the time Josiah returned to the group, the manager was interrogating the kids—one of whom was his own son—about where they'd purchased the alcohol.

I told you what would happen if I caught you using a fake ID again! He'd yelled at his son, a blond boy who looked deceptively innocent.

I didn't buy it or use a fake ID, Dad. That Amish guy over there—Josiah—told us he had beer in the back of his buggy and he'd look the other way if we wanted to help ourselves. We've only had a few sips.

Josiah had been almost as shocked to hear the *Englisch* kid refer to him by name as he was by his outrageous lie. *I've never purchased or transported alcohol in my life*, he'd said to the boy's father. *But you can take a look in the carriage and see for yourself there's nothing in there except a toolbox.*

The manager had climbed into the buggy and peered over the seat. He'd reached in and pulled out a half-empty bottle of gin and a six-pack of beer. Holding them up, he'd asked, *These aren't yours?*

Josiah had been appalled. Neh. *Absolutely not.* He hadn't wanted to come right out and accuse the guy's son of stashing the alcohol there when they saw the manager's car approaching. For all he knew, it could have been Stanley who'd done it. In any case, Josiah hadn't actually witnessed them doing it and God's Word warned against bearing false witness about one's neighbor. All he knew for certain was that it wasn't *his*.

Fortunately, the manager had seemed to surmise what was going on. He'd told Josiah he'd get to the bottom of the matter with the teens and their parents and assured him the youth would face consequences for their behavior. He'd offered to bring them to Josiah's house to apologize for lying once they'd sobered up, but Josiah had said it wasn't necessary and he hadn't supplied his address. He'd just wanted to leave with Stanley.

Make sure you don't come back here again, the manager had warned the teenager. *Or I'll pay your elders a visit and let them know what you've been up to.*

Clearly the *Englischer* had a strong understanding of how to intimidate an Amish boy—Josiah had seen by how nervous Stanley was that he wouldn't make the same mistake twice. So on the way home, he'd promised that if Stanley agreed he'd never drink or trespass again, Josiah wouldn't tell anyone about what he'd done or where he'd been.

However, Josiah later discovered that someone had videoed the entire episode on a cell phone and it went "viral," as the *Englisch* would say. Both Stanley and Josiah worked for Emery in his door-making shop and before long a customer came in and played the clip for the three of them.

Astonishingly, Emery demonstrated less faith in Josiah than the golf club manager had shown him. After the customer left, Emery hadn't even asked to hear Josiah's side of the story before reproaching him. *You know our* Ordnung *prohibits drinking any alcohol whatsoever!*

Trying not to respond in anger, Josiah had stated evenly, *It wasn't mine—I believe the kids put those bottles in my carriage because they saw the manager coming and they didn't want to be caught red-handed.*

Emery had then turned to Stanley and questioned, *Is it true? Did the* Englischers *put the bottles in Josiah's buggy?* Josiah noticed he'd automatically assumed it was the *Englischers*, and not his son, who had been drinking.

The teenager had somberly shaken his head. *If they did, I didn't see them do it.*

On one hand, Josiah understood Stanley's reluctance to snitch on his friends and to face the consequences of his own behavior, too. On the other hand, he was disgusted. Didn't the teenager have any conscience at all?

Emery had turned his attention back to grilling Josiah. *If you had nothing to hide, why didn't you tell me about this incident yourself? Why did I find out about it from an* Englischer*?*

Josiah had hesitated in order to give Stanley a chance to speak up. He'd hoped the boy would have confessed the real reason Josiah never reported the incident to Emery, but Stanley had just silently looked down at his feet.

The club manager knew their claim didn't have any merit and he assured me he'd hold the kids accountable for their drinking. As far as I was con-

cerned, the matter was over, so there was no need to mention it, Josiah had said at last.

But he knew how feeble his excuse sounded. Emery hadn't come right out and said he didn't believe him, but the older man began giving Josiah the cold shoulder. He must have told others in their district about it, because Josiah sensed some of them looking askance at him, too. It disappointed him, but not nearly as much as Jana's response did.

I know you don't drink, so you must have been hiding the alcohol for someone else, weren't you? she'd asked after Emery told her about what had happened. *Is it someone in our district? Or was it for your sister's husband—they were visiting from Ohio last week, weren't they?*

Josiah was angry she hadn't believed him and appalled she'd assumed the alcohol belonged to someone in *his* family. He'd considered telling her about her brother's drinking. Yet no matter how irresponsible and cowardly Stanley's behavior was, Josiah couldn't break his word to him. After all, God was always faithful to *His* promises and Josiah wanted to try his best to follow the Lord's example. However, he had decided he couldn't court someone who didn't have more trust in him than what Jana had demonstrated, so he'd broken up with her.

Shortly afterward, Emery said he no longer needed Josiah's services. He'd claimed it was because business was slow, but Josiah believed the real reason was that the video had received so much attention, so more and more customers recognized him when they came into the shop. (It wasn't difficult, considering Josiah was one of only two men in the district who had red hair.) They'd whisper to each other, *Isn't he the one who was hanging out and drinking with the underage kids on the golf course?*

Josiah had hoped the whole fiasco would blow over and people would lose interest, but it seemed to drag on. Meanwhile, even the Amish business owners who believed he'd been telling the truth were reluctant to hire him because they were worried his notoriety would reflect poorly on them, too. As a result, for the past year Josiah had been taking whatever odd jobs he could get, so he was going to be strapped for cash until he began working for Victor.

"Do you know anyone who might be hiring?" he asked as his brother applied the buggy's brake and simultaneously slowed the horse in front of the bus station.

"*Neh*, but you can ask around at *kurrich* on *Sundaag*." Victor reached into the back to pull out his luggage. He and Josiah said goodbye and Victor hopped out of the buggy. But then he stuck his head back in for one last piece of advice. "The *leit* in New Hope are very friendly. The teenage youth attend singings, but there's another group closer to your age who go on outings together. Bowling, hiking, canoeing, they've even hiked Mount Katahdin together. I know they'd *wilkom* your company. When you go to *kurrich*, Honor Bawell will probably tell you all about their next outing."

Honor must be the community matchmaker, Josiah thought as he pulled out into traffic. There was one in every district, which was helpful if you were looking for a courtship, but he definitely wasn't. He'd recently turned twenty-five—the age when most Amish men he knew were married with two or three children. Josiah hadn't been in any rush; he'd wanted to wait until he'd met the right woman. *Unfortunately, I'm not a very* gut *judge of character*, he thought.

Or more accurately, the problem was that *Jana* wasn't a good judge of character. She didn't know what kind of man Josiah really was and she had a huge blind spot in regard to her brother.

How could he have actually believed she might have been the Lord's intended for him? That she'd be the kind of spouse who'd support him through thick and thin, just as he would have done for her? In hindsight, Josiah was grateful they'd broken up before their courtship had progressed any further. And now that he thought about it, losing his job wasn't so bad, either; if Emery hadn't relieved him of his responsibilities, Josiah never would have moved to New Hope. Originally, he'd regretted having to leave Illinois. But now that he was here, he felt relieved that no one would question his commitment to following the *Ordnung* or wonder whether he or his loved ones had a drinking problem. This was going to be a fresh start.

Maybe by autumn, I'll have enough money to pur-

chase lumber to build a small one-bedroom house on Laura and Victor's property, he thought. Instead of a *daadi haus*, it would be a bachelor *haus*; he could picture himself living alone there indefinitely.

The possibility energized him so much he decided to stop at the newly opened Amish hardware store to price some of the materials he'd need to put in a new kitchen floor for Laura. His brother had left him cash to pay for the supplies and wood, but he still intended to shop around for the best deal.

As he was browsing the aisles, he overheard an Amish woman talking to the man at the cash register. "I understand that you don't have the time to help me. And I'd really prefer someone from our *g'may* to work on the project. But since all of the skilled *menner* seem to be busy, too, I'll have to settle for an *Englisch* carpenter. So why won't you let me post an advertisement on the bulletin board by the door?"

Before the young man could reply, Josiah stepped forward. *"Guder nammigdaag,"* he greeted them both. "I'm Josiah Mast, Victor Mast's brother."

The man introduced himself as Keith Harnish, son of the hardware store owner.

Then the woman said, "*Wilkom* to New Hope, Josiah. My name is Anke Bachman." She had dark blond hair, blue-green eyes and ears that stuck out ever so slightly. He wouldn't have even noticed, except they were as pink as her cheeks; despite the soft smile she gave him, her flushed face indicated she was upset about something.

"It's *gut* to meet you both. I don't know if Victor mentioned I was coming to New Hope, but I've just moved here permanently. I overheard you saying you needed a carpenter. In Illinois I worked in a door-making shop and I'm looking for a temporary job until the spring, when I'll join my *bruder*'s crew installing fences. Can I ask what kind of project you need someone to do?"

Anke's smile grew wider. "*Jah.* I'll tell you all about it. Let's step outside so we can talk without disturbing Keith."

As they stood on the sidewalk in front of the store's big glass window, she told Josiah about her family's run-down *daadi haus*. From what he could understand, Anke's sister was undergoing some kind of treatment and she needed someone to care for her son while she was recovering in Portland, which was located about two hours south from New Hope. Anke's family's house was too small to accommodate everyone while the boy was in town, so Anke was going to stay in the *daadi haus* with him for the next six weeks or so.

"There's only one problem—we need to move into it on *Muundaag.* The rest of the repairs can be done over time, but by *Muundaag* we need a roof over our heads—one that doesn't leak, that is."

"From what you've described, I don't think that will be a problem," Josiah told her. They agreed on his hourly salary and he said he'd come to her house the following morning.

Denki, *Lord, for providing for my need before I even expressed it*, he silently prayed as Anke walked down the street. Then Josiah headed back into the hardware store to continue browsing.

"Did you tell her you'd repair the Bachmans' *daadi haus*?" Keith asked as soon as Josiah shut the door behind him.

"*Jah*. It's perfect timing, since I can't help my *bruder* install any fences until the weather warms," he replied. "And she seemed desperate. I'm surprised no one in the community wanted to take the job—or that her *familye* isn't hosting a frolic."

"Well, several of us might have made it a priority to help her, but because we don't agree with what she's doing..." Keith turned up his hands, as if there was no need to say more, but Josiah was completely confused.

"I don't understand. Is there a dispute over who owns the *daadi haus* or something?"

Keith snickered. "She didn't tell you about the controversy, did she? No wonder she wanted to speak with you about the project in private. She didn't want *me* to tell you, either."

"Tell me what? Is she doing something wrong? Is Anke violating the *Ordnung*?"

"Not exactly. But her *schweschder* Clara went *Englisch* five years ago. She had a *bobbel* out of wedlock and now she's an alcoholic. According to Anke's *schweschder*-in-law, Velda, the court is making Clara go into a program to get sober, so Anke is caring for Clara's *suh* for the six weeks—against her *familye*'s wishes. And against what many of us in the community believe she should do."

"I honestly had no idea her *schweschder* was an *Englischer*—or that she's an alcoholic," Josiah said, shaking his head in disbelief. "If I did, I would have had reservations about helping Anke, too. But I can't go back on my word now."

"Don't feel bad. It's not your fault. She should have been more forthcoming," Keith said. "But a word to the wise… Anke's very kind but sometimes her kindness clouds her better judgment. Be careful it doesn't cloud yours, too."

"I'll bear that in mind," Josiah solemnly replied, shaking his head in disbelief. How was it possible that he'd traveled over one thousand miles, only to find himself right back at square one?

Chapter Two

Anke hopped out of bed bright and early on Wednesday morning. She couldn't wait to get over to the *daadi haus* and begin cleaning it up. But first, she helped Velda make breakfast and serve it to the four children, all of whom were fussy eaters—except for Charity, the baby. At eight months old, she seemed to consume more than any of her three siblings. The twins, Millie and Micah, were barely four and they did almost everything together. Asher was almost six and next year he'd go to school, since that was when Amish children enrolled in first grade in New Hope. But for now, he was still home during the day. He was such a sweet boy that Anke couldn't help but hope he and Will would become friends, since Asher's behavior was more mature than the twins' was.

"Tell me about Victor's *bruder*," Velda said as she wiped oatmeal from Charity's chin and forehead. "You told us you'd found someone to repair the *daadi haus* but then you dashed off to your room last night before I could ask any questions."

"That's because I'm working on a special apron order for a customer for Valentine's Day," Anke replied. It was also because she didn't want her sister-in-law to object to her hiring Josiah. Velda really shouldn't have had anything to say about the matter, since Anke was paying for his labor with her own money, but that wouldn't have stopped her from offering an opinion. Even though Velda had ultimately agreed it would be permissible for Will to stay with Anke in the *daadi haus*, Anke knew Velda's feathers were still ruffled about it.

She had undoubtedly complained about it to Keith's sister-in-law Ruth, who'd stopped by the house on Tuesday morning to drop off her daughter's hand-me-down clothes for Charity. Otherwise, how had Keith found out so quickly about Anke's intention to watch Will? She suspected if they'd still been courting, he would have gladly helped mend the *daadi haus* roof, but since she'd broken up with him, he'd said he didn't have time.

Oh, well. I don't need to figure out if he had an ulterior motive for turning down the project, she thought. *I'm just grateful that the Lord provided for my needs through Josiah's help.*

Velda snapped her fingers in front of Anke's nose. "Are you awake? I asked you where Josiah lived before he moved here."

"Illinois, I think." Anke signaled Millie to close her mouth while she chewed her toast.

"Does he have a beard or mustache?"

Anke rolled her eyes. Amish men traditionally only grew beards after they were married; in Maine, they were also allowed to wear mustaches if they chose, although they weren't required to. So what Velda was really asking was whether he was single or not. Presumably, she didn't want the children to understand her question. "*Neh.* No beard." Before her sister-in-law could question her further, Anke added, "We didn't have a lot of time for chitchat. Mostly, I just described what I needed him to repair on the *daadi haus*."

"Was he a carpenter when he lived in Illinois?"

"Kind of. He worked in a door-marking shop for four years and *kumme* spring, he's going to work for Victor installing fences. So I'm sure he can handle patching up a roof or replacing a few risers on the staircase, if that's what you're worried about."

"Why are you going to stay in the *daadi haus*?" Asher asked his aunt.

Anke, Ernest and Velda had agreed in advance they'd be as honest as was appropriate with the children about the situation. So yesterday during supper, they'd told them about Will's visit.

"Don't you remember what your *mamm* and *daed* and I told you?" Anke softly prodded. She'd noticed when Asher repeated explanations aloud in his own words, he absorbed them better. She started him off with a hint, "You have another *ant* you've never met…"

"And her name is *Ant* Clara. She was your little *schweschder* 'cept she went to live with the *Englisch*."

Millie chimed in, "That's something an Amish person should never, ever do."

"It's very, very bad." Micah shook his index finger with each word, just as Velda had done yesterday.

Although Anke understood why her sister-in-law had felt it was necessary to emphasize this point, she hoped her nephews and nieces wouldn't repeat it to Will. "*Jah*, but that's not your *gschwischderkind's* fault, so we aren't going to talk to him about it. Otherwise he might feel sad," she reminded them.

"Jah," Asher agreed. "And he's probably already sad because his *mamm* had to go to a special hospital. That's why you're going to take care of him—"

"Why can't his *daed* take care of him?" Millie interrupted her brother.

The adults hadn't addressed the topic of Will's father with the children yet. They weren't sure what the boy had been told, so they didn't want to present conflicting stories. However, now that Velda was put on the spot, she blurted out, "Will doesn't have a *daed*."

"Why not?" Millie pressed.

Micah tilted his head. "Did his *daed* die?"

"Well…" Velda had worked herself into a corner, so Anke knew she had to jump in.

"What your *mamm* meant was Will's *daed* is out

of town. He's very far away, in a place called California. So I—"

Millie cut in, "Is his *daed Englisch*, too?"

"Jah," Anke answered matter-of-factly, hoping the less she said, the less she'd have to say. "So I get to take care of Will. Isn't that *wunderbaar*?"

"*Jah.* But why can't he stay in our *haus* with us? He can have my bed and I can sleep on cushions on the floor."

Asher's offer made Anke want to throw her arms around him. *If only your* mamm *were as welcoming as you are*, she thought.

"That's very generous of you, but Will's going to be here a long time. After a while, you'd get a crick in your neck from sleeping on the floor." Anke walked her fingers along her nephew's shoulder, up his neck and beneath his chin to tickle him.

"But we'll be able to play with him, right?"

"*Jah.* When your *mamm* allows you to."

Millie held up three fingers. "Is he coming in this many days?"

"*Neh*, in this many." Anke showed her there were five more days to go until Monday.

Velda stood up and started collecting the bowls. "You *kinner* go wash your hands and brush your teeth. I'll be there in a minute." Once they were out of earshot, she complained, "Will isn't even here yet and they're already so excited they hardly slept last night. Didn't I tell you having him here was going to be disruptive?"

"They're always this excited before their other *gschwischderkinner* visit, too," Anke said. "His *mamm* may have made some *baremlich* choices, but every *kind* deserves a warm *wilkom.* And every *kind* needs a warm *haus.* So if you'll excuse me, I'm going outside to wait for Josiah so we can walk over there together."

"Aren't you going to do the dishes? I need to help the children brush their teeth."

You're going to have to get used to running the household by yourself when I'm not here, Anke thought and then she immediately felt guilty. "*Jah.* I suppose there's no sense waiting out in the cold. I told Josiah to go ahead and stable his *gaul*, so I have a few minutes to spare."

"Denki." Velda walked down the hall toward the bathroom, leaving Charity in her high chair.

"Ma-ma-ma-ma," the baby sang, banging a spoon on the tray. "Ma-ma-ma-ma."

Anke sang back to her as she washed and dried the dishes. When she finished and there was still no sign of Velda, she lifted the toddler from her chair. "Up you go, my little dumpling. Uh-oh. You *schtinke*—I need to change your *windel.*"

"Da-da. Da-da," Charity babbled as Anke carried her upstairs to get a fresh cloth diaper. Velda and the children passed her on the way down. Apparently she'd been reading them a story. "I have to get going but Charity needs a fresh *windel*—"

"Okay." Velda smiled. "*Kumme* find me in the

kitchen when you're done. I need a second cup of *kaffi*—do you want one?"

Neh, *I need you to change Charity*, Anke thought and once again, she felt guilty for being so irritable. Changing a diaper only took a few seconds; it wasn't as if Josiah was going to turn around and leave if she wasn't at the *daadi haus* exactly at eight o'clock, as they'd agreed.

On the contrary, when she came downstairs, Anke found him standing near the door in the kitchen, drinking a mug of coffee that Velda apparently had poured for him. She was across the room, leaning against the counter as they conversed, while the children stood off to the side, shyly looking up at their tall visitor.

Asher seemed especially awed, and Anke couldn't blame him. Josiah had removed his hat and his dark red curls—unusual for an Amish person in this part of the country—were eye-catching. Although he had baby blue eyes and a boyish spray of freckles across his wide forehead and cheeks, he appeared more commanding than juvenile; maybe that was due to his size.

Wait till Honor Bawell meets him, Anke thought. *She'll find some reason to host a winter activity for the older singles in our* g'may *and the Serenity Ridge district.*

She'd undoubtedly ask Anke to go, too—and Anke would say no. It wasn't that she begrudged her unmarried friends an opportunity to enjoy a time of recreation and fellowship with each other. It was that their underlying motivation more often than not seemed to be that they wanted to find someone to court. Anke figured since she wasn't interested in having a suitor, it was better if she didn't participate. Not to mention, she was usually busy doing something with her family anyway.

"*Guder mariye*, Josiah," Anke said when Velda finished telling him all about Ernest's butcher shop.

"Guder mariye," he replied stiffly.

Am I just imagining it, or is he acting different than he did yesterday? she wondered. *Maybe he's annoyed because I'm late?* "Sorry to keep you waiting. I'll get my coat and then we can go." She handed the baby to Velda. After donning her wool coat, she twisted a scarf around her head and neck and then pulled on a pair of mittens.

"*Denki* for the *kaffi*." While Josiah placed his cup on the counter near the sink and then donned his hat, Millie pulled on Anke's arm.

Anke bent down and the girl cupped her hands over Anke's scarf by her ear. "Did you see his hair?" she asked in a loud whisper. "It looks just like a rooster's comb."

Hoping Josiah hadn't heard the little girl, Anke swallowed a giggle and whispered back, "*Jah.* Isn't it *wunderbaar*? But it's not polite to tell secrets in front of other people, remember?"

Anke and Josiah had barely made it off the porch before he gruffly remarked, "It's not polite to keep secrets behind people's backs, either."

"Ach. I'm sorry—I didn't realize you could hear us." Anke was surprised by his sternness; didn't he take Millie's age into account? "We expect the *kinner* to mind their manners, but sometimes they forget. But I know what Millie said was intended to be a compliment."

"I don't mean *that*," he replied scornfully. "I'm referring to the secret you kept from me about why you really needed to move into the *daadi haus*."

Anke stopped walking. "But I—I told you why. I distinctly remember saying I needed a place to stay with my nephew while my *schweschder* was in a recovery program."

"You didn't say it was because she has a drinking problem. I thought she was *sick*."

"I'm sorry if I wasn't clear. I didn't deliberately try to deceive you—although, to be honest, I really don't believe my *familye*'s situation is any of your business."

When Anke huffed and crossed her arms over her chest, steam rose from her nostrils and despite being pretty, she reminded Josiah of an angry bull. Why was she acting so indignant? She was the one who hadn't been forthcoming with him, not the other way around.

"Your *familye*'s situation became my business when you asked me to work on the *daadi haus*," he explained. "If I had known your *schweschder* had gone *Englisch* and that allowing her *suh* to live with you was creating conflict in your *familye* and upsetting the community, I might not have agreed to be a part of it by repairing the *haus*."

Anke narrowed her eyes at him and stuck her hands on her hips. "For someone who just arrived in town, you're better versed in the local gossip than I am. I didn't realize anything I was doing was upsetting members of our community, but I assure you, I'm not breaking any ordinances."

"Even though your *schweschder* went *Englisch*?"

"Right—because she's not under the *bann*. She ran away on *rumspringa*, had a *bobbel* out of wedlock and last year, her boyfriend dumped her. She turned to alcohol for comfort and developed a drinking problem. Recently, a judge ordered her to go into a recovery program—to be very clear, that's a place where the *Englisch* help alcoholics become sober. If she didn't go, she'd lose her *suh* to foster care. And I didn't want her or my nephew to suffer that kind of separation." Anke's eyes welled, and for a moment, it seemed as if she might break down in tears.

She turned and took a few steps toward the *daadi haus*. Then she stopped and whirled to face him again. "One more thing. Despite what Keith or anyone else may have told you, some of my *familye* members aren't *hallich* about me caring for my nephew, but we came to a mutual agreement. I can keep Will with me for six weeks, provided he and I live in the *daadi haus*. So that's the full story straight from the *gaul*'s mouth. If you don't want to work on the *haus* now that you have a clearer understanding of why I need to live in it, I won't hold you to your commitment. There are plenty of *Englisch* carpenters who'd appreciate having a job during the winter."

Anke stomped off across the yard. The snow was deep and crusty and her footsteps sounded angry as she made her way toward the ramshackle structure. Josiah heaved a sigh. Now what? On one hand, he had to consider that he was a newcomer in this town; he didn't want to start off on the wrong foot with the majority of the community members. On the other hand, he really needed the money. More important, despite the fact that Anke had said she wouldn't hold him to his commitment, Josiah felt obligated to honor his word.

I suppose it won't take very long to fix the roof and do a few basic repairs inside to make the place livable, he decided. *Besides, Keith knows I didn't deliberately choose to go against the community's preference in this matter. As long as I keep my distance from Anke and her nephew socially, I shouldn't experience the same kind of treatment I received in Illinois.*

"Anke, wait!" he called as he bounded across the yard. When he caught up to her, he said, "I still want the job."

She nodded, but didn't say anything else. They continued until they reached the *daadi haus*, but when she started up the porch stairs, Josiah warned,

"Don't step there!" The board was so rotted it might have given way beneath her. If the condition of the porch was this poor, he could only imagine what the inside of the house was like.

A second later, Anke pushed open the door and Josiah had his answer: devoid of furniture, the interior was thickly coated with dust and he immediately noticed mice droppings on the windowsills, many of which were as rotten and chipped as the porch steps.

"Stay here by the door," he advised her. "I want to make sure this place isn't going to *kumme* crashing down on our heads before you go any farther."

She giggled, as if she thought he was joking, but he was serious. The *daadi haus* was so small, it only contained four rooms. The front door opened into the small living room on the left side of the house; behind it was the kitchen. On the right side were two tiny bedrooms, with a bathroom in between them. It didn't take Josiah long to make his assessment.

"The *gut* news is that the woodstove seems to be in working order," he said. "And there's no issue with the plumbing, either. But the leak has affected both bedrooms and I'm going to need to take out part of the wall to check for mold, as well as replace some floorboards and window frames. I can patch up the roof by *Muundaag* well enough to get you through the winter. But you're not going to be able to sleep in the bedrooms until the following week, at least."

Anke twisted her mouth to one side, and nodded slowly. "Okay, then we'll just have to sleep in the living room. It'll be warmer by the woodstove anyway."

"I doubt two beds will fit in here."

"Oh, we don't have beds. I intend to borrow a couple of cots. And if no one has any to spare, I'll put extra blankets down for padding and Will and I will bundle up in quilts. We'll be fine once I give this place a *gut* cleaning," she said cheerfully. "Now *kumme* with me to the barn—I'll show you the wood and supplies my *bruder* said you can use."

As Josiah stepped out of the drab, dilapidated little dwelling, he thought, *If she's willing to live in there for over a month in this weather, taking care of her nephew must be really important to her.* By the same token, if her family was forcing her to stay in this *daadi haus* with a child, they must have been adamantly opposed to inviting the boy into their house with them.

It's understandable they'd both have strong feelings about the matter, Josiah thought. But, as Anke had pointed out, her family's situation was none of his business. His only task was to make the tiny house livable again—and that was going to be a big enough challenge.

By late Friday afternoon, Josiah was nearly done repairing the roof. It hadn't been easy; the temperatures were well below freezing and the windchill factor was even lower than that. But he couldn't wear gloves because they'd interfered with his ability to hold nails in place. So it was just easier to go barehanded. It was also slower, because every couple of minutes he kept having to stop and blow on his fingers to warm them.

Also, he'd had to make several trips to the hardware store. Although he'd been able to use some of Ernest's tools, lumber and supplies, he had needed to purchase an equal amount of materials brand-new.

Additionally, there were interruptions from Anke, who seemed to constantly be asking him if he wanted more coffee or something to eat. While he appreciated her consideration, he was concerned if he accepted her offers, she'd take a break with him, too. He was here to work and he didn't want to give Anke the impression he was interested in socializing.

Nor did he want her sister-in-law—who seemed to spend an inordinate amount of time shaking out rugs on the porch—to glance over and see him and Anke standing beside the *daadi haus* eating muffins and drinking coffee together. If she did, Velda might have concluded Josiah was friendlier with Anke than he really was. Or even that he sided with her in regard to the issue of bringing an *Englisch* child into their family and *g'may.* So he always turned down Anke's offers of treats and drinks, even when his stomach was rumbling and it would have warmed his fingers to wrap them around a mug of hot coffee.

Sometimes when he was up on the roof, he could hear Anke singing indoors below him as she scrubbed the floors or washed the windows. He couldn't hear the words, but he could tell by the tune how joyful she was.

I don't understand how she can be so hallich, *knowing that the* leit *are judging her for what she's about to do*, he thought. *If I had a choice, I never would have willingly gone through what I experienced in Illinois. Yet it doesn't seem to make any difference to her.*

Josiah shifted his position on the steep incline and a couple of loose shingles slid over the edge to the ground below. *What this place really needs is metal roofing*, he thought. *It's more durable and it would keep the* haus *a lot warmer.* But he supposed since Anke only intended to stay in it for a month and a half, it wasn't worth the investment.

He descended the ladder and even before he'd reached the bottom, he heard the children's voices nearby and his heart skipped a beat. He had asked Velda to be sure to announce her arrival if she came in the area with the kids. What if one of the falling shingles had landed on them? By the time he got down, they had gone inside.

"Wilkom," Velda greeted him when he opened the door, as if she was the queen of the castle. "*Kumme* in quickly—you're letting the heat out and this place is already too drafty as it is."

"Hello, *kinner*." He tugged on Millie's hat and gave Micah a playful nudge before turning to their mother. "Hello, Velda. You know, you really should be more careful bringing them here," he warned her. "It's not safe—"

Velda's eyebrows shot up and she didn't allow him to finish his sentence. "It's not safe for Anke to live here with Will?"

Josiah could hear the eager hope in her voice. "*Neh.* I was going to say it isn't safe for you to bring the *kinner* here without announcing your presence. I try to keep an eye out for anyone entering the area, but I didn't hear you *kumme* over. A couple of shingles slid off the roof—they could have hit one of you on the head."

"Sorry, I forgot," Velda blithely apologized. "The *kinner* were so excited about seeing where Will and Anke will be staying. Although we can't see all that much—it's awfully dark in here, isn't it?"

"That's because it's a dreary day," Anke explained. "But once the sun comes out again, or when I get a lamp in here, it'll be brighter."

"A kerosene lamp? Won't that be dangerous with a small *bu* in the *haus*? Especially an *Englischer* who isn't used to them? You know how curious some *kind* can be about fire." For some reason, Velda's tone sounded more critical than concerned.

"I wasn't planning to use a kerosene lamp—"

"Well, don't get any ideas about using our propane lamps," Velda interrupted. She seemed to do that quite often. "*We* need them."

Most of the Old Order Amish people Josiah knew didn't use kerosene lamps, either. They utilized gas-powered lights that were built into their walls. Or else they used a different kind of propane lamp; it was attached to a rolling stand that also contained a cabinet where the tank was stored. The entire contraption could be wheeled from room to room. This was the kind of lamp Velda said she couldn't spare for Anke's use.

Josiah noticed that she seemed stingier than her husband when it came to helping Anke prepare the *daadi haus* for Will's arrival. He wondered if she was normally so closefisted or if withholding something Anke needed was Velda's way of expressing disapproval. In this case, Velda's refusal to allow her sister-in-law to use the lamp might have been for the best anyway; using a propane tank in such a small, enclosed area didn't seem like the safest idea.

Apparently, it made Anke nervous, too, because she said, "I had no intention of using a propane lamp in here. I'm going to buy a battery-operated one."

Velda clicked her tongue against her teeth. "My, my. Between paying Josiah to work and all the things you'll need to buy to make this place inhabitable, I'm concerned that the expenses are really adding up."

"It won't cost you a penny, so the worry's all mine," Anke said. She smiled sweetly, but Josiah knew full well what she meant; she was politely indicating her sister-in-law should mind her own business in regard to how Anke spent her money.

Quite honestly, Josiah kind of felt that way about Velda himself. *Why did she bring up the topic of my salary?* It was insulting: almost as if she thought he shouldn't be paid. Granted, if he'd been at a work frolic, he wouldn't have received compensation. But this wasn't a frolic—it was his livelihood.

Before he knew it, he heard himself saying, "My *bruder* has an extra battery-operated lamp you can borrow while he's away, Anke." As soon as the words were out of his mouth, Josiah regretted them. Would Velda tell the others he was going out of his way to help Anke host her nephew?

"Will can use my flashlight so he can find his way to the bathroom in the dark," Asher volunteered. "Or if he wants to look at a book beneath his covers like I do sometimes."

"Denki," Anke replied, grinning at both of them. Then she turned to the twins and asked, "What do you think of this *daadi haus*?"

"I like it," Millie said. "But where are you going to sit?"

"I'm going to bring the folding table and chairs over from the barn."

"I can help you," Asher offered.

"Me, too!" echoed Micah.

"That table's too heavy for you *buwe* to carry," Velda informed them. "*Kumme.* Let's go back to the house and have some hot chocolate."

After the door closed behind them, Anke turned to Josiah, her expression shining. "That's very kind of you to allow me to use your *bruder's* lamp. *Denki.*"

"Don't mention it. As I said, he has a spare," he

said, shrugging off her appreciation so she'd understand he wasn't showing her any preferential treatment. Since he needed to go buy groceries and run a couple of other errands, he told her he'd finished the roof so he was going to leave for the day. "What time is Will coming on *Muundaag*?"

"Around three o'clock, I believe."

"*Gut.* I'll have plenty of time to rehang the front door on *Muundaag* morning." Josiah had noticed it was hanging crooked, so it was letting in a draft. By rehanging the door, he'd create a better seal and the *daadi haus* would feel at least a degree or two warmer.

"Aren't you coming tomorrow, too? It would be *wunderbaar* if you could get a start on the bedrooms. As you mentioned, it's going to be tight quarters for us in here."

"*Neh.* I can't. I'm attending a work frolic tomorrow." Keith had told him about it during one of Josiah's return trips to the hardware store. "I think almost all of the young *menner* from New Hope will be there."

Anke appeared surprised. "*Jah*, they will be. But it doesn't take that many *menner* to raise a workshop—you're the only person who's repairing my *daadi haus*. One day could make a big difference to me, but they probably wouldn't even notice if you're not at the frolic."

Actually, I think they would. But even if they don't, I'm not going to risk it, Josiah thought. "I didn't realize you expected me to work on *Samschdaag*, so I already told them I was coming. I can't change my plans now. It wouldn't be right."

I certainly can't fault him for wanting to keep his word, Anke thought after Josiah left. *And since he's new in town, the frolic will be a* gut *opportunity for him to get acquainted with some of the other* menner *in our district.*

Yet she was still disappointed that he wasn't going to make more progress on the *daadi haus* before Monday. As she'd pointed out, Omer Wilford already had plenty of men—including Anke's own brother—who would help him raise his workshop on Saturday, but she had no one except for Josiah. And now she didn't even have him.

It wasn't for a lack of trying. She had asked Ernest to put out the word that she needed additional help. She'd hoped that some of the older men who weren't assisting Omer might be able to pitch in on the *daadi haus* repairs on Saturday, but they'd all claimed they couldn't. Anke didn't doubt they were busy, but she had the feeling they would have made time to help her if it wasn't for the fact that she was taking in an *Englisch* child.

After all, her sister-in-law wasn't the only person in their district who'd been very outspoken about the decision Anke had made. Just this week while she was out running errands, she'd been stopped on four different occasions by people from her *g'may* who questioned whether she was really doing the right thing by taking care of Will.

Her answer was always the same—"I've prayed about it and it's not a violation of the *Ordnung*, so I believe it's what the Lord would have me do."

But as she looked around the shabby little *daadi haus*, she had her doubts. *Velda's right. It's too dark in here. And there's no furniture.* The folding table and chairs would be fine for mealtimes, but where were they going to sit to relax?

I might as well bring in some bales of hay to use as armchairs, Anke thought ruefully, fighting back the tears. *Despite all the money it's costing me to have this* haus *repaired, it's really not much better than a stable.*

Her intention was to provide a healthy, loving home for Will, but she hadn't fully considered how the boy might feel to live in such a rickety little building. Furthermore, how would Velda's attitude affect him? Anke didn't want Will to feel as if he was less precious in *Gott*'s sight—or in hers—than any of her other nieces and nephews were. But how could he not feel that way if he was rejected by most of his family?

For the first time since she'd made up her mind that she'd watch Will, Anke wondered if she was making a big mistake. So she dropped to her knees and prayed aloud.

"Dear *Gott*, if I'm wrong to keep Will here, please make that very plain to me. It would be very painful to release him into foster care, but if that's what's best for him, please allow it to happen." She stopped praying to dry her cheeks with her apron and then she added, "But if it's best for him to stay here, please protect him from hurtful attitudes. And help us reflect Your grace to Will, and to each other."

As she rose to her feet, Anke noticed a little patch of sunlight dancing on the floor. It was as if the Lord was reminding her He was the source of all the light and love the little home needed, and it made her feel like dancing, too.

Chapter Three

On Sunday, Anke bustled about in the basement kitchen, helping the other women prepare platters of bread, bologna, cheese, Amish peanut butter, egg salad, pretzels, beets, pickles and an assortment of cookies for the after-church meal. Unlike in most Amish districts in the country, some of the Amish communities in Maine, including the one in New Hope, met every other week in a church building instead of taking turns hosting worship in their homes. The central location was one of the advantages of the church and its large, spacious kitchen was another.

"Anke, is it true that Clara is abandoning her *bobbel* with you because she has a drinking problem?" Faith Smoker asked nonchalantly as she filled a pitcher with water. Almost instantly, a hush fell over the room and the other women continued performing their tasks in silence.

Anke would have preferred to keep the particular

details of Clara's situation private within her family, but since that had been impossible from the start she figured it was best to set the record straight honestly and matter-of-factly. "That's not exactly accurate," she clarified. "But *jah*, as you've apparently heard, I did meet with Clara recently and she told me she gave birth to a *bu*, Will, out of wedlock five years ago during her *rumspringa*."

"For shame," one of the older women exclaimed and someone else clicked her tongue. Apparently, this was the first time the two of them had heard the news about Clara, but no one else seemed surprised.

"*Jah*, it is a shame. It was very upsetting to learn about the kind of life Clara has been living since she left New Hope and our *familye*. Especially because we've been praying faithfully for her," Anke acknowledged openly, her face growing hot. As she sliced a loaf of homemade wheat bread, she didn't look up, but she could feel the other women's eyes on her. Although she felt disgraced by her sister's story, she repeated it as straightforwardly as she could, ending, "So that's why Will is coming to stay with us for six weeks."

"Not with *us*," Velda clarified when she entered the kitchen just as her sister-in-law finished speaking. "He's staying with Anke in the *daadi haus*."

"In the *daadi haus*?" Arleta Lehman repeated incredulously. "Is that what Iddo said the *Ordnung* requires?"

Iddo Stoll was New Hope's deacon. After Ernest

and Velda agreed that Will could stay with Anke in the *daadi haus*, Ernest had discussed the situation with Iddo, too, because Velda wanted to be sure they weren't violating any ordinances. "*Neh.* Iddo told my *bruder* it would have been permissible for Will to visit our *familye* on a temporary basis in our home," Anke answered.

"But I think most of the *mamms* here can understand why I don't want Will to live in the same *haus* with my *kinner.* I'm worried about his influence on them," Velda asserted and several of the other mothers of young children indicated they agreed with her concerns.

Anke understood why it was so important that they protect their families from the *Englisch* influence, but she hoped this didn't mean they wouldn't allow their young children to play with Will at all. She assured them, "I'm going to do my best to see to it that my nephew behaves himself and abides by our customs while he's staying with us—with *me*, I mean."

"Of course, you will. Although he's bound to misbehave from time to time, just as all our *kinner* do." Arleta gave Anke a sympathetic smile. "I'm sorry to hear about your sister's situation, but it must have been such a blessing for you to see her again? And to know that as long as she's alive, there's still hope for *Gott* to change her heart."

Anke was almost moved to tears by Arleta's empathy. The young mother of a young daughter seemed to understand what it had meant to Anke to see her sister again—and to focus on God's redeeming power, instead of on Clara's wrongdoings. "*Denki* for asking. You're right—I was overjoyed when Clara reached out to me. Even though I regret the circumstances, I'm *hallich* that I get to care for her *suh*."

"But how will you stay in the *daadi haus*? Is it even habitable?"

"Not yet, but it will be by *Muundaag.* Victor's *bruder* Josiah has been repairing it. He just moved to New Hope from Illinois."

"So *that's* who that *mann* was sitting over by the window," Honor Bawell blurted out, snapping her fingers.

Several women chuckled at her blatant curiosity about New Hope's newest bachelor and then they resumed their separate conversations with each other. Relieved she was no longer the center of their attention, Anke began chatting with Honor, who said a group of singles was going snowshoeing together that afternoon.

"It's going to be a lot of *schpass*," she said. "Faith, Jacob, Keith, Glenda and Ervin are all going. I should invite Josiah, too. His *bruder* must have snowshoes he can borrow. Would you like to *kumme*?"

"I can't. I told Velda I'd watch the *kinner* so she and Ernest can take a nap. Charity is teething so neither of them has gotten much sleep lately."

"Oh, that's too bad. It seems like you hardly ever get to socialize with us single people." Honor stacked a plate high with the bread Anke had been slicing and set it on a tray. "So, tell me, what's Josiah like?"

Anke chuckled, realizing that Honor was already trying to determine if he'd be someone she'd consider as a suitor. "I'll let you decide that for yourself after you meet him."

"Just tell me a little bit," Honor wheedled. "Like if he's quiet or talkative? Serious? Funny?"

Anke certainly wouldn't describe him as talkative. She'd tried to be cordial, but he hadn't accepted any of her offers of coffee or sweets. He seemed rather standoffish and she was inclined to think he wasn't very personable, except he always gave Velda's children a warm hello and sometimes he'd playfully tease them. And he volunteered to allow her to use Victor's lamp, which was considerate of him. Still, Anke didn't have a strong sense of his character, so she simply told Honor, "He's been too busy working on the *daadi haus* for me to chat with him. All I really know is that he's a *gut* carpenter. Very thorough." *He's also very strong and he has the prettiest hair I've ever seen on a* mann, Anke thought. But it would have been an inappropriate remark for her to make. Besides, Honor could see that for herself.

"Humph." Honor made a dissatisfied sound and muttered, "If I didn't know better, I'd think you're deliberately being evasive because you're interested in a courtship with him yourself or something."

"Believe me, I'm not," Anke replied with a

chuckle. Not that she'd tell Honor if she *was* interested in having Josiah as a suitor, but that was beside the point. "I appreciate his work on the *daadi haus*, but right now my sole focus is on preparing a place for my nephew to stay with me."

"All right, but I hope you don't regret it if Josiah winds up courting someone else," Honor warned.

"As I said, courting is the last thing on my mind," Anke reiterated. "But I'm *hallich* to introduce you to Josiah after lunch, if you'd like me to."

"That would be *wunderbaar*." Honor beamed, obviously as determined to enter into a courtship as Anke was to avoid one.

Josiah pushed his hat farther down on his head as he stepped out of the church and crossed the yard. He had almost reached the hitching post when he heard a woman call his name. Turning, he spotted Anke and another woman approaching him. Even before Anke introduced him to the tall, smiling, dark-haired woman, Josiah guessed she was Honor Bawell, the one Victor had told him about.

She welcomed him to New Hope and then invited Josiah to go snowshoeing with a group of young men and women from the district. When she listed their names, he noticed she didn't mention Anke's. "We're going on the trails in the woods by the gorge. It's beautiful there and the conditions should be perfect because of last night's snowfall," she told him, gesturing toward the pristinely white field in the distance.

Among the Amish, Sunday was traditionally considered a day for socializing as much as it was considered a day of rest. But after the incident at the golf course, Josiah had grown so accustomed to keeping to himself on the Sabbath that he'd gotten used to being alone. Also, after a week that included making a long trip, working on the *daadi haus* during the day and his brother's kitchen floor during the evening, as well as attending a work frolic, he was worn-out. He'd been looking forward to stopping at the phone shanty to call his family. Afterward, he intended to go home and relax with a cup of hot cocoa as he read Scripture or one of the books about Maine that he'd found on his brother's shelf. So he declined, saying, "*Denki*, but I don't have snowshoes."

"Doesn't your *bruder* have a pair you can use?" Honor pressed him.

"I—I'm not sure—I haven't looked around for any. But even if he does, I've never gone snowshoeing before. I should get some practice, first, so I don't slow everyone else down."

"You don't have to worry about that—I'm not very fast, either." Honor peered at him from beneath her lashes. "You and I can keep each other company if we lag behind the others."

It dawned on Josiah that maybe she wasn't the community matchmaker after all; maybe she was looking for a suitor for *herself.* Or was she just being friendly? He couldn't tell, but either way, he didn't want to do anything that might result in the two of them spending time alone together. "I appreciate the offer, but I've had a long week and I was planning to go call my *familye* and then relax for the afternoon."

As he was speaking, Keith came up to where the trio was standing and echoed Honor's sentiments. "You definitely should *kumme* with us, Josiah. The way the weather changes around here, you might not get another opportunity like this again until next year."

Before Josiah could refuse for a fourth time, Anke, who had been quietly shifting from foot to foot and rubbing her arms as if she was cold, spoke up. "Quit pressuring him, you two! The poor *mann* just traveled halfway across the country. He probably needs a little time to adjust to being here before he goes mountain climbing on the coldest day of the year with you."

Anke's tone was lighthearted and she was clearly exaggerating so they'd let Josiah off the hook. He shot her a grateful look and she acknowledged it with a discreet little smile and nod of her head.

Josiah was about to remark that she was right, but Keith cut in. There was an edge to his voice as he needled her, asking, "What's the matter, Anke? Are you worried he'll fall and injure himself and then he won't be able to repair the *daadi haus* for you?"

Anke's mouth fell open and she took a step back before replying, "*Neh*, of course not. If Josiah—or anyone else—injured himself, I'd be far more concerned about his well-being than about the *daadi haus*." The ribbon of Anke's winter church bonnet blew across her cheek and as she smoothed it down, Josiah noticed the hurt look in her sea-green eyes. Backing farther away from the group, she said, "My *familye* must be wondering what's keeping me, so I'd better go. Have *schpass* snowshoeing, everyone."

As she walked out of earshot, Keith mumbled, "She's awfully defensive about the *daadi haus*—that's the sign of a guilty conscience."

Josiah had actually found Keith's comment to Anke to be unsettling, too. It was understandable if he disagreed with her plans to care for her *Englisch* nephew, but why had he brought it up when they'd all been talking about a completely different subject? It was almost as if he was antagonizing her, which would have been unkind. *Maybe he was trying to be funny*, Josiah thought, trying to give him the benefit of the doubt.

Instead of acknowledging Keith's remark, he said to Honor, "*Denki* again for the invitation, but as I said, I'm going to relax at home this afternoon. I'll look around the *haus* and barn to see if Victor has any snowshoes. If he does, I'll be able to join you the next time you go."

"Gut." Honor batted her lashes at him. "We'll hold you to that—no excuses if you're tired or the weather's bad."

"Don't worry. No matter how unpleasant the circumstances, Josiah always keeps his word, don't you?" Keith asked.

Puzzled by what he meant, as well as by the sarcasm in his voice, Josiah answered, "With *Gott*'s help, I try."

It wasn't until he'd walked away that Josiah caught on—Keith had been alluding to the fact that Josiah was honoring his word to repair Anke's *daadi haus*, even if it wasn't for an ideal purpose. It was the second time Keith had brought up the topic out of the blue, so it must have really been troubling him. *How many other people in New Hope feel as strongly about Anke's decision as Keith does*? he wondered. No one had mentioned anything about it at the frolic. But then again, no one had done much talking at all—they were too busy racing to raise the workshop before it began to snow. So Josiah couldn't make any assumptions about their opinions on the matter.

I wish I'd never taken the job, he thought as he unhitched his brother's horse from the post. *Fortunately, it won't be long until I'm finished with it and then I won't have to worry about whether or not people are judging me as being guilty by association.*

On Monday morning, Anke was so nervous and excited she could hardly eat anything for breakfast. However, pudgy little Charity leaned forward in her high chair as far as she could, reaching for the untouched slice of French toast on Anke's plate.

"*Neh—neh*, you little *schnickelfritz*." Anke

laughed as she pushed the dish out of reach. "You've had enough bread and syrup. Here, try a little bit of scrambled egg."

"Are there this many days until Will gets here?" Millie asked, holding up her index finger.

"*Neh.* He's coming today, so there are zero more full days left. Like this." Anke curled her fingers into a circle and then peered through them, making Millie giggle. She loved how joyful her nieces and nephews were about Will coming to New Hope.

"He's coming at three o'clock. That's after lunch but before supper," Asher said, repeating to his younger siblings what Anke had told him the night before. "You two might still be napping."

"I don't want to still be napping. I want my eyes to be wide-open so I can see him," Micah objected.

Millie nearly tipped her glass of milk over as she set it on the table and announced, "I want my eyes to be wide-open when Will *kummes*, too."

"You'll all get a chance to see your *gschwischderkind*, but not until your *ant* shows him where he's going to live. He needs to get settled into the *daadi haus*, first." Velda had taken every opportunity to remind her children that Will was only allowed into the main house at her invitation. So Anke was amazed when her sister-in-law added, "Your *daed* and I decided last night that Will and Anke should have supper here in the *haus* with us today. You can meet him then."

Anke suspected her brother was the one who'd

made the decision a long time ago. He'd probably been trying to convince Velda all week that it was the hospitable thing to do. Regardless of how the decision came about, Anke couldn't have been any happier and the children were thrilled, too. They spontaneously erupted in a collective cheer.

"That's a *wunderbaar* invitation, Velda. *Denki*," Anke said.

"Don't get used to it," Velda warned them all sternly. "It's just this one time, in celebration of Valentine's Day."

In New Hope, the Amish usually marked the holiday with homemade cards and special desserts. But because she'd been so focused on preparing the *daadi haus* for Will's arrival, Anke had completely forgotten today was Valentine's Day. "Oh, *neh*!" she exclaimed. "I just remembered that I have to deliver the special-order apron I made to Millers' Restaurant by noon."

The eatery was too far away for her to walk to it and Ernest had taken the buggy to his butcher shop, which was three miles across town. In warmer weather, Anke could have made the trek, but today there was a stiff wind and she still had so many things to get done before Will arrived. *I can't risk upsetting a customer or I might lose business*, she fretted. *And I'm going to need the income now that I'll be buying extra food for Will and me.*

As much as she hated to impose on Josiah, there was no way around it—Anke was going to have to ask if she could take his horse and buggy.

* * *

Josiah was surprised Anke hadn't come to the *daadi haus* yet; it was almost ten o'clock and usually she showed up by nine. He had to give her credit; by cleaning the walls, windows and floors, and by painting the cupboards, she had brightened the dingy kitchen and living room considerably.

But the lack of furniture kept the place from being very cozy. Right now, there were only a folding table and four chairs in the kitchen and a rocker in front of the woodstove in the living room. *Are they really going to sleep on cushions if no one has any cots or beds they can use*? he wondered. He'd rehung the front door, but he could feel a draft coming from one of the living room windows—and the bedroom windows were even draftier.

Ideally, most of the windows in the *daadi haus* should have been replaced. But since he knew Anke didn't have the time or money for him to do that, Josiah decided he'd talk to her about putting plastic wrap over them once he'd finished recaulking the frames. *I need to get more caulk at the hardware store*, he suddenly remembered. *I could pick up the plastic then.*

As he was dithering about whether to go into town now or wait until he'd talked to Anke about purchasing plastic wrap, she burst through the door with two cardboard boxes in hand. *"Guder mariye,"* they greeted each other as she carried the boxes into the kitchen. When she returned he noticed her forehead was puckered with lines and she was biting her lower lip. Was she dissatisfied with the work he was doing?

"I'm afraid I have to ask a favor," she began, before explaining that she needed to deliver an apron she'd made to Millers' Restaurant by noon. "Would you mind if I borrowed your *gaul* and buggy?"

Josiah hesitated, calculating how many miles Victor's horse would have to travel in the blustery weather if Anke went out and returned and then he made a second trip to the hardware store, as well as back home at the end of the day. He supposed he could offer to drop the apron off on his way to pick up the caulk, but he didn't know where the restaurant was. Besides, then he'd have to explain to the Millers why he was running Anke's errand. He didn't want to draw attention to the fact he was working on her *daadi haus*. Finally, he answered, "I have to go to the hardware store, so you can *kumme* with me and drop it off."

"*Denki*, Josiah," she exclaimed and dashed back to the house to get the apron while he went to the stable to hitch the horse and buggy.

Once they were underway, it occurred to him he should have asked if Velda and the children wanted to come with them, too. In his district in Illinois, it wasn't necessarily unusual for an Amish man and Amish woman who were single to share a daytime ride into town in a buggy and no one thought much of it. But Josiah was aware that in some Amish communities, people assumed it meant they were courting. He was so worried about it that he didn't realize Anke had asked him a question until he noticed her eyeing him. "I'm sorry. What did you say?"

"I asked whether Honor talked you into snowshoeing after all or if you were able to go home and get some rest."

"I went home." A moment passed and Josiah recognized he'd sounded cranky, so he asked, "Have you ever been snowshoeing with the group?"

"Once or twice. I enjoyed it, but I couldn't go yesterday because I was watching the *kinner* so Velda could rest."

"Oh. Is she ill?"

"*Neh.* But Charity is teething, so she hasn't been getting much sleep. Neither has my *bruder* Ernest. I'm a little worried about how they'll fare without me around to help—ack! That sounds so boastful, doesn't it? I don't mean it like that. I just know how difficult it can be to care for four young *kinner* when you're overly tired. So for their sake, I hope Charity cuts those teeth soon."

You're the one who probably isn't going to be getting much sleep in the near future, Josiah thought. "At least you'll be right next door if your sister-in-law needs your help—or if you need hers."

"*Jah*, but since she's limiting how often I'm allowed to *kumme* to the *haus* with—" Anke stopped speaking midsentence and pointed out a potato farm owned by the Wittmer family. Then she rambled on about other Amish families who owned farms in their community. But Josiah wasn't fooled. He knew she was trying to distract him because she was embarrassed she'd let it slip that her sister-in-law was limiting her visits with her nephew to the main house.

He certainly understood why Velda wouldn't want her children living with or being influenced by an *Englischer.* But from what he understood, Anke was the owner of both houses on the property and she had voluntarily relinquished the main residence out of regard for her brother and sister-in-law's reservations about Will. So it seemed strange that Velda would feel she had the need or right to impose restrictions on Anke's visits, especially if her intention was to help care for Velda's children.

Josiah reminded himself that their family dynamics were none of his business and he began explaining his observation about the windows in the *daadi haus* to Anke. "It's going to be awfully cold sleeping on the floor, even if you have cushions," he said. "That's why I think it would be wise to put plastic wrap over the windows."

"*Neh*, you can't do that—it will block out the light. Besides, Arleta Lehman said she has two spare cots I can use, so we won't be on the floor after all. She's bringing them over this afternoon. Isn't that *wunderbaar*?"

Josiah didn't have to turn his head to see that Anke was smiling—he could hear it in her voice. *She's so excited about having cots to sleep on that she doesn't even seem to mind that they only have a rocker and a couple of uncomfortable folding chairs for sitting.* He might not have agreed with her decision to take Will in, but Josiah had to admire her grateful, upbeat attitude.

When they reached the Millers' Restaurant, Anke dashed inside to deliver the apron. He hoped when they got to town she'd wait for him in the buggy, just in case people saw them out together. But when they pulled into the parking lot, she said she had to run down the street to buy cocoa for a cake she was making that afternoon. Josiah went into the hardware store and quickly found the caulk he needed, but Keith was helping an *Englisch* customer load something into his car. While Josiah was waiting at the register, Anke came in and stood beside him, pink-cheeked from the wind.

"It's so cold I thought I'd warm up in here until you're ready to leave," she said blithely. Her eyes were sparkling and she gave him such a fetching smile that Josiah felt guilty for wishing she hadn't come into the store. He wasn't worried that Keith would think they were courting, but Josiah suspected he'd have something to say about them being together anyway.

He wasn't wrong. After Keith entered the store and greeted them, he cracked, "So, you're not letting Josiah out of your sight today, eh, Anke? Afraid he's going to walk off the job before he finishes repairing the *daadi haus*?"

His remark instantly drained the exuberance from Anke's features. Her mouth fell open and she blinked several times, but before she could respond, Josiah spoke up. "I believe Anke trusts that I wouldn't walk off a job I agreed to undertake. If anyone seems concerned about my work on the *daadi haus*, it's you, Keith." Realizing he sounded harsher than he'd intended, Josiah grinned and added, "Don't worry—I intend to complete what I started, which is *gut* for business, since I'll probably be back in here buying more supplies again."

Keith furrowed his brow, as if he wasn't quite sure how to take Josiah's comment. It had clearly disconcerted him, though, because he gave him the wrong change after he rang up Josiah's purchase. But he let the matter drop, said goodbye and quickly scurried off.

Josiah and Anke returned to the buggy and neither one of them spoke as they made their way back to her house. They were almost there when she said, "You're right, you know, Josiah. I *do* trust that you won't walk off this job without completing it. And that means a lot to me, especially because…because some people in the community don't agree with what I'm doing. But with the exception of Keith, I don't think anyone will give you a hard time about helping me. *I'm* the one who's hosting an *Englischer*, not you."

Josiah knew from experience that that didn't necessarily mean he was in the clear. He also thought,

I'm not exactly sure that I *agree with what you're doing, either.* But when he glanced sideways and caught sight of Anke fretfully studying him, he said the one positive thing he *did* know for sure. "I think it was *Gott*'s timing that you needed a carpenter and I needed a job."

"*Jah.* Otherwise, Will and I might have had to sleep in the barn," she said with an effervescent giggle that again indicated how good-natured she was being.

Something tells me that still wouldn't have stopped you from taking him in, Josiah thought and he grinned at her before turning his attention back to the road.

Chapter Four

Anke was beside herself with anticipation and nervousness as she paced the gravelly stretch of lane near the end of the driveway. In deference to Velda's concerns, she had agreed to meet Yolanda and Will out of sight from the main house—her sister-in-law hadn't wanted them to see their cousin arrive in a car. Her request didn't make much sense to Anke, since the children already knew he was *Englisch.* Furthermore, Ernest occasionally received a ride in a car from one of the *Englischers* who took him to various fairgrounds where he sold sausages. But Anke was determined not to give Velda any reason to complain that she wasn't being respectful of her wishes. So, she walked back and forth near the road, stamping her feet to keep her toes from going numb.

It must be closer to four o'clock than to three by now. What could be keeping Yolanda? she wondered, hoping it wasn't that Clara had changed her mind. A knot of anxiety tightened in her stomach. *She wouldn't do that, would she?* Suddenly, Anke wished she had asked Josiah to stop at the phone shanty so she could have checked if she had any messages. Her fear that Will might not be coming after all made her stomach cramp and she stopped walking to clutch the fence post.

Please, Lord, bring Will to me soon, she silently prayed. She knew she should also ask for God to give her the grace to accept it if Clara had changed her mind, but Anke couldn't bear the thought. Not after all she'd done to prepare for Will's arrival. And not after harboring so much hope in her heart that her sister was on her way to changing her life around.

Her anxiety subsided and when she heard a car pulling up, she opened her eyes. Yolanda waved to her from behind the steering wheel. Before Anke reached the vehicle, Clara's sponsor had opened her door and stepped out. "Hello, Anke," she called. "Sorry to keep you waiting—my GPS kept rerouting me. Apparently it doesn't recognize this lane as a street."

"It's fine—I'm just glad you're here now."

Yolanda opened the passenger door behind her and a little boy hopped out. He was wearing a blue synthetic jacket and a blue knit hat with orange around the brim and an orange pom-pom on the top. Somewhere in the back of her mind, Anke registered the bright color, which was considered so flashy that some of the Amish men in New Hope had petitioned the state to allow them to wear yellow vests while they were hunting deer, instead of orange. *His hat will be the first thing to upset Velda*, she thought. But Anke's only concern at the moment was drawing near enough to see her nephew's face.

When she did, it took her breath away: he looked almost exactly like Clara had at that age—wide-set blue eyes, wispy blondish hair and an upturned nose. But unlike his mother, Will was slight—even though he was almost Asher's age, he appeared to be Micah's height and weight. His smallness made him seem especially vulnerable and Anke had to refrain from overwhelming him by gathering him into her arms.

"Will, this is your aunt Anke," Yolanda said. "She's going to take really good care of you until your mom is out of the hospital."

"Hello, Will. I'm very happy you're here with me." Anke spoke in *Englisch* and stepped closer. The little boy peered up at her.

"Are you Mommy's big sister? The one who pushed her really high on a swing?"

Anke was caught off guard, moved by the childhood memory Clara must have told him. "Yes, that's right, I am. I can show you the swing and all the other places where your mom used to play when she was a little girl."

Instead of replying, Will ducked into the back seat again and for a second, Anke's heart sank, thinking he wanted to leave. But then he pulled out a green backpack and adjusted it over his shoulders. "Can I go sledding on the really fast hill, too?"

Anke smiled. "*Jah*, once the weather gets a little warmer." She had noticed he was wearing sneakers instead of boots and his synthetic coat didn't appear very thick.

"It sounds like you're going to have a lot of fun here, Will," Yolanda remarked. She removed a small overnight bag from the trunk and handed it to Anke, along with her business card. "That's my cell phone number. I know it isn't easy for you to call, but if you need me for anything, don't hesitate to get in touch. I'll do the same if I…have any updates at all," she said discreetly.

After thanking her, Anke took Will's hand in hers. There wasn't any traffic and she wasn't worried he would slip, but she wanted him to feel a connection to her. Anke expected he might be shy at first since they'd never met and he was in an entirely new location, but he peppered her with questions as they tramped down the long driveway.

"Is this a farm?" he asked, pointing to the big yard.

"*Neh*. But we do grow vegetables for our family to eat in the spring and summer. And we have chickens and a horse and two milk cows."

"Can I pet them?"

"Yes, if an adult is with you and says it's all right. I can show you the animals tomorrow."

"What are their names?"

"We call the cows Brownie and Blondie. The

horse's name is Star and you'll have to ask your *gschwischderkinner* what the chickens' names are because I can't remember them all."

Will stopped to bounce his book bag farther up on his back. "What's a *scwisher-kinner*?"

Anke hadn't realized she'd inserted an Amish word into her sentence. "*Gschwischderkinner* means cousins. You'll meet them later when we eat supper together."

"What are their names? Are they big like me?"

Anke smiled because he'd referred to himself as big and she told him his cousins' names and ages.

"Are they allowed to ride the horse?"

"No one here rides the horse, but he does pull the buggy and you can ride in that someday."

"Is it like the sleigh Santa rides in?"

Anke winced at the reference, but she didn't want to tell him there was no such person as Santa Claus and make him upset before they'd even reached the porch of the *daadi haus*. So she replied, "A buggy isn't open like a sleigh. It has a roof and walls and windows. You'll see one soon."

Anke hadn't realized quite how many Amish customs would be foreign to an *Englischer* Will's age. Hadn't Clara told him anything about their lifestyle? Even if she hadn't mentioned it to him while he was growing up, it seemed she should have told him this week, in preparation for his visit.

Suddenly, Will stopped cold and dropped Anke's hand. "Wow!" he exclaimed.

She immediately stopped, too, concerned he'd seen a moose along the edge of their property. Late afternoon or early evening was about the time of day when they were sometimes spotted in that part of Maine. "What is it?"

"That house is *huge*! Is that where I'm going to live?"

Anke's breath caught and for the briefest second, she had the impulse to tell him, *Yes. Yes, it is—just as soon as I tell my brother and sister-in-law I've changed my mind about staying in the* daddi haus.

"No. That's where your *gschwischderkinner* live. They have six people in their family, so they need more room than you and I do. You're going to live with me, over there." She pointed to the *daadi haus*.

"Wow!" he exclaimed again. "I never got to live in a log cabin before."

Anke's heart was ready to burst with delight over his reaction. *If living in a log cabin makes him that* hallich, *I'm not going to tell him it's called a* daadi haus, she thought as they continued toward it. When they reached the porch, she had to help him climb onto the first step because it was so high and his legs were so short. She could hear Josiah scraping the bedroom window inside and she paused before she opened the door. She hoped Will wasn't going to be disappointed when he saw the inside of his temporary home.

Arleta Lehman had brought over two folding cots shortly after Anke and Josiah returned from their trip to town this morning. So Anke had made up the narrow beds with the heaviest quilts she could find in the linen closet; fortunately, they had so many that Velda couldn't claim she couldn't spare them. Arleta had also given Anke an old armchair that had belonged to her husband's grandmother. She'd said she felt bad that the upholstery was threadbare in spots and that one of the springs poked out in the back, but Anke was very grateful to receive it. She figured it could be Will's chair and she'd take the rocker. In her estimation, they had all the furniture they needed, but Anke didn't know how an *Englisch* child, even one as poor as her sister's son, would feel about living in such a sparsely decorated house.

She turned the handle and pushed the door open, explaining, "Right now, we have to share this room until our bedroom walls and floors and windows are repaired. That's why there are beds in here."

"Me and mommy live in a studio 'partment, too," he knowingly informed her as he unzipped his jacket. "She lets me watch cartoons in bed."

"Hmm." Anke figured she'd better break the news to him sooner rather than later. "I'll let you read in bed, but you can't watch TV because we don't have one here."

"Why not? Did a bad guy steal it?"

"No..." Anke stalled, trying to recall the simple explanation she'd prepared in anticipation of questions like this. "You see, we're Amish. And Amish people don't live the same way other people do. We don't wear the same kinds of clothes or drive cars or use electricity or watch TV."

"Why not?"

By and large, the Amish didn't claim their lifestyle was the right way to live, nor did they claim theirs was the only true faith—doing so would have been considered prideful. So Anke chose her words carefully. "Well, because we believe that God wants us to be different from most of the world. He loves us so, so, so much and He wants us to love Him back—and to love other people, too. But if we're distracted by worldly…by the things a lot of other people do, sometimes we forget to focus on God and on our neighbors. Or sometimes we're tempted to do bad things God wouldn't want us to do."

"Does God think it's bad to watch cartoons?"

Anke had expected Will would have questions about the Amish lifestyle, but she wasn't expecting the boy to be quite so inquisitive. If she had been speaking to an *Englisch* adult, she would have replied that she didn't know the mind of God; she only knew and acted on her own beliefs. But how was she going to put that into an explanation a child could understand?

Having overheard much of Anke and Will's conversation, Josiah recognized what a spot she was in. He'd been waiting for the right moment to introduce himself, because he didn't want to interrupt them. But now it seemed an interruption might be welcome, so he put down his caulking scraper, opened the bedroom door and stepped into the living room. "Hello," he said affably to Anke and the small blond boy she was crouching down beside. There was a look of relief in her eyes as she stood up.

"Hello, Josiah. I'd like you to meet my nephew Will." She put her hand on the boy's shoulder. "Will, this is Josiah."

Will craned his neck to look up at him. "Hi… Are you Aunt Anke's boyfriend?" he asked.

Josiah was startled by the question, but he realized in the *Englisch* world, it wasn't considered unusual, even for a small child, to ask something like that. And he knew Will was probably just trying to get a sense of who was who in his new surroundings.

Anke seemed startled, too. "No, he's not. I don't have a boyfriend," she blurted out, confirming Josiah's hunch that she wasn't courting anyone. Then she added, "Adults here don't discuss things like that with children, Will. But Josiah is a carpenter. He's fixing the bedrooms so we can sleep in them."

"What happened to them?"

"A big branch fell on the roof, so then it had a leak. Some of the water warped the floor. And some of the wood around the windows is rotting out. I need to fix everything to make it nice and safe and warm for you and your *ant*."

"Did it rain on your head when there was a leak?" Will asked Anke, causing Josiah to realize the boy had thought Anke had always lived in the little house.

She probably didn't tell him she had to move into it because she didn't want him to know they've been banished from the main house, he thought. Catching her eye, he mouthed, "Sorry."

Anke gave him a small shrug and then looked down at Will. "*Neh.* I wasn't here when the tree fell onto the roof. No one has lived in this house for a long time. I usually live in the other house, but remember that I told you it's kind of crowded? So Josiah is fixing this house for us so we have room to stretch our arms and legs."

"Thanks, Mr. Josiah," Will said so gratefully it made Josiah feel guilty that he'd ever had second thoughts about working on the *daadi haus.*

"You're *wilkom.* But you don't have to call me mister," he told him. In most Amish communities, children didn't use titles to address their elders the way *Englisch* children did. "You can just call me Josiah."

"Okay," he agreed. "You can call me Will. But not Bill or Billy. That's what my mommy calls my daddy and it makes her very sad."

Josiah felt a mix of compassion and discomfort. On one hand, it was painful to imagine what kind of family life Will must have had. On the other, the child didn't seem to have any understanding about what was appropriate to disclose to a stranger and what wasn't. Granted, most children revealed information that was embarrassing to their parents from time to time. But for the child's sake—and for Anke's, too—Josiah hoped Will wouldn't be this forthcoming about his home life with everyone else in the district. *Anke's sure got her work cut out for her training Will how to conduct himself,* he thought.

She was holding her chin, as if trying to decide what to do next. Figuring she might want to speak with Will in private, Josiah excused himself to the barn. As he was sorting through the lumber Anke's brother said he could use, Ernest returned from the butcher shop early and unhitched his horse and buggy. They chatted briefly and he helped Josiah find the kind of wood he needed. Then he invited him to stay for supper.

"I brought fresh meat home. We're having noodles and sausage," he said, reaching into his buggy and pulling out a thermal bag with one hand and a big pot of cyclamen with the other. "It's a Valentine's Day tradition in our *haus*—the flowers are Velda's favorite and noodles and sausage are mine."

Just the mention of the word *sausage* made Josiah's mouth water. Other than the cold church lunch, he hadn't had a homemade meal since he'd left Illinois. But did he really want to be with the Bachman family on Will's first night there?

Ernest seemed to read his mind. "I can understand your hesitation. It's been a…a tense situation and we've all had to make some difficult decisions. That's partly why I'd like you to join us for a special supper—because I appreciate that you're renovating the *daadi haus*. I would have liked to help, but I didn't have the time. And honestly, I've had to do what my wife and I thought was best for my *kinner*—just like Anke is doing what she believes is best for our nephew and *schweschder.*"

Reading between the lines, Josiah could sympathize about what an untenable position Ernest must have been in. Essentially, he'd had to choose between his wife's and both of his sisters' preferences. "There's no need to explain. No need to thank me, either. Anke is paying me well to repair the *daadi haus.*"

"Then *kumme* join us for supper just because there's nothing that hits the spot on a cold night quite like fresh pork sausage. If we're fortunate, the *weibsleit* will surprise us with a special dessert, too."

Josiah already knew that Anke had made a chocolate cake with buttercream frosting; the tantalizing aroma had filled the *daadi haus* all afternoon. "Sounds too *gut* to miss," he said to Ernest. "Count me in."

Ernest had carried Anke's dresser down from the house on Saturday when he returned from the frolic. She'd asked him to set it in the closet, so she and Will would have easy access to it. Her intention was to use the top two drawers and give him the bottom two. But when she helped him unpack his duffel bag, she realized he hardly had enough clothes to fill half of one of the drawers. *Is that because Clara knows most of his wardrobe wouldn't be appropri-*

ate in our community or is it because that's all he owns? she wondered.

Glancing at his book bag, she said, "You can put the rest of your things in this drawer, here."

"Okay," he agreed and proceeded to shove the entire book bag into the bottom drawer.

"Don't you want to unpack it first?"

"Do I have to?"

Realizing that Will might have brought something from home he didn't want her to see yet, Anke didn't force the issue. "Well, I guess it's okay if we keep your book bag in the closet for now. You can unpack it later. Let's clean up and then you can help me with my surprise. But you have to keep it a secret."

"What is it?"

"You'll have to wait and see."

After they'd washed their hands and Anke had given Will a snack, she told him she needed help decorating the special cake she'd made for Valentine's Day. They frosted it together and then she allowed him to line heart-shaped pink candies around the circumference of the cake and some on top, as well.

"It looks perfect," she told him. "I think your cousins will like it."

"You mean my shwisher-kinner?"

"*Jah*, your *gschwischderkinner*," Anke replied, impressed that he was already trying to imitate her *Deitsch*. She had intended to introduce him to a few words each day, but maybe he'd be ready to learn more rapidly than that. It certainly would be to his advantage, since most young Amish children in New Hope primarily spoke *Deitsch.* Some, like her brother's children, understood conversational *Englisch,* but the majority only learned a few *Englisch* phrases here and there until they went to school. "Do you remember what I told you their names are?"

"Micah and Millie and...Charity and Ashes."

"Asher, *jah.* Your *onkel* is named Ernest and your *ant* is called Velda. They're all very happy to see you so I think it's time for us to walk up there," Anke suggested, setting the cake in a cardboard box she'd used that morning to carry utensils and a couple of pots and pans from the main house. She was half-tempted to suggest that Will leave his orange and blue hat at home and just zip his hood up instead. But she was more worried about his ears getting cold than she was about how her sister-in-law might react to the bright color.

Just as they were ready to walk out the door, Josiah walked in, carrying wood. To Anke's surprise and delight, he said Ernest had invited him for supper. *With Josiah there, everyone will be on their best behavior—and I don't necessarily mean the* kinner, she thought facetiously. But in all seriousness, she appreciated the patient and diplomatic way Josiah had answered Will's many questions. His interactions with the boy had a calming effect on *her* and she felt like Josiah's presence during supper might make Velda feel more comfortable, too.

"I've got a few things to finish and then I'll *kumme* over a little before six," he said.

"No hurry. We're going early so Will can meet his *gschwischderkinner*."

"That means my cousins," Will informed Josiah, as if he didn't know. He pointed at Josiah's head. "Is that a cowboy hat?"

"*Neh.* This is an Amish hat. It keeps my ears warm and the sun out of my eyes."

"I like it," Will remarked.

As they headed toward the main house, the wind whipped right through Anke's coat and Will crossed his arms against his chest. *He must be freezing*, she thought. Usually, Micah received Asher's hand-me-down clothes and shoes. If they were still usable by the time he outgrew them, Velda would pass them on to another boy in their district. But Anke hoped her sister-in-law still had a pair of boots or a coat that Will could use. A couple wool sweaters, too.

When they reached the house, she hesitated on the porch and shifted the box in her arms. She almost felt as if she should knock to announce their arrival, yet something within her rebelled at the idea—it was still her home, after all. But as it turned out, Asher flung the door open from the inside.

"Hi, *Ant* Anke. Hi, Will," he said in *Englisch* and Millie and Micah copied him. Anke introduced them by name and when Velda came into the room carrying Charity, she introduced both of them, too.

"You *kinner* may play in the gathering room. I

don't want you going upstairs," Velda cautioned her children in *Deitsch*. Then she instructed Will in *Englisch*, "When Amish men and boys come into the *haus*, they always take off their hats because that's the polite thing to do. They take off their shoes and boots at the door, too, so they don't track in snow and get the floors wet."

Ideally, jah. *But I've seen Micah and Asher wear their boots in bed while they've been taking a nap,* Anke thought defensively, but she held her tongue. In Amish communities, it was commonplace for adults to instruct and correct all children, not just their own offspring. Will would be expected to mind Velda, just as Velda and Ernest's children obeyed Anke. And if Anke had any qualms about Velda's instructions or vice versa, the women would address them in private, not in front of the children.

Will pulled off his sneakers, revealing a hole in the big toe of his left sock. Straightening up, he asked, "Can I keep my coat on? I'm cold."

"Coats are for outdoors, too," Velda said, but she softened her tone and added, "Asher, go bring Will a sweater from your bottom drawer. And another pair of socks, as well."

Asher charged down the hall just as Ernest came around the corner. When he saw Will, he stopped and did a double take. Anke knew why; it was because of Will's resemblance to Clara. But what surprised her was that Ernest's eyes welled—usually, it was more difficult to read his emotions. *This entire situation with Clara and Will must be troubling him more than I've realized*, she thought.

Ernest blinked and cleared his throat. "Hello, Will. I'm your uncle Ernest. I'm glad to see you," he said.

"Are you my mommy's brother? The one who runs faster than a black cow with big horns?"

Ernest chuckled. "Yes, one time when I was young, I made the mistake of crossing a field with a bull in it and he gave chase. I had to run really fast to make it back over the fence."

"Is a bull going to chase me across the field?"

"No. We don't have a bull here, just cows."

As Ernest reiterated the list of animals Anke had told Will they had on the property, she set the cardboard box down so she could remove her coat and go help Velda in the kitchen. Meanwhile, Asher bolted back down the hall with the sweater and socks for Will. When he'd put them on, the three children ushered him into the gathering room. Listening to their excited commotion, Anke beamed. *Denki, Lord, for helping Will's initial introduction to the* familye *go so smoothly*, she silently prayed. *Please continue to bless our time together.*

When Ernest opened the door, Josiah immediately noticed two things. The first was the sound of the children laughing. The second was the most delectable aroma he'd smelled since he'd left home in Illinois. His uneasiness about eating with the Bachmans immediately lifted.

He barely had time to wash his hands and say hello to the children before the women called everyone to come to the table. As they entered the kitchen, Anke greeted them with an enormous smile. Looking at her, Josiah suddenly remembered that during their teenage years, his mother occasionally told his sisters that nothing was more becoming on a young woman than a joyful heart. It was certainly true in Anke's case this evening; she was radiant with happiness. *I'm so glad everything seems to be going well*, Josiah thought, sitting in the chair Velda indicated was his.

"I hope everyone's *hungerich*, because we made a double batch of everything," Anke announced, practically singing.

"Even the special dessert?" Ernest teased.

"Dessert?" Anke feigned ignorance as she sat down across from Josiah. "Who told you we have dessert?"

Will looked worried. "*I* didn't tell him."

"*Neh*, he didn't," Ernest confirmed. "I guessed it because we always have a special dessert on Valentine's Day."

"There won't be dessert for anyone who doesn't eat their supper. So let's stop chattering and say grace," Velda admonished them.

Everyone bowed their heads, but as Ernest began to pray, Will asked, "Why is everybody hiding their eyes?"

"That's what we do when we thank God for our food," Anke whispered. "Shh."

Ernest began again in *Deitsch*, *"Gott—"*

Will piped up again. "Why doesn't God want us to see Him?"

"Shush," Velda scolded and clapped her hands together so sharply that even Josiah flinched.

He heard movement on the other side of the table, but Josiah didn't open his eyes until Ernest had completed his brief prayer. Then he realized that Will had slunk down beneath the table.

Anke was bending sideways in her chair, saying, "Will, come out from under there." The other children were absolutely silent, except for Charity, who was grunting as she leaned forward, trying to reach the plastic bowl of plain noodles her mother had set aside for her.

While Velda passed the serving dish to Josiah as if nothing had happened, Anke repeated, "Will, come out from under there."

"No," he refused, crying. "I don't want to. I want my mommy."

Velda leaned sideways to look under the table, too. "In this house, children do *not* tell their elders no," she barked. "If you don't behave, you won't be invited back."

"I'm handling this, Velda," Anke snapped, at which point Ernest pushed back his chair, got down on all fours and slid the boy out from beneath the table. He set him on his feet. Will's chin was dropped to his chest and his shoulders bounced up and down as he sobbed.

"Why don't you go with your Aunt Anke and she can get you a tissue," Ernest said quietly into his ear.

Anke took his hand and the pair left the room. Velda's face was scarlet, whether from the blood rushing to her head because she'd been tilting sideways or because she was upset. She continued passing the food around and serving it to the children. But Asher looked as if he was about to cry and Josiah had lost his appetite, too.

It's true that Will needs to learn gut *behavior and follow their household rules*, he thought. *But considering his age and that he's been separated from his* mamm *for the first time in his life, couldn't Velda have been little gentler about it?* Better yet, he thought she shouldn't have interfered at all, since Anke was already addressing the boy's behavior.

"Eat your noodles and sausage, Asher," Velda said.

"My *bauch* hurts."

"If your *bauch* hurts too much to eat supper, then it hurts too much to eat *kuche*, too."

Apparently, Asher's stomach really did hurt that much, because he nodded, but didn't pick up his fork. Josiah asked Ernest about how his business was doing, but he was too distracted by the muffled sound of Will sobbing in the gathering room to pay attention to his answer.

A few minutes later, Anke came back into the

kitchen. "Will has had a long day and I think it's better if we eat alone this evening. I'm going to put some food in a container and we're going back to the *daadi haus*."

Velda pinched her lips together, but she didn't say anything as Anke moved about, filling a glass dish with enough noodles and sausage for her and Will. But when Velda noticed she had taken out a long knife, she objected, "You're not going to slice into the *kuche* before everyone has finished eating supper, are you?"

"Well, it's too cold outside for us to come back later to get our dessert, so *jah*, I am—unless you're willing to bring us two pieces when you're done?" When Velda didn't respond, Anke lifted the cake from the counter and brought it to the table. "Look, *kinner*. Before I cut it, I want you to see the special *kuche* your *gschwischderkind* helped me decorate for you and your *mamm* and *daed*—and for Josiah, too—for Valentine's Day."

Millie and Micah craned their necks and made awed sounds, but Asher said, "Can I be excused from the table so I can give the cards we made to *Ant* Anke and Will?"

Velda was chewing, so she held up a finger indicating she'd answer in a moment, but before she could swallow, Ernest said, "*Jah*, go ahead, *suh*." As the boy quickly left the room, Josiah caught Velda scowling at her husband.

"*Gut nacht*, everyone," Anke said once she had cut and wrapped two pieces of cake for her and Will.

"Gut nacht," everyone except for Charity and Velda chorused.

"Happy Valentine's Day," Josiah added weakly, because nothing about the occasion felt happy anymore.

Chapter Five

Will's sobs had subsided by the time he and Anke returned to the *daadi haus*, but he was shivering so she decided to give him a warm bath. It calmed him down, but afterward he hardly ate three bites of his supper.

"I'm tired. Can I go to bed?" he asked.

Since he was already in his pajamas, Anke said, "Yes. You can go into the living room and I'll come tuck you in in a moment." They had been carrying the battery-operated lamp from room to room, but now she lit a kerosene table lamp in the kitchen so Will could take Victor's lamp with him. She hastily finished her meal and then brought their dishes to the sink.

When she came into the living room, Will was already in bed. He was squeezing his eyes shut tightly, so she knew he wasn't really asleep. She sat down beside him and stroked his head. "Are you going to go to sleep without saying *gut nacht* to me?" she asked.

He opened his puffy eyelids. "Does that mean *good night* in Amish?"

"*Jah*—yes. The language we speak here is called *Deitsch*. Would you like me to teach you more *Deitsch* words?"

"Jah." He propped himself up on his elbow. "How do you say *mommy* in *Deitsch*?"

"Mamm," she replied softly.

"*Mamm*. That sounds kind of the same as *mom*." When he dropped back against his pillow again, Anke heard a faint but definite *clunk*.

"Uh-oh, I must have left something on your bed when I was making it up." She couldn't imagine what it could have been. A book? A kitchen utensil? She slid her hand under the pillow beneath his head.

"No, that's okay. You didn't leave any—" he started to protest.

Anke pulled out a framed, close-up photo of Clara and Will. It must have been what the *Englischers* called a "selfie," because it appeared to be taken at arm's length, above their heads. Clara had one arm wrapped around Will and they were both looking upward, grinning.

"Mommy—*Mamm* said I could keep it under my pillow. She said I could," he wailed, sucking his bottom lip in and out. Anke wanted to cry, too. She'd had her share of experience with young children and she knew even the best-behaved ones were prone to trying to get their way. Often, they used tears to do it. But this wasn't manipulation; this was a little boy expressing utter loneliness for his mother.

Their *Ordnung* prohibited the Amish to be photographed, but Anke thought, *Since he's not Amish, the* Ordnung *doesn't apply to him.* The *Ordnung* was less clear about whether that meant it was permissible for him to keep the photo in her house. Anke's sister was aware of that, too—it was probably why she'd instructed him to keep it hidden beneath his pillow. Or was it because she knew her son would feel loneliest at night?

Either way, Anke felt conflicted. She didn't want to encourage Will to hide the photo, because that seemed as if she'd be encouraging him to be deceptive. Nor did she feel it was prudent to allow him to display it openly, because it would offend her family and visitors. Finally, she handed him the photo and he hugged it to his chest. "You may keep it in your book bag for now and look at it before you go to sleep," she said. Careful not to use the word *hide* or *secret*, she added firmly, "When you're done looking at it, you can give it to me and I'll put it in your backpack in the closet. You can see it again tomorrow night."

Will nodded. He pulled the frame away from his chest and studied it for a long moment before relinquishing it to Anke. She set it aside so she could tuck him in, taking another quilt from her bed and adding it to his. "You must miss your *mamm* very much, don't you?" she said, and he nodded again. "When your *mamm* moved away from me, I missed her very much, too. I still miss her a lot and it makes me sad. When that happens, do you know what I do?"

"Look at a picture of her?"

"*Neh.* Amish people don't have photos. But I do something even better than that. I pray to *Gott* and tell Him how sad I feel." Anke's voice wavered. She paused before continuing, "And sometimes He gives me a picture in my mind of your *mamm* smiling and that makes me not so lonely. I also ask *Gott* to keep her safe and not let her be too lonely, either. I think I'll do that now. Do you want to listen to me pray?"

"Should I close my eyes and do this?" He steepled his hands beneath his chin the way everyone had done while saying grace. Anke seized the opportunity to answer the question he'd interrupted Ernest's prayer with at supper.

"*Jah.* When we talk to *Gott*, we close our eyes and fold our hands because it helps us concentrate on Him. And we're very quiet because we want to hear each other praying."

"I'll be very quiet," Will said, so Anke prayed briefly for her sister and nephew and for herself, too.

When she finished she kissed him on the forehead and said good night and turned the lamp to the lowest setting. Then she went into the kitchen to clean the dishes. She spotted the container of cake on the counter, but she didn't feel in the mood for dessert. *It will just remind me of how hopeful I was and how joyful I felt that everything seemed to be going so well*, she thought.

Once she'd put the dishes away, she went into the living room to complete an apron she'd nearly finished making. *If I can sell a few more of these this week, I should have enough cash to buy Will a warmer coat*, she figured. But the light was too dim for sewing and she had to give up.

Although it was still early, she was so weary and cold she decided she might as well go to bed. As she lay in the dark listening to Will breathe, she ruminated over what had happened at the supper table. She appreciated that Velda was sensitive about the boy's behavior. It wouldn't be good if Asher, Micah and Millie began to imitate Will and interrupted the adults while they were praying. Or if they refused to obey an adult's instructions the first time they were told them, the way Amish children were taught to do from a very young age. But Anke felt resentful that Velda had been so stern about his conduct, considering it was Will's first evening in a new culture with complete strangers.

It wasn't as if Anke had any intention of allowing him to continue to have tantrums at the table, or anyplace else, for that matter. But if he didn't know what was acceptable and what wasn't, how could he be expected to follow the rules? That was why Anke had planned to take him into another room and speak to him in private. But when Velda butted in and chastised him so shrilly, she'd made matters worse. *I guess it's best for everyone if I don't bring Will to the* haus *anymore until I've spent some time helping him understand what's permissible and what isn't*, she decided. Not that her sister-in-law necessarily wanted her and Will to visit anyway, but Anke knew it was unrealistic to keep the children apart indefinitely.

At least Ernest seemed to be a little more patient with Will than Velda was. And if Anke wasn't mistaken, Josiah had seemed sympathetic, too, even though it must have been uncomfortable for him to be in the middle of such a tense family situation. *He really is a kind* mann. *Honor would be very fortunate to have him for a suitor*, she thought.

But as she pictured Honor riding in Josiah's buggy the way Anke had done that morning, she felt a peculiar heaviness in the pit of her stomach. It couldn't be envy, could it? *Neh*, she told herself. *It's just because I ate supper when I was upset.* So she clutched a pillow against her stomach, rolled over and went to sleep.

Josiah waited an extra hour before going to Anke's in the morning. He figured that she and Will might not have gotten a good night's rest and needed to sleep in. But when he arrived, he found them both in the barn, where he stabled his horse because the weather was too cold to tie him to the post outside.

"Good morning," he greeted them in *Englisch* after he'd unhitched the buggy.

"Gudermariye," they both said in unison.

Anke had dark circles beneath her eyes, but her

cheeks were rosy and she was smiling. "Will's learning to speak *Deitsch*," she explained.

"And I learned to *millich* the *kieh*," he added happily, using the plural form of *cow* as the three of them walked outside into the bright sunlight. "*Onkel* Ernest showed me. *Ant* Anke and I collected *oier* from the *hinkel*, too."

After Will took off across the snowy yard toward the *daadi haus*, Josiah remarked, "You must have gotten up pretty early for him to *millich* the *kieh* with Ernest. I thought you might have needed some extra sleep. Otherwise I would have been here at my usual time."

"I'm just glad you came back after last night's supper," Anke said softly. From the lines on her forehead, Josiah could tell she was serious. He was touched that she was so concerned about his comfort, when she was the one dealing with so much. "I'm sorry if it was upsetting for you to be in the midst of all that…that chaos."

"Don't apologize. I have eight young nephews and nieces in Illinois, so I know that not every *familye* meal is a picnic."

"I'll have to remember that—not every *familye* meal is a picnic," Anke said with a chuckle. "I hope you at least enjoyed the *kuche*?"

Josiah had only eaten a small piece and honestly, he'd hardly recalled swallowing it. He didn't want to offend Anke, nor did he want to lie. "I, um…"

"Be honest—it was dry, wasn't it? I was afraid of

that. It's such a rich cake that I worry about getting it done enough. As a result, sometimes I keep it in the oven too long."

He stopped walking and met her eyes. "*Neh.* It wasn't dry. Or if it was, I didn't notice. I sort of ate it fast and then I left, so..."

"Ah, I see. I hardly remember eating supper when I got back to the *daadi haus*, either. However, I saved my dessert. I know you don't like to take breaks when you're working, but you can have my slice with your lunch. If you like chocolate, I think you'll really enjoy it." She looked expectantly at him. Josiah noticed that instead of appearing greenish, today her eyes were closer to the frosty-blue color of the sky.

"Actually, I don't know if I can wait until lunchtime. I'm already *hungerich,*" he said. "But I don't want to eat your entire dessert, because then you won't have any. Let's share it when I'm done repairing the sills on windows in the front bedroom, okay?"

"Perfect." Anke turned and they continued walking toward the *daadi haus* where Will was climbing the porch stairs.

"I should add another step. Those are too high. He can hardly get up that first one."

"*Jah.* Neither can Micah and Millie. They have to use their hands to boost themselves up. It reminds me of bear cubs climbing trees."

When Will had reached the top, he turned around and called, "*Ant* Anke, how do you say *log cabin* in Amish?"

"Daadi haus," she called back. When Josiah tipped his head at her, confused, she waved her hand and said, "Don't ask, cowboy." Her answer gave Josiah such a belly laugh he had to stop to clutch his sides.

"What's funny?" Will questioned.

"We're both just very *hallich* this morning," his aunt answered.

"I'm *hallich*, too," Will said and from the smile on his face, Josiah knew he understood what *hallich* meant.

For the next couple of hours as Josiah worked in the front bedroom, he could hear Will asking Anke questions. She never seemed to get exasperated, even though her nephew was far more outspoken about his curiosity than most Amish children Josiah knew in his district. But then, Will probably had more questions because he hadn't grown up in this culture. *I might be a newcomer to this district, but Will's a newcomer to this entire lifestyle*, Josiah realized. *For such a young* bu, *he's awfully brave.*

After a while, Anke's and Will's voices died down and then he heard the front door close and he figured they went outside. They were back within fifteen minutes, no doubt because the boy's flimsy jacket didn't keep him warm enough in the subfreezing temperatures. Josiah waited a few minutes so they could warm up by the stove before he emerged from the bedroom and announced, "I'm *hallich* you're back. I was about to take a break."

Anke put on a pot of coffee and warmed some

milk for Will. She was going to split her slice of cake between Josiah and her, and allow her nephew to eat the smaller slice she'd cut for him. But Will insisted he wanted to share his cake with Josiah, too. Since the child was still cold, Anke suggested they eat in front of the woodstove. Will allowed Josiah to use the armchair and he dragged in a chair from the kitchen. Anke sat in the rocker.

"Do you think Asher and Micah and Millie are going to *kumme* outside and play with me pretty soon?" Will asked his aunt with his mouth full.

"It's not polite to speak when you have food in your mouth, Will," she said, holding a finger to her lips. "I don't know if your *ant* Velda will allow your *gschwischderkinner* to play outside today. It might be too cold."

"Aww." Will opened his mouth again to complain, even though he hadn't swallowed his cake.

"You know what I like to do when I'm eating *kuche* that tastes as *appenditlich* as this tastes, Will?" Josiah asked, so Anke wouldn't have to correct the child again. "I like to take a nice big bite—not too big, but big enough to taste the frosting *and* the cake—and I just let it melt in my mouth for as long as I can. That way, all of my taste buds can really enjoy how sweet and rich it is. Like this." He showed Will what he meant and the boy imitated him.

After that, the three of them quietly ate their cake, with no sound except for the fire crackling and their forks scraping against their plates. After he'd taken the last bite, savoring its dense, chocolate texture, Josiah glanced up to see Anke watching him. He smiled and gave her a satisfied nod to indicate how much he enjoyed the dessert.

Actually, it wasn't just the dessert he enjoyed; it was the coziness of the fire and the pleasure of being in Anke's and Will's company. Unfortunately, ever since the incident at the golf course, Josiah was on the defensive, so he rarely felt this relaxed around anyone outside his family. While Anke and Will continued to eat their cake, he stretched his legs out in front of him, in no hurry to get back to work.

"That was *gut*," Will said, smearing chocolate across his face as he wiped his lips with the back of his hand. Anke handed him a napkin.

"That's for sure," Josiah agreed.

"*Denki.* I'm *hallich* you both enjoyed it."

She had no sooner finished her sentence than there was a knock on the door. Will flew across the room to open it before Anke could put her plate down. It was Honor Bawell, of all people, and she was holding a plastic container in her hands.

"Gudermariye," Will exuberantly greeted their visitor.

Anke shot across the room behind him and Josiah hopped up from his chair, too. "*Gudermariye*, Honor," she echoed.

"Hello, Anke. Hi, Josiah." Honor looked down at the boy. In *Englisch* she asked, "Are you Clara's son?"

"*Jah.* This is Will, my nephew," Anke piped up.

"I can get a chair for you," the child offered Honor.

"*Neh.* She can use mine. I need to get back to work," Josiah said.

"You do? But I made Long John Rolls." She held up the container. "They're best when they're eaten fresh."

Ordinarily, it was true; the oblong frosted donuts were best when eaten the same day they were made. However, Anke knew there was no good day to eat anything Honor baked—she had an uncanny talent for ruining virtually every recipe she attempted. As her own mother once joked, "Honor can't serve a cup of *kaffi* without getting eggshells in it." But that didn't stop her from trying and from handing out her confections to unsuspecting bachelors like Josiah. Anke hoped for his sake he was too full to accept.

"What's a Long John Roll?" Will asked.

"It's a doughnut with frosting on the top, but it's long instead of round," Anke explained in *Englisch.*

"Yum. Can I try one, please?"

"You've just had a piece of *kuche.* No more sweets for you," his aunt told him.

"I've just had a piece of *kuche*, too, so I'll have to pass," Josiah said, putting on his coat. "I'm going to be working on the window frame from outdoors."

Honor's face fell. "That's too bad, but I'll leave you these for later. By the way, did you find out if your *bruder* has snowshoes?"

"Uh, I believe I saw a pair hanging in the mudroom, *jah*."

"*Wunderbaar!* We've got another trek planned this *Sundaag*. We're meeting at the gorge at one thirty, after everyone has finished their home worship services and eaten lunch."

"Oh, well, I..."

"You can't say *neh*. You promised me, remember?"

Josiah promised Honor he'd go snowshoeing with her? Anke wondered. *Is that why he's turning red—because he's interested in her already?*

"*Jah*, that's right. I'll be there, weather permitting." Josiah walked toward the door, but Honor was in his way, and as he tried to go around her, she stepped in the same direction. When she moved to the other side at the same time he did, accidentally blocking him again, she giggled. "Excuse me," he mumbled and squeezed by her and out the door.

Honor unbuttoned her coat and began to take it off, but then changed her mind. "It's chilly in here. I'll keep this on while we're having *kaffi*," she said, which meant she was staying.

She's never kumme *to visit me at this time on a weekday before*, Anke thought as she went into the kitchen to pour Honor a cup of coffee. *I'm sure her primary purpose in coming was to see Josiah, not me. Not that I care—I told her I didn't mind if they ended up courting and I meant it.* But she, Josiah and

Will were having such a nice, peaceful time together that Anke wished it hadn't been cut short.

When she returned to the living room, she found Will reciting all the Amish words he knew to Honor. How was Anke going to keep him occupied while the two women were visiting? Like most Amish people, she didn't believe a child should be privy to adult conversation, nor did she believe children should have to be constantly entertained. However, she couldn't send him to one of the bedrooms, because both of them were in various states of disrepair and they were drafty. Nor could she send him outside to play because it was too cold. Once again, she wished she would have checked some picture books out of the library.

After serving Honor coffee, Anke asked Will to come into the kitchen. "While I'm visiting with my friend, you may sit in here and use these crayons to draw a picture for Asher and Millie and Micah, since they made Valentine's Day cards for us." This morning, she and Will had opened them and taped them to the wall above the boy's bed. Since the children were so young, it was difficult to tell what they had drawn, but the pictures added a splash of color to the room.

Once Anke had Will situated, she returned to the living room to visit with Honor, who chattered almost nonstop. After an hour she wished her visitor would be on her way. But because Anke was no longer responsible for keeping a big house and she wasn't helping Velda care for her children, she didn't have any pressing reason to excuse herself. *I hope Honor doesn't stay until lunchtime in hope of visiting with Josiah during his break*, she thought.

Fortunately, Will came into the living room a few minutes later. "I finished all my pictures. Want to see them?"

Impressed that he'd been working so intently for this long by himself, Anke said, "*Jah.* Show us what you drew."

Although childlike, his pictures had an astonishing amount of detail for someone so young. Even if he hadn't announced what he'd drawn as he presented each sheet of paper, Anke would have been able to discern what he'd depicted. A mother rabbit with a baby bunny for Charity. Two birds in a tree for Millie—the tree also had a wooden swing, like the one Anke had shown him Clara used to swing on. A frog and a dog for Micah.

"This is for Asher," he said, holding up the last one.

Anke immediately recognized what he'd meant to illustrate, but Honor questioned, "What are all those horses pulling? A plough?"

"Those aren't *geil*," he told her, recalling the Amish word for horses that Anke had taught him. "They're reindeer. That's Santa's sleigh. See? He's got lots of presents."

Honor's eyes grew wide. To Anke, she said, "You're not going to let him give Asher that, are you?"

Anke discreetly shook her head, but Will caught

her. Wide-eyed, he cocked his head and said, "But I made it for him."

"I'll explain after Honor leaves," Anke said pointedly, standing up and retrieving her and Will's coats from the closet. "Let's walk her to her buggy, Will. We can see her *gaul*."

The promise of seeing a horse was enough to temporarily distract Will. He set the pictures on his bed and hurried to put his coat on. When they stepped outside, Honor said, "I'm just going to pop around the corner to say goodbye to Josiah. You go ahead and show your nephew my *gaul*. I'll be right there."

It's one thing if she wants to speak with Josiah in private, but she should do that on her own time, Anke thought, annoyed that Honor was dismissing her as if *she* was the visitor. *It reminds me of how I felt about being in my own* haus *yesterday evening.* But since she wanted to be a good example to her nephew, Anke complied and led him to the barn so Honor could be alone with Josiah.

I should have brought the stepladder out here, Josiah thought, stretching to pound a stubborn nail into the window frame. He didn't hear anyone approach so he flinched when Honor touched his shoulder. "Sorry," she said. "I said your name, but you didn't answer."

"You're fortunate I didn't swing my hammer farther back than I did or you might have gotten a black eye," he told her, and she laughed, as if he was trying to be funny. Honor didn't seem to have any more sense about safety than Velda did.

"I'm leaving now, but I wanted you to know that Anke put your Long John Rolls in the kitchen—I hope she doesn't allow her nephew to get into them. He doesn't seem to understand what's forbidden here."

Of course he doesn't. He hasn't even been here for twenty-four hours, Josiah thought. "*Denki.* I'll take them home with me. Bye, Honor."

She didn't budge. "I also wanted to remind you about snowshoeing at the gorge. One thirty on *Sundaag.* Okay?"

"*Jah.* I said I'd be there and I will."

"Because you always keep your word," she said, giggling as if it was some kind of private joke between them.

Josiah turned back to the window frame and raised the hammer. "Watch yourself. You're too close," he warned. So she stepped away, said goodbye and finally left.

Josiah was frustrated for a number of reasons. First, as careful as he was being in his work on the *daadi haus*, he regretted repatching the holes in the roof and essentially tacking on windows. The place needed a complete overhaul, not just a few coverups here and there. Second, he was really cold and he wouldn't have come outside at all to work right now if Honor hadn't stopped by. Third, he wished he hadn't committed to going snowshoeing with her and the other singles their age. He didn't intend to be vain, but it was relatively clear to him that Honor was behaving flirtatiously toward him.

And Josiah was *not* interested in courting again. But if he was, it wouldn't be with someone like her. Honor was certainly attractive and generous and friendly. But he preferred someone who didn't seem so…so frivolous. Someone who had priorities that she pursued as intently as she pursued a suitor. Someone who was more mature. Someone like Anke.

Where did that thought kumme *from*? he asked himself. *This cold weather must be getting to me.* His fingers were numb and he couldn't get anything else done out here, so he headed inside. As usual, he closed the bedroom door behind him to prevent the warm air from escaping from the living room. A few minutes later, he heard Anke and Will come in.

"Can we bring my pictures to my *gschwischderkind* before we take our coats off?

"*Neh.* It's almost time for lunch," Anke said, but Josiah guessed she was stalling. He could have been wrong, but from the little he knew of Velda, he figured it would be a while before she'd let Will play with her children again.

"After lunch?"

"*Kumme* sit here with me, Will," Anke said. Even though Josiah knew he shouldn't listen in, the softness of her voice made him curious. "I like the pictures you made for Micah, Millie and Charity. But Amish *kinner* don't believe in Santa Claus, so I'm afraid you can't give the picture of the reindeer to Asher."

"But…but if he doesn't believe in Santa Claus, who gives him presents at Christmas?"

"Well, his *mamm* and *daed* give him a gift. I do, too. But Amish people celebrate *Grischtdaag*—that means Christmas—by worshipping *Gott.* We sing and pray and at *schul* the *kinner* have a pageant, which is a lot of fun. And we have *gut* things to eat and we spend time with our friends and *familye*."

In the long pause that followed, he imagined Will was trying to absorb what Anke had told him. Josiah didn't move, afraid that it would be obvious he'd been eavesdropping. Finally, Will said, "If I draw a picture of something else for Asher, then can we take them to my *gschwischderkind* after lunch?"

"We'll see."

"But I won't draw Santa—"

"Will." Anke's voice was firm. "When an adult gives you an answer, you may not argue with them. Do you understand me?"

He must have nodded because the next thing Josiah heard Anke say was that he should go wash his hands so he could help her crack eggs into the pan for lunch.

"Oier?" he asked.

"*Jah.* That's right. *Oier.* Very *gut*."

When he heard footsteps scampering down the hall, Josiah resumed his assessment of the work he still needed to complete on the window. But first, he was going to have his lunch. He set down his hammer on the sill and the entire board fell off from the tool's weight. "Arg," he moaned, louder than he'd intended.

The door suddenly opened and Anke questioned, "Are you okay?"

"*Jah.* But this sill isn't." He pointed to it.

She chuckled. "That must be exasperating, but I'm *hallich* it's only the wood that fell off and nothing happened to you."

"*Jah.* At least the window is reparable, so I shouldn't be upset. But I think I need to take my lunch break now. I'll be back when I'm done."

"Did you leave your lunch in your buggy? It will be frozen. You're *wilkom* to join Will and me for scrambled *oier.*"

Josiah hesitated. Usually he ate his lunch in the barn, because he hadn't wanted to give her the impression he was interested in socializing with her. Nor did he want Velda to read anything into his actions and decide he was siding with Anke. But now that he'd been a guest at the Bachmans' table, Josiah wasn't as worried anymore about what Velda thought of him. And this morning it had been so pleasant taking a break indoors with Anke and her nephew. *Why not?* he asked himself.

To Anke, he said, "*Denki.* That sounds *gut.*"

In fact, it sounded terrific.

Chapter Six

After four days, Anke still hadn't seen Velda or the children outside once, not even to hang her laundry. *She must be hanging her clothes in the basement to dry because it's so cold outside*, she thought. But Anke couldn't entirely rid her mind of the nagging feeling that her sister-in-law didn't *want* to see her. Or, more likely, that she didn't want her children to see Will. Anke wouldn't push, since she had previously agreed she wouldn't visit the house with Will without an invitation. However, by Thursday, she needed to retrieve additional sewing supplies and material from her room.

She decided she'd run over to the house while Josiah and Will were eating, since he agreed to keep an eye on the boy while she was gone. Josiah had been joining them inside for lunch all week. Sometimes he brought his own and sometimes he ate eggs or grilled cheese sandwiches with Anke and Will. She considered their lunch hour to be the best part of the day, primarily because Will was so enraptured by everything Josiah said and did. But also because Anke appreciated having another adult around to chat with and she enjoyed learning about Josiah's family and life back in Illinois. So she regretted missing any part of their time together and she dashed up to the main house as quickly as she could.

Rapping once on the door to announce her presence, she let herself in, calling, "It's me."

Asher raced down the hall in his stocking feet, almost knocking into her as he skidded to a stop. "Hi, *Ant* Anke." He hugged her around her waist. "I missed you. Where's Will?"

She tousled his hair. "He's eating lunch. I just popped in to ask your *mamm* a question."

The boy released her. His shoulders drooping, he led her to the kitchen. "She's making *supp*."

When Anke entered the kitchen, she found her sister-in-law opening a store-bought can of cream-of-chicken soup. Was that what she was serving the children for lunch? Usually, Anke only used canned soup in a pinch if she needed to make a gravy base for a casserole.

Charity was banging a spoon against her high chair with one hand and mashing a piece of banana into her mouth with the other. The twins were nowhere to be seen.

"Hello, Velda. I came to get some material from my room." When her sister-in-law didn't turn around to face her, Anke knew it was time to clear the air. So she said, "Asher, could you please go get my sewing bag for me? It's the big blue one in my closet. It's kind of heavy—do you think you can carry it?"

"*Jah*, I can. *Daed* brought us steak last night for supper. He said protein makes us strong."

After the boy disappeared down the hall, Anke asked, "Are you still upset about what Will did the other evening?"

"*Neh.*"

Velda's curt answer wasn't convincing, but Anke decided to take her at her word. As long as her sister-in-law considered the matter to be over, she figured she might as well ask if the children could spend time together that afternoon. "*Gut.* Because I know the *kinner* would like to play together—even it's only for twenty minutes or half an hour. They could make a snowman or run around in the yard. I've been teaching Will what kind of behavior is expected here and he seems to understand. I can't promise he won't misbehave, but I'll address it quickly if he doesn't."

Velda finally turned around to face her and Anke noticed immediately how frazzled she appeared. Also, she had something—oatmeal?—crusted on her forehead. "Okay, I'll give him another chance. But you'll have to supervise them, because as you can see, after lunch, I still have breakfast dishes to do."

Anke was so thrilled that Velda was allowing the children to play together that she offered, "If we let the *kinner* play indoors, I could do the dishes and you could take a nap. You look a little tired. Besides, it's so cold out there."

"I shouldn't nap. I have laundry I haven't put through the wringer, yet."

Anke recognized a hint when she heard one, but again, all she could think about was how happy Will and his cousins were going to be to spend time together. "I'll take care of that, too. It's fine."

"Oh, all right," Velda said with a sigh, as if she was the one doing Anke a favor instead of the other way around.

Asher trudged back into the room with Anke's canvas bag and Micah and Millie followed on his heels. They enveloped their aunt from opposite sides of her legs and told her they'd missed her, too, just as Asher had done.

"Guess what? When you're done eating your *supp*, I'm going to bring Will back here to play with you."

The three children's cheers startled Charity and she flung a handful of banana onto the floor.

"Now look what you made her do!" Velda scolded and Anke wasn't sure whether the comment was directed at her or the children.

She really must be exhausted to be so easily agitated, Anke thought. *The sooner she takes a nap, the better for everyone.* "It's okay. I'll wipe it up." When she was done, she hurried back to the *daadi haus* to tell Will the good news.

"Where's your bag?" he asked and Anke noticed his mouth was full. Fortunately, he wouldn't be eating at the main house, so she still had time to work with him on table manners.

"I was so excited I forgot it at your *ant* Velda's."

"Why are you excited?"

"Because she invited you over to play with your *gschwischderkinner*!"

Instead of the joyful outburst she was expecting, Will knitted his brows together. "Aren't you coming with me?"

Anke noticed that his question made Josiah wince. Like Anke, he must have recognized that Will was apprehensive about receiving another scolding from Velda. "*Jah.* Of course, I'm coming with you. I'm going to help do *Ant* Velda's housework while she's napping. Maybe I'll have time to work on my aprons, too."

"I'll bring my pictures." Will had made a second drawing for Asher to replace the first; this one was of two boys chasing chickens.

"First, go wash your hands so you don't get them sticky."

After Will left the room, Anke said, "*Denki* for keeping him company while I was gone, Josiah."

"It was no trouble."

"Did he ask you one hundred and one questions?"

"One hundred and two," Josiah joked, his blue eyes twinkling. "But it was fine. He's just trying to make sense of his new world."

If Honor had asked me today what Josiah is like, I would say he's very patient and understanding and he's got a gut *sense of humor*, Anke mused, recalling the question her friend had posed to her in the kitchen at church. To Josiah, she said, "Still, he's so curious that it can be tiresome for an *eldre* to respond to him after a while. At least, I feel that way sometimes. I'm *hallich* I'll get a little break while he's playing with his *gschwischderkinner*."

"Seems to me that Velda's the one getting the break, not you."

Anke didn't understand what he meant at first and then she realized she'd mentioned she was going to help Velda with her housework. "Oh, I don't mind doing a few dishes. I'm so used to managing a bigger household that it feels strange for me just to have two people to clean up after. My *schweschder*-in-law looked utterly beat and I know she'll feel better after a nap. Besides, I'd gladly clean the *haus* from top to bottom if that's what it takes for Will and his *gschwischderkinner* to spend time together."

I know you would. Your dedication to doing what's best for Will—and for others—is one of your most winsome qualities, Josiah thought, peering into Anke's eyes. He couldn't say it, though, so he broke his gaze and stood up. "I'm going into town to pick up some PVC windowsill protectors. They'll last longer than these wooden sills. Is there anything else you need at the hardware store while I'm there?"

"*Neh*. But *denki* for asking."

Will returned to the room and the three of them

put on their coats and stepped outside at the same time. Josiah noticed the boy was pulling on Anke's hand like a puppy on a leash, dragging her toward the main house.

Dear Lord, he's so excited—please help him to have a gut *time and for everyone, including Velda, to be kind and forbearing to each other*, he prayed as he walked toward the barn to hitch his horse and buggy and ride into town.

Josiah entered the hardware store less than half an hour later, just as Ben Nisley, Victor's nearest neighbor in New Hope, was coming toward the exit. The men stopped to greet each other and exchange small talk before Ben said, "My wife and I are aware you're on your own for a while. Would you like to join us for worship this *Sundaag*?"

The Amish only met together for worship every other week. On "off-Sundays" they met with their immediate family members in their own homes. Because Josiah was alone and didn't have anyone to worship with, he gratefully accepted Ben's offer. "I'd appreciate that. But I made a commitment to go snowshoeing at one thirty—will your wife be offended if I leave right after lunch?"

"*Neh.* Of course not. She's still young enough to remember what it was like when we were courting age—she'll be *hallich* you're getting out and having *schpass* with your peers."

Although Josiah was surprised by Ben's mention of courting, he let the comment pass. After saying goodbye, he browsed the aisles until he found the windowsill protectors he'd come to buy and set them on the register in front of Keith.

"I heard you making plans to worship with Ben's *familye* on *Sundaag*," Keith remarked. "Is Anke going, too?"

"Anke? Why would she worship with the Nisleys? She lives clear across town from them."

"*Jah*, but birds of a feather."

"What do you mean by that?"

He shrugged. "You know. The Nisleys rent out their *daadi haus* to *Englischers* and Anke allows her *Englisch* alcoholic *schweschder*'s *suh* to stay in hers. My *schweschder*-in-law Ruth said Anke won't be allowed to worship with her *familye* on *Sundaag* since Velda doesn't want her nephew being part of their service. I figured the only people who might not mind if she brings the *bu* with her would be the Nisleys—and you."

Josiah responded quietly but firmly. "As far as I know, Anke won't be worshipping with us. But neither the Nisley *familye* nor Anke is violating the *Ordnung* because it's not a violation to allow a guest to worship with the members of this district on occasion, whether at home or in *kurrich*."

Omer Wilford, the man whose workshop Josiah had helped raise the previous Saturday, had come up to the counter beside Will. "It may not be a violation of the *Ordnung*, but that doesn't mean it's a *gut* idea," he interjected. "Frankly, I'm surprised Iddo Stoll didn't discourage Anke more strongly from taking the *bu* in. It seems unfair to those *familye* with small *kinner* that just because she has chosen to allow an *Englischer* into her *haus*, the rest of the district has to allow him into our worship services."

"He's only a young *bu* and he won't be in New Hope for very long. I don't think he'll lead the other *kinner* astray," Josiah argued. "Most of them don't even speak *Englisch* well enough to converse with him."

"They don't have to speak with him—temptation usually starts with the eyes," Omer said. "My *kinner* are old enough to recognize the differences between the *Englisch* and the Amish. It might seem innocent on the surface to invite an *Englischer* to worship with us, but before we know it, our *kinner* will want to wear bright clothes and talk on cell phones, too."

Will is only five years old so he doesn't have a cell phone—but both of you *do. Even if you only use them for business purposes, your* kinner *might be just as tempted to wish they had a cell phone by watching you make calls as they are by anything Will does*, Josiah thought. But he felt too intimidated to voice his opinion.

"It's not just young *kinner* who can be led astray by socializing or worshipping with *Englischers*." Keith stared directly at Josiah, even though he was replying to Omer. "If *eldre* spend too much time around *Englischers*, they can be tempted to blur the lines between the world and us, too. Especially when it involves someone an Amish person cares about, the way Anke cares about her alcoholic *schweschder*. But it's not long before a person starts making excuses and compromises they wouldn't have made if they'd stayed away from the *Englisch* altogether."

"Amen!" Omer uttered. "That's why I'm opposed to an *Englischer* living in our community. I sure won't let my *kinner* go anywhere around the *bu*—or even around other *kinner* who go around the *bu*. And I intend to arrive early to *kurrich* and sit in the front row so my *kinner* won't be able to see Anke's nephew."

Keith snickered. "Problem is, there are so many other people in the district who feel the same way that the front bench might already be filled, no matter how early you get to *kurrich*."

When Omer cracked up, Josiah forced himself to chuckle, too. Then he paid for his purchase and said goodbye. He hurried out the door and down the street to his buggy, his stomach churning. It was clear to him that no matter how fond he was growing of Will and Anke, he had to distance himself from them. If he didn't, other people in his new community would distance themselves from *him* and he'd wind up as miserable in New Hope as he'd been in Illinois.

I can't fault Velda for napping for so long, Anke thought. *I'm the one who told her to sleep as long as she needed to.* But she would have weighed her words more carefully if she'd known her sister-in-law was going to sleep for almost three hours.

During that time, Anke had washed, dried and put away the breakfast and lunch dishes, as well as run the laundry through the wringer and hung it up in the basement to dry. She'd also scrubbed the kitchen floor, which was encrusted with the same oatmeal she'd noticed on Velda's forehead, and cleaned the bathroom.

She'd completed most of these tasks while lugging Charity around on her hip—the baby was unusually clingy because she needed a nap, but she refused to take one. Anke didn't want her wailing to disturb Velda's rest, so she gave up trying to put her down. In between these chores, Anke had supervised the children as they'd colored and played with blocks. She'd also let them help her scrub potatoes for supper, which really amounted to allowing them to splash around in the sink. Finally, Charity fell asleep, so after putting her in the crib upstairs, Anke suggested the children quietly look at the books Velda had checked out of the library.

Anke had barely sat down and sewn ten stitches on an apron hem when she heard Charity fussing. She went upstairs again to discover the baby was in urgent need of a diaper change. As Anke cleaned her up, she could hear the children getting rambunctious downstairs, but by that time, she didn't care if they woke Velda, so she continued dressing the infant. Now Charity was wide awake, so Anke decided to take her back downstairs.

"Did you have a *gut* rest?" she asked when she saw Velda coming out of her bedroom.

"*Jah*—until the *kinner* woke me up. What in the world are they doing down there?"

"They were reading when I came to see why the *bobbel* was fussing." Anke followed Velda down the stairs.

When they entered the gathering room, they found Micah and Millie sitting on the floor, clapping in awe as Asher and Will jumped so high on the couch it seemed their heads would hit the ceiling. For some reason, Will had the apron Anke had been sewing tied around his neck.

"Absatz!" Velda commanded sharply and Asher immediately stopped jumping and landed on his bottom on the couch cushion. Velda repeated the Amish word, louder this time. *"Absatz!"*

"That means *stop*, Will," Anke told him. He immediately stopped jumping, too. Anke thrust Charity into Velda's arms and walked over to where the boys were sitting on the couch, both red-faced and staring at their knees. Untying her apron from Will's neck, she said, "Hold still or you'll stick yourself—this has pins in it. What were you thinking to tie it around your neck?"

"It's my cape. I was being a superhero so I could jump higher than Asher."

Velda gasped. "That's it. I want that *bu* out of this house right now. It's bad enough that he got Asher to jump on the couch, but introducing him to such nonsense as a superhero is inexcusable. He is *not* allowed to be around my *kinner* again," she ranted to Anke in *Deitsch*.

Although Will couldn't have understood what she'd said, Asher burst into tears and then Micah and Millie did, too. "But, *Mamm*—" Asher began to object.

Velda snapped her fingers and pointed at her son. "Quiet," she said, silencing him before speaking to Anke in *Deitsch* again. "See? Look how much influence he's already had. My *kinner* are talking back to me and having tantrums because they saw *him* do it. I warned you and Ernest this would happen. But would you listen? *Neh!*"

"*Kumme*, Will. Let's go," Anke said, collecting her sewing bag on the way out of the room. They put on their hats, coats and mittens and walked back across the snowy lawn in silence, except for Will's sniffling. Anke glanced over and saw a few tears rolling down his cheeks, but she didn't console him. If he was crying because he regretted that he'd jumped on the couch and taken Anke's apron, then she considered his tears a sign of a healthy conscience.

Besides, she was too angry about the way Velda handled the situation to say anything comforting to Will. She thought both boys should have been admonished for jumping on the couch. Then Anke could have addressed the issue of Will taking her apron and superheroes, too. *They deserved to be scolded, but banishing Will from the* haus *for the rest of the time he's here seems unnecessarily stringent,* she thought. *And Velda can't blame her* kinners' *crying on him—they're probably crying because they're tired. Or because* she's *been short-tempered with them lately.*

When they got inside, Anke realized Josiah had returned and was working in the next room. She hoped he didn't overhear their entire conversation. She'd been working so hard all week to help shape Will's behavior, but obviously, she hadn't done a good enough job of it and it made her feel like a failure.

After they'd taken off their coats, she told him to sit down. Standing in front of him, Anke asked, "Does your *mamm* allow you to jump on the couch in your apartment, Will?" She knew she couldn't really fault him for jumping on Velda's couch if he'd never been forbidden to do it at home.

He looked at her and shrugged his shoulders, fat tears beaded on his lashes.

"I want you to think about it and then answer *jah* or *neh*." She repeated, "Does your *mamm* allow you to jump on the couch at home?"

"I—I don't know. Our couch doesn't bounce. It's called a futon. Mommy sleeps on it at night. It's kind of hard and it's got wood under it."

"I see." Anke noticed he'd reverted to calling his mother *mommy*. "Well, jumping on the furniture is not allowed here. In fact, you should never do it anywhere. Furniture is for sitting on. If you jump on it, you could get hurt. Or you could get the furniture dirty or even break it. You are not allowed to do that again. If you do, I'll take away your soft armchair and you can sit on a hard kitchen chair from now on so you won't be tempted to jump on it. Do you understand?"

"Jah." He hung his head and his tears splotched the legs of his pants.

Anke dropped into the rocking chair beside him. "Will, look at me." When he did, she said, "You're also not permitted to take anything that belongs to someone else without their permission. That's not right. How would you feel if someone went into your backpack and took something that belonged to you?"

Will cried harder, his chin quivering. "Please don't take my picture of Mommy, *Ant* Anke. Please? You said I could look at it at night. You said so."

Anke got up so she could lift the child onto her lap. Cradling him against her, she said, "I'm not going to take your photo, Will. I promise. I only asked you how you'd feel if I did take it. And I can tell it would make you very sad. That's how I felt when you took my apron."

As she rocked back and forth, a few tears rolled down her cheeks and dripped off her chin onto his fine blond locks. Anke was torn up inside because she knew how hard Will was trying to fit in and how much he missed his mother. She was also angry at her sister because the consequences of Clara's decisions were hurting her son even more than they'd hurt her Amish family. *Dear* Gott, *please heal Will's heart*, Anke prayed. *Help me to be a comfort to him and give me wisdom about how to guide him during his time here.*

Eventually, the boy quieted down and pulled back so he could look her in the eyes. "I'm sorry I took your apron, *Ant* Anke," he apologized.

"I forgive you. And I trust you not to take anything of mine again."

"I won't," he said, solemnly shaking his head.

Anke gave him a hug before she told him, "I know you might see superheroes on TV at home, but Amish *kinner* don't believe in superheroes who can fly or who have special powers to fight evil."

"They don't?"

"*Neh.* The only One who can do such mighty things is Jesus, or *Gott.* He can do miracles and He always opposes sin—that means the things people do and say and think that are wrong. Yet even though He hates sin, if we believe in Him, He forgives us for all those bad things. But Jesus is real and superheroes are pretend. That's one of the reasons *Ant* Velda got so upset—she doesn't want you telling Asher about someone who's make-believe."

"I didn't tell him. The book did."

Anke tipped her head. "What book?"

"From the library. It has a superhero cat in a cape in it. It's for the letter *C*."

"So that's why you tied my apron around your neck?"

"*Jah.* I'm sorry." Will dropped his head again.

"It's okay. I said I forgave you and I did." She cupped Will's chin and lifted his head. "But I need to understand what happened. You tied my apron around your neck and then you jumped on *Ant* Velda's couch and Asher did, too?"

Will couldn't move his head because Anke was holding his chin, but he averted his eyes to the side and down, his lashes fanning his cheeks.

"Will, when I ask you a question, you must answer me. Who jumped on the couch first? You or Asher?"

"Asher." His voice was raspy as he added, "He said he could jump higher than a superhero because he ate a whole lot of steak at supper."

Anke tensed her jaw, absorbing what she'd discovered. It occurred to her that Asher had tried to tell his mother what had really happened, but she had silenced him. *This* was the very reason why Anke had wanted to speak to the boys about what they'd done, instead of flying off the handle like Velda. "Okay, well, we'll talk to your *ant* about this later."

"So I can say sorry about jumping on the couch?"

"*Jah*, that's one reason." Anke touched the tip of his turned-up nose. *I just hope Velda is as contrite about her mistake as you are*, she thought.

From what he'd overheard of Anke and Will's conversation, Josiah could picture the events that unfolded at Velda's house earlier in the afternoon. He sympathized with her and the boy because it sounded as if Will had been blamed for something that wasn't entirely his fault. He'd been listening to Anke instruct her nephew all week in the ways of the Amish and he had no doubt that she was committed to helping him fit in. More important, she was clearly teaching him about God's love and forgiveness.

But he couldn't deny it troubled him to hear her and Will talk about a photo in his book bag. From what Josiah deduced, it seemed she was allowing him to take the photo out when no one else was around and that seemed deceptive. He recalled what Keith had said about how Amish adults were sometimes tempted to make excuses for *Englischers*, especially *Englischers* they spent a lot of time with or cared deeply about.

I think that may be what's happening with Anke and her schweschder *and nephew,* he thought. *In a way, it happened to me, too—I got involved with* Englischers *when I tried to help Jana's* bruder. *I would have been better off if I had just kept going past the golf course that day.*

Anke and Will's conversation reaffirmed what Josiah had decided earlier that afternoon; he was going to have to severely limit his connection to them. That meant no more lunch breaks together anymore. While Josiah didn't relish the idea of eating in the barn again, on the plus side, the cold weather would force him to take a quicker break, which meant he'd finish his work on the *daadi haus* quicker, too. He estimated that he could complete everything by Friday or Saturday of next week, if he hurried.

After that, the only time I'll see Anke and her nephew will be in kurrich—*unless I sit in the front row so I won't be led astray by the sight of them, too,* he thought wryly.

Chapter Seven

"Why isn't Josiah eating lunch with us today?" Will asked on Friday afternoon when he returned from washing his hands and discovered that Josiah had left for the barn.

I don't know, Anke thought. *But he certainly has been acting odd. Yesterday he hardly uttered goodbye when he left and this morning he barely greeted us, either. He must have something on his mind.* She'd considered asking him if anything was wrong, but she didn't want to pry, especially not with Will around.

"He said he wanted to check to be sure his *gaul*'s water isn't frozen. He wasn't planning to take a very long break anyway."

"Can we go to *Ant* Velda and *Onkel* Ernest's *haus* after lunch?"

Anke was impressed by Will's self-restraint. Even though she knew he was eager to see his cousins again, this was the first time he'd asked her about it today. But Anke had decided to wait until tomorrow to go over to the main house, since Ernest only worked until noon on Saturdays. She figured it would be better to discuss the boys' behavior when her brother was present, as he was more reasonable and calmer than Velda was.

Also, Saturday afternoon was when either Velda or Anke would typically use the buggy to go to the supermarket, while the other woman stayed home and watched the children. So Anke would have to go to the house anyway, to either give her grocery list to Velda, or to get Velda's list from her.

"We're going to their *haus* tomorrow, when *Onkel* Ernest gets home from his butcher shop."

"But why can't—" Will started to ask and then he clamped his hand over his mouth, apparently remembering he wasn't supposed to argue with a grown-up's decision. From behind his fingers he mumbled, "I forgot."

"That's okay. We all forget what we're supposed to do or what we're not supposed to do sometimes. But if we practice, it becomes a habit and after a while, we don't even have to think about it—we just do what we're supposed to do," Anke said. "Now, let's bow our heads and I'll say grace."

"Don't forget to pray for *Mamm*," Will reminded her, just as he'd done at every meal and again every evening when she prayed with him before he went to bed.

"Dear *Gott*," she prayed. She could hear the front door open and close again—Josiah must have returned from the barn. She waited for his footsteps to fade as he walked into the bedroom before continuing, "*Denki* for this food and for Your love. Please help us to do the things we should and to repent when we do the things we shouldn't. Please heal Clara in all the ways she needs healing and bring her home to us soon. Amen."

"How many more days until I get to see Mommy?" Will asked when he opened his eyes. Anke noticed he always reverted to the *Englisch* word when he felt lonely.

Clara hadn't even been in the recovery program for a week yet, so Anke didn't want to discourage Will by saying he had thirty-some days left before she came home. Instead she told him, "In about five weeks."

"Is that a really lot of days? Is it this many?" He held up all ten of his fingers.

"*Neh.* It's more than that."

His jaw dropped. "But that's too many days."

"I know it seems that way, *jah*. But sometimes it takes that long for…for someone to get completely better. Otherwise, if they leave the hospital too soon, they might end up getting sick again and then they'd have to go back into the hospital. We don't want that to happen." Anke gestured toward Will's bowl, hoping to distract him. "Your *supp* is getting cold."

He picked up his spoon and stirred the broth, but

he didn't lift it to his mouth. "If *Mamm* eats lots of steak, will she get better?"

Now Anke felt too sad to eat, too. She set down her spoon. "Your *mamm* needs more than protein to get better. She needs help from the people at the hospital."

"Can't *Gott* help her get better?"

"Absolutely. That's why we pray about it every day and every night. But even with *Gott*'s help, sometimes it takes a while for a person to get better." Anke knew the conversation was becoming too intense for the child, so she said, "I know you want to see your *mamm* very soon and so do I. But I'm glad that while we're waiting for her to *kumme* back, we get to be together. I love having you here and teaching you about being Amish. And I also have lots to do, so I really need your help."

"You do?" Will slurped a spoonful of his soup. "Like what?"

"I want to make snickerdoodle *kuchen* this afternoon and I'd like you to crack the *oier* for me."

"Okay. I'm *gut* at mixing, too." Will's countenance brightened considerably.

"Ah, but are you as *gut* at eating *kuchen* as you are at making them?"

He giggled. "*Jah.* I can eat this many." He held up his ten fingers again.

"That many? You'd get a *bauchweh* if you ate ten *kuchen*."

"Does that mean a tummy ache?"

"Jah."

"Then I won't eat ten. I can give some to Josiah."

"What a *wunderbaar* idea," Anke exclaimed.

But at the end of the day when Will presented the cookies to him, Josiah's half-hearted thanks made Anke wish they had saved the cookies for themselves. *Can't he see how eager Will is to share with him*? she thought. *I don't care if Josiah got up on the wrong side of the bed or not. He could show a little more enthusiasm than that when a* kind *gives him something he made.*

"I don't think he likes snickerdoodles," the boy surmised after Josiah left. "Maybe he's 'lergic."

"That could be. But maybe he's just tired from all the work he's been doing. When he gets home and his *bauch* starts growling this evening, he'll probably be really *hallich* he has a plate of *kuchen* all to himself."

"He won't share them with his wife?"

"*Neh.* He isn't married. Josiah lives alone right now."

"That's sad." Will hugged his aunt's legs. "I'm *hallich* I get to live here and help you until my *mamm* gets home."

"I'm *hallich*, too," Anke agreed, so touched by the child's sentiment that even as she was saying how happy she was, she had to wipe a tear from the corner of her eye.

Josiah knew that Anke had sensed the change in his attitude toward her and Will because he'd seen the way she'd set her jaw after he'd barely mumbled *denki* when Will had given him the plate of cookies he'd made.

In contrast with Anke's stony countenance, the child's expression was one of perplexed sweetness. Josiah knew Will looked up to him and the boy was undoubtedly confused by his sudden indifference. He so regretted offending Anke and hurting the boy's feelings that he'd almost returned to the *daadi haus* to apologize. But how would he excuse his behavior? He couldn't very well have said, *I'm concerned that if I continue being friendly with you, I might be ostracized. And not just me, but my* bruder *and his wife, too.* No, that would only hurt Anke and Will further. It was better to pull back without any explanation.

On the way home Josiah stopped at the smaller of the town's two grocery stores because its deli department offered premade meals. While not nearly as delicious as homemade food, they were a lot tastier than anything Josiah could have made for himself, but they were costlier, too. *What would I have done if Anke hadn't given me the job repairing the* daadi haus? he ruminated as he stood in line, still feeling guilty about his behavior. *I would barely be able to afford to eat butter and noodles every night.*

While he was thinking, someone behind him tapped his shoulder. He turned around to see Iddo Stoll, New Hope's deacon, standing behind him. "Are you in line for the bachelors' special?" he asked, gesturing toward the glass display case of heated, precooked food.

Josiah laughed. "*Jah.* I'm buying supper."

"I am, too. My wife, Almeda, is out of town, so I've got to hunt and forage until she returns from visiting her *schweschder* in Serenity Ridge," Iddo joked.

"How long is that?"

"She's coming back tomorrow. And to be honest, she had prepared four days' worth of meals before she left." The older man patted his stomach. "But I doubled up on yesterday's supper so here I am now."

"Well, I'd recommend the beef stroganoff over the *hinkel*," Josiah suggested. "By this time of evening, the *hinkel* is a little dried out from sitting beneath that warming light."

"Sounds like you've been getting your food here often. No one has hosted you for supper yet? That surprises me. Usually the *leit* in New Hope are a little more welcoming."

Josiah didn't want to mention that he'd been too busy working on Anke's *daadi haus* to really connect with any of the people from the district during the week. "Oh, the *leit* have been very welcoming—a group of them invited me to go snowshoeing with them. And one of the *weibsleit* brought me Long John Rolls."

The deacon raised an eyebrow. "Honor Bawell?"

"Jah." Josiah was perplexed by how he'd guessed.

"She brought me some, too, in Almeda's absence." He stroked his beard thoughtfully. "It was very kind of her and I appreciated the gesture…a lot more than I appreciated the taste."

Josiah had to laugh at that; he'd been so hungry he'd eaten two of the donuts the first night, just to keep his stomach from growling. But after he had finished them, his stomach made even more unsettling noises, so he'd broken the rolls in pieces and fed them to the chickens. "I'm surprised you didn't like them—Victor's *hinkel* gobbled them up."

"*Hinkel* eat bugs, so that's not saying much." The deacon smiled. "Since we're both on our own, why don't we eat our meals at my *haus*? It's not more than a mile and a half from here."

Josiah had been planning to make more progress on Victor and Laura's kitchen floor that night. He was also nervous that the deacon might question him about his work on Anke's *daadi haus*. But he knew it would have been rude to turn the deacon down, so he accepted. And it turned out that he was glad he did—he enjoyed getting to know Iddo and learning more about the New Hope district's history.

"I wish I would have remembered to get dessert," Iddo said after they'd finished their meals and he was making decaf coffee.

"I happen to have snickerdoodle *kuchen* in the buggy. We might have to wait until they thaw out a little, but I can go get them if you want me to?"

"Honor didn't make them, too, did she?"

"*Neh.*" Josiah hesitated before he added, "They're from Anke."

"In that case, bring them in!"

The men finished off the plate of cookies long before they'd drunk their coffee. Iddo leaned back in his chair with a contented sigh. "I'd been hankering for something sweet. Almeda didn't leave me any dessert—she's trying to help me lose weight. So you'll have to tell Anke those *kuchen* hit the spot."

"*Jah*, they did," Josiah said noncommittally, since he didn't want to agree he'd pass along the deacon's compliment to Anke and Will. It might encourage them.

"How is the work coming on her *daadi haus*?"

"Fine. I should be done by the end of next week," Josiah said. Even though he knew the deacon had told Anke's family it wasn't a violation of the *Ordnung* for her to take care of Will, that didn't necessarily mean Iddo agreed with her decision. So Josiah quickly explained, "I wouldn't have taken the job, except I can't install fences in this weather."

"Well, then, I'm *hallich* that it's working out, for both your sakes. Almeda and I were praying someone would help her." Iddo looked Josiah squarely in the eye. "We knew that the work wouldn't be easy and it would take a strong man to do it."

Josiah immediately recognized what the deacon meant. Although he was being careful not to say anything that might seem to disparage the members of his district, Iddo was indicating he thought it was weak of them not to help Anke. He was acknowledging that he understood it took a man of strong character to associate with her by repairing the *daadi haus*. But Iddo was wrong about Josiah; he'd been cowardly. He'd been so afraid of how people would judge him that he hadn't really spoken his mind or stood up for Anke when he had the opportunity.

"I—I don't know if I'm as strong as you think I am," Josiah confessed.

"Your *bruder* told me in confidence what happened in Illinois," Iddo replied bluntly. "You're stronger than *you* think you are."

As the deacon raised his cup to his mouth and took a long pull of coffee, Josiah rubbed his eyes with his palms, simultaneously embarrassed and relieved that Iddo knew about the incident at the golf course. Mostly, he felt grateful that the deacon clearly wasn't judging him for what he'd done or making assumptions about his commitment to their Amish faith and lifestyle.

He also felt even more ashamed because *he* hadn't supported Anke in a similar manner. But that was about to change.

"*Neh*, I'm weak," Josiah insisted. "But *Gott* in me is strong and He'll help me repair what needs repairing."

On Saturday morning, Anke was surprised when Josiah knocked on the door half an hour earlier than usual. "I'll open it," Will volunteered.

"You haven't finished your breakfast yet. Your *oier* will get cold. I'll let Josiah in." The fact of the matter was that Anke didn't want Josiah's crankiness to affect Will's mood. The child was so excited about the prospect of seeing his cousins after lunch that he'd woken up at first light and asked her if it was almost time to go say he was sorry to his aunt for jumping on her couch. *If only we adults were that eager to apologize*, she thought ruefully as she opened the door for Josiah.

"*Gudermariye*, Anke. I'm sorry I'm early but I wanted to give something to Will before I got started working on the bedroom floor. I brought something for you, too." He reached into his pocket and pulled out a handful of fat batteries. "I noticed you've only been using the kerosene lamp lately, so I figured you might need these."

"That's thoughtful, but I'm going to town after lunch today, so I planned to pick up fresh batteries then."

"But I want you to have them as a small token of my appreciation for all the meals you've made for me. Including the *kuchen* you and Will baked yesterday. I shared them with the deacon last evening and he said to tell you they were *appenditlich*—and I agree."

As Josiah studied her, his reddish eyebrows nearly touched in the middle of his forehead and she realized he was anxiously awaiting her reply. It was clear he wasn't just offering her batteries; he was offering an apology for how he'd behaved the previous day. "*Denki.* That's a lovely gesture." As she took the batteries, her fingertips brushed his calloused palm, sending a shiver up her arm and down her spine.

"I finished my *oier*," Will announced as he came around from behind her. "Hi, Josiah. Did you know I'm going to see my *gschwischderkinner* after lunch?"

"I hope you have *schpass*."

"Does that mean a snack?"

Josiah's curls seemed to bounce when he laughed. "*Neh.* It means fun."

"Oh, I'll have lots and lots of *schpass*."

"I brought you something." Josiah held out two mason jars. One was empty and the other was filled with long screws.

Will reached for the jars. "Is this so I can build something?"

"*Neh.* This is so you will know how many days until your *mamm* is better and *kummes* home. You won't even have to ask your *ant* Anke." Josiah showed Will that he'd put forty-two screws, one for each day Clara was expected to be gone, into the jar. He explained that each evening before he went to bed, Will could take one of the screws from the clear mason jar and put it into the blue mason jar. "When you run out of screws in the clear jar, that's when your *mamm* will come home."

"But the blue jar doesn't have any screws in it at all." Will looked upset.

"You're right. How many nights have you been here?"

The boy glanced at Anke. "Five," she said. "Do you need me to help you count them out?"

"*Jah.* I can only count in *Englisch*," he replied.

Anke couldn't stop smiling. How she felt reminded her of the day her father had hung the swing in the tree for Clara. Her mother was delighted to see her young daughter enjoying herself so much. At the time, Anke was almost courting age and she never forgot that her mother had told her, *The way to a man's heart might be through his* bauch, *but the way to a woman's heart is through her* kind.

Now Anke knew exactly what she'd meant. Not that she thought Will was her child or that Josiah was trying to win her heart. But what he did for her nephew was so sweet she hummed her way through the morning.

For lunch she used the rest of the leftovers to make a "haystack casserole" and she was pleased when Josiah joined her and Will for lunch. The boy could hardly sit still and he practically inhaled his food.

"Slow down, Will," she told him. "There's no sense in hurrying—you're still going to have to wait for me to finish before we go next door."

After finishing what was on his plate, Will chatted away, informing Josiah, "*Ant* Anke's going to bring me some books from the library. She's going to teach me to read by myself. Not just the alphabet. Whole words—" He stopped suddenly and put a finger to his lips as if Josiah had been the one speaking, not him. "I hear *Onkel* Ernest's buggy!" he exclaimed.

Anke hadn't heard anything. "Are you sure? He usually doesn't get home from work for half an hour."

"Can I be 'scused to go look out the window?"

"Okay," Anke allowed. When he'd left the room, she said to Josiah, "I'm surprised your ears haven't fallen off yet. I'm sorry he's so talkative—he's just excited about seeing his *gschwischderkinner*. But if you're tired of listening to him, please feel free to tell him it's time to be quiet."

"I don't mind. The more he talks, the less he eats and the more there is for me," he joked. Or maybe he wasn't joking; he'd had three helpings of casserole and showed no signs of slowing down.

"We have *kuchen* for des—"

Anke was interrupted by Will wailing, "Where are they going?"

"Excuse me," she said, rising to go find out what Will was talking about, but he'd already returned to the room, a look of utter rejection on his face. "Did you see *Ant* Velda and the *kinner* go somewhere with *Onkel* Ernest?"

"*Neh*. They—they—they—" Will was obviously trying not to cry in front of Josiah.

"Take a deep breath," Anke instructed, giving him time to regain his composure. "That's right. Now, tell me what's wrong."

"They all got into a buggy and they went down the driveway."

Anke couldn't figure out what had happened. "Are

you sure it wasn't *Onkel* Ernest's buggy? They all look similar."

"*Neh.* The *gaul* wasn't Star. It was kind of yellow."

Yellow? Anke wondered, trying to picture who owned a pale-colored horse in their district.

"Do you mean tan? Like this color?" Josiah asked Will, touching the table.

"*Jah.* And it had black legs up to its knees. Like socks."

"That was the Harnish *familye*'s buggy," Anke uttered.

"Keith Harnish?" Josiah asked.

"*Neh.* His *bruder* Saul. His wife, Ruth, is friends with Velda and they have two *kinner*, Eileen and Phineas, around the twins' age," she explained. "I don't know where they went, but don't worry, Will. I'm sure they'll be back soon."

But Anke was the one who was worried. It wasn't like her sister-in-law to go somewhere with all the children on a Saturday. *I hope none of the* kinner *is ill and they aren't on their way to the doctor*, she fretted. But then she told herself, *That can't be it—Velda would have told me. Besides, how would Ruth have known Velda needed a ride? They must have prearranged this trip to wherever they're going.* Otherwise, Velda would have let her know, because she would have had to give Anke her grocery list so Anke could do her shopping for her. She silently asked the Lord to keep Velda and the children safe and healthy.

After Josiah resumed his work on the bedroom floor and Anke had cleaned up the kitchen, she played a card-matching game with Will. She was still so distracted by wondering where Velda was that her nephew matched five times as many cards as she did.

"Do you hear that?" Will asked, halfway through their second game. He hopped down from the kitchen chair and ran into the living room. A moment later he returned, his shoulders slumped. "It was only *Onkel* Ernest."

They finished playing the game and then Anke laid the cards out side by side on the table again. "This time, you get to see how long it takes you to find all the pairs yourself—no peeking. I'm going to go next door to ask your *onkel* if he knows where everybody went."

Before leaving, Anke stuck her head in the bedroom to let Josiah know she'd be right back.

"You want me to play cards with Will?" he volunteered.

"*Neh.* He's fine by himself. Please keep doing what you're doing. I just wanted you to know where I was. I'll only be a minute."

She dashed across the lawn and into the house. "Is everything okay?" she breathlessly asked Ernest when she found him the kitchen.

He set down the glass of milk he'd just poured for himself. "Hi, Anke. Everything's fine as far as I know. Why?"

"Because I think Velda and the *kinner* went somewhere with Ruth Harnish in her buggy. I thought there might be an emergency."

Her brother put the glass bottle of milk into the fridge and then turned and scratched his bearded chin. Sometimes his slow, thoughtful responses were comforting. Other times, they drove Anke to distraction. "*Neh*, not as far as I know," he said. "She told me last night they were going to the market together. Then the *kinner* were going to play for a few hours at Ruth's *haus*. Didn't she mention it to you?"

"Neh," Anke spat out the word as if it was bitter on her tongue. "She didn't tell me. Apparently, she's not speaking to me at all."

Ernest shook his head. "I doubt that's true. Why wouldn't she be speaking to you at all?"

"Didn't she tell you about what happened the other day?"

"She said the *kinner* were misbehaving and she'd asked you to take Will home."

As calmly as she could, Anke relayed the entire story of what had happened, including what Will had told her about the illustration of a superhero cat wearing a cape like in the library book Velda had chosen for her children.

"Are you sure?" Ernest asked. "Velda is usually very careful about what the children read and look at."

Anke closed her eyes and let her breath out through her nose in a huff. She understood why her brother would be careful about jumping to conclusions, especially involving his wife. But it irritated her that he couldn't see how Velda was behaving. "I'll go get the book and we can take a look at it," she offered.

She went into the living room, found the book and brought it back. Maybe it was misplaced, but Anke had so much trust that Will had been telling her the truth that she didn't even need to open it to the page that contained the letter *C*. She simply handed her brother the book and watched his face as he flipped to the illustration in question. He shook his head, his mouth settling into a grim line.

"I'll speak with Velda," he said. "I'm sorry, Anke."

You're not the one who should be sorry, she thought. But after an urgent prayer for God to help her control her tongue, she replied, "I'm sure that when Velda understands what really happened, she'll remedy the situation right away."

At least, Anke hoped she would—for the children's sake.

Realizing he'd left a piece of equipment he needed on the porch, Josiah came out of the bedroom where he'd been working to retrieve it. Will must have heard the front door open because he came sailing into the room before Josiah had even stepped outside.

"Oh. I thought *Ant* Anke was back." His disappointment was almost palpable.

"*Neh.* But she should be here any second."

"Could you help me get a glass from the cupboard, please? I'm thirsty. And I can't stand on a chair to reach it—chairs are only for sitting on."

Josiah grinned; Anke's instructions obviously were sinking in. "Have you ever used a stepladder?"

"What's a stepladder?"

"It's a short ladder that carpenters use if they can't reach something by stretching."

Will shook his head. "*Neh.* I never used a stepladder. Just a ladder for climbing a slide."

"Would you like to use my stepladder to get a glass from the cupboard?"

"Jah." He jiggled his head up and down, so Josiah retrieved the ladder from the bedroom.

Setting it up in front of the sink, he cautioned, "Before you step on this, it's very, very important that you remember you're not allowed to use it without an adult like me around."

"I know. You have to say I can use it first."

"Right. Okay, I'll hold it steady and you can climb up."

The boy scaled the ladder quickly. When he reached the third step, he turned around. "I'm almost as tall as you," he said, even though his head barely came up to Josiah's chin.

"Almost. But every carpenter knows when he uses a ladder he's supposed to pay attention to what's in front of him, not what's behind. So turn around and open the cupboard."

Will retrieved a glass and handed it to Josiah. Then he backed down the ladder. "That was *schpass*," he said as he jumped off the bottom rung. Josiah folded the ladder, but Will protested, "I need to use it again so I can turn the faucet on."

"*Neh*, one climb per day," Josiah said. "I'll fill your glass for you."

As the boy was chugging down his water, the front door opened. "I'm back," Anke called. Right away, Josiah recognized the note of false cheerfulness in her voice. When she came into the kitchen and saw him there with her nephew, she said to Will, "Uh-oh. Did you disturb Josiah when he was working?"

"Neh," Josiah quickly answered for him. "I let him use my stepladder to get a glass since he didn't want to climb on the furniture. But don't worry—he knows he isn't allowed to use the ladder without me here to help him up and down."

This time, the cheerfulness in Anke's voice was genuine. "Wow, that's really nice of Josiah to share his ladder with you, Will. Isn't it?"

"*Jah.* I was as high as him," Will replied. "Where did *Onkel* Ernest say everybody went?"

"Well, because they didn't know we were coming over to see them after lunch, they all went shopping."

Josiah figured there was more to the story than Anke was letting on, but it wasn't any of his business, so he excused himself and picked up the stepladder. As he was leaving the room, he heard Will ask, "Are they coming back soon?"

"*Neh.* They…had some other places to go."

"After they go other places, can I play with them?"

"It will be too dark outside by then. But guess what you and I are going to do? We're going to go for a ride in the buggy. Won't that be *schpass*?"

Josiah quickly closed the bedroom door behind him so he wouldn't feel so sad when he heard the boy's disappointed reply.

Chapter Eight

Anke hoped Velda would come over and speak to her on Saturday evening, after Will had gone to bed. She even set the light in the window, so Velda would know she was still awake, but where it wouldn't shine in Will's eyes and disturb his sleep.

Not that he'd had any trouble dropping off; the day had been emotionally exhausting for the child. First, he'd gotten all wound up in anticipation of seeing his cousins, only to have his hopes dashed when they went to Ruth's house without him. Anke had been relieved that he'd perked up again when she took him to the store in the buggy. After that, they stopped at the library, where she'd checked out the maximum number of children's picture books permitted.

Their final stop was the wool shop because Anke wanted to buy yarn to knit a warmer sweater for her nephew. That was when his mood took a downturn. *That was really my fault*, Anke thought as she rocked in front of the fire. *I shouldn't have told him he could choose the color.* Rather, she should have shown him which colors were acceptable, and then allowed him to choose from among them.

Instead, she'd made the mistake of saying he could choose any color he wanted, the way she would have told Micah or Millie or Asher. But that was only because they would have known they weren't allowed to choose orange, the way Will did. Then she had to tell him no, orange wasn't permitted. He'd burst into tears, drawing the attention of two women from her district who'd exchanged looks that Anke took as criticism.

It was my fault, she told herself again as she relived the scenario in her mind. *I got his hopes up and then pulled the carpet out from under him—and he'd already experienced that once today.* She could almost cry, just thinking about how when they'd arrived home, she'd suggested he look at a book while she made supper. By that time, Josiah had already left for the day. The *daadi haus* seemed so still and quiet that Anke popped her head into the living room to make sure Will hadn't fallen asleep while he was reading. Instead, she found him standing at the window; he'd been watching for Velda and the children to return.

"Will, it's almost supper time," she'd said. "Even if your *gschwischderkinner kumme* home, they won't be able to play. They'll have to go inside and eat." But he'd insisted on staying there, even after the sky grew dark.

"Why didn't Asher and Millie and Micah and Charity and *Ant* Velda *kumme* home yet?" he'd asked after they'd eaten supper and she'd read him three of his library books.

"Maybe they did *kumme*, but you didn't hear them."

"*Neh.* I have really *gut* ears. I didn't hear the buggy *kumme* up the driveway."

Anke knew he was right; he would have heard them. But she couldn't tell him what she really thought: that they'd come home *before* Anke and Will did, but Velda didn't want the two of them to know. So she'd kept everyone inside.

Now she wondered, *Why would she be so stubborn as to refuse the* kinner *to play together? Doesn't she realize she's punishing* them *as much as she's punishing Will?*

Whatever reason Velda had for still avoiding them, Anke hoped she got over it by tomorrow morning. She wanted to settle their differences so she and Will could join her brother's family for home worship on Sunday morning.

She finally turned out the light and crawled into bed. *Has it only been six nights that Will's been here*? she thought. It felt a lot longer than that. Yet in some ways, it also felt as if the time was passing too quickly. She already felt lonely when she imagined Will leaving.

That's not going to happen for over a month, she reminded herself. *And I've got a jar of screws to prove it.* Anke smiled when she recalled how happy Will was to take one of them out of the clear jar and drop it into the blue jar before he went to bed this evening. It even seemed to make him happier than looking at the photo of Clara.

The screw jars were such a gut *idea. Josiah really has a way with* kinner. *He'll make a* wunderbaar daed *someday*, she mused. For the briefest moment, as she pictured Josiah and his wife, along with their brood of curly red-headed children, Anke felt a wistfulness she'd never experienced before now.

That's lappich *of me to feel this way. I don't want a husband or* kinner. *Right now I've got my hands full taking care of Will*, she thought. And if the Lord answered Anke's prayers, Clara would return to New Hope and she and her son would stay there for good. *She'll need my help raising him, which I'll be overjoyed to do. And even if that doesn't happen, Velda and Ernest will still need me to help them with their* kinner.

No, Anke didn't want a family of her own—she loved the family she already had. But as she drifted off to sleep, she caught herself wishing that Velda would go visit her relatives in Canada and leave Will's cousins behind so the children could play together whenever they wanted.

On Sunday morning as Josiah directed his horse toward the park near the gorge, he reflected on what a meaningful time of worship he'd had with the Nisley family. They'd read a passage in Scripture from the Sermon on the Mount and they'd sung a couple of his favorite contemporary hymns together. Not to mention, Hope and her daughters had prepared leftovers for lunch that were far more flavorful than the best meal he'd bought from the supermarket.

Between eating with Iddo the other night and worshipping with the Nisleys this morning, Josiah was beginning to feel a lot more comfortable in New Hope. However, he wished he didn't have to go snowshoeing with the other single people in the district this afternoon. Actually, he was looking forward to going snowshoeing for the first time—especially since today was a good fifteen degrees warmer than it had been all week—but he wished he didn't have to go with Keith and Honor.

Josiah found it difficult to believe that only a couple of days ago, he was afraid of being excluded from his peer group, but now he was regretting that they'd included him. It wasn't that he was ungrateful or that he meant to be unkind, but he wasn't receptive to Honor's flirtations or to Keith's comments about Anke.

Anke. If Josiah had his way, he'd prefer to spend the day with her and Will. As he turned down the last road before the park, Josiah imagined him and Anke taking her nephew sledding or skating. Then he found himself imagining what it would be like to go out with Anke alone—to take her out to a restaurant or for a buggy ride, the way he might do if they were courting.

I can't let myself get carried away, he thought. *Just because I'm no longer concerned if the* leit *in New Hope will judge me for working on Anke's* daadi haus *doesn't mean I'd want to be her suitor. Besides, she's too wrapped up in caring for her nephew.*

Although Josiah admired Anke's dedication to supporting her sister, there was something about it that reminded him of how loyal Jana had been to her family, too. Of course, being committed to one's family wasn't just admirable—it was essential, as far as Josiah was concerned. However, in Jana's case, she was so loyal to her family that she couldn't even consider that her father might have been mistaken or that her brother could have done something wrong. Instead, she'd suspected one of *Josiah's* family members had been drinking. While he had no good reason to believe that Anke would act in a similar manner, there was something about her relationship with Clara that made him wary anyway.

If I learned anything from courting Jana, it's that I'll spare myself a world of hurt by staying single, he thought as he spied several other buggies in the parking lot. *Now, if I can only get that message across to Honor, I might actually have a pleasant afternoon.*

Maybe Velda is waiting for me to kumme *to her*, Anke thought as she dried the last of the lunch dishes. Since her sister-in-law hadn't dropped in to speak about what had happened, Anke had assumed Velda didn't want her and Will coming to their home worship service earlier that morning. She realized that may have been an incorrect assumption, but she wasn't going to take any chances of being turned away at the door and crushing her nephew's hopes once again.

So Anke had conducted her own home worship service with Will. First, she'd read to him from the Bible and then she'd taught him the simple *Englisch* song "Jesus Loves the Little Children."

After they'd sung the line about all children being precious in His sight, Will had asked, "Does Jesus love *kinner* like me as much as He loves Amish *kinner* like Asher and Millie and Micah and Charity?"

"*Jah*, every bit as much," Anke had answered unequivocally. "And I love you every bit as much as I love your *gschwischderkinner*, too."

"Can I play with them today?"

"I'm not sure. The Sabbath is a day of rest, so they might have to stay inside and take long naps." Anke had known how weak her excuse sounded and she'd expected Will to ask a stream of questions, but he hadn't.

"Maybe when they wake up, *Ant* Velda will let them *kumme* out to play," he'd said, but he didn't sound convinced.

Now as Anke returned the clean lunch plates to the cupboard, she thought, *It's a lot warmer outside today. Maybe I can take Will for a walk—I could pull him on the sled.*

She went into the living room to find him bent over a picture book on his lap, his blond head like a little ball of sunshine. Sitting in the big chair, the boy appeared even smaller than usual; he appeared out of place. And suddenly Anke felt a surge of anger at her sister-in-law. *If it weren't for Velda, Will would be playing with the other* kinner, *not reading alone in an* eldre*'s chair.*

She cleared her voice and asked, "How would you like it if we went outside and I gave you a ride on the sled?"

Will shrugged. "I don't know."

"It's a lot warmer out today and I'll put a blanket over you so you won't get cold," she assured him. "I can't gallop as fast as Star can, but I can trot nice and steady. It'll be *schpass*."

"Okay." His tone was one of resignation, not excitement.

As they were putting on their coats and hats, Anke heard the unmistakable sound of an approaching buggy and her stomach dropped. *Please,* Gott, *let that be Josiah*, she prayed. There wasn't any reason for the carpenter to drop by the *daadi haus* today, but he was the only person Anke could imagine visiting them. Whoever else may have arrived would be coming to see Ernest's family—and that meant Will would likely be excluded from playing with the children again.

The boy had heard the buggy, too, and he darted to the window, one sneaker on, one off. "Somebody's here!" he shouted.

"It's probably one of the *weibsleit* from *kurrich* coming to see your *ant* Velda," Anke told him. "*Kumme* away from the window—it's not polite to stare."

Will reluctantly obeyed, dragging himself over to where Anke was holding out his sneaker for him. *These shoes aren't warm enough for him to go tromping through the snow—it's a* gut *thing I'm pulling him on the sled.*

When she handed him his hat, he said, "I can't wear that. It's got orange on it. Orange is too bright and it makes me get attention."

He was more or less repeating what Anke had told him about the yarn he'd chosen yesterday—that the Amish considered it prideful to draw attention to oneself by wearing bright colors. "I think it would be okay for you to wear your hat since you aren't wearing it because it's bright. You're wearing it to keep warm."

"Can't I just wear my hood?"

Anke vacillated. "Okay. But I'll bring your hat with us, just in case—" She stopped talking when she heard footsteps on the porch. Will had heard them, too, and he tried to open the door, but he couldn't get a grip on the knob because he was wearing mittens. Anke was almost as excited as he was to see who was there. She gently nudged him out of her way. "Here, I'll open it."

"They're home, *Daed*!" a blonde girl even littler than Will shouted. It was Sovilla Lehman—Arleta's four-year-old daughter. Standing at the bottom of the stairs was Noah, Arleta's husband.

"Hello, Anke. I hope we're not interrupting your naps?" he asked.

"Not at all. We were just getting ready to go outside."

Anke was about to introduce her nephew to Sovilla and Noah, but he'd already squeezed past her and announced, "Hi, I'm Will."

"I'm Sovilla. Can I see inside your *haus*?"

"*Neh*, Sovilla," Noah forbade his daughter. For one halting second, Anke was afraid he didn't want her going into the house because an *Englischer* lived in it. But then he added, "You weren't invited and it's not polite to invite yourself."

"She's *wilkom* to go in. Will, show Sovilla the living room and kitchen." Anke moved aside, allowing the little girl to enter. Then she stepped onto the porch and pulled the door almost shut behind her so the heat wouldn't escape. "I'd invite you to look around, too, but it's so small in there I'm not sure everyone would fit."

Noah chuckled. "That's okay. I don't plan to stay. We just stopped by to ask if Will wanted to go sledding with us over by the *schul.* Arleta couldn't *kumme*—she has a *koppweh.*"

"I'm sorry to hear that. I hope she feels better soon." While Anke appreciated the invitation to go sledding, she was surprised Noah had invited her to go with him without Arleta present. It didn't seem appropriate for her to accompany a married man on an outing without his wife, but Anke didn't know how to express that or what other excuse to give for declining.

"I sense Arleta will feel much better once she's had some rest. She said she thought you might need a little peace and quiet for yourself, too. She gave me a very firm reminder to tell you I promise not to allow the *kinner* to go down the hill too quickly."

Relieved to realize Noah wasn't inviting *her* to go sledding with him and the children, Anke laughed. "I trust you," she said. "My only concern is that Will doesn't have decent boots. But I suppose he'll be okay if he puts on another pair of socks."

"That should help. And if he's anything like Sovilla, he'll want me to give him a ride up the hill on the sled, instead of walking through the snow himself."

"In that case, maybe I should give *you* another pair of socks," Anke joked. Her heart felt ten pounds lighter. And when she told Will he got to go sledding with his new friend, his elated reaction made her feel as if her heart might float away altogether.

For the duration of their snowshoeing excursion, Josiah had managed to avoid engaging in any conversation with Keith except friendly, superficial small talk. Nor had he fallen behind the others and gotten stuck alone with Honor. Instead, he'd kept pace with two other young men, Ervin and Jacob. They'd given him a few pointers about how to dig his toes into the snow as he was going uphill, but other than that, he was surprised at how naturally easy it was to transverse the snowy terrain.

"*Denki* for inviting me to *kumme* with you," he said at the end of their hike. The group was crossing the final field together, at a slower, leisurely pace. "It's really beautiful here and I felt like I got a *gut* workout."

"Jah," Keith agreed. "All this exercise has made me *hungerich*. I wish there were someplace nearby where we could get a bite to eat, don't you, Glenda?"

"You mean like my *familye*'s restaurant, don't you?" she said. Her parents owned Millers' Restaurant.

"I hadn't thought of that," Keith said, even though he clearly had. "But now that you mention it…sure, I guess I could stop there, since it's on my way home."

Josiah couldn't keep the disbelief from his tone when he asked, "Your *familye*'s restaurant is open on the Sabbath?"

"Only for pleasure, not for business. That's why Keith dropped his very obvious hint—he knows my *mamm* sometimes allows my siblings and me to bring our friends there to eat *Samschdaag's* leftovers," Glenda explained.

"Oh. That makes sense. For a minute though, I was thinking, *Whoa—the* leit *in New Hope conduct business on* Sundaag*? That's a lot different than in the district I came from*," Josiah admitted. "I should have known better."

"Ha!" Keith guffawed. "Of *course* we don't conduct business on a *Sundaag.* Most of us don't associate with *Englisch* alcoholics, either…or with other people who do."

Josiah's pulse thumped in his ears. *How does Keith know about what happened at the golf course in Illinois?* he wondered. But then he realized that Keith was actually referring to Clara. As usual, he had found a way to bring up the topic of Anke's decision to care for Will. Josiah decided not to take the bait and kept tramping toward the parking lot as if he hadn't heard Keith's remark.

"Who else is going to the restaurant?" Honor asked. Everyone said they'd go, except for Josiah, who remained silent. So Honor pressed him, questioning, "How about you, Josiah? Are you coming, too?"

"*Denki*, but *neh*. Not this time."

"But you must be *hungerich*, aren't you? Just *kumme* and hang out with us for a little while. The food will be *appenditlich.*"

Josiah appreciated being included, but he wished Honor would accept his decision without arguing. *Even Will has already learned that* neh *means* neh, *and he's only a* kinner, he thought. An *Englisch* one, at that. But Josiah realized she wasn't going to stop pestering him until he gave her a reason for not joining the group.

"*Jah*, I've heard *gut* things about Millers' Restaurant and I plan to eat there one day soon," he said, so he wouldn't offend Glenda. "But I'd like to spend part of the Sabbath resting in preparation for the long week I have ahead of me."

"Pfbt." Keith made a scoffing sound. "How much work can there be to do on Anke's *daadi haus* anyway? It's the size of a bread box. If I didn't know better, I'd think you were drawing the job out because you *enjoy* working for her."

"Actually, you'd be right. I *do* enjoy working for Anke," Josiah blurted out. Then, because he realized that it sounded as if he was interested in her romantically, he added, "She's been a *gut* employer. She pays me a generous salary and she's not unreasonable or demanding, the way some homeowners are."

"I'm sure that's true. She's always been very kind to everyone." Honor panted as she tried to keep up with them and simultaneously insert herself into their conversation. "But sometimes, she lets people take advantage of her *gut* nature."

Josiah stopped short. "You think I'm somehow taking advantage of Anke's *gut* nature?" he spoke louder than he intended. Or maybe his voice just rang out because they were in an open field.

"*Neh*, I didn't mean you, *lappich*." Honor playfully nudged his shoulder, setting him into motion again. "I meant her *schweschder* and her nephew. She loves Clara so much she allowed Will to live with her. And I think she spoils him. Like the other day when I came over and the three of you were sitting there eating chocolate *kuche* first thing in the morning."

So says the weibsmensch who'd stopped by at ten-thirty with Long John Rolls, Josiah thought, scanning the field. Another hundred yards and he'd be at his buggy—he lengthened his stride.

"Josiah was having breakfast with Anke and Will?" Keith questioned Honor.

"*Neh*, not breakfast." Jabbing both poles into the snow, Josiah came to a standstill. He was fed up. "I was taking a short break from work and Anke was thoughtful enough to offer me a piece of *kuche.* You're right, it was chocolate and Will and Anke had some, too. As for her spoiling him—only *Gott* can judge whether that's true. But from what I've overheard while I've been working, Anke constantly instructs and corrects the *bu.* She's doing her best to educate him about our lifestyle and customs. And she's trying to teach him about *Gott*'s love and forgiveness—she's modeling it for him, as well. Which, as I understand it, is something we're all called to do."

Josiah looked back and forth from Honor to Keith, almost daring them to contradict him. In his peripheral vision, he saw their peers shift their stances and Josiah regretted making them uncomfortable, but he felt this was something that he'd needed to express. In fact, he should have said it long ago.

When neither Keith nor Honor said anything else, Josiah yanked his poles from the snow. "As I said, I really enjoyed snowshoeing with everybody. I hope to join you again soon. But I'm tired now and I'm going home. See you later."

He'd advanced maybe fifteen yards when he overheard Faith giggle. "There's only one reason a *mann* defends a *weibsmensch* like that—he must really like her. He probably wants to be her suitor."

Josiah was tempted to turn around and tell her she couldn't be more wrong. But the fact was, she may have been more right than he wanted to admit.

It was almost three thirty and Anke knew that at any minute Noah would bring Will home. As delighted as she was to know he was out having a fun time with another child close to his age, for the past two hours Anke had felt an overwhelming sense of loneliness for the boy. She was aware it wasn't because he'd left for the afternoon—it was because she knew it was a foretaste of how she'd feel once Clara got out of the recovery program and took him back to Portland with her. *That day hasn't* kumme *yet. I don't know what* Gott *has in store for us*, she reminded herself. Then she'd spent the next half an hour praying for her sister; in particular, she'd asked the Lord to urge her to return to New Hope and to her family for good.

Anke had also asked God to help change her own attitude toward Velda. She'd been wrestling with resentment because her sister-in-law was apparently still refusing to allow Will to come to the house, even though Asher was as responsible for their behavior as Will had been. *Maybe she's not being stubborn*, Anke thought. *Maybe she's ill.*

Then again, yesterday she'd been worried that something had happened to Velda or the children—and they'd been fine. *Neh, she's deliberately distancing herself and her* familye *from us.* It seemed so immature. So spiteful. Almost cruel. The more Anke dwelled on it, the worse Velda's behavior seemed to her and the angrier she became. *So much for enjoying an afternoon to myself,* she thought. The house may have been quiet, but Anke's thoughts were hardly peaceful. Suddenly, she recalled the verse that began "Blessed *are* the peacemakers..."

Anke knew that for her own good, as well as for Velda's and the children's, she had to be the one to go make peace with her sister-in-law. And she had to do it quickly, before Noah returned with Will. She pulled on her coat and dashed across the yard. When she reached the porch, she knocked on the door, even though doing so really got her goat. A moment later, Velda opened it.

Her eyes were pink rimmed, there were three pins sticking out crookedly from her hair and she wasn't wearing a prayer *kapp.* "Are you ill?" Anke immediately asked.

Velda burst into tears. *"Neh."*

Alarmed, Anke put her arm around her and led her to the couch, where they sat down beside each other. "Then what's wrong? Did something happen to Ernest or the *kinner*?"

"*Neh.* They're all upstairs napping." Velda covered her face with her arm, crying as she spoke. "Or they're pretending to nap—they're probably afraid to *kumme* down. I've been so short-tempered. I even raised my voice to Charity this morning and made her cry. I feel *baremlich* about it…and about how I treated Will. And you. Oh, Anke—I'm so sorry!"

Velda continued to weep as she explained that she'd wanted to come over to apologize and to set things right. But she'd been too ashamed for blaming Will for being the one to suggest jumping on the couch. And because she was mortified about the book she'd allowed the children to check out of the library.

"It's okay," Anke comforted her. "Will is eager to apologize to *you* for jumping on your couch. He knows it's not acceptable behavior—and that he's not allowed to talk about superheroes with your *kinner*. As far as your checking out a book with a picture like that in it…you didn't know. It's not as if you did it on purpose."

"I *should* have known. I should have read it thoroughly first." Velda sobbed even harder. "I know it's prideful, but I feel like such a failure as a *mamm*."

"I understand you're upset, but I doubt that picture will have a lasting effect on your *kinner*. So you made one tiny oversight, but that's absolutely nothing compared to all the love and guidance and nurturing you've given your *kinner*."

"*Neh*, you *don't* understand," Velda insisted. "It's *not* a tiny oversight, don't you see?"

Anke shook her head, puzzled by why her sister-in-law was so upset. "I'm sorry, but I don't."

"Be-because for five years, I've listened to the pain in your *bruder*'s voice every single night when he's prayed for your *schweschder*," she explained. "I was so determined not to ever allow our *kinner* to be influenced by the *Englisch* because I couldn't stand the thought of Ernest bearing that kind of burden again..."

She cried so hard she had to stop speaking, but she didn't need to say anything else anyway. Anke understood now why she was so upset about the book and about Will visiting New Hope. As moved as she was by her sister-in-law's disclosure, Anke still didn't think it was fair to forbid the children to play with one another.

"*Denki* for sharing that with me, Velda," she said. "It helps me understand why you feel so strongly about protecting your *kinner*. And I respect your decision in the matter. But I really don't believe Will is going to negatively influence Millie and Micah and Asher. If anything, in the past week, I've seen how living here has positively influenced *him*."

She paused while Velda lifted her apron to her face and dried her eyes. But when her sister-in-law didn't say anything, Anke suggested, "What if one—or both—of us is always present when the *kinner* are together? What if we never let them out of sight or earshot like I had to do the other day? *Then* will you be more comfortable occasionally allowing them to play together?"

"I—I don't know," she said. "I need to talk to the Lord about it."

"That's a *gut* idea—but you'd better put on your prayer *kapp*, first."

Velda lifted her hands to pat her bare head. "Ach! What a mess I am," she uttered. "The house is, too. I'm going to pieces without you here."

Even though her sister-in-law's remark bordered on being a complaint, Anke understood it was Velda's way of saying she appreciated how much work Anke did, and she smiled to herself.

When she got back to the *daadi haus*, she was surprised to see it was almost four o'clock and Noah still hadn't returned with the children. *I've had enough peace and quiet for one day—now I want Will here*, she thought. *And it will be nice to have Josiah back again tomorrow, too.*

Closing her eyes, she pictured his curly locks and the dusting of freckles on his forehead. Then she reminisced about him bringing her batteries for the lamp and how she'd felt when her fingers had brushed his skin…

Her thoughts were interrupted when Noah's buggy came up the lane. *I shouldn't be thinking about such things anyway*, she told herself. Those were the kind of daydreams a woman had about her suitor, not about a man she hardly knew. Besides, she had her sister's child to focus on—and when he came in the door, she forgot about everything except his smile.

"Sovilla's *daed* is so strong. He walked up the

hill with me riding on his shoulders and he pulled Sovilla on the sled at the same time! And he gave us big pushes down the hill. But he said they were only medium-fast because Sovilla's *mamm* didn't want us to go full speed," Will raved. Hardly pausing to take a breath, he asked, "Is it time for supper? I'm *hungerich*."

Anke laughed. "*Jah*, it's almost time to eat. We're having *supp*. While I'm heating it, I'd like you to take off your shoes and warm your toes in front of the fire. Your feet must be awfully cold."

"*Neh*. Only a little."

Noticing he had a knot in his laces, Anke helped him remove his sneakers. She pressed her hand to his toes and could feel they were cold even through two pairs of socks. Buying him a pair of boots was essential, especially if the weather stayed warm enough for him to go outside to play. But how would Anke get into town this week? She supposed she could pull Will on the sled. Or better yet, she could ask Josiah to borrow his buggy. *Then I could repay him by inviting him to stay for a nice supper*, she absentmindedly schemed before she realized her mind had drifted to romantic thoughts of Josiah again.

I can't believe I'm contriving ways to bribe him to spend more time with us, she thought as she went into the kitchen and began stirring the pot of soup. *It's completely* lecherich. *He has other things to do in the evening.*

"Someone's here!" Will yelled and by the time

Anke entered the living room, he'd already opened the door.

"Hello, Will. Hi, Anke," Velda greeted them both and so did Asher, who was standing at her side.

Will apologized before he even said hello. "I'm sorry I jumped on the couch, *Ant* Velda. I won't do it ever, ever again. Furniture is for sitting on. And we don't believe in superheroes. Only *Gott*." Then he added, "Hi, Asher. I missed you."

Anke noticed he used the word *we* instead of *you* or *Amish people*. In the back of her mind, she wondered whether that meant he considered himself to be Amish, now, too. But she was more interested in hearing how Velda and Asher responded to Will's apology.

"Hi, Will. I missed you every day." Asher spread his arms and embraced his cousin. When he let go, he gazed up at Anke. "I told Will to jump on the couch. He didn't tell me to do it first."

Anke nodded. "*Jah*. I know. I imagine you're not going to jump on furniture again, either, are you?"

"*Neh*. Never."

"And I'm not going to jump to conclusions," Velda joked nervously, but the boys were too young to understand her pun. They looked at her blankly, so she crouched down by Will and said, "I'm sorry I thought you told Asher to jump on the couch. I made a mistake."

"It's okay." Will wrapped his arms around her neck, practically hanging on her. Anke was just about to tell him he needed to let go now, when he murmured, "You feel soft, *Ant* Velda. Just like my *mamm*."

Velda patted his back and stood up so he had to release his grasp, but Anke noticed her eyes were swimming with tears. "Would you two like to join us for leftovers?" Velda asked.

"I was just warming up a pot of *supp*, but we'd much rather have leftovers at your *haus* with all of you. Wouldn't we, Will?" Anke asked. But the boy was too preoccupied with putting his sneakers on to answer.

Chapter Nine

When Anke opened the door on Monday morning, Josiah could tell right away that she and Velda had reconciled their differences. Her eyes sparkled like spring grass after a fresh rain and her lips danced with a smile. But in case he had any doubt, Will came charging into the room and exclaimed, "Hi, Josiah. Guess what I did yesterday?" Without waiting for him to guess, the child said, "I went sledding with Sovilla and her *daed* on a big hill and then *Ant* Anke and I ate supper with Asher and Micah and Millie and Charity and *Onkel* Ernest and *Ant* Velda."

Will could have just said he'd eaten supper with his cousins and aunts and uncle, but Josiah recognized that the child considered each of his relatives so special, he had to list them by name. "That sounds like quite a *schpass* day."

"*Jah.* It was. And we got to have leftovers for supper—those are my favorite," Will said earnestly.

Josiah caught Anke fighting a smile, obviously trying to contain her amusement.

"Would you like a cup of *kaffi*?" she asked Josiah.

"I probably shouldn't since I had two at breakfast, but I'd like one anyway. It's supposed to get to thirty-five degrees this afternoon, but it's still chilly out there this morning—a cup of *kaffi* will warm me up."

"You should take a seat by the stove," Anke suggested. "If you have the time to visit, I mean."

I'll take *the time if it means I get to bask in the glow of your smile*, Josiah thought dreamily. Anke's vivaciousness was so charming this morning it was almost making him dizzy. "I have a few minutes, sure," he said.

"You can sit in my chair," Will offered, as generous as always. He followed Anke into the kitchen. A second later, there was a loud scraping sound as Will dragged the chair into the living room and placed it next to where Josiah was sitting. The boy perched on it and asked, "Did you have a *schpass* day yesterday, too?"

"*Jah*, I did." He took the mug from Anke, who'd come back into the room. After giving it to him, she settled into the rocker.

"Was it more *schpass* than going sledding and eating leftovers?"

"Hmm. Probably not. But I did go snowshoeing."

"What's that?"

"It's when you wear special shoes that allow you to walk on the snow without sinking into it. And you use poles to help you move forward and to balance." Josiah sipped his coffee—it was nice and strong, even by Amish standards.

"Did you go with somebody?"

"Will, It's not polite to pry." Anke held a finger to her lips. Why had her smile suddenly disappeared? Was she that upset about her nephew's manners?

"That's okay. I don't mind telling him," Josiah said, and listed the name of each person who'd gone snowshoeing, just as Will had done.

"That's a lot of people."

"*Jah.* It was." Josiah addressed Anke. "Have you ever gone snowshoeing, Anke?"

"On occasion, *jah.*" Her answer seemed a little curt and Josiah had no clue how to account for the sudden change in her mood.

"Did you enjoy it?"

"Jah."

"Did you have leftovers when you were done snowshoeing?" Will wanted to know.

"Well, everybody else did. Glenda's *familye* owns a restaurant. It was closed because it was the Sabbath, but her *mamm* and *daed* allowed her to bring her friends there to eat."

"But not you?"

"*Neh.* I wasn't very *hungerich* yet. So I went home and ate a bowl of chili."

"What kind of restaurant was it?"

He's asking so many questions this morning—

usually Anke would have told him he had to stop by now, Josiah thought. "It was an Amish restaurant."

"I never went to an Amish restaurant before. Sometimes my *mamm* takes me to a pizza restaurant. That's my favorite kind. But it's *Englisch*."

Josiah was suddenly inspired. "Well, I'll tell you what. Since you like going out for pizza so much, when I finish making all the repairs I need to make on the *daadi haus*, I'll take you to a pizzeria to celebrate—but only if your *ant* Anke doesn't mind?" He raised his eyebrow at her.

"That's generous of you, but it's not necessary."

"But if you let me take you and Will out for pizza, you'll get a break from making supper in that tiny kitchen of yours. Wouldn't that be nice?"

Will leaned over and whispered loudly to Josiah, "*Ant* Anke says when an *eldre* makes a decision, we aren't supposed to argue."

"Will, *kinner* are not supposed to tell *eldre* what to do, either!" Anke exclaimed.

Josiah couldn't help it; he burst out laughing. "He's right, though. I shouldn't twist your arm. If you'd rather not go, there's no pressure." *Even if I'd really like to take you and Will out*, he thought.

Anke hesitated before she answered. When Josiah had first started telling Will about how much fun he'd had snowshoeing with Honor and the others, Anke had felt an undeniable twinge of envy. She could envision Honor flirting with him and she'd wondered if he had felt flattered or had reciprocated her attention. She was so curious that she'd even allowed Will to ask Josiah more personal questions about his afternoon than she ordinarily would have permitted.

Then, when he'd mentioned taking the boy out for pizza, Anke had thought Josiah just meant he was going to take Will out alone, kind of as a male bonding experience. But now that she knew he wanted to take her, too, it felt a little awkward. Almost as if he was leading up to asking her to walk out with him. In which case, she'd have to say no. Because no matter if she *had* been playing with thoughts of what it would be like to have him as a suitor, she didn't have time for courting. Not now, when Will was here. And not in the future, either—Velda had already admitted she couldn't manage her household without Anke.

Or was she reading too much into his invitation? She supposed since the three of them had been eating meals together all along, it seemed only natural that Josiah would include Anke, too. She was the child's aunt and Josiah's friend; that was probably all there was to it. In any case, it was a gracious invitation and Anke decided to accept.

"*Denki.* You're right—it would be nice not to have to cook supper in such a tiny kitchen for one evening," she said.

"Wunderbaar," Will and Josiah both exclaimed at the same time, making Anke laugh.

For the next few days, she felt as if she could

hardly contain her happiness. She had reconciled with Velda, the children were allowed to play together, the repairs were progressing smoothly *and* she had a celebration of sorts to look forward to at the end of the week with Josiah and Will.

Denki, *Lord, for Your abundant provisions*, she prayed on Thursday morning when she knelt beside her bed. He had given her so many blessings she felt greedy asking for any more. But she had determined long ago that she would never stop requesting for the Lord to bring Clara home. So she added, *Please give my* schweschder *a deep desire to repent and return to us for* gut*...after she's completed her recovery program.*

Even as she rose from her knees, Anke realized the last part of her request was for her own benefit, as much as it was for Clara's. Yes, Anke wanted her sister to meet the requirements the judge had set for her. And yes, she wanted Clara to be free from her addiction to alcohol. But she also wanted her sister to remain in the recovery program so Anke could spend the full six weeks taking care of Will by herself.

Although she loved all of her nieces and nephews equally, Anke felt a special closeness with Will. Almost as if she was more like a mother to him than an aunt. Maybe that was because his mother wasn't always around, like Velda was. Or because Anke and Will lived in a separate house where she didn't have to divide her attention between multiple children. In any case, she wanted to make the most of every day with him.

"Gudermariye, Ant Anke," he said, interrupting her thoughts. "Why were you looking at me?"

"Because I love you so much I like to look at you even when you're asleep. But I'm *hallich* you're awake because I need you to help me gather *oier* for breakfast."

"Is Josiah going to eat with us?"

"I don't know." Josiah had accepted Anke's invitation to have pancakes with her and Will yesterday morning, even though he'd already eaten breakfast at home. "Why?"

"Because I like it when he eats with us. My *daed* never ate with me before."

Anke caught her breath. She knew Will's father must have eaten with them all of the time. So it was clear what the boy was actually expressing was that he didn't *remember* his father eating with him. It was also clear that Will was associating Josiah with a father figure. *I don't know if that's* gut *for him*, Anke fretted.

But then Will added, "If Josiah is going to eat with us, we need to gather lots and lots of *oier* and then Asher and Micah and Millie and Charity and *Ant* Velda might not get any."

Anke chuckled and her fears about Will becoming too attached to Josiah quickly dissipated. "Josiah doesn't need *that* many *oier*. We'll be sure to leave plenty for your *ant* and *gschwischderkinner*."

"Even enough for Charity?" The day before, Will had been astounded to see the infant shoveling double fistfuls of scrambled eggs into her mouth.

"*Jah.* Even enough for Charity. Now hurry and go get dressed so Josiah doesn't think you're a *schlofkopp.*" Anke teased, using the word for *sleepyhead. And I'd better brush my hair and wash my face so he doesn't think* I *look like something the cat dragged in*, she thought. And while she was at it, she decided to put on a fresh apron, too.

Josiah had only been working for half an hour when he realized he'd forgotten to bring the pneumatic drill he needed back to the *daadi haus* with him. He'd taken it home with him last night to drill pilot holes in the wood of the floor he was laying for Laura and Victor. He hoped Ernest had one he could borrow, otherwise, he'd have to go all the way back home to get it and that would slow his progress considerably.

Not that he was in any hurry to finish this project. He'd had such a pleasant week listening to Anke and Will talking, reading and laughing together as he worked. He always knew when Anke was baking; not just because of the delicious aromas that permeated the air, but also because he could hear her humming or singing to herself. When the treats had cooled, she'd allow Will to knock on the door to the bedroom and ask if he wanted to take a break and have a sweet with them. Of course, Josiah always said yes and he ate lunch with them, as well.

His experience of repairing the *daadi haus* this past week with Anke and Will nearby was similar to how Josiah had pictured his life would be after he married Jana. Except in a way, this was better because...well, because Anke wasn't going to betray him and devastate him the way Jana did. How could she? They weren't courting and he hadn't opened his heart to Anke.

But he *did* like being in her company. So he wasn't concerned if he didn't finish the repairs on Saturday as he'd projected he would do. However, he disliked making extra trips. Even if the temperature was a couple of degrees warmer than the day before, so much back and forth was hard on the horse. And in general, Josiah didn't relish traveling in *Englisch* traffic when the roads were wet or snowy. But after Velda gave him permission, Josiah looked through Ernest's tools and equipment and didn't find the kind of drill he needed.

"I'm afraid I'm going to have to go home and get mine," he told Anke, who was hanging Will's socks in front of the woodstove while the boy was reading in his chair. She wrinkled her forehead and parted her lips as if she wanted to say something, yet she didn't. *Is she upset because I made such a* dumm *mistake?* Josiah wondered. "I'm sorry I forgot it. I know you're eager to have your own bedroom, so I can work a little later tonight to make up for lost time."

"*Neh*, there's no need to do that. I was just wondering..."

Josiah was intrigued. What could she be so hesitant to ask him? "Wondering what?" he prompted.

She held up a sock. "Will's feet keep getting wet when he plays outside because he only has sneakers to wear. Unfortunately, my sister-in-law gave her *buwe*'s boots away, so we don't have any hand-me-downs for him to use. I was wondering if he and I could go with you and we could swing by the shoe store in town?"

"*Jah*. It would be my pleasure." Josiah really meant it. "While you're getting your coat on, I'll go hitch the *gaul*."

"I'll help you!" Will scrambled for his coat and mittens.

"Josiah doesn't need your—" Anke started to say, but Josiah waved his hand to indicate it was fine if Will came with him.

In the barn, the boy stayed to the side, as he was told, and he listened intently while Josiah explained everything he was doing as he hitched the buggy to the horse. Josiah explained that his father had taught him the same way. "Once I was tall enough to fasten all the straps, it was my responsibility to hitch the horse and buggy every *Sundaag* before we went to *kurrich*."

"Didn't you have *kurrich* in your *haus*?" Will was obviously unaware that last week was an off-Sunday.

"*Jah*. But every other *Sundaag*, we met at someone else's *haus*. Here in New Hope, every other *Sundaag,* we meet in our *kurrich* building."

As soon as the words were out of his mouth, Josiah wished he could take his explanation back. What if Anke hadn't been planning to bring him to church? He couldn't imagine *her* missing a service, but maybe she had arranged for a member of the Serenity Ridge district to watch him, since their church schedule was the opposite of New Hope's. *I'm such a* bobbelmoul, he lamented. But there was nothing he could do about it now; he'd have to mention his blunder to Anke later, when Will wasn't around.

After boosting Will into the buggy, Josiah got in, too. "Would you like to help me hold the reins and guide the *gaul* up the lane?"

Of course, Will was ecstatic and when they came to a halt near the *daadi haus*, he exclaimed, "Wait till I tell my *mamm* I drove a *gaul*—and I'm only five!"

Josiah laughed, just as Anke came down the porch steps. She was watching her feet to be sure she didn't slip on the icy surface, but when she reached the bottom, she glanced up and caught him watching her. Her face broke into a brilliant smile that made Josiah's pulse quicken.

"You've got to scoot into the back now," he told Will. "It's your *ant*'s turn to ride up front with me."

"Denki," Anke said as she settled beside Josiah, tucking the wool blanket he'd handed her around her lap. But after that, she didn't utter a word for the first

two miles of their trip. Funny that she couldn't think of anything to say, since she was never at a loss for conversation while Josiah was working on the *daadi haus*. He was quiet, too—the only one making any noise was Will, who was singing, "Jesus Loves the Little Children" in the back of the carriage.

Still, their silence wasn't unpleasant, just different. *It's so much more relaxing than riding with Keith. That* mann *talked so much it made my head spin*, Anke thought. *And most of the time, he was talking about other people's business.*

Startled to find herself comparing Keith to Josiah, Anke began to sing along with Will. A moment later, Josiah joined in and before she knew it, they'd arrived at his brother's place. Josiah dashed into the barn and returned with the drill, lickety-split. This time when they got back underway, he gave Anke an update on Laura's father, saying he seemed to be doing better and that Victor and Laura were expected home the week after next. After that, conversation flowed easily again until they arrived in town a few minutes later.

They pulled into the lot designated for buggies, which was half a block from the *Englisch* apparel store. As Anke and Will were waiting for Josiah to hitch the horse to the post, a young man and woman buzzed through the field across the street on a snowmobile.

"Did you see that?" Will asked Josiah. "They were going really fast—but I think Star can run even faster. I wish we could race them, don't you?"

"Neh." Josiah sharply chided him, "The *gaul* could get hurt and so could you. And so could the *Englischers* on the snowmobile. That would be *baremlich* for everyone."

"Oh." Will momentarily looked dejected, but Anke knew she couldn't coddle him. It was as important for her to learn to allow others to instruct the child as it was for Will to receive instruction. Yet she was surprised by the severity of Josiah's warning. Will, however, seemed to take it in stride: when she told the boy he had to hold her hand to cross the street, he grasped Josiah's hand, as well. And even after she'd let go of his fingers on the sidewalk, Will and Josiah stayed linked together until they reached the store.

"Are you sure these are Amish boots?" Will asked Anke after she'd selected three pairs from the shelves for him to try on.

"Shoes aren't Amish or *Englisch*, only people are," she warily replied. Sometimes, it seemed there was no end to the amount of explaining she had to do each day in order to help Will understand the difference between the Amish and the *Englisch*. "But *jah*, these are the kind of boots Amish *buwe* wear."

"Is this where Asher and Micah got their boots?" Will crammed his foot down into the first one Anke gave him to try on.

"*Neh.* They got their boots from someone who outgrew them. The *bu* who gave them their boots moved here from another district. You get to have brand-new boots—that's why these might seem different." Anke was crouched down in front of Will, trying to help him get the second boot on. Why didn't it fit? They were both the same size.

"That hurts," Will complained loudly, drawing the attention of the *Englisch* sales clerk who was hovering near the belt and purse racks, indiscreetly watching them.

"*Ach*—that's because you have two socks on this foot and only one sock on the other." Deciding this pair of boots wasn't a good fit anyway, she told Will to take them off. "Let's see if this pair works instead."

"Did *you* get your boots here?" Will asked Josiah as he pushed his feet into the second pair of boots.

"*Neh.* They don't carry my size. I had to order mine from a catalog."

"I want to order my boots from a catalog, too."

Anke was losing patience. "You're not getting your boots from a catalog—it will take too long for them to arrive. You need new boots now." She noticed an Amish couple milling about in the area, but she didn't recognize them. Maybe they were visitors from the Serenity Ridge district?

"But I want the same kind Josiah has," Will demanded loudly and the Amish woman spun around to glare over her glasses at them.

"Shh. Stop arguing," Anke hissed, pointing a finger at him. "Or you won't get any boots at all."

Will burst into tears. "I don't want any boots. They hurt. They're pinching me."

"Then stand still so I can take them off." Anke tugged the boot, but it wouldn't budge. She tried again, pulling harder. Will's foot abruptly slid free of the boot, but in the process Anke toppled backward and landed on her rump. Physically, she wasn't hurt, but her pride was injured. Especially when the Amish woman clucked her tongue and mumbled something about her not being a good example. Tears sprang to Anke's eyes.

"Here. Let me help you up." Josiah extended his hand and pulled Anke to her feet. For a moment, she was overwhelmed with the desire to nuzzle her face against his chest and weep. Instead, she inched backward, but Josiah still didn't release her hand. "Are you okay?"

She nodded. Will was covering his face with his arm, hiccupping more than he was crying. Anke wanted to say she thought they should leave now. But she regretted that Josiah had taken them this far out of his way for nothing. "I'm afraid this was a bad idea."

"Do you have anything else you need to buy?" he asked her softly. "You could go browse and I'll help Will try on the last pair of boots. We'll meet you by the cash register."

Anke didn't know if she should accept his offer. "Are you sure?"

Josiah nodded and Anke inched away. Ordinarily, she would have expected an Amish child to behave better than Will was behaving—Amish children learned quite young that tantrums weren't acceptable. But Will *wasn't* an Amish child. As Anke browsed the fabric section of the store, she realized *that* was exactly the problem. Will wasn't being contrary because he wanted his way; he was insisting on wearing the kinds of boots that were exactly like the other boys wore because he wanted to fit in. All along, she'd been emphasizing how important it was that he do what was considered appropriate for Amish children in their district, so of course he'd be upset if he thought he wasn't going to get the "right" kind of boots. She suddenly understood why Velda said she'd felt like a failure as a mother the other day.

Meandering among the bolts of fabric, Anke was struck by an idea: she'd make Will a pair of pants that were *exactly* like Asher's and Micah's. He could wear them with the sweater she'd been knitting for him.

By the time she reached the cash register, she was smiling again—and so were Will and Josiah, who were waiting for her there. The child was hugging a shoebox. "If at first you don't succeed, try, try again," Josiah whispered to Anke over the boy's head. His breath tickled her ear, making her insides quiver.

"Denki," she whispered back as Will placed the box on the counter. "I'll stand in line—could you two wait for me near the exit? I need to talk to the clerk about something in private."

Josiah took the hint and led the boy away. A few

minutes later, she found them sitting side by side on a bench just inside the door. She handed the shoebox to Will, who cradled it in one arm and jumped off the bench to wrap his other arm around her legs.

"*Denki* for the new boots, *Ant* Anke."

"You're *wilkom*. Do you want to put them on before we go outside?"

He arched his back to look up at her, wide-eyed. "I can wear them *now*?"

"That's why we bought them—to keep your feet warm."

So he sat back down on the bench and removed his sneakers. But before he put on his boots, Anke said, "Wait a second. I have something else for you." She held up a paper bag containing the small gift she'd bought on the sly. But before letting him have it, she said, "There's something in here for Josiah, too. So maybe we should let him open it."

Will nodded eagerly. "This is for me, too?" Josiah repeated in surprise. He reached into the bag Anke gave him and pulled out two pairs of soft dark woolen socks. One pair was child-sized; the other pair was made for an adult.

"Even if you're wearing *gut* boots, it's important to wear warm socks, too," she explained.

"Mine are just like Josiah's," Will noticed, which was why Anke had bought them both a pair. The boy began pulling them on right away.

"*Jah*, except his are bigger." She turned to Josiah and showed him the label. "You said this store didn't carry boots in your size, so I figured you needed extra-long socks. Do you think these will fit all right?"

"They'll fit perfectly. That was very thoughtful. *Denki*, Anke."

She may have given him a pair of wool socks so his feet wouldn't get cold, but the way Josiah said her name made *Anke* feel warm all over.

It was almost one o'clock by the time Josiah, Anke and Will turned into the lane leading to the Bachmans' property.

"I'm sorry that we kept you out so long," she apologized. "But since your work has been interrupted, you might as well have lunch before you get started again, right? I made beef stew last night. It will only take a minute for me to heat it up if you'd like to join us."

I'm in no hurry, Josiah thought. "*Jah*, stew sounds better than the sandwich I brought." He dropped her and Will off in front of the *daadi haus* and then went to stable the horse. As he was walking up the driveway, he noticed Asher and Will running across the lawn to Velda's house.

"Did Will abandon us?" he asked Anke when he came into the kitchen.

"*Jah.* Asher came over and invited him for lunch, so it will just be you and me." Anke gestured for him to take a seat. After she'd served them each a steaming bowl of stew and set a basket of bread in the center of the little table, she said grace. As she buttered a piece of bread, she remarked, "I hope that when Will went inside the main *haus* he remembered to take his boots off. He really loves them. I don't know how you talked him into getting them, but I'm *hallich* you did."

"It wasn't difficult. I just told him that when I was a *bu*, I wore a pair of boots exactly like those." Josiah took a bite of beef; it was incredibly tender. He wondered if that was because Anke was such a good cook or because her brother was a butcher and brought them such great cuts of meat. "I think he was so resistant to the first two pairs because he was scared they weren't 'Amish enough.'" Josiah gave a wry laugh, but Anke set down her spoon, a frown tugging at her mouth.

"*Jah*, I figured that out, too—but not until after he'd had a tantrum. And after *I* did, too." She lowered her eyes. "I'm sorry you had to witness that."

"It's okay. Everyone loses their patience on occasion. But you probably felt a lot more frustrated than how you actually came across." Josiah tipped his head to try to catch her eye, but she still wouldn't look up at him. "For what it's worth, I think you're doing a *wunderbaar* job caring for Will and teaching him about our faith and lifestyle."

"*Denki* for saying that, but..." She shook her head, as if having an argument with herself. "But sometimes I wonder if I've made a mistake in keeping him with me. I wonder if this has all been too hard on him. Too big of an adjustment. I question whether he would have been better off in foster care. At least that way, he only would have had to adjust to new people, not to an entirely new lifestyle. I think maybe I was being selfish to bring him here."

"Pah!" Josiah snorted, immediately dismissing the notion. "You weren't being selfish, Anke—you were putting your *familye*'s needs first, trying to do what's best for your *schweschder* and nephew. *Jah*, Will might be struggling to adjust to being here, but..." Josiah remembered what Iddo Stoll, the deacon, had said to him the evening they'd eaten supper together. "But he's a lot stronger than you think he is. Besides, you're his *familye* and I doubt any stranger could ever love him the way you do. He's very blessed *Gott* put you in his life."

Even with her head dipped, Josiah could tell the frown was melting from Anke's face. And when she finally looked up, her cheeks were flushed and her eyes were sparkling. "He's very blessed *Gott* put *you* in his life, Josiah—and so am I."

That's how I feel about both of you, too, Josiah thought. But he didn't dare express it, since the last time he'd felt this way about a woman was when he was courting Jana, and look how that turned out. So instead he replied, "That's very kind of you to say—*denki*." Then he scooped up another spoonful of stew, even though Anke's sentiment had given him such butterflies in his stomach that he hardly felt hungry anymore.

Chapter Ten

"Bye-bye, see you in a while!" Anke waved to Will, Asher, Micah and Millie, who were chasing each other through the snow under Ernest's watchful eye, before she climbed into the buggy with Velda.

It was Saturday afternoon and instead of stabling the horse when he got home from the butcher shop, Ernest had hitched it to the post closer to the house, since Velda and Anke had planned to leave for the grocery store right away. Usually one of the women took turns staying behind with the children, but Ernest said he could manage them on his own, especially since they played together so much better when Will was there with them.

"If it weren't for his jacket, someone passing by would never know Will was *Englisch*," Anke remarked as they pulled down the lane. On Friday afternoon, she had completed making a pair of "Amish pants," as he called them, for the boy. Once he'd put them on, he hadn't wanted to take them off—he would have slept in them if Anke had let him.

"*Jah*, but does *he* know he's *Englisch*?" Velda asked. "And do *you*?"

Anke twisted sideways to look at her sister-in-law. "What do you mean by that?"

Velda lifted her shoulders in a small shrug. "I wouldn't want him—or you—to forget that just because he dresses and behaves like an Amish *bu* doesn't make him one."

"I'm well aware of that," Anke snapped. "First you were worried he'd be too much of an *Englisch* influence on your *kinner*. But now you're criticizing him because he appears too Amish? You know, sometimes it seems as if there's just no pleasing you." She'd never spoken so bluntly to Velda before, but her sister-in-law had really struck a nerve.

Surprisingly, Velda's response was as gentle as Anke's was harsh. "My intention isn't to be critical. I'm just concerned that one or both of you are losing sight of the fact that he's only going to be here for four more weeks. If he gets the idea he's staying here for *gut*, when Clara returns and takes him back to the *Englisch* world, he'll be crushed. And so will you."

Anke had already had concerns about that herself, but she didn't like to admit them. "We don't know for sure that Clara *will* take him back to the *Englisch* world. We've been praying all this time that she'll repent and return to us and I have faith that will happen."

"I hope it does, but if it doesn't..." Velda wisely didn't complete her sentence. Anke already had gotten her point and she didn't care to talk about it any longer—in part because she knew Velda was right. As fervently as she'd been praying that when Clara completed her recovery program, she'd return home for good, Anke knew that might not happen. The Lord wasn't going to *force* Clara to repent; she had to make that choice for herself. After they'd traveled about a mile, Velda asked, "How much longer until Josiah completes his work on the *daadi haus*?"

"He'll finish sometime this week. Maybe by *Dunnerschdaag*." Even though Josiah had intended to wrap up the repairs this afternoon, their trip to the shoe store had set his schedule back. Also, he'd mentioned a few other things he'd noticed needed fixing. For instance, he still wanted to add another step to the porch staircase so it wouldn't be so difficult for Will to get up it. So Josiah estimated he'd be finished with all the extra repairs by Thursday.

"Dunnerschdaag?" Velda giggled. "At this rate, Will's going to be long gone by the time Josiah finishes the repairs."

Now Anke was doubly irritated; first, because of Velda mentioning Will leaving again and second because it sounded as if she was criticizing Josiah. "He does excellent work and he's actually very efficient. But the *daadi haus* was in worse shape than we thought it was. There's a lot to do."

Velda threw back her head and laughed. "You

don't really believe that, do you, Anke? He's stalling on purpose so he can spend more time around you."

Do you really think so? Anke wanted to ask, suddenly feeling as giddy as a schoolgirl. Just because it was impractical for her to court anyone didn't mean she wasn't flattered about the possibility of Josiah being drawn to her.

"Oh, look at you blush! You want him to be your suitor, don't you?" Her sister-in-law teased. "Maybe I should *kumme* over with the *kinner* during the day and chaperone the two of you?"

"There wouldn't be room for you to *kumme* over with the *kinner*. We'd have to squeeze together like sardines in a can," Anke told her.

Velda grew serious. "*Jah*, I know the place is really tiny…and I feel bad you've been cramped up in there, but I hope you understand why I still think it's prudent to keep a little space between the *kinner* and Will."

"*Jah.* I do," Anke assured her. "And don't worry about us. We're not cramped—we're cozy." And by that, she didn't just mean her and Will; she meant Josiah, too.

From Anke's remark yesterday, it's safe to assume she's as fond of me as I am of her, Josiah thought as he moved a handheld manual sander across the floorboards in the bedroom. *Just because I had a* baremlich *experience courting Jana doesn't mean the same thing is going to happen here.* Moving to

Maine was supposed to be a fresh start for him, so why shouldn't that include a new romantic relationship, as well as a new district and a new job?

These were the same thoughts he'd been thinking all morning. Actually, they had kept him tossing and turning throughout the night, too. Now his mind was made up: he was going to ask Anke if he could be her suitor. The question now was, *when* could he ask her? Will was always around. *I know—I could ask if she wants to go snowshoeing with me tomorrow after* kurrich *and talk to her about it then! I'm sure Velda and Ernest would take Will home with them.*

Having figured out his strategy, Josiah was so eager to put his plan into action that he stopped sanding and went outside to see if he could spy Anke and Velda returning from the grocery store in the buggy. Instead, he spotted the children and Ernest gathered beneath a barren maple tree halfway across the yard. Ernest was holding Charity in one arm and using his other arm to push Millie on the swing. It seemed like a strange winter activity, but the children apparently were enjoying it because they'd formed a line to take a turn.

Josiah was crossing the yard to ask if Ernest needed a hand, when the buggy rolled up the driveway. So he switched course and went to help Anke carry the groceries inside, instead. *Now is my chance*, he thought, hoping Will would stay outdoors a little longer.

They'd made it to the porch when the little boy

called out, "*Ant* Anke, look at me! Am I going as high as my *mamm*?" He was pumping his legs and sweeping back and forth in an arc through the air without any help from Ernest.

"You're going even higher!" Anke answered.

Josiah followed her into the house and set the two bags of groceries on the table. She thanked him and immediately began putting the food away, buzzing around the kitchen as quickly as a hummingbird. It made him so nervous he almost retreated into the bedroom to resume sanding the floor again. But he knew Will could return at any minute and he didn't want to waste this opportunity. So, without even waiting to get Anke's attention, Josiah hastily blurted out, "Would you like to go snowshoeing with me after *kurrich* tomorrow?"

She turned from the cupboard to face him, a surprised look in her eyes. "I would, but..." she said slowly, indicating she was about to give a reason why she couldn't. Josiah braced himself for disappointment. "But I don't have any snowshoes. Whenever I've gone snowshoeing, I've borrowed a pair from Faith's *schweschder*."

Relieved, Josiah offered, "You could use Laura's—I'm sure she won't mind. I'll bring them with me to *kurrich*."

"In that case, I'd love to go, provided Velda and Ernest don't object to taking Will home with them."

Why should they—you've been taking care of their kinner *for years*, Josiah thought. But for what felt like the hundredth time, he reminded himself that that was none of his business. Besides, even if Anke couldn't go snowshoeing this Sunday, the important thing was that she'd said yes in the first place. Emboldened, Josiah inwardly resolved, *If tomorrow doesn't work out, then I'll just keep asking her until we finally get time together by ourselves.*

After supper, Anke rocked in front of the woodstove as she continued knitting the sweater she'd begun for Will. The boy, meanwhile, bent over the pad of paper on his lap, drawing something he said he didn't want Anke to see yet. He was so intent on sketching that for once, he didn't ask her any questions, which allowed Anke's mind to wander.

For someone who'd claimed she didn't need romance in her life, she was exceptionally happy that Josiah had asked her to go snowshoeing with him tomorrow. In New Hope, there were only two reasons why a single Amish man spent an afternoon alone with a single Amish woman. The first was that he was about to ask to be her suitor and the second was that they were already courting. Of course, Anke wasn't sure what the customs were in Illinois, so she didn't want to make any assumptions. But just the fact that Josiah wanted to spend his day off with her made Anke believe he liked her in a special way—which was how *she* felt about him, too.

Still, enjoying someone's company wasn't the same as courting and if Josiah did ask her to walk out, Anke was no longer sure how she'd answer. Up until Thursday, if he had proposed courtship, she would have turned him down. She would have said she didn't have time for a suitor—she had her family's needs to focus on. She would have explained that the men who'd courted her in the past wound up resenting the way she'd put her family's needs above her courtship with them. Anke might have told Josiah she valued his friendship too much to risk falling out with him.

However, on Thursday after they'd come home from town, Josiah had made it very clear that he understood Anke's commitment to doing what she thought was best for her family. He even seemed to appreciate that quality in her. And he'd been a huge help with Will, especially in the apparel store, when the child had thrown a tantrum. Anke couldn't imagine anyone else she'd courted ever being that patient with the child—or with *her.*

Maybe it's possible to serve my family and *have a suitor after all*, she mused. *Maybe I just needed to find the right* mann.

Realizing she'd dropped a stitch, Anke set her knitting on her lap and reminded herself that Josiah *hadn't* asked to court her. Furthermore, she hadn't even asked Velda yet if she and Ernest could take care of Will after church. So Anke didn't need to decide right this minute what she'd say if Josiah happened to bring up the topic of courtship tomorrow. She'd have to pray about it later, so she'd be better prepared to respond if necessary.

"It's time for you to go to bed, Will," she told her nephew. "We have to get up early for *kurrich* tomorrow. Do you want to show me what you've drawn?"

Will slid off his chair and brought the paper to her. "It's you and me and Josiah. See? That's his hat."

"I see. And we're all holding hands, aren't we?" Anke surmised the picture was inspired by their trip into town on Thursday.

"*Jah. Mamm* and my *daed* used to hold hands with me, too. *Mamm* said they'd swing me really high."

Anke was troubled that Will seemed to be associating Josiah and her with Clara and her boyfriend. Did that mean he felt like Anke and Josiah were replacing his parents? Maybe her sister-in-law was right. Maybe he was beginning to think that he was staying here permanently. "It's a very nice picture," she said. "Now let's go wash your face and brush your teeth."

After Will had gotten into his pajamas and Anke had prayed with him, the boy crawled into bed. "Didn't you forget something?" she asked him. When he stared blankly at her, she prompted, "The screw jars." Although he'd looked at the photo from his book bag, he hadn't transferred a screw from the clear jar to the blue jar the way he did every night to mark how many days were left until he saw his mother.

"Do we have to do that?"

"*Neh*, I guess not." *Maybe he's adjusting better now*, Anke thought hopefully. But she decided she'd better not assume. "Why don't you want to?"

"Pretty soon there won't be any screws in the white jar. That means I have to go back to the 'partment."

Anke inhaled sharply, realizing that by not transferring a screw, Will thought he could somehow keep his visit from ending. As earnestly as she was praying that he could stay there permanently, too, she realized it might not happen. Clara might complete her recovery and return to the *Englisch* world. Velda was right—if Anke didn't keep that possibility in the forefront of Will's mind, when it happened, he'd be devastated. So she said, "*Jah.* But it also means you get to see your *mamm.* And she can't wait to see you."

Will blinked a few times, thinking. Then he got up and went over to where the jars were balanced on the low end table Velda had given them to use. He reached into the clear jar, took out a screw and deposited it into the blue jar. *Tink.*

One more day gone, Anke thought. After she'd tucked Will in, she sat on the edge of his bed for a long time, watching him sleep and thinking about how attached he'd already grown to his family here. It was what Anke had wanted: for them to be close and to come to love each other. She hadn't really considered how brutal it would be for them to separate if Clara didn't return to the Amish.

What am I supposed to do? Her question was part prayer, part lament. It wasn't as if Anke or his cousins could pull back from the child; that would be cruel. They were his family. *But maybe I could at least put a little distance between him and Josiah, so he doesn't grow even more attached.* Anke realized that meant for now—with the exception of when the three of them went out for pizza together—she was also going to have to put more distance between Josiah and herself, so that Will wouldn't see them as parental figures.

I suppose that resolves the issue of what my answer will be if Josiah asks to court me, she thought sadly. But why put either of them in that position? It seemed kinder to cancel their snowshoeing expedition altogether, yet she didn't know what reason to give him. She didn't want to say she was afraid that Will was beginning to see them as his substitute parents, or even as a couple—that would have sounded too forward, especially if he wasn't considering asking to court her. *I guess I could tell him I didn't want to be away from Will for that long after all*, she decided. And it was true; the more she thought about her nephew going back to the *Englisch* world in four weeks or so, the less willing Anke was to miss even an afternoon with him now.

On Sunday morning, Josiah remembered what Omer and Keith had said about scrambling to take the front row at church so their children wouldn't have to be distracted by looking at an *Englisch* boy. He was concerned Anke's and Will's feelings would be hurt if they recognized other people were avoiding them. So he decided he would sit beside them during the service. But when he entered the church's large gathering room, he realized that not everyone seemed to feel the same way Omer and Keith felt; with the exception of an elderly couple, no one else had joined them in the front row.

However, since Josiah didn't have any relatives to sit with, he figured it wouldn't be inappropriate for him to join the Bachman family anyway. Anke was sitting at the end of the bench; Will sat on her left. Asher was beside him, then Velda, who was holding Charity. On the other side of Velda were Millie, Micah and Ernest. There was just enough space to Anke's right for Josiah to slide onto the bench beside her. Looking straight ahead, she gave a slight nod to acknowledge his presence, but didn't say hello because it would have been considered rude to chat with each other after they'd entered the gathering room.

Josiah said a silent prayer, asking God to keep Will from feeling overwhelmed. Amish mothers usually brought handkerchiefs to tie into various shapes to keep their little ones quiet during the service, which lasted for three hours. They also brought pretzels or crackers and raisins for the children to snack on. Still, three hours was a long time for a child to sit still, especially for an *Englisch* boy who wasn't even school age yet and who had never been to an Amish church.

When everyone rose to sing the opening hymn, Will stood on cue, copying his cousin Asher. The second song sung in every Amish service was always "The *Loblied*." It sounded more like a chant and in New Hope the Amish sang the traditional German version. During the opening verse, Josiah heard Will's voice, soft but distinct. *I hope he's not going to ask Anke a lot of questions*, he worried. *Otherwise, there are bound to be complaints and criticisms about her bringing her nephew to church.*

Anke leaned toward the child and then stood up straight again. Even as the other men's and women's voices filled the room, Josiah could still hear the child's voice in the background. *Isn't Anke going to quiet him?* Josiah wondered. But then he realized the boy wasn't talking; he was singing, too. He strained to hear him incant the words perfectly in German, although he couldn't have known what they meant. Will stopped singing after the third verse, but Josiah was astounded that Anke had taught him to memorize as much of the song as she had.

In the corner of his eye he saw her hand move up to her cheek time and time again—she was blotting tears from her skin. That was when it struck him that she hadn't taught him the song at all. Josiah would have heard them practicing. He figured out that Anke was crying because it was Clara who must have taught Will to sing like that, and Josiah got a little choked up, too.

For the rest of the service Will was very quiet. But toward the very end, he whispered loudly enough in Anke's ear for Josiah to hear him say, "I have to go to the bathroom." As soon as the closing hymn was sung, Josiah stepped aside to allow Anke and the boy to scramble out of the room. He would have liked to at least say hello to her before lunch preparations got underway, but knowing they were going snowshoeing later curbed his disappointment. *If a little* Englisch bu *has the patience to remain quiet through a three-hour church service, I suppose I can wait another hour to ask Anke if I can be her suitor*, he decided.

Lovina Bawell, Honor's mother, came up to Will as he stood with Anke in line to use the bathroom. "I heard you singing," she remarked. "Did your *ant* Anke teach you that song?"

"*Neh.* My *mamm* sings it at nighttime when her nerves feel bad," Will answered openly. "It makes her sleepy."

Anke cringed to herself, wondering how Lovina would react to the child's frank admission about Clara. But the older woman just nodded and said, "It's *gut* to sing hymns or to pray when we're upset." Then she smiled and walked away.

Clara must have been upset frequently for him to learn the first three stanzas, she thought. Yet she also felt a little surge of hope; at least her sister had taken *something* about her Amish faith and background to heart.

After Will had used the bathroom, she sent him off to play with the other children under the care of three teenage girls whose turn it was to keep them occupied while the older women prepared lunch. Anke felt so dismayed that she was going to have to cancel her snowshoeing outing with Josiah that she could hardly concentrate on what the other women were chatting about. But when it was her turn to eat and she sat down beside Velda, her sister-in-law whispered, "Have you heard what everyone's saying about Will?"

"Neh," she replied, bristling. *And I don't think I want to.*

"They were amazed that an *Englisch bu* knows 'The *Loblied*.' Someone even said you'd put them to shame by teaching him that song before they've taught their *kinner*."

"I didn't teach him—Clara did."

"*Jah*, that's what Lovina told us," Velda said, sitting up straighter. "You should have seen the looks on the other *weibsleit*'s faces!"

Anke had to smile to herself; just two weeks ago Velda was ashamed of being associated with Clara. Now she was bordering on being prideful about her *Englisch* sister-in-law. Changing the subject, Anke told her that she had to speak with Josiah briefly and asked if Velda could take Will to the buggy with the other children.

After Velda agreed, the two women finished their meals quickly so they could return to the kitchen to help with the last of the dishes. Then Anke dashed outside to the hitching rail. She saw Josiah's horse, but she couldn't find him. She hurried back toward the church to look for him inside again, but before she rounded the corner of the building, Keith Harnish stopped her.

"Whoa. Where are you going so fast?" he asked.

"Hello, Keith. Have you seen Josiah?"

"He may have taken off so he could go hang out with some *Englisch* alcoholics like your *schweschder*."

Anke crossed her arms against her chest. "First of all, if you're going to refer to my *schweschder*, please call her by her name. It's Clara. Secondly, I don't know what you mean by your remark, but I don't think you're at all funny."

"I'm not trying to be—I'm completely serious. Last year, Josiah was caught red-handed supplying beer to *Englisch* teenagers in Illinois. It was in the back of his buggy. Somebody captured the entire incident on their cell phone and posted it on social media. It went viral, which is the *Englisch* way of saying it spread like wildfire. I've watched the clip myself."

"Now I know you're joking. You've always claimed that you never use your cell phone to look at *Englisch* social media," Anke challenged him. "You only use it for business purposes."

"I didn't watch the clip on *my* phone. A customer showed it to me. He came into the hardware store the same day Josiah did and he recognized him from social media right away because of his flaming mop of hair."

"I'm sure he's not the only Amish man with red hair in Illinois." Anke rubbed her forehead. The combination of the frigid breeze and Keith's nonsense was giving her a headache. "I've gotten to know Josiah well enough that I'm certain that when he makes a commitment, he sticks to it. That includes his commitment to abide by the *Ordnung*. He'd never do what you're describing."

"He's only been here two weeks, so what makes you think you know what he's really like?" Keith challenged. "I'm telling you, Anke, you should stay away from Josiah. People are known by the company they keep. And you've already got a strike against you because of your alcoholic *schweschder*."

She balled her gloved fingers into a fist to keep herself from shouting, *My* schweschder*'s name is Clara and I don't care what you saw on social media, I know what kind of* mann *Josiah is*! Anke's head was really throbbing now, so she took a deep breath and let it out. She was about to say that she'd be glad to be known by the company she kept because she considered Josiah to be compassionate, industrious and funny, but just then, someone cleared his throat behind her.

Although he'd only caught a snippet of their conversation, it was clear to Josiah that Keith had been warning Anke to stay away from him. *But why would he say that unless...unless he somehow found out what happened in Illinois?* Josiah realized that must have been it: why else would Keith have said that people were known by the company they kept? Feeling both mortified and infuriated, he could barely keep his voice from shaking as he greeted them. "Hi, Anke. Hi, Keith."

Anke said hello, but Keith muttered, "See you." Then he walked way.

Figuring he could talk to Anke about what Keith had told her once they were in the buggy, Josiah asked, "Are you all set to go snowshoeing?"

"I—I'm afraid I can't g-go with you today after all," she stuttered nervously.

"Really? Velda and Ernest wouldn't agree to watch Will for you?"

"*Neh*, that's not the problem. It's that…it's that Will's only here for a few weeks and I want to spend as much time with him as I can."

Josiah wasn't buying her excuse. It seemed to him that she'd changed her mind because of what Keith had told her. She wouldn't do that, would she? He bluntly replied, "I don't understand why that didn't occur to you yesterday. Did something else happen to change your mind?"

She rubbed her brow and closed her eyes and then opened them again before answering. "*Jah.* I'm getting a *koppweh*, so I'm sorry I'm not really up for discussing it right now. But what it *kummes* down to is that, well, I don't know how to say this exactly…"

With a sinking feeling in his gut, Josiah said it for her. "You don't think we should socialize together."

"*Jah.* But only because of Will. He's so young and impressionable and I wouldn't want him to get the idea that, you know, that we're a couple—"

Josiah had heard enough. Cutting Anke off, he snidely retorted, "I wouldn't want him to get that idea either, because we're *not.* So it's fine by me if we keep our distance from each other." He turned on his heel to leave, but she caught him by his arm.

Anke's eyelashes were beaded with tears. "I'm sorry if my decision upsets you, Josiah. But I thought you'd understand that I have to do what's best for my nephew and—"

"I understand all right. And as soon as I finish the repairs on the *daadi haus*, I'll be out of your hair. But *you're* going to have to be the one to tell Will we're not going out for pizza together, because when *I* agree to do something, I don't break my word." Josiah yanked his arm from her grasp and strode across the lawn to his buggy, both hurt and seething.

He unhitched his horse from the rail and as he started toward home, Josiah brooded, *This situation with Anke reminds me almost exactly of what happened with Jana—but at least Jana gave* me *the benefit of the doubt, even if she did assume it was a member of my family who had been drinking.* Anke hadn't even heard his side of the story before she decided she no longer wanted to associate with him. And for her to use Will as an excuse was like rubbing salt in Josiah's wounds. All he'd ever done was try to have a good influence on the child!

It was maddening to him that he'd risked his own reputation by helping Anke host her alcoholic sister's son, yet she had the nerve to distance herself from *him*, when Josiah had never even had so much as a drop of fermented cider. He felt every bit as betrayed as he did after he'd tried to help Jana's brother. He also felt incredibly foolish to have made the same mistake twice. *I just don't learn, do I?* he chastised himself. *How could I have thought Anke was someone I'd want to court? Anyone who behaves like that isn't even a friend!*

But she was his employer—for a couple more days, at least. *Tomorrow I can put the finishing touches on the bedroom floor and I should be able to wrap up the rest of the repairs by* Dinnschdaag *afternoon*, he thought. Yes, he'd claimed it would probably take him until Thursday to complete a few extra projects he'd agreed to do—but that was because he was drawing them out so he could spend more time with Anke and her nephew. Now he couldn't finish them fast enough.

Once they arrived home and got out of the buggy, Ernest stayed in the barn to unhitch the horse. The four older children ran toward the house, while the two women strolled up the driveway behind them. "Are you okay?" Velda asked, shifting Charity in her arms. "You seem upset about something."

Anke had managed to contain her tears all the way home. But she was afraid that the floodgates would open up if she told her sister-in-law why she really felt so crushed, so she said, "I have a *kop-pweh*, that's all."

"Then you should go take a nap. Will can play with our *kinner*. Ernest told them they can all take two turns on the swing, then they'll *kumme* inside to color some pictures, have a snack and take a nap. Asher will be thrilled to let Will use his bed so he'll have an excuse to sleep on a cot like Will gets to do in the *daadi haus*."

After claiming she intended to spend as much time as she could with her nephew before she left, Anke felt too guilty to accept Velda's offer. "*Neh*. That's okay. It'll probably go away once I warm up and have a cup of tea."

"Then you should just go have a cup of tea by yourself and enjoy a little peace and quiet," Velda suggested. "You've always helped Ernest and me with our *kinner*. I don't think I've ever appreciated it as much as I have these past two weeks, when you haven't been in the *haus* to give me a hand. So why not allow me to return the favor? Or is it that you don't want Will to play in such a messy *haus*? Because I promise you, I've been keeping up with my housework a lot better these past couple of days and I won't serve him soup from a can, either."

Anke gave a wan smile. "I'm not at all worried about those things. I suppose a nap might be a *gut* idea, if you're sure you don't mind?"

"Not at all. Sleep as long as you like."

So Anke returned to the *daadi haus* alone. But by the time she'd stoked the fire in the woodstove and made a cup of tea, she was weeping too hard to drink it. *I thought Josiah was different*, she cried to herself as she pushed the rocker back and forth with her feet. *I really believed he respected that I have to put Will's needs above my own.*

She could have accepted it if Josiah expressed disappointment because she'd changed her mind about going snowshoeing. After all, she'd really been looking forward to spending time with him alone, too. But he'd acted even sulkier than Keith or her other suitors had acted, not even allowing her to finish her sentences. *Keith was right—I don't know him as well as I thought I did.* Not that she believed there was an iota of merit to what Keith had said about Josiah supplying alcohol to *Englisch* teenagers. But Anke never would have expected him to react to her decision the way he did.

And she certainly never expected him to cancel their plans to go out for pizza when he completed the *daadi haus* repairs. It was completely unreasonable for him to pin the blame on her because she'd been the one to say she didn't think they should socialize. *I didn't mean we couldn't still go out for pizza. Or even that we should* never *socialize again*, she thought. Josiah would have known that if he had allowed her to finish talking instead of being so defensive. *How am I ever going to tell Will we're not going out to his favorite kind of restaurant*? she cried to herself. *He's going to be crushed.*

Once again, Anke remembered what her mother had said about how a man could win a woman's heart by how he treated her child. *A* mann *can break a* weibsmensch*'s heart by the way he treats her child, too*, she thought. And that was exactly what Josiah had done to her.

Chapter Eleven

The good thing about Will sleeping in the same room with Anke was that she was so concerned he'd hear her weeping that she couldn't give in to her tears on Sunday night. However, she'd cried so much on Sunday afternoon that she still woke with puffy eyes and a pink nose on Monday morning.

After dressing and brushing her hair, she returned to the living room to wake her nephew. "Will," she said, touching his shoulder. "It's time to get up. We're taking your *onkel* to work, remember?"

Yesterday afternoon, Anke had grown so distraught about the idea of being around Josiah all day when he came to work on the *daadi haus*, she asked Ernest if she could use the buggy. She decided she could stop in at Millers' Restaurant to collect her money for any aprons that had sold the previous week. Later in the afternoon, she intended to take all the children to the library, while Velda stayed home with Charity. But first, she and Will had to bring Ernest to the butcher shop.

"Will," she repeated. "Wake up."

As the boy drowsily rose and got dressed, Anke went into the kitchen to scramble eggs. "Aren't we going to wait to see if Josiah wants to eat with us, too?" he asked when he came into the kitchen.

"*Neh.* By the time we return, he'll be hard at work. If we keep distracting him every morning the way we've been doing, he won't be able to finish our rooms. We don't want that to happen, do we?"

Will shrugged. "I like sleeping in the living room."

"I think you'll like sleeping in your own bedroom just as well, now that Josiah has fixed it up." Anke had to admit that he had done beautiful work; the floors looked nicer and smoother than those in the main house and she could no longer feel a draft coming from any of the windows. "You'll be as snug as a bug."

"How many more days until Josiah's finished?"

"I—I'm not sure," she hedged. "A couple, maybe."

"*Gut.* Then we get to go out for pizza!" Will exclaimed. Anke still didn't know how she was going to break it to him that they weren't going out for supper together. Will must have noticed her frowning because he asked, "What's wrong, *Ant* Anke?"

"Nothing, but no more talk about pizza. You haven't even eaten your breakfast yet," she said, rising from the table to get a piece of paper and a pen.

"What's that?" Will asked when he saw her affix

the note she'd written on the outside of the door with a tack some twenty minutes later as they were leaving.

"It's a message for Josiah, so he knows we're not going to be here today."

"Not at all?"

Not if I can help it, Anke thought. "Well, this morning we have errands and then *Ant* Velda invited us to eat lunch at the other *haus*. And after that, we're going to the library. So we won't be coming back until later this afternoon and then we'll have to pick up your *onkel* again. Why do you ask?"

"Because I have to give Josiah the picture I made for him," Will said and hopped down the porch steps.

Anke had forgotten all about the picture, so on the way to the barn she silently prayed, *Please, Lord, don't let Josiah's anger at me affect the way he responds to Will.* Then she reluctantly added, *And please help me not to feel so angry at Josiah, either.*

When Josiah reached the *daadi haus*, he pulled a note with his name on it off the front door. The note read, "Will and I will be gone for most of the day until around two or three o'clock. If he says anything about going to the pizzeria, please don't let on that we aren't going—I haven't told him yet."

Don't worry—I won't, Josiah thought. As he'd said yesterday, it was Anke's responsibility, not his, to break the news to Will that she didn't want them to socialize anymore. *Apparently, she doesn't want to be in the same* haus *with me, either*, Josiah concluded, because she'd never been away for so long during the day. He might have found her avoidance to be insulting, except he didn't want to be in her company, either.

Without Anke and Will there to invite him to join them for a snack or lunch break, Josiah got a lot more done than usual. So at two forty-five when he accidentally cracked the final length of floor molding he was installing, he decided he'd call it a day. *I need to purchase more molding and by the time I go into town and return, it will be after four o'clock anyway,* he rationalized. More important, he wanted to leave before Anke and Will returned.

On the back of the note Anke had written to him, Josiah scribbled, "Went to the hardware store. Be back tomorrow." Rather than posting it to the door, he decided to leave it on the coffee table in the living room. When he set it down, he noticed one of Will's drawings. Although the picture was rudimentary, it was still far better than any Josiah had ever seen a child make. He could easily tell that it was an illustration of three people: a man and a woman holding hands with the boy in between them.

That's Anke, Will and me, he thought, recognizing himself because the boy had depicted him wearing a hat. Immediately, he was overwhelmed with regret. *I've always done my best to keep my word. Now I'm going to break a promise to a* kind? Just because Anke was the one who had decided they shouldn't socialize any more didn't alleviate Josiah's guilt. *Will is going to feel as let down by me as I felt by her.* It wasn't an experience he'd wish on anyone, especially not a child.

Is she really so fearful of associating with me that she'd rather allow Will to get hurt than to go out together for one meal? It seemed a hypocritical thing to do, considering how much it had hurt her when other people behaved that way toward her and Will, but Josiah figured there wasn't anything he could do to change her mind. He set the drawing back on the table and headed out to the barn to hitch his buggy.

His intention was to go to the *Englisch* hardware store because even though the prices were higher there, he wouldn't have to listen to Keith make wisecracks about his past. But halfway into town, he thought, *I'm sure Keith has already spread the word about the golf course video, so I might as well get used to whatever he or anyone else says about me.* Josiah was tired of trying to hide his past, as if he'd done something shameful. *Maybe it's better if people know sooner rather than later, because that's how I'll find out who might be my friends and who might be...like Keith. Or Anke.*

So ten minutes later, he strode into the hardware store, his head held high. "Hi, Omer. Hi, Keith," he loudly greeted the two men. They were standing near the front counter, huddled over a cell phone. "What's new?"

Keith hid the phone from view and began fiddling with the receipt tape on the cash register. But Omer blatantly confessed, "Keith just showed me a video of a red-headed man who was caught with beer in the back of his buggy. He's tried to tell me it was you, but he's pulling my leg, isn't he?"

Josiah shook his head. "*Neh.* That was me all right. But it wasn't my beer. I've never touched any alcoholic drink in my life. Although I can't prove it, I suspect those *Englisch* teenagers you also saw in the video stashed their beer in my buggy so they wouldn't get in trouble."

Keith ridiculed, "Do you really expect anyone to believe that?"

"*Gott* knows that it's the truth and His opinion of Josiah is the one that matters most," a man's voice said loudly as he emerged from a side aisle. It was Iddo Stoll, the deacon, and he was glaring at Keith and Omer. "Whether you choose to believe it or not is your business. But when I hear you spreading falsehoods in our community, then it becomes *my* business, too. So you *menner* can expect a home visit to discuss what *Gott*'s Word has to say about slandering your neighbor." He stepped past the cash register and doddered out the door, leaving all three men slack jawed and speechless.

A few minutes after Josiah had purchased the molding he needed and he was on his way home, he reflected on what had transpired in the hardware store. He was very grateful that Iddo had come to his defense, and he expected today would be the last time Keith or Omer would have anything disparaging to say to him about the incident in Illinois. He also appreciated that the deacon had pointed out what Josiah should have concluded a long time ago: God's opinion of him was the one that mattered most.

But that didn't mean he wasn't affected by people's opinions of him, too. Especially when one of those people was someone he'd grown to like very much. Someone he'd dreamed of courting. Someone who had seemed so trustworthy that even now, he couldn't believe he'd been as wrong about her as she was about him.

On Tuesday morning, Anke was so distraught about anticipating telling Will that they wouldn't be going out for pizza with Josiah that she got sick to her stomach. And while she was in the bathroom, the boy happily answered the front door when the carpenter arrived.

"*Gudermariye*, Josiah." Will's enthusiastic greeting was loud enough for Anke to hear down the hall. Then he announced, "*Ant* Anke has a *bauchweh*. She's in the bathroom getting sick." Anke quickly rinsed her mouth and opened the door.

"Oh. Are you sick, too?" Josiah sounded concerned.

"*Neh.* Look, I made this for you."

In the quiet pause that followed, Anke stood in the hallway, holding her breath and praying that Josiah wouldn't be as ungracious about receiving the picture as he'd been about accepting the cookies Will had made for him the previous week.

"I like this drawing. You put a lot of detail into it. I notice the *mann* and *bu* are wearing the same-colored socks," Josiah finally said, and Ankle exhaled in relief.

"That's because it's me and you. And this is *Ant* Anke. See her eyes? That color is called turtle blue."

Anke pressed her hand over her mouth, suppressing a giggle.

"You mean turquoise blue?" Josiah asked.

"*Jah.* Isn't it pretty?"

Anke stepped into the room before Josiah could answer. *"Gudermariye,"* she said coolly to Josiah. "Will, *kumme* into the kitchen to have your breakfast. Let Josiah get to work."

"Do you want to eat with us?" Will invited him.

Anke quickly spoke up. "I'm not making breakfast this morning because I have a *bauchweh*, remember? I doubt Josiah wants to eat cold cereal."

"*Neh*, I don't," he confirmed just as quickly. "I'm going to get right to work. I'll be finished with Will's bedroom today. I can move his bed in there when I'm done if you want me to."

Anke was surprised that Josiah was being so accommodating. *It must be because I prayed he wouldn't take his anger at me out on Will.* Then she remembered she'd also prayed that *she* wouldn't feel so angry at Josiah, either, and she said, "*Denki.* I'd appreciate that."

"I can help you move it," Will volunteered.

"You probably won't be here—we're going to Sovilla's *haus* today with your *gschwischderkinner*." After church on Sunday, Arleta had invited a group of mothers with young children to go to her house on Tuesday after lunch. The adults were going to work on sewing projects while the children played outside.

Their neighbor down the road, Martha Ropp, was going to pick them up and take them home, since she and her three children had been invited, too. Anke knew it would be a tight squeeze in the buggy, but she didn't care. Nor did she mind that she'd had an upset stomach. The only thing that mattered was spending as much time away from the *daadi haus* as she could until Josiah was done with the repairs and left for good.

It was nearly four o'clock and Josiah had completed everything he'd agreed to repair inside the *daadi haus* and he'd moved Will's bed into the bedroom, too. If he hurried, he could add an extra step to the porch stairs and leave before Anke and Will returned. Although he still had misgivings about not following through with his commitment to take Will out for pizza, Josiah knew he didn't have any other choice in the matter. But he didn't want to be around when the child realized it was his last day there.

As he was prying the board off the bottom step so he could reconfigure it, he heard a vehicle drive up the lane. *Someone must have turned down into the driveway by mistake*, he thought. *I hope they're not lost, because I don't want to take the time to give them directions.*

Unfortunately, when he glanced over his shoulder, he noticed an *Englisch* woman with purplish hair get out of the back seat. "Nobody's home," he shouted to her as she began walking toward the main house. "Can I help you with something?"

The woman turned to face him. "I'm looking for Anke Bachman," she called back.

Josiah took a few steps closer so he wouldn't have to keep yelling to be heard. As he approached, he thought, *She looks familiar. Have I seen her in town before?* Just as he reached the driveway, he realized why he seemed to recognize her. *She looks just like Will—that's his mother! That's Clara!* Josiah came to a dead halt.

"Anke's not here," he said. "No one is. They should be back within an hour."

"An hour?" she repeated, biting her thumbnail. "Okay, well, I'll just have to wait, then."

Josiah was so stupefied he couldn't seem to move as he watched her return to the car. She opened the door and got in, but the driver didn't reverse direction. *Are they just going to idle there until Anke returns?* Josiah wondered. He couldn't imagine Velda's reaction to finding an *Englisch* car in the driveway, much less, to seeing Clara with purple hair. But a moment later, Anke's sister got out of the vehicle again. "That's the last time I ever use your service!"

she shouted, slamming the door. The car sped away as Clara hurried across the lawn to the main house again.

Josiah shook his head and resumed his work on the porch step, but his mind could hardly concentrate on what his hands were doing. *Why is Clara here? She couldn't have completed the recovery program already—she's only been there a little over two weeks.* His stomach felt knotted up with dread. *What is Anke going to do when she sees her? And how is Will going to feel?*

"It's locked," Clara announced, jarring him from his thoughts. Josiah hadn't realized she'd crept up right beside him.

"What?" He stopped what he was doing and stood up to speak to her.

"The door to the main house is locked. We never locked the door when I lived here," she explained, biting her pinkie nail this time. Didn't she have any gloves? It was freezing out here. "I'm Clara, Anke's sister. She's been taking care of my son, Will."

"*Jah.* I know," Josiah replied flatly. He begrudgingly told her his name, too.

"It figures. Everyone knows everything about everybody here. You probably know *why* she's been taking care of him, too, don't you?" After Josiah nodded, Clara momentarily glanced down at her feet. Then she looked up and changed the subject. "So, did you buy this place from my family or are you just renting it?"

"Neither. Anke hired me to make repairs so it's livable for her and Will."

Clara's eyes went big and round, just as her son's always did when he was astonished. "They've been staying out here?" After Josiah nodded, she mumbled dolefully, "I should have known Velda wouldn't allow them in the main house with her."

Regardless of how he felt about her sister, Josiah didn't want Clara to worry about her son's living conditions. "It's actually pretty cozy inside," he consoled her.

She immediately perked up. "Good. Then I'll wait in there where it's warm." Bypassing the bottom step, she bounded up the stairs and into the *daadi haus* before Josiah could object.

It's not my haus *anyway, so I can't stop her*, he thought. Besides, now that Clara was there, he had an even more urgent reason to finish his work and leave before Anke and Will returned, so he got back to it. Even though his mind was swirling with concerns about why the boy's mother had returned, Josiah managed to stay focused and he finished installing the step within fifteen minutes. *Now all I need to do is collect my tools from the bedroom and I can get out of here.*

When he pushed open the door, he discovered Clara holding a handful of Will's socks over an open duffel bag. Maybe it was because he noticed she had dropped the pair that Anke had given to the boy—the socks he loved so much because they matched

Josiah's—on the floor, but he couldn't stop himself from blurting out, "What do you think you're doing with those?"

"I'm packing. That's why I'm here—I came to get Will. I want to have his things ready so we can leave as soon as he returns." She deposited his clothes into the bag and added defiantly, "Not that it's any of *your* business—or anyone else's. Will is *my* child."

Josiah had been telling himself the same thing for two weeks; he wasn't a member of the Bachman family, so what they did wasn't any of his business. But he no longer cared whether he had any right to voice his opinion or not. For Will's sake, he was going to speak his mind. "*Jah*, Will *is* your *kind*. But if you take him away from here before you've completed your recovery program, you'll risk losing him for *gut*. Is that what you want?"

Clara turned her back to Josiah and zipped the duffel bag, wordlessly indicating she was going to carry through with her intention to take the boy away from New Hope. Away from Anke.

Softening his tone, Josiah pleaded, "Please don't do this, Clara. It wouldn't be fair to your *suh*. He's been so brave, adjusting to an entirely new home and lifestyle. He's really *kumme* to love it here, even though he's counting down the days until you can be together permanently again. Don't do something rash now that might result in the two of you being separated for a much longer period of time."

Her back still turned, Clara didn't respond for several moments. Just when Josiah decided there was no sense in trying to get through to someone who was ignoring him, she asked, "Do you…do you really think Will's happy here?"

"I *know* he is," Josiah responded without hesitation. Nor did he give it a second thought before saying, "Your *schweschder* has seen to that. You couldn't have trusted him into the care of anyone more capable, loving and devoted than Anke is. I've seen how much she has joyfully sacrificed in order to provide a *hallich* home for Will until you can complete your program. And frankly, it would be selfish of you drop out of it now."

Clara broke out in tears, her shoulders heaving as she sobbed into her hands. "But I miss him so much…" Knowing that her loneliness was at the heart of her actions, Josiah kept quiet, allowing her time to weep. But meanwhile, he kept peering out the window, anxious that Anke and Will would return any minute.

When Clara's crying subsided, he said, "I can tell how much you love and miss your *suh*. And I can't imagine how difficult it is for the two of you to be separated. But you'll miss him even more if he's put into foster care for the long run."

She finally turned around and looked Josiah in the eye, nodding. "You're right—I know you're right. I shouldn't have *kumme* here. If Will sees me, it's going to make him lonely all over again when I leave. Could you give me a ride to the other side of town so I can meet my sponsor in the diner where none of the other Amish people in New Hope ever go? She'll pick me up and take me back to the center."

Josiah suppressed a groan. *I can just hear the rumors that will crop up if anyone sees me with another* Englisch *alcoholic*, he thought. But Clara was right; if Will saw her, it would be twice as hard for them to part a second time. *"Jah,"* he agreed. "But we'd better hurry."

"Just let me put Will's things back in the drawer." No sooner had she unzipped the duffel bag than a buggy came up the lane. "Oh, no! I can't let him see me! What am I going to do?"

Josiah's stomach lurched, but he said, "Quick—go into that room there and don't make a sound until Anke *kummes* to get you."

"Look! Josiah put in an extra step for me!" Will exclaimed as he and Anke approached the *daadi haus* and Velda and the other children walked in the opposite direction toward the main house.

"That's *wunderbaar.*" Since Martha had dropped everyone off in the driveway, Anke hadn't been able to peek inside the barn to see if Josiah's buggy was there. But since the step was installed, she figured he'd left for the day.

However, just as they reached the porch, he stepped outside, closing the door behind him. "Hello. As you can see, I finished the last of my projects," he said cheerfully.

Anke scowled in response. *Why did he have to announce that? Couldn't he just have said goodbye as if it were any other day?* she silently carped. *Now Will is going want to go to—*

Even before she'd finished her thought, Will asked, "If you're all done, does that mean we get to go out for pizza?"

"We—we can't," Anke faltered. "Not today."

"Oh, that's right, your *bauch* probably still hurts, right?" Apparently, Josiah must have realized his blunder and he was trying to backpedal.

"*Jah*, it does." She pressed a hand against her abdomen.

"That's too bad, because I really had my heart set on pizza. Didn't you, Will?" Josiah asked, causing Anke to wonder if he was being spiteful or if he was really just obtuse. When her nephew agreed that he'd been looking forward to pizza, too, Josiah suggested, "I suppose you and I could go out—if your *ant* didn't mind staying home by herself?"

Will gave Anke a hopeful look. "Can we, *Ant* Anke?"

What in the world is Josiah thinking to suggest something like that in front of Will? Anke wondered. Yet she realized he'd actually come up with a perfect solution for avoiding being together, while also avoiding disappointing her nephew. *He doesn't want to hurt Will's feelings any more than I do...but what if the* bu *has such a great time that he grows even more attached to Josiah?*

As she was internally dithering, Josiah piped up again, "You know what, Will? We should give your *ant* a few minutes to make up her mind. I think I dropped some nails over there in the snow. Let's go see if we can find them while she comes to a decision." As he passed Anke on his way down the steps, he discreetly pressed a piece of paper into her hands.

She unfolded it to read, "Clara is inside the house. She'll explain everything. She doesn't want Will to see her." Anke gasped, her knees almost buckling beneath her.

Several yards away where he'd begun searching the snow for nails, Will jerked his head up. "What's wrong, *Ant* Anke?"

"My—my *bauch* feels really funny. I think you *buwe* should go ahead to the pizzeria without me."

"Denki!" Will cheered, charging forward to hug Anke before racing back to Josiah's side again.

"We won't be back until at least seven thirty. I promise," Josiah said with a pointed look that Anke took to mean he expected Clara would be gone by then.

"Okay. Have *schpass*." She held on to the porch railing to steady herself as she watched them disappear into the barn. She waited in that position until she saw Josiah's buggy pull out into the driveway and down the lane. Then she darted up the stairs and into the house. She didn't see her sister in the living room, but when she flung open the bedroom door, Clara dove into her arms.

"Oh, Anke," she cried. "I almost made a huge mistake—*again*."

"*Kumme*, sit with me in the living room and tell me all about it."

So her sister spent the next hour pouring out her heart. She told Anke how much she missed Will, what a struggle it had been to stop drinking and how ashamed she felt for making such poor choices and causing everyone so much pain. In turn, Anke recounted everything she could think of that Will had done since he'd come to live with them, including singing "The *Loblied*" in church. She reminded Clara of Christ's love and forgiveness for everyone who chose to put their faith in Him. And she encouraged her to stick with the recovery program.

"I have no intention of quitting again," Clara assured her. "Although now I'll probably have to stay an extra week or two because I'll have to start over from the beginning. Is it okay if Will stays with you a little longer?"

"Don't be *lappich*. Of course he can!"

Clara checked the time on her cell phone. She had called Yolanda almost forty-five minutes earlier, so she projected if they left now they'd arrive at the diner at about the same time as her sponsor did. "Even if we get there a little early, it's better if I go before Will returns, otherwise, I might not be able to leave at all."

Anke refrained from saying that was her exact wish: for them both to stay in New Hope permanently. The last thing she wanted was for her sister to feel trapped or pressured. Clara was already extremely emotional. "I'll go tell Ernest I'm taking the buggy. Don't worry—I'll be discreet."

"Can you…can you ask him to *kumme* out for a minute? I'd like to say hello."

So their brother met them in the barn, where he and Clara shared such a sweet embrace that Anke had to turn away, for fear she'd start crying.

Once the sisters arrived at the diner, they chatted in the buggy until they spotted Yolanda's car turning into the parking lot.

"*Denki* for everything you're doing for me and Will," Clara said, giving Anke a goodbye hug. "As Josiah said, I'd never find anyone more loving, capable and devoted to care for my *suh*."

"Josiah said that?"

"Yeah. I can tell he thinks the world of you." Clara pulled back to look her in the eye. "Tell me the truth. He's your suitor, isn't he?"

"*Neh*. He's not."

"That's too bad. He's the kind of man I wish I had chosen. He seems like he'd be a really positive role model for a young boy like Will."

The first thing Anke did after her sister and Yolanda drove away was to bow her head and thank the Lord that Clara had decided to return to the recovery program, and to ask Him to give her strength to start over again. On the way home, Anke's thoughts turned to her sister's observation about Josiah. He really had gone out of his way to protect Will from getting his feelings hurt tonight—both by encouraging Clara to return to her recovery program and by taking Will out for pizza as he'd promised. Nothing about Josiah's behavior or what he'd said to her sister indicated that he resented Anke's commitment to her family.

Maybe I misjudged him. It's possible that he just reacted poorly in the moment on Sunndaag *because he was disappointed I decided not to go snowshoeing*, she thought. *And Clara herself said she'd like Will to have someone like Josiah for a role model. So maybe we don't have to keep our distance from him after all.*

If her sister had the courage to admit her mistakes and try again in her recovery program, then with God's help, Anke was going to try again with Josiah, too. The question was, did *he* want to start anew with her?

Josiah softly rapped on the door of the *daadi haus* so he wouldn't wake Will, who was asleep in his arms. They had returned later than he'd expected because they'd stopped at the apparel store before going to the pizzeria so Josiah could buy the boy a hat similar to his own. He supposed he should have asked Anke if it was okay first. But he figured she wouldn't be opposed to him giving the boy a traditional Amish piece of clothing as a gift. In any case, they'd gotten to the pizzeria later than he'd intended and it was very crowded, so they'd had to wait for a booth. By the time they'd finished their meal, Will was so full and tired that he'd fallen asleep in the buggy on the way home.

Anke was smiling when she opened the door. "Hello, *buwe*—" she started to stay. But when she saw that her nephew was sleeping, she covered her mouth and whispered, "Oops, sorry."

She gestured for Josiah to follow her into Will's newly finished bedroom. He laid the boy down on his cot and then helped Anke remove his shoes and coat. After they'd tiptoed into the living room, Anke held up the hat and asked incredulously, "You got this for him?"

"Jah." Josiah stiffened his spine. "I didn't think you'd object."

Anke wrinkled her forehead. "Why would I object? It was very thoughtful...like so many things you've done for us. Especially tonight." She took a step closer and looked him squarely in the eyes. "I can't thank you enough for encouraging Clara to return to the recovery program and for keeping Will from discovering she'd been here."

Josiah brushed off her compliment, saying, "There's no need to thank me. I did it for her *suh*." He reached for the doorknob, but before turning it, he remarked over his shoulder, "Since you don't want to associate with me anymore, you can put my final paycheck in the mail once you have a chance to write it out. I also left the receipts for the materials I bought on top of the fridge."

"Wait!" Anke placed her hand over his. Her touch was gentle and warm. "I never said I didn't want to associate with you—I said it wasn't a *gut* idea for us to socialize, but I didn't mean forever. I only meant while Will was here. Even so, I made a mistake and I'm very sorry."

Josiah slid his hand out from under hers and dropped it to his side. Facing her, he asked, "You're sorry—what changed your mind? Did the deacon set the record straight with you, too, like he did with Keith Harnish?"

Anke scrunched up her face and tipped her head in what appeared to be genuine bafflement. "Iddo Stoll? Keith Harnish? What do either of them have to do with my decision about whether to socialize with you?"

Now Josiah was perplexed. "I—I thought I heard Keith telling you about the video of me getting caught with alcohol in the back of my buggy. Isn't that why you wanted to distance yourself from me?"

"*Neh*, of course not. As I told you, I didn't think it was *gut* for Will to get the idea we were a couple. You saw the picture he'd drawn of us holding hands... I was afraid he was beginning to feel like we were replacing his *mamm* and *daed*. Or that he was growing too attached to you, in particular. I didn't want to make it harder for him to leave when the time came."

"But Keith *did* tell you about the video, right?"

"*Jah*. But I assumed that was just a case of mistaken identity."

As relieved as Josiah was that he'd been wrong about Anke's motivation for not wanting to socialize with him, he realized she might change her mind again when he told her what had really happened at the golf course. But it was important to him to know whether she trusted he was telling the truth, so he admitted, "It wasn't a case of mistaken identity. It really was me in the video clip. But the beer in the buggy wasn't mine. I've never had a drop of alcohol in my—"

Anke interrupted. "You don't have to explain. I believe you. I told Keith that, too—I said you'd never break your commitment to abide by the *Ordnung*." She scowled as she added, "I think he was part of the reason I had a *koppweh* that afternoon."

Josiah's legs felt weak when he realized how wrong he'd been about her, so he asked if they could sit down. Anke perched on the edge of the rocker and he took a seat facing her in Will's armchair. Leaning forward on his knees, he peered into her eyes and confessed, "I'm the one who made a mistake—I wrongly assumed that *you* believed a lie about me. That's why I got so upset after *kurrich* on *Sunndaag*. I'm sorry for how immaturely I behaved. I should have heard you out instead of storming off, but I was defensive because…because of things that happened in my past."

Anke's face blossomed with a smile. "That's okay. I was defensive, too. I assumed you were angry because I was putting my *familye*'s needs above my desire to have *schpass* with you."

"Are you kidding me? Your commitment to your *familye* is one of the qualities I appreciate the most in you." Josiah sat up straighter. "I feel very blessed to have been part of your *familye*'s life. And I'd really like to continue to hang out with you and Will... but aren't you still concerned he'll grow too attached to me?"

"*Neh.* Not since Clara mentioned that she wished Will had a role model like you in his life. That's when I realized that even if he only knows you for a short amount of time, the influence you have on him now could last his entire life. Besides, a *kind* can never have too much love. And the fact of the matter is, he's *already* grown attached to you."

"I've grown attached to him, too." Josiah gazed into her sea-green eyes, adding softly, "And to you, Anke."

Her voice barely a whisper, she replied, "I feel the same way about you, too."

Josiah took her hand in his. "Then will you accept me as your suitor?"

"Jah." She gently squeezed his fingers. "As long as it's okay if Will sometimes comes with us when we go out?"

"Sure. He can be our chaperone—to make sure we don't do too much of this." Josiah leaned forward and gave her a soft, lingering kiss.

"In that case, forget I asked," Anke teased. "He can stay home with his *gschwischderkinner*."

Epilogue

"I can't believe you're actually moving out," Clara said to Anke as she helped her pack. The sisters and Will had been living in the *daadi haus* together for a little over a year and a half, ever since Clara completed her recovery program and returned to New Hope. But tomorrow was Anke's wedding. After that, she'd live with Josiah in the house he'd built on property he'd bought from his brother. "How will I ever manage without you?"

"You'll do just fine," Anke assured her. In the past year, she had witnessed her sister growing more and more responsible, mature and faithful to the baptismal commitment she'd made to God and her Amish community. "*I'm* the one who's going to feel lost without you and Will."

"*Gott* willing, soon enough you'll have *bobblin* of your own to care for—and you'll have your own *haus*, too. You'll forget all about us. You know what they say—out of sight, out of mind."

"*Neh*, that's not true," Anke insisted somberly, even though she recognized that her sister had only been teasing. "The entire time you were gone, you were never out of my mind, Clara. You were always in my prayers. And as far as having *bobblin* of my own… I hope I do. But that won't change how much I love Will or any of my nieces and nephews. Or you."

"I know it won't," Clara replied just as seriously. Then she smiled a playful smile. "Do you think your *bobblin* will have hair like Josiah's?"

Before Anke could answer, the two women heard footsteps on the porch. They went into the living room just as Josiah and Will entered from outside. They both wore identical hats, which they swept off their heads and hung on two pegs by the door. Although Will's peg was lower than Josiah's, he no longer had to stand on tiptoe to reach it, the way he did two months ago.

"I'm *hungerich*," the boy announced. "May I have *kuchen,* please?"

After Clara took him into the kitchen to give him warm milk and a cookie, Josiah asked, "Did I hear someone saying my name when I walked in?"

"We were just talking about your hair." Anke stepped closer to him and reached up to finger a curl.

"You mean my rooster's comb?" he asked.

Anke laughed, remembering what Millie had said the first time she'd seen Josiah's vivid red spirals. "I love your hair."

Josiah encircled her waist and pulled her a little nearer. "I love your turtle-blue eyes," he joked, using Will's word for *turquoise*. "But not as much as I love your ears."

"My ears? But they stick out."

"Exactly. It makes them easier to kiss." He demonstrated several times, which tickled and made Anke giggle so hard that she was afraid Will and Clara would return to the room to see what was so funny.

"Absatz," she whispered.

"Okay, I will," he agreed reluctantly. "But I'm only going to keep my word about that until tomorrow, when we're married..."

* * * * *

Get 4 FREE REWARDS!
We'll send you 2 FREE Books plus 2 FREE Mystery Gifts.
The Maverick's Marriage Pact
STELLA BAGWELL
Secret under the Stars
ELIZABETH BEVARLY
FREE Value Over $20
The Cowboy's Ranch Rescue
Lisa Childs
His Partnership Proposal
Both the Harlequin® Special Edition and Harlequin® Heartwarming™ series feature compelling novels filled with stories of love and strength where the bonds of friendship, family and community unite.
YES! Please send me 2 FREE novels from the Harlequin Special Edition or Harlequin Heartwarming series and my 2 FREE gifts (gifts are worth about $10 retail). After receiving them, if I don't wish to receive any more books, I can return the shipping statement marked "cancel." If I don't cancel, I will receive 6 brand-new Harlequin Special Edition books every month and be billed just $5.49 each in the U.S. or $6.24 each in Canada, a savings of at least 12% off the cover price, or 4 brand-new Harlequin Heartwarming Larger-Print books every month and be billed just $6.24 each in the U.S. or $6.74 each in Canada, a savings of at least 19% off the cover price. It's quite a bargain! Shipping and handling is just 50¢ per book in the U.S. and $1.25 per book in Canada.* I understand that accepting the 2 free books and gifts places me under no obligation to buy anything. I can always return a shipment and cancel at any time by calling the number below. The free books and gifts are mine to keep no matter what I decide.
Choose one: ☐ Harlequin Special Edition (235/335 HDN GRJV) ☐ Harlequin Heartwarming Larger-Print (161/361 HDN GRJV)
Name (please print)
Address
Apt. #
City
State/Province
Zip/Postal Code
Email: Please check this box ☐ if you would like to receive newsletters and promotional emails from Harlequin Enterprises ULC and its affiliates. You can unsubscribe anytime.
Mail to the Harlequin Reader Service:
IN U.S.A.: P.O. Box 1341, Buffalo, NY 14240-8531
IN CANADA: P.O. Box 603, Fort Erie, Ontario L2A 5X3
Want to try 2 free books from another series? Call 1-800-873-8635 or visit www.ReaderService.com.
*Terms and prices subject to change without notice. Prices do not include sales taxes, which will be charged (if applicable) based on your state or country of residence. Canadian residents will be charged applicable taxes. Offer not valid in Quebec. This offer is limited to one order per household. Books received may not be as shown. Not valid for current subscribers to the Harlequin Special Edition or Harlequin Heartwarming series. All orders subject to approval. Credit or debit balances in a customer's account(s) may be offset by any other outstanding balance owed by or to the customer. Please allow 4 to 6 weeks for delivery. Offer available while quantities last.
Your Privacy—Your information is being collected by Harlequin Enterprises ULC, operating as Harlequin Reader Service. For a complete summary of the information we collect, how we use this information and to whom it is disclosed, please visit our privacy notice located at corporate.harlequin.com/privacy-notice. From time to time we may also exchange your personal information with reputable third parties. If you wish to opt out of this sharing of your personal information, please visit readerservice.com/consumerschoice or call 1-800-873-8635. Notice to California Residents—Under California law, you have specific rights to control and access your data. For more information on these rights and how to exercise them, visit corporate.harlequin.com/california-privacy.
HSEHW22R3